# THE BALL AT VERSAILLES

Danielle Steel has been hailed as one of the world's most popular authors, with a billion copies of her novels sold. Her recent international bestsellers include *Joy, Resurrection* and *Only the Brave*. She is also the author of *His Bright Light*, the story of her son Nick Traina's life and death; *A Gift of Hope*, a memoir of her work with the homeless; and the children's books *Pretty Minnie in Paris* and *Pretty Minnie in Hollywood*. Danielle divides her time between Paris and her home in northern California.

# By Danielle Steel

Joy • Resurrection • Only the Brave • Never Too Late • Upside Down • The Ball at Versailles
Second Act • Happiness • Palazzo • The Wedding Planner • Worthy Opponents • Without a Trace
The Whittiers • The High Notes • The Challenge • Suspects • Beautiful • High Stakes
Invisible • Flying Angels • The Butler • Complications • Nine Lives • Finding Ashley
The Affair • Neighbours • All That Glitters • Royal • Daddy's Girls • The Wedding Dress
The Numbers Game • Moral Compass • Spy • Child's Play • The Dark Side • Lost And Found
Blessing In Disguise • Silent Night • Turning Point • Beauchamp Hall • In His Father's Footsteps
The Good Fight • The Cast • Accidental Heroes • Fall From Grace • Past Perfect
Fairytale • The Right Time • The Duchess • Against All Odds • Dangerous Games
The Mistress • The Award • Rushing Waters • Magic • The Apartment
Property Of A Noblewoman • Blue • Precious Gifts • Undercover • Country
Prodigal Son • Pegasus • A Perfect Life • Power Play • Winners • First Sight
Until The End Of Time • The Sins Of The Mother • Friends Forever • Betrayal
Hotel Vendôme • Happy Birthday • 44 Charles Street • Legacy • Family Ties
Big Girl • Southern Lights • Matters Of The Heart • One Day At A Time
A Good Woman • Rogue • Honor Thyself • Amazing Grace • Bungalow 2
Sisters • H.R.H. • Coming Out • The House • Toxic Bachelors • Miracle
Impossible • Echoes • Second Chance • Ransom • Safe Harbour • Johnny Angel
Dating Game • Answered Prayers • Sunset In St. Tropez • The Cottage • The Kiss
Leap Of Faith • Lone Eagle • Journey • The House On Hope Street
The Wedding • Irresistible Forces • Granny Dan • Bittersweet
Mirror Image • The Klone And I • The Long Road Home • The Ghost
Special Delivery • The Ranch • Silent Honor • Malice • Five Days In Paris
Lightning • Wings • The Gift • Accident • Vanished • Mixed Blessings
Jewels • No Greater Love • Heartbeat • Message From Nam • Daddy • Star
Zoya • Kaleidoscope • Fine Things • Wanderlust • Secrets • Family Album
Full Circle • Changes • Thurston House • Crossings • Once In A Lifetime
A Perfect Stranger • Remembrance • Palomino • Love: *Poems* • The Ring
Loving • To Love Again • Summer's End • Season Of Passion • The Promise
Now And Forever • Passion's Promise • Going Home

## Nonfiction
Expect a Miracle
Pure Joy: *The Dogs We Love*
A Gift Of Hope: *Helping the Homeless*
His Bright Light: *The Story of Nick Traina*

## For Children
Pretty Minnie In Hollywood
Pretty Minnie In Paris

# Danielle Steel

# THE BALL AT VERSAILLES

PAN BOOKS

First published 2023 by Delacorte Press
an imprint of Random House
a division of Penguin Random House LLC, New York

First published in the UK 2023 by Macmillan

This paperback edition first published 2024 by Pan Books
an imprint of Pan Macmillan
The Smithson, 6 Briset Street, London EC1M 5NR
*EU representative*: Macmillan Publishers Ireland Limited, 1st Floor,
The Liffey Trust Centre, 117–126 Sheriff Street Upper,
Dublin 1, D01 YC43
Associated companies throughout the world
www.panmacmillan.com

ISBN 978-1-5290-8552-5

1 3 5 7 9 8 6 4 2

A CIP catalogue record for this book is available from the British Library.

Typeset in Charter ITC by Palimpsest Book Production Ltd, Falkirk, Stirlingshire
Printed and bound by CPI Group (UK) Ltd, Croydon, CR0 4YY

Visit **www.panmacmillan.com** to read more about all our books
and to buy them. You will also find features, author interviews and
news of any author events, and you can sign up for e-newsletters
so that you're always first to hear about our new releases.

To my special children,
Beatrix, Trevor, Todd, Nick,
Samantha, Victoria, Vanessa,
Maxx, and Zara,

May there always be magic in your lives,
and people who love you,
and whom you love.

If you do your part beautifully,
with open hearts,
the magic will come.

May you be ever blessed.

I love you with all my heart,
Mom /d.s.

*Dear Friends,*

The Ball at Versailles was a very special night in 1958 when the first debutante ball was held at the Palace of Versailles in Paris. Young ladies from socially important families and nobles were presented to society. At that first glittering ball, a few more than thirty American girls were invited to join them, with all the young girls in gorgeous white evening gowns. It was a Cinderella night, and also fraught with all the tension that eighteen-year-old girls, and their male counterparts, can create! I'm sure it was an unforgettable and truly fabulous event.

Debutante balls are as old as history and have existed for centuries. As recently as the twentieth century, their purpose in English society was for young women to find a husband. The young men would court them for the brief social season, and girls were expected to be engaged by the end of it and to marry shortly after. They married while barely knowing each other, and trusted the outcome to chance. And often, being of the same social 'status' was not enough!

Today, there are still debutante balls, which are a tribute to tradition. The goal is no longer to find a husband but simply to mark a grown-up moment in their lives – a rite of passage – as they turn eighteen, and celebrate their entry into a grown-up world, still wearing a beautiful white gown, and having an evening they will always remember. Even today, it is still a Cinderella night.

I hope you love the story as we travel back to that first very special night in 1958, at the Palace of Versailles, where memories were made.

Love,

Danielle

# THE BALL AT VERSAILLES

# Chapter 1

Jane Fairbanks Alexander saw the creamy white envelope sitting on the silver tray on the table in the entrance hall, where the part-time housekeeper who came three times a week had put it. Gloria was Irish and had worked for them daily when Jane's daughter Amelia was still in school, but now that she was in college, Jane didn't need Gloria as often and she had another part-time job the other two days of the week. She bought the groceries she knew Jane liked, did the laundry, and cleaned the apartment. Amelia only came home now for the occasional weekend. It was her freshman year at Barnard. The apartment seemed strangely quiet without her. It was small, neat, and elegant, and had two bedrooms, in a prewar building in Manhattan on Fifth Avenue and Seventy-sixth Street, with a doorman, which made Jane feel safe. On the days that Gloria was there, it was nice for Jane to come home to a clean, tidy apartment, with her laundry neatly folded on her bed. Having an orderly home was some slight compensation for the fact that Amelia wasn't there anymore. She was uptown in the dorm. Barnard was the female sister school of Columbia University.

Amelia was loving her freshman year. She was an English literature major, which made sense since Jane was the second-in-command of a venerable publishing house in the city. Amelia's father had been in publishing too, and Amelia had clear goals. She wanted to go to law school when she graduated from Barnard, and hoped to get into Columbia, which had been one of the first law schools to accept women. For the past nine years, Jane had brought Amelia up on her own. She had been nine years old when her father, Alfred, died. She had never known him as her mother had. Jane had warm memories of him before the war, when he was still a whole person, before he had gone to war and everything had changed.

Jane had met him when she was a junior at Vassar. He had been getting a master's in English at Yale. Once they met at a deb ball in New York, he had courted her for a year and a half and traveled from New Haven to visit her in Poughkeepsie as often as he was able. They got engaged during her senior year, and married as soon as she graduated, in 1939. Alfred was twenty-four then, and Jane was twenty-two. He had an entry-level job in publishing at G. P. Putnam's, and he had a bright future ahead of him. He had started as an editorial assistant and was rapidly promoted to junior editor. He loved his job and looked forward to being a senior editor or even editor in chief one day.

Jane got a job fresh out of college, working at *Life* magazine as an assistant copy editor. Their interests had always been very similar and they both loved their jobs in publishing. Alfred was assigned to the more literary books, and the manuscripts he worked on were loftier than the work Jane did at *Life*. But her work was lively, fun, and she found it exciting. She got pregnant three months after they married and had an easy pregnancy. She was at the magazine for a year, until she gave birth to Amelia in the summer of 1940, and never went back to work after that. She was happy staying home with their baby daughter and caring for her herself, and Alfred's job, along with the money he had inherited, provided them with a very pleasant life. He didn't expect her to go back to work.

Alfred didn't have a great deal of money, but his grandparents had left him a handsome bequest that provided some luxuries as well as necessities. And later, after his parents died, one of cancer and the other of a stroke, they had left him some more money too. He still had to work, but he and

Jane weren't dependent on his job, and it was comforting to know that they had a tiny amount of savings in the bank, invested safely and conservatively. Their backgrounds were very similar. Jane's father was the president of a bank in New York, and her mother was from a distinguished family in Boston. She came from "old money" too. Jane's parents were from families that had once been more comfortable than they were now. They had lost most of their fortune in the Crash of '29, but there was still enough left to provide their heirs with a comfortable, secure life. Alfred's family were part of the Old Guard of New York. He had several cousins who had more money than he did, but his was among the best-known names of New York Society. He was by no means the richest among them, but he had enough to support his wife and daughter and there was no need for Jane to work. Alfred's father was an investment banker on Wall Street, and like Jane's mother, Alfred's mother had never worked.

The two sets of parents knew each other. Alfred's and Jane's fathers belonged to the same club, where they often met after work, and both their mothers volunteered once a week together as Gray Ladies for the Red Cross. It was work they enjoyed. They liked sharing a granddaughter once Amelia was born and took her to the park together sometimes to see the animals at the zoo or ride on the carousel. Jane and Alfred were only children, so Amelia's arrival was met with wonder and delight by both sets of grandparents.

Jane and Alfred's lives rolled along smoothly from the moment they married for two and a half years, until Amelia was eighteen months old. At night they talked about Alfred's job, his progress and latest promotions, and the manuscripts he was assigned to work on. But when Pearl Harbor was hit, Alfred enlisted within days afterwards. It was a few months before he shipped out, first to England and from there to Italy. He and Jane corresponded faithfully, and it was only once he was in Italy that she noticed that his tone had changed. He sounded discouraged, and alternated between fear and rage, and he couldn't tell her what he'd seen, so she could only guess how hard the war was for him. Both his parents died in the first year he was away, which upset him deeply too. There were long periods when she didn't hear from him at all, depending on where he was and if there was mail service. Then he would surface again. After he'd been in Italy for a few months, she noticed the tremor in his handwriting. The letters no longer sounded like him, and when he returned from the war in the summer of 1945, she could see why. He was a changed man. Amelia was five years old, didn't remember him, and cried each time she saw him or he tried to pick her up, which either made him cry, or storm out of the room, slamming the door behind him.

The doctors said he was suffering from shellshock and battle fatigue and it would heal in time, but it never did. He was thirty years old, and the death of his parents in a relatively short time after he left had added to his trauma. Once he came back, he no longer saw his old friends or went to his club. His job at the publishing house had been filled by a woman, who was doing an excellent job, for a lower salary than they'd paid him. She was a war widow now and they didn't want to upset her and let her go. The job market was flooded with young, healthy men looking for work, and Alfred was turned down for every job he applied for. It was clear that he hadn't recovered yet. He either flew into a rage over something they asked him, or, as at one interview, broke down in tears when they asked him about his war experience. Eventually he stopped going to interviews, and sat at home, brooding and drinking all day, while Jane struggled to find ways to cheer him up. His preference was gin, but he would drink anything he could lay his hands on. Jane would throw away the bottles when she found where he concealed them, but he always had more hidden somewhere. Without a job and drinking heavily, and Jane not working either, Alfred went through much of the money his parents and grandparents had left him very quickly. He did some gambling at a private poker club, and a lot of drinking, and sat in a chair in a haze all day, lost in thought, staring into space. At night he usually fell asleep listening to the radio. His return was nothing like Jane had imagined it would be, with two kindred spirits finding each other again and picking up where they left off. Alfred never found his way back to that place. He was lost, never to be found again.

At thirty-four, four years after he returned from the war, he was driving to Connecticut to visit a friend from his army days that Jane had never heard of before when he drove off a cliff into a ravine and was killed. He didn't leave a note, so she was never sure if it was suicide or an accident because he was drunk. She suspected the former but could never prove it. He had been profoundly depressed for four years, with night sweats and nightmares almost every night, and he refused to get treatment for it. He insisted he was fine, but they both knew he wasn't.

Jane found herself a heartbroken widow at thirty-two. Her own parents had died by then, so she had no one to turn to for help when she discovered that Alfred had gone through almost all his money and had no life insurance. What he had left she put in an investment account with his military benefits, for Amelia's education and emergencies that might come up. Fortunately, he had purchased their apartment from his inheritance from his grandparents before the war, so she and Amelia had a roof over their heads, but very little more than that.

Amelia was nine when her father died, and attended the Chapin School, an exclusive private girls' school on the East Side. Jane had attended Chapin too, and Amelia never suspected her mother's terror when she discovered Alfred's circumstances. They barely had enough to live on with the little that was left. Jane tried to get another magazine job and couldn't find one. She hadn't worked in nine years, and only had had a year's experience before that.

She finally found a job as a junior editor in a well-known publishing house, similar to Alfred's first job when she married him. She found she had a talent for editing, and young writers liked working with her, and she enjoyed encouraging them. Beyond that, she had a keen eye for manuscripts that were submitted that she was sure would be commercial successes, and she was often proven right. She had an uncanny knack for finding the proverbial needle in the haystack, discovering unknown authors whose novels became bestsellers. She rose quickly in the ranks of the publishing house she worked for, Axelrod and Baker. Phillip Parker, her boss, was impressed by her abilities, and she got regular promotions and raises. She learned to live frugally and provided everything Amelia needed. Within six years, she became the assistant publisher, and since her boss was nearing retirement, she had an eye on his position, and he hinted to her regularly that she was almost sure to get it. In fact, she had been doing his job more than he was for the past three years. He had frail health and he told her it was only a matter of time before she'd get his position as publisher. She worked hard in order to be worthy of it and took work home at night. She was doing the work of two people, his job and her own.

She was proud of the work she did and loved working with the authors. She knew many of them personally, made a point of getting to know the new ones, and continued encouraging young writers. It was rewarding work, and she made a decent salary. She'd had several offers from literary agencies to become an agent, which might have been more lucrative, but she was loyal to the house she worked for, and they paid her well. She was able to provide all the things Alfred would have if he hadn't blown most of his money before drinking himself to death. The autopsy had shown that he was drunk when he drove over the cliff. She had been angry at him for a long time afterwards but had finally made her peace with it. Alfred's death was due to the war. It wasn't his fault.

Neither Alfred nor Jane had grown up with extreme luxury. Their families' fortunes had dwindled, as had the fortunes of many aristocratic families after the Great Depression. But both their families were still comfortable before the war and had provided for their children. Jane and Alfred came from blue-blooded lineage, had been educated at the best schools and colleges, knew the right people, and lived on the edge of New York Society, among people of their own kind. They had never been deprived growing up, and Jane was determined to see to it that her daughter lacked for nothing. She had sent her to one of the best private schools in the city too. Amelia had pretty dresses when she went to birthday parties. They were invited to the finest homes, and Amelia to the best parties. Jane was a member of the Colony Club, one of the most exclusive women's clubs in New York. And she saw to it that the girls Amelia met and made friends with were from the "right" families. The New York Social Register was Jane's bible, and she made sure that the people they socialized with were in it. Given her background, people who didn't know her well assumed she was a snob, but she wasn't. She was kind to everyone at work, but where Amelia was concerned, she wanted her to have the best opportunities, and tried to be sure that she grew up among the same kind of people her parents had grown up with. Jane never strayed far from that safe, familiar world, and didn't allow Amelia to do so either. When the time came, she wanted Amelia to marry someone from that world.

Giving Amelia the best of everything had been a fierce struggle for Jane. Her existence since Alfred's death had been a life-and-death battle to make ends meet, and she never wanted Amelia to go through that when she grew up.

# The Ball at Versailles

Amelia never knew how often Jane deprived herself of a new coat or dress or hat or shoes, or even a new skirt for work, for her daughter's benefit. Jane was a pretty woman and she dressed up what she had with a bright scarf, or her mother's jewelry. She always wore her mother's pearls to work. She looked and sounded like what she was, a beautiful, ladylike, distinguished, aristocratic woman from an upper-class background, with an excellent education. She had been grooming Amelia all her life to appeal to the right man one day and to marry someone who would care for her and protect her and support her, so she would never have to make the sacrifices her mother had after Alfred's death. Jane was willing to sacrifice everything for her daughter.

Only a month before, on Christmas, Amelia had made her debut at the Infirmary Ball, one of the most exclusive debutante cotillions in New York, where Astors and Vanderbilts had made their debuts before her. Many of the girls Amelia had gone to school with had come out with her. She had worn a beautiful dress that they had picked out at Bergdorf Goodman. It was a simple heavy white satin gown by Pauline Trigère with a tiny waist that showed off Amelia's slim figure and a skirt shaped like a bell. Amelia was a beautiful girl, with a perfect body, long blonde hair, and big blue eyes. She was a younger, almost exact replica of her mother. Jane was beautiful at forty-one, and they looked like sisters.

Amelia was exquisite coming down the stairs with her escort, to curtsy as she was presented, under the crossed swords of the West Point cadets. Teddy Van Horn, a childhood friend, had been Amelia's escort, and he looked handsome in white tie and tails and was a year older than Amelia. She had no romantic interest in him whatsoever. They were just friends, which made the evening easier than if there had been romantic sparks between them. Jane had made her debut at the same ball twenty-three years before. And even now, at forty-one, she remembered how excited she had been. It had been the high point of her life until she married Alfred.

The beautiful dress had put a strain on Jane's budget, which she never discussed with Amelia. Alfred's remaining money, which she'd saved and invested, paid for college. Amelia's dorm room, everything that went with it, and her expenses were a stretch on Jane's current salary, but as soon as her boss retired and she got the position she'd been waiting for as publisher, her finances wouldn't be quite so tight. She was looking forward to it and knew it would be soon.

Jane could manage in the meantime, just as she had for the past nine years. Amelia was eighteen now, and once she finished college and got through law school in seven years, Jane could heave a sigh of relief. They had made it this far, and she knew that she could hang on for another seven years of keeping a hawk eye on their budget, without Amelia ever feeling the pinch of it or being deprived. Jane would die before she would ever shortchange Amelia and make her aware of her mother's struggle. She wanted Amelia to make a brilliant marriage, so she would never have to worry about anything. She wanted her to marry for love of course, but it was as easy to love a rich man as a poor one. Amelia was well behaved, so Jane wasn't worried about who she'd meet in college. She was always in the library working to keep her grades up, and she had done well so far. Jane was proud of her. Amelia was a serious student with good morals and values, and a kind heart. She would have been devastated if she had known of her mother's struggles to support her.

Jane had worn a plain black velvet evening gown to Amelia's debut just before Christmas. She had found it in a secondhand shop where wealthy women often sold their cast-off clothes. It was by Charles James, and she'd found a handsome short mink Galanos jacket to go with it. She looked just as elegant as all the other mothers at the cotillion and was prettier than most of them. Amelia and Jane were both beautiful women and looked well in whatever they wore. Amelia's dress was one of the most beautiful there.

Amelia had been pleased to be invited to the cotillion and had expected to be. She and her friends had talked about it with anticipation all through high school. It didn't have deep meaning for her the way it did for her mother and some of

13

the other girls, but she knew it would be fun. It was a rite of passage into adulthood. She had chafed for a while about the origins and purpose of the cotillion in the past. Debutante balls were originally meant to introduce young women of good families to Society, with the intention of finding husbands for them. It had always been the case in the United States and Europe. But few young girls married at eighteen anymore, "fresh out of the schoolroom," as they used to say. Many or even most went to college now, and a number of them met their husbands there, as Jane pointed out when Amelia complained briefly about the cotillion being archaic. She was bothered too that anyone who was not from their white upper-class milieu was excluded. It seemed wrong to her.

"It's a cattle market, Mom," Amelia had grumbled briefly, "and all the cattle are just like us. Why is that okay?"

"It is *not* a cattle market. It's a night designed to make you feel like Cinderella, and if you meet your Prince Charming, then that's wonderful. It's a rite of passage for people like us, like a club, to show off our daughters we're so proud of. And you know all the girls coming out with you. You went to school with many of them." The others went to schools like Spence and Brearley, the rival schools to Chapin. Amelia had given up her reservations. She couldn't change the rules, even if she disapproved that all of the debutantes were white and Christian. The year before, Amelia had been deeply moved by the nine brave students who had been the first students to desegregate Central High in Little Rock, Arkansas. She had followed it closely on the news and took their situation very much to heart.

"It's not right, Mom, that they're not included too."

"No, it's not right," Jane agreed with her, "but history moves slowly. It will change one day, but most people in this country aren't ready for that to happen yet. One day integration will be the norm. The whole country isn't there yet."

"They need to hurry up. We're no better than they are."

"It will happen in your lifetime," Jane reassured her. "Probably by the time you're my age. Little Rock was a first big step toward that. But we can't fight everyone's battles, we can only fight our own, and that's not our battle to fight." Jane's struggle every day was to do the best she could for her daughter and support them both.

"Maybe it should be our fight too," Amelia had said earnestly, only a month before. The inequities of segregation had upset her since she was a young child. She hated the idea that some people were treated differently. And there was no question that events like debutante balls excluded many people and were only open to a select few. It was a very exclusive club. The purpose of deb balls and presentations of marriageable young women hadn't changed for centuries.

15

It was an antiquated tradition, and a thinly veiled effort to find husbands for young girls as they came of age.

In the end, despite her reservations, Amelia had had fun, particularly since so many of her friends from school were there, and she had stopped complaining about it. She had fun with Teddy and the many girls that were debs with her. She didn't consider it an earth-shattering event that would change her life, but it was a fun party, and she loved her dress.

As Jane sat down at her desk with the thick cream-colored envelope with her name on it in elegant calligraphy, and a French stamp, indicating it had been sent from Paris, a new door opened to Amelia, beyond her mother's deepest hopes for her. Jane read it carefully and smiled. In the presence of the President of France and Ambassador Hervé Alphand, the French Ambassador to the United States, with the Duchesse de Maillé and the Duc de Brissac, as co-chairmen of the event, two hundred and fifty French debutantes were to be presented to Paris Society at a ball held for the first time at the Palace of Versailles, and Miss Amelia Whitney Alexander was on the list of forty American young women who were included in the number of invitees. It specified that the Americans had to have been presented as debutantes in the U.S. in 1956 and '57, which was Amelia's case, having just come out in December 1957 a month before, and debutantes who would be presented later in the year in December 1958 were acceptable. Debutantes from earlier or later years were not included. And more specifically the girls had to be from seventeen to nineteen years of age. Jane's smile widened as she read down the list of the Honorary committee and the ball committee, which included several Bourbons, among them the pretender to the throne of France, if there were still a king. On the list were a number of royals, and Miss Mary Stuart Montague Price was General Chairman on the American side. And one could assume that almost all on the list of debutantes were from aristocratic families. The American debutantes whose names Jane recognized were from the most distinguished families in the country. It was not a list which reflected wealth or fame, but bloodlines and ancestry. And it was a great honor and compliment for Amelia to be invited.

Jane's mind raced immediately to what the event might cost her, in terms of plane tickets, the hotel, expenses while they were in Paris, and possibly another lighter, more summery dress than the heavy satin one Amelia had just worn to the cotillion. But there was no way that Jane would deprive her daughter of the experience if Amelia wanted to go. Jane intended to do everything she could to convince her if Amelia hesitated. She didn't speak French and might feel shy about it. But it was a fantastic opportunity for any girl her age, to be presented at the Palace of Versailles, formerly the Court of Louis XIV. It would be an unforgettable event for her to experience, and an amazing opportunity for her to meet young men far beyond her usual circle of friends. She might marry a French prince, or an English duke, Jane fantasized. Her mind raced at the thought of all the advantages for Amelia that might come of it.

She vaguely remembered that the young Queen Elizabeth had recently stopped the presentation of debutantes at the Court of Saint James and declared it an antiquated tradition, so the French had risen to the occasion, and this would be the first Debutante Presentation at the Palace of Versailles. The ball was to be held on the twelfth of July. Jane carefully set the invitation down on her desk, to show Amelia when she got home. She was coming to spend the weekend with her mother, so the timing of the arrival of the invitation was perfect. The favor of a reply was requested by February first, from those who wished to participate. She hoped that Amelia would be as excited as she was. It was an honor to be chosen as one of the forty Americans being invited.

Jane read through the rest of her mail, made some notes of things she had to do, and looked out the window at Central Park in the dark. There was still snow on the ground, and she stood thinking about the ball as she heard Amelia's key turn in the lock. She bounded into the room in saddle shoes and a plaid skirt, a navy twin set, a pea coat with a white wool cap and mittens, and a face red from the cold. Her long blonde hair hanging down her back made her look like Alice in Wonderland, as she walked into the living room and smiled at her mother. The two women looked strikingly alike. Jane went to hug her daughter and smiled happily to see her. It was the first week of school after the Christmas holidays, and Jane had missed Amelia once she went back to the dorm. They had spoken several times that week. They usually spoke every day. They were very close, enjoyed each other's company, and got on well.

"How was school?" Jane asked her as they sat down on the couch in the living room. The room wasn't large, but it was elegantly arranged, with antiques Jane had inherited from her family and Alfred's, and it had a warm, welcoming feeling to it. Amelia loved their apartment. It was just big enough for the two of them and felt cozy and inviting.

"Long," Amelia answered. "I already have three papers due. It feels like they're punishing us for having had a vacation." The cotillion already felt light-years away. "I have to work all weekend," she said, looking disappointed. She wanted to see her friends and go to a movie with her mother. They had promised to go on Sunday before Amelia went back to school. And there was a movie theater that was playing *Funny Face* with Audrey Hepburn and Fred Astaire again, and they both wanted to see it.

"That's fine. I have some things to do too. This week was crazy in the office. We have several important books coming out in the next few months." Amelia had grown up with only her mother, so they were friends now as well as mother and daughter, and allies in most things. They rarely argued and both had easygoing personalities.

They chatted for a few minutes, and Jane couldn't hold back any longer. She walked to her leather-covered antique English desk that had been her father's, picked up the invitation, and walked back to the couch and handed it to Amelia.

"Look what came in the mail today," she said, unable to conceal her excitement. Amelia took it from her, read down the lists of all the names, and the explanatory cover letter, and looked up at her mother.

"Are they kidding? They're all princesses and countesses. Why would they want me there?"

"Because you have distinguished ancestors, and maybe they got the list from the Infirmary Ball. It sounds incredible. The first debutante presentation at the Palace of Versailles. That's so exciting." Amelia looked considerably less enthused than her mother.

"It sounds too fancy to me, and I don't speak French. I knew most of the girls I came out with. I wouldn't know anyone there."

"You don't need to speak French. It's not a speaking part.

You walk down the aisle or a staircase on the arm of your escort, you curtsy just like you did at the Infirmary Ball, and that's it, and you've made your debut in France too. At Versailles."

"I don't know any boys there to be my escort," Amelia said, trying to back out. It sounded intimidating to her. Most of the French debutantes had titles. Some were even princesses.

"Read the letter. They will supply a suitable escort for the debutantes coming from abroad. There will be five hundred escorts for two hundred and ninety girls. Amelia, you have to do it. You can't miss an opportunity like that. You'll have the memory of it forever."

"I already did it here, Mom. How many times do I have to be presented? It'll be the same thing all over again, with French subtitles." Amelia shrugged and handed the invitation back to her mother, unimpressed and unenthused about going.

"It's at Versailles. Nothing you've ever done will equal that," Jane insisted. She could already envision it, with Amelia looking like a princess too.

"Why do you want me to, Mom?" Amelia looked discouraged.

"Because when life gives you an opportunity like that, I think you have to embrace it. And I'll be there with you. You won't be alone."

"It sounds scary to me."

21

"It's a chance to make friends in another country."

"And marry a duke or a prince, right?" Amelia teased her, but she knew she wasn't far from the truth. "I don't want to be Cinderella, Mom. I did the cotillion, that was enough. I didn't meet a handsome prince. I had fun. The whole concept is out of another century. I don't need to come out twice. Once was enough and I don't want a husband for about another ten years. I want to finish college and go to law school."

"You'll be too old to be a deb at Versailles by then. This is the year you're supposed to do it. After that you'll be a post-deb and they won't want you."

"This is 1958, Mom, not 1850. It's ridiculous."

"No, it's not. Consider it a fabulous costume party. You'll even meet some American girls, you can speak English to them."

"And what do I say to my escort after 'Bonn-joor,' when I have no idea what he's saying to me?"

"You give him that killer smile of yours and he'll melt at your feet." Amelia smiled at her mother's romantic illusions and faith in her, and then looked worried.

"Are you going to *make* me, Mom?" Amelia looked stubborn for a minute, and Jane could see that this wasn't going to be as easy as she'd thought. Amelia was sounding obstinate.

"I'm not going to *make* you do anything, but I am going to try to convince you. I think it's a fantastic opportunity, and I don't want you to miss it. I think you'll regret it forever if you don't go."

"No, *you* will," Amelia said pointedly. She knew her mother. She wanted the best of everything for her daughter, sometimes too much so.

"It's one night out of your life. How terrible could it be?" Jane wheedled, trying to sway her.

"It sounds boring, and pompous. They're probably all snobs. And it's expensive. The letter said there's a five-hundred-dollar fee if I do it. I'd rather have the money for new ski equipment. We have a long weekend coming up. I want to go to Vermont with friends from school." Amelia was athletic, which was often costly.

"You can rent the equipment, and five hundred dollars isn't a lot for an opportunity like this," but the rest of the expenses would be, Jane knew. She didn't care, she wanted Amelia to have the experience.

"I'll think about it." Amelia didn't want to argue with her mother about it, and she could see that Jane was determined. Jane nodded. She knew how rigid Amelia could be if she dug her heels in, and she didn't want her to refuse.

"We'll talk about it on Sunday," Jane said, with a determination Amelia knew only too well. When her mother wanted something badly enough, she was relentless, especially if it was for Amelia.

"I'll probably have my promotion by then, and a nice big fat raise," she reassured her, "and we can go on a little trip afterwards, in Provence or somewhere, just the two of us. It'll be fun." Amelia smiled. She could see a ball at the Palace of Versailles in her future, with a lot of stuck-up French people who didn't speak English and would probably snub her and be rude to her and consider her some kind of hick and treat her like a tourist, but once her mother got that look in her eye, wild horses would be easier to deal with. "Come on, let's go have dinner. Gloria left us a roast chicken. I'm starving," Jane said, and gave her daughter a hug.

"Me too," Amelia said. She put an arm around her mother's waist, and they walked to the kitchen together. Jane gave her a quick kiss, and started to organize dinner, and not another word was said about the ball at Versailles that night, but Amelia knew her mother wasn't going to forget it. It was beginning to seem unavoidable, and she would have to be presented as a deb, again. She felt like she was about to be auctioned off to the highest bidder, or a handsome prince, according to her mother.

The plan sounded stupid to Amelia, and she didn't want a husband, especially not a French one. It was all just too weird.

She forgot about it after that and spent the weekend working on her papers.

Jane didn't mention it again until shortly before Amelia had to leave to go back to the dorm on Sunday. She wanted to go to the library after dinner.

Jane picked the invitation up from her desk and waved it at her. "And the ball at Versailles?" Amelia let out a terrifying groan.

"Oh God, why do I have to? Stop trying to marry me off, Mom."

"I'm not. I just want you to have fun." Jane looked determined, and Amelia knew she wouldn't win, so she might as well give in.

"Do I have a choice?" Amelia said, with a glance of resignation at her mother. She'd been hoping she would forget or give up.

"Actually," Jane smiled at her, "no, you don't. Trust me. It will be fabulous. You'll be glad you went. And we'll do something fun afterwards, a little trip in France."

"Okay, I give up," Amelia said, rolling her eyes, and went to get her bag. She was wearing jeans and saddle shoes, a heavy Irish sweater, and the pea coat.

"I'm sure you won't regret it," her mother promised.

"*Argghkkk*. You are the stubbornest person I know," Amelia said, exasperated.

"Thank you." Her mother smiled at her. "I love you too. And you'll thank me when you're a duchess with your own château."

"I think I hate you," Amelia said with a grin, kissed her, and hurried out the door to go back to her dorm. July was so far away, it didn't seem real anyway.

Jane filled out the form that night, wrote the check, and mailed it from her office in the morning. She was absolutely certain that the ball at Versailles was going to be amazing, and Amelia was going to love it.

# Chapter 2

The enormous Colonial-style home of Charlene and Bailey Smith was in Highland Park, the wealthiest suburb just north of Dallas, and was reminiscent of *Gone with the Wind*. It was certainly not subtle, and they made no attempt to hide their money, but they had taste as well. Charlene was third-generation oil money from Houston, and was one of the richest women in Texas. And Bailey came from wealth of more human scale, made from land development, commercial real estate, and more recently shopping malls. He had a sixth sense for great investments. His fortune didn't match his wife's, but he had enormous personal wealth, and together they were a force to be reckoned with on the Dallas social scene.

They were civic-minded and philanthropic and had built a hospital for handicapped children and given millions to breast cancer research. Charlene was on the board of countless worthwhile charities. At forty-six, she was strong, sure of herself, and outspoken, and had a good heart. Bailey tended to be more diplomatic, and gentler with people. Whenever someone wanted money for a charitable donation of Olympic proportions, or an angel investor to start a business, they went to Bailey. He was brilliant in business, but also had a soft heart. He was fifty-one, and they had just celebrated their twenty-fifth anniversary. They had a solid marriage, and two daughters, Araminta and Felicity.

Their oldest daughter, Araminta, was twenty-two years old. She had gone to the best private girls' school in Dallas, was a lackluster student, and had opted not to go to college. Neither of her parents was surprised, though her father was somewhat disappointed. He would have liked to see her at least try to get an education, or even pretend to. Araminta loved going to parties and drinking too much, staying out late, dating all the rich, handsome bad boys in Dallas, wearing beautiful clothes, and stealing her mother's most expensive gowns when she could get away with it. She was a gorgeous girl with raven dark hair, translucent white skin, and big blue eyes.

She could have been a model if she'd wanted to bother, which she didn't. Neither work nor school appealed to her, and she made no pretense that they did. She was a fabulous dancer, loved to have fun, and men flocked to her like mice to cheese. She loved to have a good time. She had come out at the Idlewild Club debutante cotillion four years before in a dress her mother had had made for her in Paris by Givenchy. She was the belle of every ball she went to, including the one her parents gave her, for six hundred people, when she came out. She had a second haute couture dress for that. The second one was made for her by Christian Dior, and so was the gold gown her mother wore to their party. The shocking pink one Charlene wore to the Idlewild Club cotillion was by Yves Saint Laurent.

The Smiths never did anything quietly, or by half measures. They entertained a lot and gave grand parties. They loved to travel and had their own plane. They had an apartment in New York, a house in Palm Beach. They were avid skiers, and they had a house in Aspen too. Their homes were beautifully decorated, their art collection was legendary, and Charlene was beginning to worry slightly because although Araminta never lacked for dates, no serious suitor had emerged from the crowd in the four years since her debut. She had been sure that Araminta would be engaged within six months of her ball. Her parents thought that a husband and babies would ground her and settle her down, but so far nothing had.

Bailey was somewhat wild in his youth before he married Charlene, and Charlene's father had been a notorious player, gambler, and drinker in his day, especially after Charlene's mother died young. He'd had three more wives after that, each progressively younger. His most recent ex-wife was twenty-five, only three years older than his granddaughter, which he made no apology for. He was nearly eighty. So Araminta came by her wild side honestly.

Charlene and Bailey's second child, Felicity, couldn't have been more different, and seemed to all of them as though she had come from another family by mistake. Even her father, who loved her, teased her that she must have been switched in the hospital. In her early teens, she had borne a certain resemblance to her older sister, with dark brown hair, though not quite as dark as Araminta's, and in her case green eyes like her mother's. Charlene had dark hair as well, and Bailey was six foot six, a powerfully built, very handsome blond man with Nordic good looks, of English and Scandinavian descent. He looked like a Viking. Charlene was delicate and fine-featured with the same dark hair as her daughters, both of whom were considerably taller than she was. But there Felicity's resemblance to her family ended. She'd had pleasant looks as a young teenager, and none of her sister's striking beauty, but she had a pretty face. And whereas Araminta's dazzling figure caught everyone's attention as much as her exquisite face, Felicity was most often described as a "big girl." She was taller than her sister, nearly six feet tall, and well over six feet in heels. And from a slim young teenager, she had gained fifty pounds in high school, which she couldn't explain. It did nothing to improve her looks.

Her mother had put her on several diets, and even hired a special chef and an exercise coach for her, to try to help her get the weight off, but nothing had worked so far, and Araminta reported to her mother regularly that she had seen a chocolate bar in Felicity's purse or seen her eating ice cream in the kitchen late at night, which certainly didn't help her lose weight.

Araminta loved to play tennis with her friends. Felicity hated sports, and spent most of her time in her room, studying. She had no interest in wearing pretty clothes and was uncomfortable at parties, but she was an outstanding student. She had been at the top of her class since she started school, she loved to read and study, and was particularly gifted in science. She had won every science prize in high school, and her crowning achievement had been getting accepted at MIT, the Massachusetts Institute of Technology. She was having a hard time choosing between majoring in biochemistry or nuclear physics, and for the moment she was headed for a career as a chemical engineer. Her father was immeasurably proud of her. No one in the family had any idea where her talent in science had come from, but her senior advisor in high school had written a glowing reference for her, and said she was just shy of being a genius. His reference had helped her get into MIT, which she loved. For the first time, she was among other students like her, and she didn't feel like a freak.

High school had been a nightmare for her. Araminta was merciless with her and harangued her constantly about her weight. Over the Christmas holiday, she had spent most of the time in her room, reading and studying, and avoiding Araminta and her friends when they came to the house and looked at her with disdain, or right through her. Felicity had her father's warm heart and sympathy for the underdog, whom she could easily relate to, since she had been in that position herself for all of her teenage years. At home, in Dallas, she felt like an outcast and a misfit, and was always referred to as the Smiths' "other daughter." Araminta was the star of the show and always had been. She was so beautiful as a child that people stopped on the street and stared at her. Felicity didn't begrudge Araminta her starring role, but it would have been nice to be accepted as she was, which had never happened. Her mother was constantly upset about her weight, and Araminta had been jealous and mean to her since the day she was born. Felicity felt constantly out of place, awkward, and too big for her own body, and whenever she felt that way, she took a pint of ice cream to her room and ate it, sometimes two pints, and then hid the empty containers in the garbage. Doughnuts were a problem for her too. They seemed to beckon to her like long-lost friends desperate to be near her. She could never resist them.

At MIT no one cared what size she was or what she ate. They were interested in her mind, her brain, and most of her friends were boys. She loved playing with physics theorems, and had a knack with them, the way other girls loved experimenting with makeup and new hairdos.

She had fought like a cat not to be presented at the Idlewild Club deb ball just before Christmas but had been pressured into it by her parents. She hadn't wanted to disappoint them, so she had given in. Other girls would have killed to be invited to come out there. Felicity dreaded it. Predictably, the evening had been an agony. She had asked her high school lab partner in chemistry, Andy Jameson, to be her escort. She knew she could at least talk to him. He was six inches shorter than she was, and weighed considerably less, but she didn't care. He was nice, from a very respectable family, although they considered him eccentric, so he and Felicity had that in common.

Andy had come to the house in white tie and tails that belonged to his father, with his hair sticking up. He had cut himself shaving in three places, and they snuck out of the party early, went back to her house, and drank beer in the kitchen while they talked about Harvard versus MIT.

He was at Harvard, and they'd met for coffee a few times in Cambridge. They had no romantic interest in each other, and he had a girlfriend at Harvard now. He had been Felicity's escort at the cotillion as a favor, and she was grateful to him. There was no one else she could ask, and she felt like a giant white iceberg in the dress her mother had picked for her. Andy had told her she looked really nice, but she knew he was lying. The hairdresser had done her hair in a crown of curls, which made her look even taller. Araminta had laughed at her when she saw her dressed. Andy had a jock brother who gave him a hard time too, so he knew the drill.

"You pay a price for being smart," Andy said over their second beer, and she nodded. They both knew it was true. Araminta had been punishing her for her entire life, and probably would have even if Felicity were beautiful and thin. She was different and couldn't hide it.

There were photographs of the prettiest debs in the newspaper the day after the cotillion and Felicity wasn't in them. She didn't even bother to look. Araminta had been all over the newspapers when she came out four years before. But she hadn't had a serious boyfriend yet, just a lot of passing romances, dates, and a few flings, and a number of boys who pursued her because she was rich. Felicity had no desire to be anyone's prey because of who her parents and grandparents were.

She couldn't wait to go back to school, where no one knew who she was. Dallas was like a fishbowl for her.

She only had three days left at home, when the invitation came from the ball committee at Versailles. Charlene saw it on her desk when she came home from a board meeting for the fund drive for a new pediatric wing for Parkland Memorial Hospital. She was the head of the committee planning the gala event. They were hoping to raise a hundred million dollars, which was what Charlene was so good at.

Charlene glanced at the envelope, opened it when she sat down at her desk, and read the cover letter carefully. At first, she thought it was a mistake. She and Bailey went to Europe several times a year, and had friends there, in London more than Paris, but they loved Paris and staying at the Ritz. And they'd taken the girls to the Hotel du Cap many times. It was Charlene's favorite hotel, and her daughters loved it too.

She saw that the invitation to a ball at Versailles was for Felicity, and she thought about it for a minute, and set it down on her desk. If she could get Felicity to agree to attend, it would give her self-confidence, and it was a huge honor to be one of forty American girls being invited. Bloodlines and ancestry were what mattered, aristocratic relatives and titles. Money didn't matter since many titled European aristocrats were practically penniless. Social connections didn't impress them either, and oil money was almost a handicap and would be politely ignored. For Felicity to be invited paid homage to the fact that the Smiths were nearly considered royalty in Dallas, and Charlene's family for three generations in Houston. It was a tribute to the whole family, and Charlene wanted Felicity to do it. She just wasn't sure how to convince her.

She went to Felicity's room to talk to her half an hour later and knocked softly on the door. When she walked into the room, Felicity was surrounded by the books she had brought with her, preparing for a big project she was planning to start as soon as she got back to school.

"Hi, Mama." She smiled at her mother. "How's your day?"

"Interesting. We're planning a big event for the hospital. They need to raise a hundred million for a new pediatric wing."

"I'm sure you'll do it." Felicity smiled at her again and sat up on her bed. She and her mother always got along. They were very different and didn't always understand each other, but her mother always tried to be fair. Felicity respected that about her. Araminta was the only real problem Felicity had in the family, and her mother tried to protect her younger daughter as best she could, although she wasn't always aware of the vicious things Araminta said, and Felicity rarely complained. It wouldn't have changed anything. It was who her sister was.

"We got an invitation today," Charlene said cautiously, still trying to figure out how to phrase it so Felicity didn't run screaming from the room. When Felicity agreed to be presented at the Idlewild Club, Charlene had promised her that she would never have to do anything like it again. And now here she was, with an even bigger opportunity to present to her, which she knew would horrify her daughter.

"An invitation to what?" Felicity asked politely, she didn't really care. She'd be back in Boston in three days, happy at school.

"An event in Paris. At the Palace of Versailles."

"That sounds cool. Are you and Dad going?"

"That depends on you," Charlene said gently.

"On me? Why?" Felicity looked innocently surprised.

"It's the first debutante ball ever held at the Palace of Versailles. It sounds very exciting. There will be two hundred and fifty French girls, and forty Americans are being invited from all over the U.S. It's quite an honor to be asked. I imagine it will be mostly royals the right age, and titled aristocrats, and some pretty fancy Americans, like Vanderbilts and Astors, and a lot of the Old Guard from New York."

"Well, thank God I'm off the hook." She smiled at her mother. "I already made my debut at Idlewild, so I'm out."

"They're inviting the girls who just came out, and those due to be presented next year. The age range is from seventeen to nineteen. They invited you, Felicity. That's an amazing honor." Felicity looked at her as soon as she said it, and backed away on the bed, as though she was afraid her mother would kidnap her and make her do it. Charlene wished she could. It would be so good for her.

"You said I'd never have to do anything like that again. I hated it, and you know it. I looked like a white elephant in the dress. The other girls were all squealing and giggling and dumb. They're all looking for husbands and none of them has a brain," Felicity said with contempt that was based on fear, and Charlene knew it. Felicity was terrified of social events where the spotlight was on her.

"First of all, you can go to parties and balls and still have a brain. We'll get you a different dress, and it's six months away so you have time to slim down a little. You can do it if you want to. No beer and doughnuts for six months, and your weight will plummet. You said you wanted to do track anyway, that will knock the weight off too. This might be a good incentive. But aside from that, it's a chance to participate in a historical event, the first deb ball at Versailles." Charlene's eyes lit up as she said it. Felicity's looked like a storm was brewing. A big one.

"They're all looking for husbands. I'm not. I don't speak French so I can't even talk to them."

"You can talk to the American girls. You might make new friends. And they're not all dumb."

"Yes, they are," Felicity said stubbornly. "Why can't Araminta do it? She'd love it."

"She's three years over the age limit, and she came out four years ago. They invited you, not your sister," Charlene said pointedly.

"I'm not doing it." She looked at her mother in terror.

"We could all go to the Hotel du Cap afterwards, for a week or two," Charlene said gently, trying to entice her.

"I want to go to summer school," Felicity persisted.

"You need a break. You can't go to school all the time."

"Why not? I have years of study ahead of me if I get a master's and a doctorate. I don't have time for events like that. And what would it do for me? I can't put it on a resume. No one cares about crap like that. I won't do it, Mom. You can't make me." She looked ready to run out of the room.

"Felicity, you need more in your life than a science lab," Charlene said firmly.

"Did Dad say I have to do it?" Felicity asked, worried. She cared more about what her father thought. Charlene and Araminta always wanted to go to balls and parties. Her father was more sensible and listened to Felicity's point of view too.

"I haven't told him yet," her mother said.

"I'd rather cut out my liver with an ice pick."

"It's just a dinner dance, Felicity. One evening out of a

lifetime." And such a beautiful evening it would be. Charlene could just see it.

"An evening wasted, and I don't have an escort. Andy's not going to come to Paris to take me."

"They have five hundred escorts available to the girls."

"It sounds like a circus." Felicity crossed her arms and glared at her mother. It was the battle of the Idlewild Club all over again.

"If it is, it'll be a beautiful circus. You might make friends that you'll keep for a lifetime, that's what these things are about."

"I don't need friends in France. You know how much I'll hate it. Why do you want me to go?"

"To broaden your world. You can't just lock yourself up with a bunch of scientists for the rest of your life." Charlene had been opposed to her going to MIT. She thought it was too narrow a focus, and Felicity needed to expand her world, not shrink it. She couldn't imagine her daughter's life as a physicist, or a chemical engineer. And she doubted that she'd find a suitable husband at MIT. Bailey had convinced her to let her go. It was Felicity's dream. "We can talk about it later."

"There's nothing to talk about. I'm not doing it. Araminta can go and pretend she's me. They'll never know."

"Araminta doesn't need another party in her life."

"Neither do I," Felicity said, and her mother stood with a determined look in her eye.

"Why does anything like this have to be such a battle?" Charlene said.

"Because it would be like torture. I don't want to get all done up in a big white dress, and meet a lot of bitchy girls, and boys I don't care about. I'm not like them, Mom, and I don't want to be. I don't care if I never get married. It's all girls like that think about. I want to do work that matters. They should have invited Araminta to do it. She'd kill to do something like that. I'd rather die," Felicity said heatedly, and an inner voice told Charlene to back down. For now, anyway. She left Felicity sulking on her bed a few minutes later, and went back to her study, just as Araminta walked in, looking beautiful and slim, in a pale blue Chanel wool suit. She looked like the cover of a magazine, and like Vivien Leigh as Scarlett O'Hara. She walked over to give her mother a kiss as Charlene sat down at her desk with a sigh. The invitation was lying in plain sight in front of her, and Araminta's eye instinctively went to it. She saw it and picked it up.

"What's that?"

"Nothing. An invitation to a party in Paris."

"Are you and Dad going? How fun. Can I come?" She read the invitation then and her breath caught. "It's a deb ball?" Charlene nodded, expecting the worst at any moment. Araminta picked up the cover letter then, and her mother

41

Danielle Steel

made no attempt to hide it. She'd find out sooner or later. "They want Felicity to come out in Paris, at Versailles?" Her eyes went wide with wonder, and she looked like she'd been slapped, as her mother nodded again.

"They're inviting forty American debs."

"Why can't I do it?"

"Because you came out four years ago. They want this year's debs and next year's." Araminta let out a bloodcurdling scream, as though she'd been stabbed.

"Oh my God, Mom, she looked bad enough at the cotillion here, you can't let her do it in Paris. She'll look like a freak. Why can't I do it and say I'm her? She'd hate it anyway."

"It'll build her confidence. This could be a turning point in her life. She might meet the man of her dreams, a handsome prince, a real one, before she winds up with some mad scientist from MIT who looks like Einstein." Charlene made it sound like the ball at Versailles was Felicity's last chance at a normal life, and it might be. After four years at MIT, she'd be so steeped in her scientific world that she'd have even less interest in the world she'd grown up in and had made her feel like a misfit all her life. She didn't want a world like theirs, and MIT was her ticket to escape a fate she dreaded. She loved her parents though, and Charlene knew that eventually they'd be able to force her into it if they had to, but she wanted Felicity to want to do it, which was too much to ask. Araminta was begging to let her go, and Felicity not to. Why did everything about the two girls always have to be complicated? Other than that, their life always seemed perfect to Charlene.

She loved their life in Dallas, and the life she'd grown up in. She and Bailey had a solid, happy marriage, and they had two daughters they loved, who couldn't have been more different, in every way.

Araminta dropped the invitation on her mother's desk, stormed out of the room, and went to her own room to sulk. She couldn't wait for her sister to leave and go back to school. She always ruined everything when she was home. She hated having her there, and for her friends to see her. She was always skulking around the house in some weird, sloppy outfit with her hair in a tangled ponytail. She looked a mess and didn't care. Every inch of Araminta was polished perfection, and she wanted to meet the kind of boys they'd invited to be escorts at Versailles. She didn't want to go as the single older sister. She wanted to be the star of the night, with every young man begging to meet her, and a few older ones.

Most of her friends had gotten engaged or married by then. Araminta was one of the last girls on the shelf, at twenty-two. Texan girls married young. It wasn't fair. The ball at Versailles would be wasted on Felicity. She didn't deserve it. Araminta had been groomed for the life of a princess. All she needed

43

now was to meet her prince. And instead, her weird sister was being handed a golden opportunity she didn't want. If Felicity didn't agree to do it, none of them would go, and life would go on just as it was now, a constant round of parties among people Araminta already knew. There wasn't a single boy in Dallas she wanted. She knew them all and had kissed and flirted with most of them.

Felicity's last three days at the end of the Christmas vacation were hell for her. Charlene kept trying to convince her of what a good time she'd have at the ball at Versailles. Araminta pelted her with snide remarks and angry looks. Their father stayed out of it. He preferred to leave important social decisions involving the girls to his wife and was sure she knew best.

Felicity finally gave in on the last night. The pressure they put on her was overwhelming. She stopped in her parents' bedroom before she went to bed. Her mother was making lists for the event she was working on for the hospital, with a list of big potential donors to contact. Araminta was hungover from New Year's Eve, and her parents didn't know it. She knew how to hide it, although Felicity could always tell from the foul mood she was in, even worse than usual with her younger sister. She made Felicity feel unwelcome in her own home. She was always the misfit and the outcast. She couldn't wait to get back to school.

Charlene looked up when Felicity walked into the room. She was wearing faded flannel pajamas that were too small for her and she loved them. They had snowflakes printed on them. Bailey was downstairs in the den, watching football.

"Thank you for a wonderful Christmas," she said in a gentle voice to her mother. Her Southern drawl was a soft purr, and she looked unhappy. It always made her feel sad that she felt so uncomfortable in her own home, as though it was her own fault, and had nothing to do with Araminta and her parents. It couldn't be their fault. It must be hers. She had failed vacation again, even after doing the cotillion to please them. It hadn't made a difference. It was just one more bad memory for her, to add to so many others. "I had a great time," she lied, as she always did, and Charlene knew it.

Felicity just didn't know how to change it. She couldn't change her parents or her sister, or even herself. She had tried. Their accepting her as she was never seemed like an option. Charlene knew Felicity hadn't had a great time at home, she never did. They were her family, but Felicity knew they were not her allies or her friends. They had never fully accepted who she was, and probably never would, Felicity realized now.

Charlene didn't mention the ball at Versailles again. She would just sign Felicity up for it, without telling her, and hope to talk her into it between now and July.

"I'll do it, Mom," Felicity said in nearly a whisper.

"Do what, darling?" Charlene asked, as she set the notepad down. "I'm going to miss you. Are you coming to Aspen in February?" It was a rhetorical question. Felicity was expected to come home for all vacations. She had no excuse not to, and no friends at school to stay with. All of her friends there were men who shared her interests, and were just pals, not dates. She didn't mind.

"Sure, Mom." She hated skiing as much as they all loved it. Araminta looked like a bolt of lightning on the slopes, slim and sexy in her ski clothes. Felicity was always scared to death and didn't have her family's natural aptitude for the sport. She was afraid of heights and terrified of the chairlift. "I meant the ball, in Paris. I'll do it." Charlene looked at her carefully, and a slow smile warmed her face.

"Thank you." Charlene reached out and touched her daughter's hand, and they held hands for a minute. Felicity liked making her happy, even if she had to sacrifice herself to do it. "I promise you'll have fun, and we'll get you a dress you love this time." She had noticed on the cover letter that the American debutantes would wear white, as was their tradition, and the French girls would wear color, which Charlene thought was unfortunate. Felicity would look better in a dark color, or even a pastel. White just highlighted the weight she could never seem to get off. Or at least not yet, but they had six months to work on it. "Your father and I are going to be so proud of you," she assured her, and Felicity smiled. That was why Felicity was doing it. She wanted to make them proud of her, no matter what it took. Araminta never would be. She didn't have it in her to be generous with her sister, or to help her through it. She would make fun of her as usual, maybe even more this time since she wanted to be a deb at Versailles so badly. "I'll come to Boston and we'll go shopping," Charlene promised. Felicity sat down next to her on the bed, and her mother hugged her. Her father came into the room then, beaming. His team had won. Felicity stood up to leave, and Charlene informed him of Felicity's decision before she left the room. Father and daughter exchanged a look and he smiled.

"Good girl," he said with his wide smile. Felicity thought her father was the handsomest man in the world. "You know how proud we're going to be. You'll be the belle of the ball." They knew it wasn't true, but she would do it anyway, just for them. And after that, she'd never be a debutante again, and she could do whatever she wanted. She was trying to buy her freedom, or their love. She wasn't sure which.

# Chapter 3

It was a brilliantly sunny day in LA the day after New Year's. Some years were like that. Spring was in the air. Caroline Taylor was just leaving her house in Bel Air in a pink blouse and matching shorts, and little ballet flats like Audrey Hepburn had worn in *Love in the Afternoon* with Gary Cooper. Caroline had a movie star ingénue quality to her, which was the world she had grown up in. Her father was Josh Taylor, the legendary Academy Award–winning producer-director. He was sixty-four years old. Her mother was Elizabeth "Betty" Wade, the movie star. Betty was thirty-nine years old and barely looked older than their only daughter, Caroline, who was eighteen. Betty had had her at twenty-one. Her career as a star hadn't given her time to have another child after Caroline, and she didn't want one. Betty and Josh agreed that one child was enough for them. Caroline was dazzling, and looked like a woman at eighteen. She had grown up in the fast-moving sophisticated world of Hollywood royalty.

The garage door yawned open, and Caroline's little red Mercedes sports car sped out onto the road. She was in a hurry. Her mother had told her about the ball at Versailles that morning after breakfast. They had sat and made lists together afterwards, of all the things they had to do. The timing was perfect. Betty and Josh were going to be on location, making a movie before that. When they finished, they would go to the Cannes Film Festival together, and then they'd come back to LA at the end of May for postproduction on the movie. They'd be finished by the end of June, in time to go to Paris with Caroline for the ball. It sounded like fun to Caroline, even though she was in a hurry as she listened. She had other more grown-up things on her mind. She was a freshman at USC, majoring in film production. She had a room in the dorm but preferred to live at home most of the time. And she had total unsupervised freedom when her parents were away. They trusted her like an adult, and their housekeeper lived in, so she wasn't alone in the house. She wanted to be a director like her father, not an actress like her mother, although she was pretty enough to be. She had a flawless figure, and long wavy blonde hair, which hung down her back as she drove to West Hollywood.

# The Ball at Versailles

The debutante ball at Versailles sounded exciting to her. Her mother had promised her a dress from Dior with a big ballgown skirt. She didn't care about meeting a man. She already had one. Her boyfriend, Adam Black, was twenty-eight years old, ten years older than she was. He had been in one of her father's movies, and they'd met when he came to the house the summer before. Their secret affair had been going on for five months, and she had discovered things with him she'd never dreamed of before she met him. She was a woman now and felt like it when she was with him. Her parents would have been furious if they'd known, but they were away a lot, and she and Adam were careful to keep the relationship a secret. They met at his apartment and went to funny little restaurants he knew. They'd gone to Mexico together for a week when her parents were away on location. They'd gone to Palm Springs and San Francisco for weekends, and no one suspected anything. They thought she was at her room in the dorm when she was at his apartment.

She looked older than eighteen, and they loved each other. It wasn't just a Hollywood romance, it was the real deal. The studio he was signed with made him escort starlets sometimes to premieres and Hollywood events, but he came rushing back to Caroline afterwards. They were going to tell her parents eventually, but not yet. It was too soon, and she didn't want them to spoil things with Adam. It was fun having

a secret life with him. She was going to tell him about the
ball when she got to his apartment. It was a short drive from
her parents' home to his small apartment in a seedy Spanish-
style building in West Hollywood. She felt very grown-up
when she went there to meet him.

She parked her car outside and rang the bell. He buzzed
her in and she raced up the stairs. He was standing behind
the open door when she got there, and as soon as he closed
the door once she was in his apartment, she saw that he was
naked, and leapt into his arms. He pulled her clothes off as
they raced toward his bedroom. They'd been managing to
find time together every day. She'd cut a lot of classes to be
with him and didn't care. Adam was the love of her life and
the most exciting thing that had ever happened to her. One
day he would be a big star like her mother. He had all the
makings of it, looks, talent, charisma. Whenever she saw his
movies or photographs of him now, it sent a thrill through
her. He felt it too. He said that he had never loved anyone
as he did her. She had been a virgin and an innocent when
they met six months earlier, and now she was an adept and
experienced lover. There was no turning back now. She
would have done anything to be with him, and their love-
making was all the more passionate because it was a secret.
They spent hours in bed together every day, and Caroline
had never been happier in her life. He made up for everything

she had never gotten from her parents, because they were important, famous, and busy. Her parents were so tightly woven together that sometimes she felt like there was no room in their life for her. Adam never made her feel that way. He said he adored her, and she knew it was true. One day he would be as famous as her parents. But for now, he was all hers, and he owned her body and soul.

The Walker Mansion at Seventy-third Street and Fifth Avenue was one of the most famous historical homes in New York. It was a beautiful structure, and an architectural wonder, and was in all the guidebooks of the city as a historical treasure. It belonged to Robert Walker, and had been built by his great-grandfather in the nineteenth century. At the time, it had been at the northern edge of the city, with gardens and fields all around it. The land around it had been sold over the years, and the house remained. There was a small elegant garden where Robert and his daughter sat and ate lunch sometimes on sunny days. On weekends, they went to their farm in Greenwich, Connecticut, where Robert kept stables with beautiful horses. He was an expert rider and polo player, and his daughter, Samantha, loved to ride too. Her father saw to it that she had gentle horses to ride, so she didn't get injured.

The house in the city had a serious feeling to it. It was filled with portraits of Robert's ancestors. They had been an important part of the industrial revolution, and their fortune had been legendary for two centuries. He was a handsome but modest man, didn't like drawing attention to himself, and had been one of the early founders of venture capital, which he found exciting and which had increased considerably the fortune he already had.

He had brought up his eighteen-year-old daughter to have solid values, and a strong sense of social responsibility. His philanthropic contributions were famous in charitable circles, and some of his largest donations had been anonymous. He had no wish to see his name on a building, a hospital, or a library. He was a serious man and his home reflected that. Samantha was the ray of sunshine that lit up his world. He had had dark times in his life and come through them.

He and his late wife, Diana, had established a charitable foundation. She was an artist, and he continued to give large amounts of money to the museums she had loved. One of the museums had curated a beautiful posthumous show of her work. She had been strongly influenced by the Impressionists and her work had a more contemporary resemblance to the paintings of Mary Cassatt. She loved painting mothers and children, and she had been a wonderful mother herself to their two children. Samantha had had a brother, Thomas, who was two years younger than she.

# The Ball at Versailles

Diana and Robert had met right after he finished business school at Harvard and Diana was recently back from two years at the Beaux-Arts in Paris. He had been starting his fledgling business, she had been painting furiously in a studio in the Village. She came from fortunate circumstances and chose to live simply, as he did. Her family had founded one of the biggest pharmaceutical companies in the country in Chicago, and she was as discreet as Robert. They were a perfect match in every way.

They moved into a loft together in the Village near her studio and married the year after they met. Sam arrived three years later, shortly after Robert had inherited his father's imposing home, and with some misgivings, they moved into the grand surroundings uptown and fell in love with the house once they lived there. Their son, Thomas, was born two years after Samantha.

Diana had added some creative touches while respecting the house's history, and painted whimsical murals in the children's rooms, and some fun trompe l'oeil in the kitchen. She had set up a beautiful airy studio on the top floor. Robert had never touched it after she died. It remained along with her memory as part of the house. The paintings she had been working on when she died were still there, among them an early portrait of Sam and Tommy. Robert seldom went up there now, but he had for a long time. He used to take refuge there when he was mourning her. Thirteen years later, he had recovered as much as he ever would.

Their life had seemed totally perfect for eight years after they married, and tragedy struck hard on an icy Connecticut road on a December morning, when a truck skidded and hit them head-on. Diana was driving the children up from the city. Robert had driven up in his own car an hour earlier. Diana and three-year-old Tommy were killed instantly, and five-year-old Samantha was in a coma for three months. Robert sat by her bedside for the entire three months and never left her, determined that she would survive, despite all evidence to the contrary. The severe injuries she had sustained had left Samantha with a slight limp, an imperfect sense of balance from the head injury, and a weak left arm she could use efficiently, but not with the strength of her right arm. Considering the condition she had been in after the accident, her recovery was nothing short of miraculous. The effects of the accident were that her subtle limp was still present at eighteen, thirteen years later, that occasionally she lost her balance and fell for no apparent reason, and that one arm was stronger than the other, which didn't bother her. As a result of her injuries, her father became hyper-vigilant and fiercely protective of her. All her life since the accident, Samantha had challenged her weaknesses and refused to let them hamper her, just as she had defied the odds of her survival. Growing up, she did what children her age did, and she refused to let the residual effects of the accident slow her down or stop her.

Samantha had some faint memories of her mother, which she cherished, but was never sure if she truly remembered her or had created the memories from things her father had told her in the ensuing years. It was evident from everything he said that her mother had been a remarkable person, giving, loving, generous, kind, devoted to her husband and children, with many talents, great beauty, and an infallible sense of humor. Unfortunately, Samantha had no memories of her brother, except for the photographs of her mother and brother scattered throughout the house.

Just as Sam bore traces of the accident, so did Robert at a much deeper level. He wanted to protect Sam forever, from all forms of harm, random accidents, and bad people. His heart almost stopped every time she fell. He could never get used to it, although she had adjusted to it as soon as she started walking again, and when she fell, she stood up, dusted herself off, and kept going. He found her to be incredibly brave. Nothing stopped her or frightened her. She was willing to try anything and tackle hard tasks that others who had no handicaps shrank from. Her brain functioned impeccably, although at first, the doctors had feared that wouldn't be the case. She had made a remarkable recovery that defied all the odds. And despite the tragic circumstances of the accident, she was a happy, well-balanced person, and very mature for her age, which wasn't surprising given what she'd been through. She was sensible and practical about her injuries.

As the years went by, she ran her father's house, firmly when necessary, but with respect for their employees, who adored her. She had grown up surrounded by loving people, and her father, who would have moved heaven and earth for her. Because of her father's fortune, hers had never been a life of struggle, but there were physical things she had to live with, and overcome, like her tendency to stumble occasionally when overtired, or even fall. She attended normal school by first grade at Dalton and had graduated seven months before.

Diana had filled the house with flowers when she was alive, and Robert continued to do so, in all the colors she had preferred. Samantha had picked up the relay on that and ordered elegant arrangements, in keeping with their home. And despite its encounter with tragedy, it was not a sad house, mostly thanks to Sam, who had been brave and determined since she was very small.

She had conducted a séance there herself once, hoping to contact her mother. She gave up the concept a few months later. She was content living alone with her father, surrounded by people who worked for him, to make their lives easier. The one thing she hated in her life were limitations, whether imposed by life, or those who wished to protect her, particularly her father. Her only quarrel with him was that he tried to curb her activities, and shield her from anything that might hurt her, physically or emotionally. Sam wanted to live a full life. The only thing stopping her was her father. Because she'd led such a sheltered life, she was shy. Even without the accident, her father's enormous fortune set her apart from others and made her the object of scrutiny and jealousy, and frequently nasty comments from other girls her age as they got older. College was socially easier for her than school had been. Anonymity gave her a sense of freedom, and she was loving her freshman year at NYU, majoring in art history. She had her mother's passion for art. She had wanted to live in the dorm, or go farther away, but her father wouldn't let her.

She loved her classes at NYU, but she hadn't made any friends yet. She was used to getting around the sprawling campus. She still wanted to live in the dorms, but her father was adamant. He insisted that it could be dangerous for her, if she fell down a flight of concrete stairs. He was never going to allow her to risk a head injury again. She might not be as lucky next time. But even going to college now, she felt as though she lived in a bubble. So did her father. It suited him.

He took refuge from the world behind his walls. He led a quiet social life and had dated very few women since his wife's death, and always said that Sam was the only long-term woman he needed in his life. Other women came and went from time to time, and he kept them away from Sam. She didn't need to know about his dating life, and he never brought the women he went out with to the house.

He had received the invitation for Samantha for the ball at Versailles. He realized that she needed more than school and her quiet life with her father, going between their city mansion and their country estate. She needed young people too. And friends, and dates, and romance. She was eighteen now, and a beautiful girl. His worst fear was that she'd fall into the hands of a man who wouldn't take good care of her, but she couldn't live like a nun forever, although she never complained about it. She longed for a bigger life.

Samantha had been invited to be presented at the Infirmary Ball and the Junior Assemblies in New York this past Christmas, but she had rapidly refused, for all the reasons they both knew. Some of her female classmates from Dalton were making their debuts, none of them girls she had been close to at school. She'd had one close friend at school, whose family had moved to London after they graduated, and since Samantha wasn't living in the dorms, it had been hard to meet people at NYU. She saw students hanging out in small groups in the Student Union, but no one had asked her to join them so far, and her slightly halting gait made her look strange at times. She didn't have the ease or physical self-confidence of other girls her age. And the thought of coming down a staircase with an escort she barely knew, and possibly stumbling and falling down the stairs, had caused her to refuse the invitation immediately. Robert was equally concerned and hadn't insisted. But she had missed out on what might have been an exciting evening for her. She had deprived herself of the opportunity to meet other young people her age, and maybe even her first romance.

She was being given a second chance with the ball at Versailles, and he wondered if maybe her European peers would be more mature and forgiving about her differences. The thought of exposing her in that way made him anxious for her, and at the same time, he thought she should give it a whirl. She might have a fabulous time and meet someone wonderful and make new friends. She might even marry European royalty. It was the kind of evening that made one dream, in a setting that made it seem even more magical. Diana had had a particular fondness for France, after her two years of studying at the Beaux-Arts, and he had a feeling that she would have approved. The event didn't have the enclosed incestuous quality of the ingrown milieu of New York Society. A ball in France in a remarkable palace seemed much more glamorous and sophisticated, although he knew Sam would have the same concerns in Paris too, with an escort she'd never laid eyes on before.

When the time came, hopefully not too soon, Robert knew it would take a special kind of man to nurture and protect Sam, and he wasn't going to relinquish his daughter to anyone until he was sure a future husband was up to it. He had not seen such a man yet, nor had Sam. She'd dated a few boys from school, but none seriously. She was mature beyond her years, which made the boys in her class seem silly to her. And the last thing Robert wanted was to have her move far away from him, but as he read about the ball in the cover letter, he didn't have the heart to deprive her of something which sounded like every girl's dream come true. It really would be a fairy-tale experience if all went well, and an unforgettable event for her, if he was brave enough to let her do it and she wanted to. He wasn't sure she would, or if he should encourage her. Part of him wanted to stop her, and a nobler part of him wanted to help her do it.

He was still debating about what to say to her about it when Samantha came into his study on New Year's Eve before dinner. He had no plans for the evening, nor did she. They were spending it together, as they had every year since she was old enough to eat in the formal dining room with him. They would bring in the new year together. He would kiss her on the cheek at midnight, and hug her, and then they would go to their respective rooms, where she would dream about the future, and he would remember the New Year's Eves he had shared with his wife for ten unforgettable years. Those years had nourished him ever since, along with his love for his daughter.

Robert was wearing a dinner jacket and black tie, as he did for all holidays, and Sam appeared in his study in a beautiful white satin and silver dress with a wide skirt with a tulle overlay by Christian Dior that she had bought at Bergdorf Goodman, and she wore little silver flat shoes, so she'd be steady on her feet. She wore high heels occasionally but not often. They were an invitation to mishaps she didn't need to risk for an evening with her father. Her hair was a light titian red, and she had big green eyes like her mother's. She was a very striking girl, and she had a tiny waist and the dress emphasized it. Robert smiled as soon as he saw her. She looked like a fairy or a princess.

"Don't you look beautiful tonight," he said admiringly, and she turned slowly in a full circle so he could see the back of the dress too. It suited her perfectly and reminded him of the invitation to the ball.

They walked to the dining room together and sat down at the long table in the elegant room that was still exactly as Sam's great-great-grandfather had designed it. Their home was similar to the Frick mansion, which was just a few blocks south of them on Fifth Avenue. One of the Frick heirs, an unmarried granddaughter who was quite elderly now, still lived there alone on an upper floor. It was the kind of fate that Robert didn't want for Samantha one day. He wanted her to have a full life with a husband and children, which he realized was never going to happen, if he kept her hidden away, and protected by him. He would have to open the door of the golden cage one day. She was too beautiful to waste it on just her father, others deserved to see her too. Sam needed the life of a normal young girl. If Robert's fortune had been less vast, she would have been out in the world, with their own kind, in her own age group long since. But the way they lived allowed her to remain hidden, whether by her own choice or his.

They had finished the first course of cold fresh crab when he brought up the subject of the ball. He still wasn't sure how he felt about it, if he wanted her to go to the ball or not, but she had a right to participate in the decision too.

"I had an interesting letter from Paris yesterday," Robert commented, as their butler set down pheasant in front of them, since Robert wasn't fond of turkey. And Henry, their butler, poured white wine into Sam's glass as well. At eighteen, her father considered her old enough to drink wine at dinner.

"Are you investing in France, Dad?" Sam asked. She leaned more to her mother's artistic pursuits, but she was always intrigued by her father's business, and liked hearing about it.

He smiled at her inquiry. She always kept abreast of what he was doing and asked the right questions. Her questions were from the heart, and she was very bright. She would make someone a good wife one day.

"This wasn't about business. It was about you."

"About me? I don't know anyone in Paris."

"Neither do I. Maybe we should change that."

"Do you want to go to France next summer?" They usually spent their summers in Greenwich, but she had been to Europe with him before. She loved the shopping and art galleries and museums. It was fun traveling with him, and he knew a great deal about art. Sam's mother had educated him on the subject.

"Maybe. We've been invited to a ball at Versailles," he explained, "or more precisely, you have, and I've been invited to tag along. It sounds very grand. It's the first debutante ball they've held at Versailles, and they are inviting forty American girls to make their debut there. And you are one of them." She looked startled for a moment, stopped eating and gazed at him intently.

"Why me? I didn't come out here, so how do they even know about me?"

"Committees like that have their ways. They talk to people and find out who the likely candidates would be for something like this. I'm not sure what their criteria are, except presumably blue blood and decent families for the Americans, since we don't have titles here, and they can't choose the girls that way as they would in England or France, or other European countries.

"It sounds like fun," he continued, "and a lot more glamorous than the deb balls you turned down here. They have a pool of five hundred distinguished young men to offer as escorts. They would assign one of them to you if you do it. It sounds like all you have to do is buy a dress and show up." He simplified it for her to make it sound less daunting. There was a part of him that wanted her to go, for her sake. It sounded like an important step and a lovely honor to him, and every young girl's dream. He didn't want to keep her from that.

"I'm sure there's more to it than that," Sam said in a small voice, toying with her food, as she thought about it.

"Not really. There's some sort of reception the day before to introduce all the girls and escorts to each other. And a tea given by the American ambassador, to honor the American girls. There will be two hundred and fifty French debutantes, and up to forty Americans. You can get lost in the crowd if you feel nervous. And at the ball, they present you, and that's it. You might meet some very nice Europeans if you do it," he said gently.

"Do you want me to?" She looked surprised. Usually, he kept her at home in the hothouse environment she'd grown up in, except for school. Robert was a great believer in education, and Sam was a good student.

"I think you should consider it. It really is a great compliment. Someone must have said some very nice things about you, if they're inviting you to make your debut in France, at such an important event. That's not something to turn your nose up at. And I'd be there that evening, so you wouldn't be lost there on your own."

"That's not what I worry about, getting lost at a ball. It might be fun, if I don't have to walk down a flight of stairs, and curtsy at the end of it. I don't want to trip and roll down the stairs and land on my bottom at the foot of the stairs, instead of making my bow," she said, looking straight at him. He knew what she worried about, and so did he, it was why she had declined to come out at the cotillion in New York.

"I know, Sam. But if your escort is a decent guy, you can tell him to keep a good grip on you." Her father had done it many times and kept her from falling, when her own sense of balance failed her. It happened less now than it used to, but it still did, and gave her no warning.

"And if he doesn't speak enough English to understand, and doesn't care, I'll make history at that ball, and wind up in a newsreel. 'Debutante from New York gets confused and slides down the staircase and does the splits in front of the honor committee. God bless America!' I'd look like a complete idiot." And then she grinned at him. "Are you trying to marry me off and get rid of me, by the way? That's what those balls are for. All those girls are looking for husbands."

"You'd probably come home with a prince, or a duke at the very least. That's better than you'd do here," he said with a laugh. "And no, I'm not trying to get rid of you. That's the last thing I want. If you married someone there, it would break my heart. I'd have to move to the Ritz in Paris so I could see you every day. I just thought it would be fun for you. You deserve better than New Year's Eve with your dad for the rest of your life. And I honestly think you'd enjoy it. They're even having a sound and light show at the presentation. Versailles is a very big deal. This will be a first. I think you ought to do it. Don't miss out on the fun, Sam. And I'll be with you." He was still of two minds about it, but he wanted it for her.

She was silent for a long time after that, mulling it over, and she finally looked at him, with most of her dinner still on her plate. The food was delicious, prepared by their excellent chef, but she'd been too nervous to even taste it, once her father mentioned the ball. She would feel like a loser now, if she didn't go. She hadn't regretted for a minute not going to the deb balls in New York, and some of the meanest girls from her school had been presented. But this would be all new faces and doing it at Versailles made it seem special. She usually tried to meet every challenge, and this was definitely one.

"What do you think Mom would tell me to do?" she asked him. It was a game they played often when she had trouble making a decision.

He didn't hesitate, he had already thought of that himself.

"I think she'd tell you to be brave and go. You can't hang around with me forever. You're a grown-up young woman, and you need to step out into the world and have some adventures, even if that's scary." Going to Versailles to be presented was much more daunting than going to college, which didn't scare her at all, although her father had had some reservations about that too, and he had flatly refused to let her live in the dorms, although she wanted to, or go to a college outside New York. She had to live at home, and he had wanted her to stay in the city. Sam had wanted to apply to Vassar and Wellesley, good Ivy League colleges for women, but he hadn't allowed it. He wanted her at home, close to him, where he knew she would be safe and protected, and he was near at hand, to help with any problem.

"What if the other girls are mean?" she asked him, and sounded like a little girl, and he smiled.

"If they are, you don't speak French, so you won't know what they said." The only thing they both worried about was if she lost her balance and fell in some very public way. Anything else she could handle and didn't care about, but falling so publicly would be mortifying.

"You can't let that stop you, Sam. Mean girls, or falling. Don't let your fears deprive you of a wonderful experience. I think you should go."

"I think so too. It sounds exciting. Scary as hell, but pretty amazing to come out in a palace." She looked at her father, as Henry set down the dessert in front of them. It was her favorite, chocolate soufflé with whipped cream. Her father had it with the thin, light vanilla sauce intended for it *à l'anglaise.* Sam preferred their cook's delicious whipped cream. She smiled at her father. "I'll do it," she said in a whisper. She felt breathless after she said it. What if it was a disaster? But if it was, she knew she'd get through it. She'd been through worse things before, much worse things.

"Just don't find a husband at the ball and get married immediately or move to Europe."

"That's not why I'm doing it, Dad." He knew she wasn't. "I'm doing it for you, to prove I can."

"And for yourself," he added. "And to have fun."

"And for Mom," she said softly, with tears shimmering in her eyes. She knew her mother would want her to do it and be brave. Her mother had been brave enough to study and live in France for two years, and to live a simple artist's life for several years in New York, although she came from a prominent, wealthy family.

It was ten o'clock when they finished dinner and went back to the library. There was a fire burning in the fireplace, and the two hours until midnight passed quickly as they talked. Robert poured her a single glass of champagne, and another for himself. She'd already had a glass of white wine at dinner, and he didn't want to get her drunk.

He kissed her on the cheek at midnight and raised his glass. "To the Belle of the Ball at Versailles," he said proudly, ignoring his own qualms for her sake.

A few minutes later, they went upstairs to their own rooms to go to bed. It was a new year, full of adventure. To both of them, 1958 was already looking promising.

# Chapter 4

The weather in New York in February was particularly bad. It rained for a good part of the month, and snowed twice. Amelia caught a bad cold and the flu and came home to have her mother take care of her, and Jane caught it from her. They both stayed home from work and school for a week, but at least they were together. It gave them time to work on their plans for the summer. One night when they sat in their bathrobes in the living room, drinking mugs of chicken soup, Jane had a pen and notepad in hand and she made some lists. They still had to shop for Amelia's dress, and Jane wanted to book their plane tickets soon, so they'd be cheaper. They made all the notes they needed to, spent much of the time sleeping, and Jane cooked and gave Amelia chicken broth at regular intervals, and vitamins. By the weekend, they were both better.

Amelia went back to the dorm on Sunday night. She had a test the next day, and Jane went back to work on Monday morning.

She had a message from Phillip Parker, the CEO of the company, asking her to meet him in his office at eleven, and she wished she had worn something more businesslike to work. She was wearing slacks and a heavy sweater, with her hair pulled back in a simple ponytail, and she still looked tired and pale after having been sick for a week. She had a pair of plain high-heeled pumps in the closet in her office, and put them on before she went upstairs to see him, instead of the flat shoes she came to work in.

His secretary said to Jane that he was expecting her, and she ushered her straight into his office. He smiled when he saw her.

"I hear you were out sick all last week," he said. "I hope you're feeling better."

"I am." She wasn't sure why he had called her to his office. He'd had a mild heart attack in November, and there were rumors flying around that he might retire earlier than planned. Either way, he had already said that he was retiring at the end of the year, and the race was on for someone to fill his shoes. Jane was the next in line and had been there for nine years. He had alluded several times to her stepping up to become the publisher and CEO. It would be a huge step up to have the position, as a woman. She was almost certain to get the job and would be the first woman to run the company in its long, dignified history. It was going to be a real tribute to her, and also meant she would be getting a big raise, since there was a vast discrepancy between her current salary and his. There were no other candidates for the position, and Phillip had assured her that he would go to bat for her. The company was privately owned, by the same family that had owned it for the last seventy years.

She had a suspicion that Phillip had called her upstairs to tell her he was leaving sooner than the end of the year and to get ready to move upstairs. It was going to be a major change in her career, and a welcome one. She was loyal to the company, loved her job, and had been struggling on her salary for years. She had stayed for the last few years because the financial struggle was going to end when she got his job. It was worth the wait, even in less than ideal conditions in the meantime.

"I wanted to meet with you last week, Jane, but you were out sick. I wanted to give you fair warning about some changes that are going to happen faster than I expected." It was exactly what she'd thought. He was leaving sooner, and she was going to have to step into his shoes pretty quickly. But she was ready, she had been preparing to take this step up for years, Phillip had more or less promised her she'd get his job when he left. He'd been saying it for the last five years, and there was no one else in-house who was up to it. Phillip knew it as well as she did, and the owners of the company did too.

The company was owned by the three Axelrod sisters who had inherited it. They were in their seventies now, and none of them had ever worked in the business. The family just lived off it, very profitably, and they had blind faith in Phillip Parker, who had worked there for twenty-nine years and had never let them down.

He met with the sisters twice a year to bring them up to date on current plans. The three women lived in Chicago, Illinois, Grosse Pointe, Michigan, and Santa Barbara, California. All were widowed now, and the eldest was turning eighty. He always enjoyed seeing them, and how reasonable and intelligent they were. None of their children were interested in publishing, and that way Phillip had no interference in how he ran the company, and its profit and loss statements spoke well for him.

Jane glanced around the room for an instant, as Phillip spoke to her, thinking about the changes she wanted to make to brighten up his office. It was a little dreary, very old-fashioned, and entirely masculine, with dark wood paneling, wine-colored drapes, and dark gray carpeting. She wanted to infuse new life into the physical space and the company. She thought it would energize their female employees to have a woman running it. She had met the three owners several times and got on well with them. She was respectful of them, and how intelligent they were. It was going to be a major coup to have a female head of a large company. Publishing was usually very traditional, so this was going to be an innovative leap into modernization. It was exactly what women in business wanted. At forty-one, it was a huge tribute to Jane that they thought she was worthy of it.

"We're going to be making some major changes, Jane, sooner than planned, and I wanted to make you aware of it, and give you a heads-up." Jane could hear the antique clock on his wall ticking loudly, and she knew she'd always remember the sound, and associate it with that moment, when she became the first female CEO of a highly respected publishing company. It had taken her nine years of dedication and hard work to get there. She had earned every minute of what was about to happen.

"You know how highly I think of you," he went on, as she hoped that her nose didn't look as red and swollen as it had to her that morning. She had worn very little makeup, not realizing that this was going to be a landmark day when she'd have to look her best. She wished she'd had some hint that today was going to be special. Phillip looked serious when he spoke. "I've been convinced for a long time that you were the right person to fill my shoes when I left. And as it turns out, I'm leaving sooner than I originally planned, after the little episode I had three months ago. I'm going to stick around till June, but we're going to have to move faster than anticipated so I can be out of here in four months. My doctor feels that I'm pushing my luck if I keep working, and Martha wants me at home. It's going to be a big change for me too." He didn't look happy about it, but resigned, and Jane was sympathetic.

"You've earned it," she said quietly. "And Martha's right. You should take time to enjoy each other." He nodded.

"I've had some unexpected news about the company. I've had no doubts that you could handle my job. In fact, I'm certain of it. But for the first time, the owners have come to me with a candidate for my job and they feel strongly about him. He's the son of their financial advisor, and he's got all the credentials, and an impressive track record in publishing, at a major house. You may know him, Ted Barnes, Yale under-grad, Harvard Business School. He's fifty-two years old, and he's the only candidate I've met who has the background and the right personality to run a place like this. The Axelrod sisters are afraid that you would meet resistance as a woman, and that having been in a lesser position in-house for a long time, the people under you may not be willing to take direc-tion from you, and the sisters have a point. I'd never thought of that because I know how good you are at your job, and I think you'd be good at mine too. But bringing someone in from outside the company, we avoid all the politics and jealousy. It would slow you down if you had to deal with that and try to do your job too. I met Barnes last week, and he's the right man for the job.

"Jane, I can't tell you how sorry I am. I know you've been looking forward to taking over from me. His Harvard MBA makes a difference, and he's already run a company bigger than ours. This will be second nature to him. And he's got ten years more experience than you do. I just can't go against what the owners want. I think it's the right move for the house. I know this isn't good news for you, and I didn't see it coming either." He looked grim and gray-faced as he told her, and she stared at him, shocked. She could still hear the clock behind him, it sounded to her like her heart beating in the room. She had just been told she wasn't getting the promotion she had waited years for.

"And what happens to me in all this?" she said in a choked voice, trying to keep her composure and be businesslike. Her heart and mind were racing. "I stay as I am?" she asked him directly. Her whole future was in the balance, and on the line.

"Ted starts next week. We've got four months to get him ready to take over, and we can't waste a minute. Technically, you could stay in your current job of course, and you're so good at it, but I think it would be a mistake and awkward for you. And I can't guarantee your old job once Ted comes in. He'll want to bring in some of his own people, and your position as Number Two would be an obvious one for him to want to fill. He would have to work very closely with you, and he knows you were slated for the job we just offered him. I think it's going to be best for both of you, not to have to deal with a situation like that. We think what makes the most sense is that you leave before he comes in." What he said sounded like a death sentence to her and she stared at him, trying to make sense of what he had just said. She wasn't getting the promotion he had promised her for years. She wasn't going to be the CEO and publisher when he left. They had given the job to someone else, and he wanted her to leave that week, before the guy who got the job arrived. She hadn't been promoted. She was being fired. She felt like he had just run a saber through her heart.

"We'll give you three months' severance of course, to give you time to find something else." He said it as though it was a magnanimous gift. Her current salary wasn't fabulous, but she could manage to live on it, barely, given all the expenses she had, and all that she tried to do for Amelia. But with this sudden change, she'd had no time to prepare for it. She had college to pay for, the maintenance on her apartment, and all the expenses associated with a college-age daughter. She could skimp for herself, but she didn't want to do that to Amelia. The big raise she thought she was going to get had suddenly evaporated, and instead she had been fired through no fault of her own.

"This is really short notice," she said to Phillip. "I wasn't expecting it at all. I've had no time to prepare. Amelia is in college, and I carry it all alone. And I may not be able to find another job at that level so quickly." He looked sympathetic and she could see that he felt awkward. He knew she'd been given a bad deal, but there was nothing he could do about it. The owners had forced a candidate for CEO on him, and he was a strong option for the job. Phillip didn't tell Jane that the owners were uncomfortable having a woman as CEO. It was a little too modern for them, as they put it.

"I might be able to get you four months' severance, but that's the best I can do." Nine years, and the promise of being made CEO had just flown out the window, which was a professional blow, a huge personal disappointment, and a financial disaster for her. She was trying to absorb the bad news and be as gracious as possible about it. She had always liked Phillip Parker, but he had just dealt her a harsh blow, and he knew it. She felt like a wrecking ball had just hit her.

"When do you want me to go?" she asked him quietly, with all the dignity she could muster.

"As soon as you get organized, by the end of the week. You can bring me up to date on the status of what you're working on. We'll make the announcement the day you leave, so the employees don't have time to make a big fuss about it. I don't expect you to come to meetings for the rest of the week." That was it. Her job was over. And somewhere deep within her, she knew that they wouldn't have dispensed with her this way if she were a man. The new CEO had a Harvard MBA, which she couldn't compete with, but she knew she could run the company just as well as he could, and Phillip Parker knew it too. But their bosses wanted their man in the job, and he couldn't argue with them. Jane knew she had been betrayed, and all she wanted to do was go home now and cry. What was she going to tell Amelia? Should she tell her now or wait until she found another job? She didn't want to scare her, but she was terrified herself.

She would have to start calling agencies immediately. She had some savings, but not enough to last forever, or for very long. She had Amelia's tuition to pay for. She'd have to get a loan if she didn't find a comparable job soon. Her mind was racing as she left Phillip's office, and he thanked her for the wonderful job she had done for nine years. He stood staring out the window, frowning, after she left his office. What he had just done felt awful. He realized now that he had been overambitious trying to put a woman in his job. The sisters had never objected, but they had found a replacement of their own. He hoped that Jane would be all right. She was a bright woman and great at her job. He told himself that she'd find a terrific new job soon. But his conscience was still gnawing at him when he thought of the look on her face.

When Jane got back to her office, she walked past her secretary Hilary quickly, and she glanced at Jane as she sped by. Hilary had been Jane's secretary for the past six years. She was an efficient woman in her fifties who had been a secretary all her life, and had never married. Jane was the first woman she had ever worked for, and Hilary was surprised at first by how self-sufficient and easy Jane was. Hilary was used to handling even personal matters for her male employers, like picking up their dry cleaning from time to time, if they were bachelors or their wives were out of town. Or they had her run to Brooks Brothers quickly to buy them a spare shirt, if they were rushing out to dinner and didn't have time to go home to change. Jane never asked her to do errands, and managed all her personal matters herself. Jane was a consummate professional, and a kind, considerate person.

Hilary followed her into the office with a look of concern. "Are you feeling all right? You look very pale."

"I think I might have a fever again," Jane said to cover her disarray after the meeting. Her mind was racing as she tried to remember what she currently had in her savings account. She had some treasury bills and bonds, and she owned the apartment Alfred had left her, but she paid a healthy maintenance for it every month. She knew she could always sell it if she needed the money, and she had a few pieces of jewelry she could sell.

"If you're feeling feverish, I think you should go home," Hilary said firmly. She tried to mother Jane occasionally, which Jane thought was sweet, and didn't expect.

"I think I will. I don't want to give this bug to anyone," Jane said. All she wanted was to get out of her office now, and away from the building. She could hardly hold back the tears. She put on her coat, wrapped her wool scarf around her throat, picked up her purse, and left the office a few minutes later. She just wanted to go home and crawl into bed. She was grateful that Amelia wasn't there. She would have known the minute she saw her mother that something was terribly wrong. The roof had caved in on her life.

Jane was almost running as she came out of the building. It was cold and there was a chill wind, and she didn't care. She decided to walk the twenty blocks home just to clear her head. What was she going to do now? How could she explain to an agency that she had gotten fired for no reason, that a man called Ted Barnes was getting the job she'd been promised for years as CEO of a publishing house, and now she was out of a job entirely.

She was chilled to the bone by the time she got back to her apartment. Her cheeks were red from the cold, and she hurried past the doorman with a nod and took the elevator to her apartment. Her feet were nearly frozen. She kicked her shoes off, took off her coat and scarf and gloves and walked into her bedroom and climbed into bed. Her world had come to an end. Her job of nine years was over. She was unemployed and she had Amelia to support and no one to help her. As the reality washed over her like a tidal wave, she lay in her bed as the sobs finally broke from her, and she cried until she felt as though the life had drained out of her, and then she fell asleep.

Her departure from Axelrod and Baker was as swift and bloodless as Phillip Parker could make it. Jane had come back to the office on Wednesday, closed her office door as soon as she arrived, and begun packing her things. She emptied her desk and left all her files in perfect order. She made an impeccable list of her pending projects, and Hilary came in to see what she was working on halfway through the morning.

"What are you doing?" Hilary asked, shocked when she saw the neat stacks of files on the desk.

Danielle Steel

"I'm leaving," Jane said quietly. She had spent the day before making lists and plans of who to call and reach out to, and figuring out her finances.

"You mean to move upstairs? Is Mr. Parker giving you an office there now? Is he going sooner than planned?" Hilary looked excited. As far as she knew, Jane had won an important corporate race, but she hadn't. She had lost. Everything.

"No, I am," Jane said in answer with a tired smile. There was no point dressing it up. They would all know soon enough, whatever story management chose to tell them, to explain Jane's instant disappearance. "I got fired on Monday. Parker is leaving in June, and they gave the job as CEO to someone else, with a Harvard MBA. He starts on Monday. And they decided that having me here with him would be too awkward, and he'll want to bring in his own people. So, they fired me. I'm supposed to leave on Friday, but they don't want me attending meetings in the meantime. They're just going to quietly disappear me and let everyone know when I'm gone. It makes it look like I must have committed some terrible crime, but I can't do anything to change that." Jane tried to look unaffected by it, but she was deeply wounded by what they'd done, and how swiftly she'd been dispensed with.

"That's horrible." Hilary looked outraged, and there were tears in her eyes too. She loved working for Jane, and she had no idea who she'd be assigned to now, when they sent her back to the secretarial pool. She had come up the ranks along with Jane for the past nine years, and Jane had always protected her and been kind to her. "They wouldn't do this to you if you were a man," she said in a whisper and Jane shrugged, as she set another stack of files on her desk.

"Maybe they would. There isn't a lot of heart in business. They do what works for them." Hilary looked worried then.

"Will you be all right? I mean . . . with Amelia and all . . ." It was sweet of her to think of it. Jane had thought of nothing else for the past two days. Her conclusion was that she would be, if she was extremely careful, and found a new job at a decent salary, in a reasonable amount of time. Phillip Parker had promised her something he couldn't deliver in the end, but she'd find a job somewhere, maybe back down the ladder, as an editor again. She'd have to take whatever she could get at some point, and no one was going to give her a job as a CEO. She realized now that that had been a pipe dream, Phillip Parker's as well as her own. The three sisters who owned the company wanted a man in the job.

"I'll be fine," Jane reassured her. She wasn't sure if that was true, but she wanted it to be. And she would make it fine, whatever it took. Hilary left her office then and came back with a steaming cup of coffee, just the way Jane liked it, with a splash of milk and no sugar.

"I'm going to miss you," the secretary said, and Jane smiled at her, and with that, the tears spilled down Hilary's cheeks. She was crying for both of them. Despite the genteel surroundings, they worked in a merciless world where any of them could be dispensed with at a moment's notice. Having never married, Hilary was careful about that. She spent very little money, had a small walk-up apartment downtown, and saved as much of her salary as she could. She never wanted to find herself unable to pay her rent if she lost her job, and secretaries were easy to come by, just as editors were. Jane wondered if she would have to start from the bottom up. Anything was possible now. She felt as though her days of glory were over, and she had college to pay for Amelia now. She had a lot to figure out.

Hilary dried her eyes, and Jane was finished packing and sorting by late afternoon.

Phillip Parker had wondered if he should call her, to make sure she was all right. She had looked so devastated when he delivered the bad news. He knew he'd never forget the look on her face, of shock and betrayal. But there was nothing he could do to change it. The Axelrod sisters had made up their minds, and Phillip was only the messenger. They wanted Ted Barnes in, and Jane out. They were very conservative women, and they didn't like the idea of a woman in a man's job.

At the end of the day, Jane called him. Her office suddenly looked impersonal and bare, and there were three boxes of her personal belongings on the floor near the door. Hilary was going to help her carry them downstairs after everyone left, to spare her the embarrassment of carrying it all out herself while everyone watched.

"Is there anything you need me to sign before I go?" she asked him, and he was surprised by the question.

"We can do it all on Friday morning," he said.

"I have nothing to do until then. All my meetings were canceled—I assume you told them to do that—and I have nothing to contribute. I emptied my office today." Her voice was neutral and cool. She was very professional, and never emotional in the office, which he respected about her. Whatever her personal problems, if she had any, he never knew about them once in nine years. All he knew about her private life was that she was a widow with a child who was apparently in college now.

"I intend to give you a glowing reference if you have any prospective employers call us."

"That's nice of you," she said, and sounded as though she meant it, whether she did or not. What he had done wasn't nice. He had promised her something for years that he couldn't deliver, and she wondered if he knew it then, and just dangled the job of CEO as a carrot to make her work harder, and she had. She had put her whole heart and soul and all her spare time into her job and had given Axelrod and Baker their money's worth and more, for all nine years, even before he promised her the top job.

"I'll have legal send up your severance papers. We can send you the check in the mail if they haven't cut it yet. I wanted to keep things quiet until Friday. But if you'd rather go now . . ."

"I would," she said calmly. She wasn't going to say goodbye to anyone. There was too much to explain. She'd seen others leave before, complaining and accusing and blaming everyone for their getting fired. It was painful to watch. She preferred to leave in silence, with dignity and grace. Phillip could dress it up any way he wanted. It wouldn't change anything now.

The papers came to her office in a confidential envelope ten minutes later. She signed them, and Hilary took them back to the legal department. The company employed two full-time attorneys for contracts and legal disputes. Phillip didn't come to say goodbye to her, which was a relief.

At six o'clock, Hilary helped her carry her boxes down to the lobby and out to the street. Jane hailed a cab, and they piled her things in, and Jane hugged Hilary.

"Stay in touch," Hilary said with tears rolling down her cheeks.

"I will. Take care, Hilary, and thank you," Jane said, hugging her again. She got in the cab with her boxes and disappeared uptown.

On Thursday, Jane called the employment agencies, and made appointments with three of them. She was applying for an executive job in publishing or any related field, not as CEO of course. And she was willing to take a job as a senior editor if there were no jobs available in management.

"What about working for a magazine?" one of them asked her.

"My first job was at a magazine, nineteen years ago. That would be fine." It might even be fun. The atmosphere in publishing houses was far more serious and dignified. Magazines were more spontaneous and more creative. She was open to whatever came her way. And she went for a long walk that afternoon. She had some ideas about how to shore things up financially, some things she could sell. And Axelrod and Baker would pay her her full salary until mid-June. Her worries would start after that, and she had time to figure it out, and even find a job before that if she was lucky.

Amelia called when she got home. She had no idea what had happened that week, and Jane wasn't sure when to tell her. She didn't want to worry her. For all of Amelia's life, Jane had shielded her from worry and bad news, as much as possible, and she didn't want to burden her now. She wanted her to enjoy her youth and her college years. Real life could always come after that. Jane's whole life had been dedicated to providing her daughter an enchanted, worry-free life. And that wasn't going to change now because she'd lost her job. With luck, she'd find a good one soon. She had a good track record, and Phillip had promised her a glowing reference.

"Do you want to go shopping this weekend?" Amelia asked her. "I finished all my papers and assignments. Maybe we can look for a dress for Versailles."

"You don't want to wear the one you wore at the Infirmary Ball?" Jane asked, suddenly panicked about the ball at Versailles. She had forgotten all about it in the drama of the moment and losing her job. She would have to figure out how to pay for that now too. Round-trip tickets to Paris, the hotel, maybe a little driving trip afterwards, and another ball gown. It was going to be an expensive trip, but maybe a good investment for Amelia's future. She wanted her daughter to have a comfortable, secure life. She didn't want Amelia to ever have to go through what she just did, where someone could pull the rug out from under her and leave her frightened and jobless with no warning. And buying Amelia a new dress was part of that investment, an insurance policy for her future. It was worth it. The ball at Versailles had suddenly taken on new meaning to Jane, although Amelia didn't know it. She was a beautiful girl, and there was no reason why she shouldn't meet her Prince Charming next summer in Paris.

"I was thinking of something kind of grand and elegant, suitable for a palace, and more summery, something floaty," Amelia said with a giggle. "Kind of Cinderella-looking, and very light and airy, since it will be summer. My cotillion dress is too serious and heavy. I'd swelter in that heavy satin. I want to float in this one," she said. She had gotten into the spirit of it in the past month, since her mother had talked her into it. She was excited about it now.

"Okay, why don't we meet on Saturday morning, we'll do all the stores that carry bridal. All the June brides buy their dresses now, so there should be plenty to choose from." Jane smiled at the excitement in Amelia's voice as they chatted about it. Amelia was fully engaged with the plan and had lots of ideas for the dress. They agreed to meet at Bergdorf's at ten-thirty, and make a day of it, with lunch at The Plaza after their first stop. Jane was pensive after they hung up, and scribbled down some numbers, trying to figure out now what the trip would cost her, and the dress. The ball at Versailles was way out of her budget now, without a job. But she wasn't going to deprive Amelia of it, whatever it took to make it possible. She was determined to find a way to make it happen for her. She always did. She had spent all of

Amelia's lifetime making up to her for the father she didn't have, to provide for them, and shepherd her through life. And Jane was determined to do it again and get Amelia to Paris for the ball, whatever it took.

At the end of February, Caroline Taylor made the rounds of the stores in Beverly Hills with her mother: Saks, Neiman Marcus, Fred Heyman's on Rodeo Drive. And they went to the big designers individually, and saw some fabulous dresses. Betty bought a magnificent Halston gown for herself. It was red, and looked ravishing on her. And they finally chose an Oscar de la Renta design for Caroline. She was going to look exquisite in it. It was a bridal design, but was perfect for a ball at the Court of Louis XIV in Paris. It was a little more daring than Betty would have chosen for her, but it suited her, and with Caroline's Alice in Wonderland innocent looks and spectacular figure, she could pull it off.

They'd had fun shopping for their dresses, and Betty enjoyed spending time with her daughter. She was leaving in a few days to go on location in Spain and Italy for her latest movie. Josh was producing and directing, and Gregory Peck and Cary Grant were starring with her. She suspected that the ball committee had chosen them to add some major international glamour and Hollywood stardust to their event. They didn't qualify as aristocrats and didn't have titles, but they were Hollywood royalty, which was even better to attract the press, and in the dresses they had chosen, whatever press was there would be all over them. Betty's name alone was enough to make that happen.

Betty had a final meeting to attend at the studio, after her last meeting with the team at Oscar de la Renta for Caroline's dress, and Caroline drove away in her little red Mercedes sports car and headed for West Hollywood. She knew that Adam would already be waiting for her. She was late. They had measured every inch of her meticulously at Oscar de la Renta's LA studio. Her mother had worn their dresses in her movies before.

She parked her car in front of Adam's house and rang the bell on the intercom. She ran up the stairs at full speed when he buzzed her in and flew into his arms. He picked her up and swung her around, and then headed straight to his bedroom and dropped her on the bed.

"Where were you? I've been waiting for you." He looked like a petulant child, and she laughed. She was addicted to his body, as he was to hers. He could never keep his hands off her for more than five minutes.

"I had to be with my mother. She's leaving this week, and we had stuff to do." She didn't want to tell him about the ball at Versailles yet. He wouldn't like the idea of her having an escort for a grand event, other than himself.

"They're leaving on location this week. She'll be gone for three months," she said gleefully, as Adam stripped her clothes off, tossed them in the air, and a minute later her exquisite body lay waiting for him, and she welcomed him readily. She was well worth the wait.

Felicity ran around the track at MIT for the third time, and nearly collapsed after she did. She was wearing men's basketball shorts and an MIT sweatshirt. It was freezing, but she was dripping with sweat. She had promised her mother that she would make a real effort this time to lose some weight. She was dieting, and running on the track twice a week. It had been agony so far, but she was sure that the end result would be worth it. A whole new body by the time she got back to Dallas.

She was starving when she got back in her car after running. She stopped at a deli to pick up a salad on her way back to her dorm. And as she walked into the deli, she was assaulted by an irresistible aroma. They were selling pizza by the slice, and it smelled fantastic. They had four different kinds, mushroom, sausage, four-cheese, and deluxe, which combined all of them, with anchovies on request. She stood on line for her turn, and the college student working at the deli counter smiled at her and took her order.

"I'll have a slice of each, but no anchovies," she said,

glancing over her shoulder as though she might see her mother or Araminta watching her, but there were only students lined up behind her who didn't care what she'd ordered. She paid for the four slices. They were warm, and she took one of them out of the box when she got in her car and ate it before she got back to her room. It was so delicious that she ate the other three slices as soon as she got there, and left the box in the trash in the bathroom. She was used to disposing of the evidence whenever she ate, but no one noticed her, or scolded her here at school. In Boston, she was an adult and could eat whatever she wanted.

She weighed herself on the scale in the bathroom after she showered the next morning, and the scale had to be wrong. She had already run twice that week, and she'd been really careful except for the pizza the night before, but that still didn't justify what the scale said. She had gained four pounds in three days. It was obviously out of whack, and the weight it reported wasn't accurate.

She dressed and left for class, thinking about the pizza again. But what the hell, the ball was still five months away. She had lots of time to diet before that. Her goal was to lose twenty-five pounds by July. That was only five pounds a month. She could do that, and the pizza was nourishing. She bought coffee and a doughnut at a coffee shop near school to take to class with her. She was too tired to run that night.

But she stopped for more pizza and took it to her room instead of dinner. Her roommate was out so no one saw her eat it. And Felicity forgot about it as soon as she did.

# Chapter 5

Felicity was second in her class at the end of spring semester. The only thing surprising about it was that she wasn't first, which was her usual placement. But MIT was harder than she had expected, and she had done less well than usual on a midterm test when she had a bad cold. She had wanted to stay for summer classes, but she couldn't because of the ball in July. She had nothing to do in Dallas. She was thinking of getting a job for a month just to keep busy and stay out of the house. She didn't want to be around her sister and her friends, hanging out at the pool, in their fancy bathing suits with matching cover-ups and flowered bathing caps. She was thinking about a job at her favorite Dairy Queen. She loved their ice cream, and in high school, a lot of kids she knew had worked there in the summer, but now that they were in college, they would get better jobs that would help them at school and look good on their CVs later.

Most of Araminta's friends hadn't gone to college, so all they had to do was look beautiful and get their hair done. Felicity had no patience with them and had no idea how to talk to them. She wasn't up on the latest makeup or beauty treatments, or hairdos, she didn't care about fashion. Almost everything in her closet had been there since junior high school and was now too small. She could still squeeze into some of it, but most of the time she wore sweatshirts and jeans, or big men's shirts with her jeans in the summer, with loafers. Araminta had commented the summer before, "How *West Side Story*!" Felicity didn't care what Araminta thought of her, she just didn't want to have to listen to it. They had seen the musical of *West Side Story* in New York.

No one at home would care how good her grades had been at the end of her first year at MIT, except her father, but she saw the wistful look in his eyes too, wishing she were slimmer, dressed better, and looked more like her sister. Felicity's parents never wished that Araminta were smarter, like her younger sister, only that Felicity was thinner and looked prettier.

She tried not to think about the ball as she packed her bags to go home. She had to empty her room for a new dorm

assignment in the fall. She didn't know who her new roommate was yet. She'd find out over the summer. She hadn't
made friends with any girls so far. She and her roommate
hardly saw each other, and had different classes and schedules, and no common interests. The only students she had
really talked to were boys in the classes where she had labs,
and none of them had asked her out. She hadn't had a date
all year and didn't expect to. Her mother said that all of that
would change when she lost weight. But she didn't want to
have to starve in order to have a boyfriend. She wasn't
unhappy alone. She kept busy with her studies and didn't
really have time to date. Or at least it was what she told
herself and had believed all through high school. Most of
the students at MIT belonged to sororities and fraternities,
although some of them had closed recently, after unfortunate
incidents involving alcohol. She hadn't been invited to join
one anyway. She wasn't crushed over it. They seemed dumb
to her, and dangerous from the rumors one heard.

She flew from Boston to Dallas and arrived late on a Friday
afternoon. After dumping all her bags in her room, she went
down to the kitchen for something to eat. She had asked
Daisy, their housekeeper, who said that her mother was out
and her father was still at work. Felicity could see Araminta
and her court sitting by the pool. There were six or seven
girls, and three boys admiring them. The boys had crew cuts

and the girls wore their hair to their shoulders in a flip, or heavily teased on top. Felicity was wearing hers in a braid down her back. She didn't go out to the pool to say hello to Araminta. She'd just make some snide remark, and Felicity was already missing the peace and quiet in her dorm, in a room where no one bothered her. She and her roommate hardly spoke. Felicity was perfectly happy that way, and she went to the library to study whenever her roommate's friends showed up and hung around.

Daisy offered to make Felicity a sandwich, and she declined. "I'm fine, Daisy, thanks. I'll make something myself. I ate on the plane." She waited until Daisy had left the kitchen, grabbed a quart of mint chocolate chip ice cream and a spoon, and headed up the stairs to her room. She ate it intermittently while she unpacked. She finished it as she put her last pair of jeans away, threw the container away discreetly in her bathroom, and saw that her mother had bought her a new scale. There would be no avoiding that while she was home, and she knew it. She had promised to lose anywhere from twenty-five to forty pounds by the time she came home, and she could tell by her clothes that she wasn't even close. In fact, she was fairly sure she'd gained.

She dropped the spoon into the sink, slipped off her jeans since she knew they had to weigh at least a pound and maybe two, and weighed herself. She might as well find out the bad news now. Her mother could tell how much someone weighed with her eyes closed from a hundred feet away.

She got on the scale, closed her eyes, and waited for the news. She didn't have long to wait. A harsh robotic voice announced it for the whole neighborhood to hear. Not only had she not lost the forty pounds she'd promised to work off, she had gained five. And now the ball was seven weeks away. She might be able to lose ten by then, or fifteen if she gave up eating entirely, but there was no way she could lose twenty or thirty pounds by the ball, let alone forty. And her mother would see it as soon as she walked through the door. She had a scale in her head.

Felicity put her jeans back on and walked down the stairs to the garage. She got her bike out and rode over to the friend who had been her escort at the cotillion last Christmas. She hadn't seen him since. She rode around to the back of Andy's house, and no one noticed her, and she threw some mid-sized rocks and gravel at his window, hoping he was home from college. He came to the window a minute later, frowning.

"Get away from—" he started to shout down, and then he saw her. "Oh, it's you. What are you doing here?" He looked happy to see her.

"Same as you," she said with a grin, pleased to see Andy. "Home for the summer, till July anyway. After that we're going to France, and then I go back to school."

"I'm going to New Zealand. My dad bought a fishing lodge there," he said.

"Sounds boring as hell," she said, and he laughed. She was like a breath of fresh air, there was nothing fake about her, like so many others they knew. She said whatever came into her head, as she just had.

She explained it after he came downstairs and got his bike out. "My summer is a bust too. I'm being presented at a debutante ball in Paris next month." He looked puzzled.

"I thought we did that. That wasn't enough?"

"Nope," she said matter-of-factly, as they rode along side by side. They didn't communicate from school, but their friendship was easy to pick up where they left off.

"Your deb ball looked pretty official to me," he said.

"It did to me too. But this one's at Versailles, the palace. My parents are all excited about it. Araminta is working on a whole list of nasty things to say the night of the ball. I'm going to fool her and wear earplugs." He smiled, he had to admit that the things her sister said to her were unthinkably mean, but Felicity appeared to be less upset about it than usual. "I thought I'd get a job at the Dairy Queen," she said, as they rolled toward a coffee shop they liked and used to go to after chemistry lab in high school.

"Do you think your parents will let you?" Her parents were all about appearances, and he couldn't imagine their being happy about her working at Dairy Queen, particularly given her mother's obsession about Felicity's weight. "So, how's MIT?" he asked, to change the subject. Her face broke into a smile when he asked.

"Fantastic. I love it. I wanted to go to summer school, but I couldn't because of the stupid ball. When do you leave for New Zealand?" At least she'd have someone to talk to while he was in Dallas.

"In two weeks." They got to the coffee shop then, left their bikes and went inside, and both had root beer floats with vanilla ice cream. He was slim and athletic and could afford the calories. She couldn't.

"I wish you were going to be at the ball in Paris with me. My escort is going to be some French guy I don't know, who probably doesn't speak English. We're going to the south of France afterwards." She missed school already and she'd only been home for a few hours. It was going to be a long summer, waiting to leave for France, being in Paris, and then in the south for a couple of weeks. She hadn't even gotten a dress for the ball yet. Her mother had wanted to wait to see how much weight she lost. She hadn't told her mother the truth before she came home, so she had that to face now, and another big white dress that made her look like a circus tent. She dropped Andy off at his house and went home. As soon as she walked in the front door, her mother was coming down the stairs and saw her. Her mother looked like she was going to cry, and Araminta was right behind her and laughed when she saw her sister.

"How much weight did you put on?" Araminta asked her in a sugary voice.

"Five pounds," Felicity said matter-of-factly, and went to hug her mother, who was trying not to look as upset as she was.

"I thought we'd go to Neiman's and try dresses on tomorrow," Charlene said. "I'm sure we'll find something you like." She tried to make it sound like it didn't matter, but it did to her, and Felicity knew she'd disappointed her again.

"Good luck," Araminta whispered to her, as she glided past her, as Felicity headed up to her room. The one thing she could always be sure of when she came home was that nothing had changed.

Jane had another interview in the first week of June. She'd been to dozens of them in the past three months. The answer was always the same. She was overqualified for the jobs they had to offer and they were sure she'd be bored and wouldn't stay in a job beneath her skills. And they didn't want to pay her what she'd been earning, for a new job as a lowly secretary. It had taken her nine years to rise at Axelrod and Baker to where she was when they fired her, and now she was starting at the bottom again. And no one would give her a chance.

She'd had lunch with Hilary a few times, who was still heartbroken that Jane had been forced to leave. The incoming CEO had hired a man to take her place. Phillip Parker was leaving at the end of June, and Hilary reported that he and the new CEO didn't get along, but it wasn't Jane's problem now. The only real problem she had was keeping everything afloat until she found a job. She had had to tell Amelia that she'd left the company, but not that she'd been fired. She sat up at night, figuring out her finances again. She had thought she'd have a job by then, but she didn't, and money was getting dangerously tight. She had just paid Amelia's tuition at Barnard for sophomore year, and she was worried she wouldn't have enough money to pay for their trip. She'd already bought their tickets on Pan Am. In mid-June, she did something she had hoped to avoid. She had made inquiries and had been given the name of a firm that was supposedly both fair and discreet.

She took a cab there one morning after Amelia had left the apartment to spend the day with friends. They were going to play tennis at the Town Tennis Club on Sutton Place. She was playing with some of her old friends from Chapin, and had told them all about the ball at Versailles. It sounded like a dream come true to them. And the dress Jane had bought her made her look like a fairy princess. They were taking the dress on the flight with them in an enormous wooden crate that had been specially made for the dress, so it wouldn't get damaged in the cargo hold.

The jeweler Jane was meeting had an office in a building on West Forty-seventh Street. He bought and sold estates, and jewelry from people who needed to sell what they had. Alfred had given her very little of his mother's jewelry. He had sold most of it himself before he died, when he needed money to pay his gambling debts, but she had a few pieces left she was saving for Amelia and had worn one of them to the meeting. It was a very handsome emerald ring Alfred's father had bought at Cartier and given his wife for their anniversary, but it would serve Jane's purposes now.

When she met with the jeweler, who looked more like a banker than a jeweler, she slipped it off her finger and handed it to him. It sat on his desk for a minute, and he took a loupe out of his pocket and examined it while Jane watched him, feeling guilty for what she was about to do. She had a very handsome sapphire set of bracelet, ring, necklace, and earrings that had been her mother-in-law's too, and she was saving it to give Amelia as a wedding present one day. Her own mother hadn't had any jewelry of any particular value. She wasn't interested in it, other than the pearl necklace Jane wore every day.

"The stone is very fine," the jeweler said politely. "It's a lovely piece. How much did you have in mind, Mrs. Alexander?"

"I don't know," she said in a crushed voice. She didn't want to tell him that her money was running out and she'd been out of a job for four months, had a daughter in college, and had an expensive trip to Europe to pay for, but Amelia's future might depend on it, if she met the right man and fell in love.

He quoted an amount that startled her. It was worth much more than she'd hoped. He was losing his margin on it and wouldn't make a profit on it. But he could afford not to for once. He'd seen women like her before, who had nowhere to turn, and nothing else to do except sell what they had to survive. Desperation was coming through her pores, although she looked poised and gracious as she sat there waiting for his verdict. He could tell how much was resting on it without her explaining it to him. He spared her the humiliation of that. He was a decent man, and he ran an honorable business. He didn't need to punish her in addition to whatever grievous situation she was in.

"That's a very fair amount," she said gratefully. She made no attempt to bargain with him. She wouldn't have dared, and the amount he had offered her would allow her to put another year of Amelia's tuition aside, in addition to the one she'd just paid, and cover their maintenance fees in the apartment for several months. The trip to Europe wouldn't be a problem now. She could cover it easily without concern. She wasn't sorry to be selling the emerald now. It was saving her life. It was better than keeping it in a locked drawer at home. She only wore it to very special events anyway. And she had none to go to, except the ball at Versailles.

The jeweler wrote her a check that felt like a fortune as she folded it and put it in an inside pocket of her purse. She looked relieved as she shook his hand before she left, and he was happy to see the relief on her face. She looked like a nice woman, and he felt sorry for her. People like her always looked so frightened when they came to him, as their worlds fell apart. The ring was a good one. He could sell it well, even if for less of a profit now, a sacrifice he was willing to make now and then.

Jane left his office and reached the street, feeling as though a thousand-pound weight had lifted off her shoulders. They would be all right for many months now, and Amelia's tuition would be paid for the next two years, including the one Jane had just paid. She could hold out for the right job now. She had no idea how long it would take, but she would find something. And in the meantime, they were going to Paris for the ball at Versailles, and with any luck at all, Amelia would meet the man of her dreams, from a good family, who would take care of her, and Jane wouldn't have to worry about her anymore. The kind jeweler on Forty-seventh Street had saved her.

Robert Walker had breakfast with his daughter that morning. They were sitting in the small protected garden, soaking up the sun. Normally they were in Greenwich on the weekends, but Samantha had errands to do, a few things she still needed for Paris. She wanted to find white satin flat shoes with rhinestone buckles to wear with her dress. She didn't want to take a chance on wearing heels for such an important event.

Robert had an important call coming from Japan that morning. It was rare for them to have a weekend in town. Samantha had finished her classes for the semester, and it was a gorgeous June day. They were going to spend a few weeks in the country before leaving for Paris.

"Are you all set for Paris?" He smiled at her, and she nodded.

"Almost, I still need shoes. I'm going to wear flats so I don't take a header down the stairs," she said matter-of-factly.

"You won't," he said gently.

"I could. I'd rather not do that in front of three hundred debs and something like nine hundred other guests, including their parents. Flats are safer."

"We need to practice your dancing," he said as they finished breakfast.

"I can't dance, not with someone I don't know. If I lose my balance, he'll think I'm drunk."

"You'll be fine," he reassured her, as he always did. "You've danced with me before."

"That's because it's you," she said. "You hold me up if I trip. I get it right in my head. But sometimes my feet don't listen and do what they want." He hoped she would have a nice escort, but there was no way to tell, and he didn't want to embarrass her by warning the ball committee that she might need help. She would have hated that. But somehow Sam always managed, and handled it with poise if something went wrong. She'd had some falls in embarrassing situations and handled them with grace.

"We'll practice before the ball," he said, and she hesitated. He couldn't always protect her in every situation, even if he wanted to. She left the house a few minutes later, and visited all her favorite shoe stores, and found what she wanted at Saks. They were perfect, white silk like her dress, with a dusting of rhinestones on them. They looked like angel shoes. They had the tiniest heel, which she thought she could manage. And she bought a pair of white satin flats just in case. She was back at the house in the late afternoon, and her father was still on his call. She called some friends from school, and arranged to go to a movie with them, and meet them at the theater.

"What are you up to tonight?" he asked her after his call, and she told him. "Do you want me to drop you off?" He was concerned.

"No, Dad, I'm fine. You can't always protect me. If I stumble or fall or lose my balance, I'll pick myself up. I know how to deal with it." It frustrated her at times to have him shield her constantly. He treated her like spun glass. She was all he had left, after losing her mother and brother. For the last fourteen years, he had protected her constantly. "You can't always be there, Dad," although she knew he wanted to be. It was so well meant, but oppressive at times.

"I don't want anything to happen to you. I couldn't bear it."

"Yes, you could, and nothing's going to happen. I'm fine, Dad. I know how to manage, and I don't lose my balance often anymore." It was just a small residual effect of the accident, and she handled it well. He knew that, but worried anyway. And he was concerned that her friends wouldn't take care of her if something happened at the movies. What if she fell down an escalator? The thought of it made him feel ill.

She left the house a little while later, and he sat in his study, thinking about her. She was the love of his life, his treasure, and he wanted to be there to protect her forever.

He wanted the ball to go perfectly for her. But life wasn't perfect, and you couldn't always protect those you loved. He had learned that lesson brutally, fourteen years before. Sam had just turned nineteen.

It was the last week in June, and Caroline had told Adam about the ball a few weeks before. She had explained to him that the ball committee selected and invited the escorts, and no one was allowed to choose their own. They wanted to be absolutely certain of who the escorts were and that there were no exceptions, or additions.

Adam was usually jealous and had been for the past year. She was surprised when he didn't make a fuss about the ball in Paris. He was perfectly relaxed about it, and about her planned three-week vacation in the south of France with her parents afterwards. She was trying to get them to let her come home early, but so far they wouldn't agree. They'd both been on location for three months, which had been heaven for Adam and Caroline. She had spent nights with him, and barely shown up for class at USC. She was in danger of failing, but she didn't care as long as she could be with him. But now her parents wanted time with her, and three weeks in the south after the ball seemed perfect to them. They still had no suspicion of her affair with Adam, or how serious it was. He had even hinted at marriage a few times, but not recently. He was getting ready to start shooting a movie and was absorbed by learning the script. She had helped him rehearse his lines and was good at it. It was all familiar to her.

She had told her parents she was spending the night at a girlfriend's and looked victorious when she got to his apartment.

"I'm yours for the weekend," she said, and playfully started unbuttoning his shirt, but he stopped her.

"I've got to get up early tomorrow for a meeting," he said vaguely.

"On the weekend?"

"I need to rehearse with the cast, tomorrow was the only day that three of them could do it," he said. She didn't believe him. He looked strange when he said it, and it was the first time in a year he hadn't wanted to make love. She eventually enticed him into it, but something was different. She could sense it. It was perfunctory and quick.

"Are you mad at me about the ball in Paris?" she asked him afterwards. He lay next to her but seemed remote, distant, absent somehow, as though he was thinking of something else and not of her.

"Not at all. I think it'll be fun for you. And you don't need to come back early for me. I'll be in pre-production by then and it'll be intense."

"That's why I want to come back early, so we can spend time together before you get started." But her parents still hadn't agreed to it anyway and were being stubborn about it. So was she.

He got out of bed then, and didn't linger with her, and after a few minutes, he handed her her clothes. "I need some space tonight, babe." She felt panic rise up in her. He'd never said that before, or sent her home. Usually, he begged her to stay.

"Is something up?"

"No, it's just the picture. I need to start working on the script." She knew how film schedules ran from her parents, and it was still early. She dressed slowly and watched him. Something had changed.

She felt sad as she dressed, wondering if it was the ball and he didn't want to admit it. She knew four weeks was too long to stay away. But she couldn't tell her parents she wanted to come back for him. They had no idea he existed in Caroline's life at all.

"What time tomorrow?" she asked Adam, as she bent to kiss him. He was sitting on the couch, naked, with a glass of wine. He hadn't offered her one, and it was obvious he wanted her to go. He didn't seem angry, just disconnected from her, which was worse.

"Let's talk tomorrow. I want to spend some time with the

others from the cast. We may want to hang together for a while." Caroline didn't say anything. She wanted to cry. She just nodded and kissed his neck. His lips brushed hers for an instant, and he watched her go. She was hoping he'd stop her and ask her to stay, but he didn't. He was silent and erotically, irresistibly handsome as she closed the door. There were tears in her eyes as she hurried down the stairs to her car. She was sobbing as she turned on the ignition and drove away.

She was halfway home when she decided to stop at a grocery store for a pack of cigarettes. She didn't usually smoke but she wanted one now. She didn't know what to do, she didn't know why he seemed so detached suddenly. She bought a pack of Marlboro Reds and was waiting at the checkout counter to pay when she saw a rack of tabloids and she thought her heart would stop beating. Adam was on the front page, kissing Fay Mallon, the young actress who was going to costar with him in his new movie. She was the hot new starlet in Hollywood, and Adam had acted nonchalant about her when Caroline had commented on it when she was chosen for the role. He said he didn't care about her, and she didn't seem so hot when he'd met her, and she had a boyfriend anyway. Caroline stared at the tabloid until it was her turn in line. She bought a copy of it and the cigarettes and hurried to her car to read the article. It said that they were an item, and there were several more photographs of them inside, one at a restaurant, two on the street, and another one on a beach near LA, and they were kissing in each picture. Caroline felt rage and panic seize her. She threw the tabloid on the passenger seat and drove back to Adam's apartment. She wanted to know what was going on.

She left her car parked haphazardly, jumped out, and raced up the stairs. She had the key to his apartment and used it. She hadn't been gone long, maybe twenty minutes. She had a straight view into his bedroom from the door, and the girl in the tabloid with him was already in his bed as Caroline stared at them in horror, and she walked toward his bedroom, blinded by pain and shock.

"What are you doing?" she said to him, and ignored the girl, who shrank away from him, covering herself with the sheet. She didn't say a word, and Caroline could see that he had an enormous erection.

"I'm doing what it looks like, Caro. Look, I'm sorry, we're done. I've been done for a while. I thought it would just die a natural death when you went to France. We had a good run, but it's over now." His eyes were cold as he looked at her. Caroline thought she might faint or throw up. "You've got to go now." There was nothing else for her to do. She never acknowledged the girl in his bed. It wasn't her fault, it was his. Caroline was clear about that. And Fay Mallon was a step up for his career. Caroline was only the daughter of a star, while Fay Mallon was going to be one. The buzz of being with her would be good publicity for him. Caroline was just a kid.

"That's it? This is how you do it? Out with the old, in with the new? You didn't even have the decency to break up with me first?" Caroline said in a shrill voice. She was shaking at the cruelty of it.

"I'll send you your things, Caroline. Now get out. You don't belong here." He looked carved in stone as he said it.

"I guess I never did," she said sadly, and looked at him long and hard before she left the room. It was her first taste of Hollywood reality. "Does she know you made love to me an hour ago, or doesn't she care?" Caroline looked at the girl then, who shrugged and glanced at Adam.

"Go!" He pointed at the door to his apartment, and feeling sick, Caroline turned on her heel and left, slamming the door behind her after throwing his key on the floor. She was shaking all over as she stumbled down the stairs. It was the worst scene she'd ever been through, like something in a cheap movie.

It made her feel sick to think of what he was doing with Fay Mallon now. He left nothing to the imagination. And he didn't care how badly he hurt Caroline. He was done, and she had been dispensed with, like so much garbage.

Actors were known for sleeping with their costars, but Caroline had thought that what they felt for each other was real. Apparently not. He was just passing time between movies, and she could have been useful to him. Fay Mallon was even more so. Caroline had been at his beck and call for a year. It made her feel like a complete fool. The worst of it was that she truly loved him, and still did, and it broke her heart to know what he was doing with his new woman.

Caroline lay on her bed all that night, smoking and crying. She never slept, and in the morning she called him. He didn't answer. She didn't know if he was out, or simply refusing to talk to her. She couldn't reach him all weekend, and by Monday she was frantic. She looked ill and her mother questioned her when she didn't come to breakfast and was shocked by how bad she looked when she saw her.

"Are you sick?"

"Yeah, I have the flu. I've been sick all weekend."

"Oh, poor baby. You should have called, we'd have come home from Santa Barbara. We were just relaxing and going to the Coral Casino for some sun. Do you have a fever?" Betty came to check and said that Caroline didn't, but she had dark circles under her eyes, and she looked even worse than she felt, which was hard to imagine. She had no way to reach Adam. He wouldn't answer his phone, and she wasn't going to go over there and beg him to talk to her. He said it was over, he had cut Caroline out of his life. He belonged to Fay now, for however long that lasted. Caroline was devastated. It was the hardest thing that had ever happened to her, and a bitter taste of adulthood in a harsh, narcissistic world.

Betty brought her a handful of vitamins and told her to take them.

"We leave for Paris in ten days. You have to be in tip-top shape. If you're not better by tomorrow, I'm calling a doctor. Maybe you need a B12 shot. But for now, get in bed and stay there," she ordered her, and Caroline was relieved to do it. She didn't want to see anyone or go anywhere. It was easier to pretend she was sick. She felt awful. All she could think about was Adam and what he was doing with Fay Mallon.

Caroline was obsessed with him and had been for a year. This was a terrible way for him to end it. The worst way she could imagine. She couldn't get the scene out of her mind, of his costar in bed with him, about to make love to her, an hour or less after he'd done the same with Caroline. And now he had shut her out, abandoned her. She wondered how long he would have gone on with the charade if she hadn't seen the tabloid and caught him. Probably till she left for Europe.

She didn't want to go out, she was afraid to run into him, and at the same time she wanted to. She wanted to see him and hold him and touch him again, but he was no longer hers. He belonged to someone else now, and she belonged to no one at all. She had never felt so lonely and broken in her life. Her protected, innocent world had shattered around her.

The letter from USC came while she was languishing in bed before they left, telling her that as a result of her incomplete attendance records, with most of her papers not handed in yet, and two exams she'd missed, she was now on academic probation for the next semester, and if she didn't make up the work and bring her grades up, she would have to leave USC. She hid the letter from her parents, shredded it, and then went back to bed. She hadn't stopped crying for a week. She was blinded by pain. Adam was cruel in the end. He was no gentleman, and not even a decent person. He had made the breakup as brutal and ugly as he could. And it was clear to her now that he was never going to see her again, unless he ran into her by accident. It was over for him. He was done. She was bereft and heartbroken and humiliated.

Caroline was still pale when she got on the plane to Paris with her parents. She looked like she'd been sick for months. Betty was afraid her dress would be too big for her. She looked like she'd lost twenty pounds in ten days. It was more likely ten pounds, but whatever it was, she could barely crawl onto the plane. Her father said he hadn't seen anyone that sick with the flu in years.

# Chapter 6

Whentifully sunny July day. The flight had stopped in
Gander, Newfoundland, and Shannon, Ireland, to refuel,
and took eighteen hours in all. They hired a large old-
fashioned cab so they had room for Amelia's dress and
their bags. They were crowded in with the dress box and
the luggage as they headed for the city. They were staying
on the Left Bank, in a quaint little hotel Jane knew, Le
Royal. She had stayed there before, when she had flown
to Paris to sign up an important French author. It was a
small hotel with charm and pretty rooms, at a reasonable
price. They had adjoining rooms and shared a bathroom.
Amelia loved it when she saw it. It was in the heart of the
7th arrondissement, with pretty little shops and bustling

bistros all around them. It was a perfect place to spend a week in Paris.

They each took a bath and changed, and then went to explore the area. They went to the Café Flore for lunch, and Jane explained to Amelia that it had been the favorite hangout of famous authors, both French and American, and Sartre, Camus, F. Scott Fitzgerald, and Hemingway had eaten there. Farther down the Boulevard Saint-Germain was the equally famous Aux Deux Magots, which had been the hangout of artists like Picasso. They were on hallowed ground. The whole 7th arrondissement was rich with history and the spirit of the famous artistic people who had lived there. Jane had given them a few days before they needed to be in Paris to explore her favorite haunts and share them with Amelia. She wanted it to be a memorable trip, and now that she could afford to pay for it, it was infinitely less stressful for her, and she could enjoy it. Amelia soaked up the beauty and delights of Paris like a thirsty flower.

For the one fancy meal they had decided to indulge in, at a fashionable restaurant, they went to Le Voltaire, which had been a secret meeting place during the Resistance, while Paris was occupied by the Germans during the war. It was a chic restaurant now, the food was exquisite, and they saw the famous fashion designer Hubert de Givenchy dining with Audrey Hepburn, which gave both Amelia and Jane a thrill.

They felt very glamorous when they went back to their hotel afterwards.

They visited the Louvre and the Musée d'Orsay, and they walked endlessly all over Paris. They strolled over from the Right Bank to the Left on the Alexandre III Bridge, which Jane thought was the prettiest in Paris, as they walked back to their hotel. They stopped to watch the Seine swirling beneath them, and the barges, cargo boats, and Bateaux Mouches for the tourists.

"I love the sense of history here," Jane said, feeling peaceful for the first time in months. She loved spending time with her daughter, and it was a relief to get away from her job search for a couple of weeks. It had been arduous and stressful, and humiliating to go to interviews. She hadn't been offered a decent job yet, in five months. There were times when she felt desperate, although less so now that she had sold the emerald ring. At other times, she told herself that the right job would turn up at the right time, and tried to believe it. No employer so far had been willing to let her take a job that was beneath her abilities. Her skills and experience were only serving to keep her unemployed for the moment. She was willing to take a lowly job as a simple secretary and not as an executive, but no one would offer her one. She had Amelia to feed, clothe, house, and educate, so she couldn't be picky, and didn't want to be. She had recently interviewed for a job as the second-in-command at a magazine, which seemed like fun, but she'd gotten the impression that they wanted someone younger. Most of the jobs she was capable of and best suited for went to men, at higher salaries than they would have paid her. It was the way of the world and a battle that was hard to win. And she hadn't so far.

Two nights before the ball, the related activities began, and Jane and Amelia had seen all the things they wanted to in Paris. They had even taken a tour of Versailles, so they'd know more of its history, as well as its grandeur. After the ball, they were going to rent a car and drive around to visit more of the châteaux in France.

It had already been a fantastic trip, even before the ball, and Amelia had enjoyed it too. She had no sense of the financial strain the trip for the ball had put her mother under, or what Jane had been obliged to do to swing it. Jane never told her or let it show. As far as she was concerned, it was her problem to solve, not Amelia's.

When Caroline and her famous parents arrived at the Ritz, the paparazzi were lying in wait for them right outside the hotel in the Place Vendôme. The Taylors scurried from the Rolls that had picked them up and into the hotel, where the paparazzi were not allowed to enter. Hotel security at the entrance stopped anyone who didn't belong there. The Ritz protected its important guests. They had given the Taylors one of their best suites. The hotel itself was beyond elegant, incredibly opulent and steeped in traditions, with antiques in the grand hallways and the beautiful rooms and suites. The Taylors had one of the best suites and a room for Caroline.

Caroline still looked like a ghost when they got there, with dark circles under her eyes. Ever since the breakup, she hadn't been sleeping well. She lay awake all night crying, stayed in bed in the daytime. She was aching to call Adam but knew she couldn't. He wouldn't take her calls anyway, and she had seen him on the cover of another tabloid at the newsstand at the airport, with his arms around Fay Mallon. Every time she saw him in the press, it was another dagger in her heart, and she felt sick. She knew she had to get over him, but she didn't know how. How did you stop loving someone after spending a year together? It was like losing a limb or a vital organ. She felt hollow inside, as though everything in her had died.

"I want you to take a nap," her mother told her. "You look exhausted after the trip." They still had no clue that Caroline was heartbroken. They had no reason to suspect it since they knew nothing about her affair with Adam. She had hidden it well. Her mother just thought she had the flu as she claimed. It seemed like a bad one, and was hanging on.

Caroline looked worse instead of better. And her mother wanted her to enjoy the ball.

Betty went to get her hair done as soon as they arrived, and Caroline's father went to the pool, and booked a massage afterwards in the room. Caroline lay on her bed and thought about Adam. She didn't even look out the window at the beautiful square with Napoleon's war monument in the center, and shops lining the Place Vendôme. She didn't want to go out despite glorious weather. She didn't care. All she wanted to do was hide under the covers, cry, and nurse her broken heart. She had never been so miserable in her life, and the last thing she wanted to do was show off in a fancy white dress, meet a bunch of American girls she didn't care about, much less two hundred and fifty French ones she'd never see again either, and an escort who probably wouldn't speak a word of English and would make her feel even worse, because he wasn't Adam. She had no idea how she would pull herself together by the next day. Their pre-ball schedule began then, with two formal tea parties and a rehearsal in the next two days. She didn't want to get out of bed. All she wanted to do was sleep and cry.

Whenever she thought of Adam and Fay Mallon, and seeing them in bed together, she felt sick, and was starting to hate him. Her parents would have killed him if they'd known, particularly her father, who had brought him home a year before in good faith, never suspecting Adam would seduce his eighteen-year-old daughter. He had trusted him with what Josh Taylor considered his greatest treasure, and Adam had betrayed him, and had even ended the romance badly and wounded Caroline severely. Neither of her parents would take it lightly. She knew that. They'd be upset with her too, for hiding the affair. She was nineteen now, but they still considered her a baby. And Adam had been so rotten to her in the end. She couldn't imagine ever feeling whole or happy again.

The manager of the Hotel George V was waiting for the Walkers when they checked in. Robert looked like a serious businessman, with Sam walking beside him. She was quiet as they arrived in Paris, worried about the next few days. Her father smiled at her reassuringly, and she smiled when she saw their two-bedroom suite, with beautiful flower arrangements and boxes of chocolates, a plate of chocolate-dipped strawberries and a tower of macarons. She helped herself to one as she looked around her room. She loved traveling with her father, although it always embarrassed her how spoiled they were. He was a very important man, and all the little extra touches were what went with it. He took it all in stride, and she was always painfully aware of it.

He had made a dinner reservation for them at Le Taillevent that night, which was one of his favorite two-star restaurants.

She wondered how many of the American debutantes had already arrived, and what they would be like when she met them. Probably they were snobs and couldn't wait to show off. She didn't expect to make any friends there, but she knew it was good practice to get out in the world, and she was determined to make the best of it, no matter how nervous she was. And she wanted to make her father proud of her. That wasn't hard to do.

The Smiths' arrival at the Plaza Athénée was pure Texas. Araminta and her mother had six large suitcases each, and a mountain of smaller bags with hats, handbags, shoes, and accessories in them. They each had a Vuitton hanging trunk, and it looked as though they had arrived by ocean liner, when in fact they had traveled on their own plane, and made all the necessary stops to refuel, which gave them a chance to stretch their legs and get some air. They made all the same stops that the airlines did. It was a very long trip from Dallas, twenty-two hours, but they preferred traveling on their own plane.

They had taken over part of a floor at the Plaza Athénée, and members of the Saudi royal family were on the floor above them. The Plaza was accustomed to large groups of highly demanding guests who were used to having whatever they asked for delivered to their rooms.

Charlene ordered tea for all of them as soon as they arrived. It came up on a rolling tray with two liveried waiters and a separate pastry cart. Felicity took an éclair to her room before the others emerged from their rooms. They had two separate suites, with two living rooms, one for Charlene and Bailey, and the other for the two girls. Araminta noticed immediately that there was one pastry missing from the tray, when she arrived in the living room. She lit a cigarette and looked glamorous as she smoked it, and Felicity made a face.

"Did you already eat one?" Araminta asked her, glancing at the pastry cart.

"No," Felicity lied, looking innocent as their parents joined them.

"We have reservations at La Tour d'Argent tonight," Bailey said happily. He loved the restaurants in Paris, all the gastronomic restaurants with Michelin stars that guaranteed an extraordinary meal.

Araminta and Charlene wanted to go shopping. Charlene invited Felicity to join them, and she shook her head. She was worried sick about the next three days, and just wanted to get it over with. She couldn't think of anything else. The beauty and delights of Paris meant nothing to her right now. All she could think of was the torture that awaited her at the ball. She was blinded by fear, and she knew just how large she looked in the white dress she would be wearing at Versailles. They

131

had found a dress at Oscar de la Renta, which the designer had modified for her. It was off the shoulders, which felt naked to her, had an empire line, and a panel in front that covered a multitude of sins, and another panel that fell from the back of the dress and provided a short train. Even Araminta had said that it wasn't bad on her, which was high praise, but Felicity knew she couldn't hide the indulgences of the past year, and she had stopped running track in May. It was too late now, but she was sorry about the pizza. As usual, her mother was nice about it, and Araminta wasn't, and called it as she saw it. "You must have eaten a hell of a lot of crap during second semester. That's a lot of doughnuts you're wearing." Felicity was used to her sister's comments, but she hated the look of disappointment in her mother's eyes. At least Oscar de la Renta had fashioned a dress that worked for her, and delivered it on time. It was in a suitcase of its own, in a mountain of tissue paper to protect it. It was almost as beautiful as a wedding dress, and would have been a very handsome one, and Felicity liked it better than the one she wore at the Idlewild Club in December. She just wished she didn't have to go to the ball at all.

She went for a walk that afternoon on the Avenue George V, looked at the shops, and tried not to think about the next few days. For once, she ate a light meal at a bistro. She was so nervous she could barely eat. Her mother nodded her approval when she ordered a simple broiled chicken dish with no sauce, and a salad. Charlene thought Felicity was trying to diet, but Araminta guessed the truth. Felicity was paralyzed by fear of what lay ahead. Araminta was still miffed that her sister was being presented at the ball and she wasn't. Life just wasn't fair at times. Araminta thought it was wasted on Felicity, who viewed it with dread.

The American debutantes who had come to Paris to be presented at Versailles were staying at various hotels around Paris, though some had rented short-term apartments and others were staying with relatives or friends. The Ritz told the Taylors that they had five of the debutantes staying there. And Charlene had heard that there were two at the Plaza Athénée. They were going to meet soon enough, the following afternoon at the United States Embassy. The ambassador and his wife were giving a tea to honor the American debutantes, without their parents, which sounded very grown up, but made it even scarier for Felicity and Sam. Amelia was looking forward to it, and Caroline Taylor didn't care. She'd been dumped by the love of her life, and nothing else mattered to her, least of all some dumb ball in France, as she said to her parents, without telling them why she was so depressed. It was her own dark secret and she intended to keep it that way.

* * *

133

The next day, Jane Alexander helped Amelia dress for the tea at the American Embassy. They had bought a pale blue silk suit almost the color of Amelia's eyes. It was simple, and Amelia wore the string of pearls that her mother had given her on her eighteenth birthday. She wore simple beige high-heeled pumps, a beige handbag and white kid gloves, and a tiny round blue silk hat with a small veil. And she wore pearl earrings that were her mother's, to match her necklace. She looked proper, elegant, and ladylike, and totally appropriate, and her eyes were alight with excitement, happy to meet the other American girls. Maybe after three intense days together some of them would be friends. Their hotel had arranged for a discreet car and driver for her, to get her to the embassy on the Faubourg Saint-Honoré, a few steps from the British Embassy, on the same street as the most luxurious shops in Paris.

At the Ritz, Betty could hardly get Caroline out of bed. She said she had a headache, and asked if she could skip it.

"No, you can't," Betty said firmly. "The show must go on, as they say. If I stayed in bed every time I have a headache when we're making a movie, I wouldn't have been in a single film. You'll feel better once you get there." She handed her an aspirin and a glass of water, Caroline swallowed it, and got up with a groan. A shower revived her a little, and she picked a very chic black linen dress with a tiny, pinched waist and a big skirt, that had been too small for Betty, and she'd given it to Caroline. Betty took a big black straw hat out of a hatbox and handed it to her daughter. The outfit was very striking, but Caroline looked more like a movie star than a debutante.

"Don't you have anything more cheerful?" Betty asked her. She went to the closet and pawed through it and came back with a beige silk dress.

"I'll look like an old lady in that," Caroline complained.

"And in the black dress and hat you'll look like you're going to a funeral. A very chic funeral in Hollywood maybe, but a burial nonetheless." Betty came back a minute later with a pink Chanel suit with black trim that had a matching hat. It was hers but she didn't mind lending it to her daughter. "Just don't lose the hat, I love it. We should have thought of today before. I forgot all about the tea at the embassy. I didn't think it would be a big deal."

"It isn't," Caroline said, looking pale, and sat down. She looked a little green as her mother stared at her.

"You don't look so great," Betty said.

"I ate oysters for lunch, and I think one of them may have been off."

"Forget about it. You can't throw up at a tea party at the embassy. Will yourself to be fine," Betty said in a determined voice. Her mother was tougher than she looked and used to working hard, in rough conditions sometimes. "It was hot today, you shouldn't have been eating oysters. Don't eat anything at the embassy and you'll be fine."

Betty helped her dress in the pink suit, and Caroline looked spectacular with her blonde hair. Betty put a little rouge on Caroline's cheeks and blended it until it looked natural, and dusted it with blush afterwards. Caroline looked healthy and just tan enough, and the hat was very stylish. She borrowed a pearl necklace from her mother and put on high heels that made the suit look suddenly sexy. Betty lent her a small black alligator clutch and Caroline looked amazing, no matter how lousy she felt. But at least she hadn't thrown up. She left the suite with a wave at her mother.

"And put on your gloves," Betty called after her. Caroline had brought her own white kid gloves, which one had to wear everywhere, particularly to a tea party.

She left the hotel a few minutes later in the Rolls that had picked them up at the airport. The driver drove down the Faubourg Saint-Honoré and turned in at the U.S. Embassy. There were several other limousines depositing elegantly dressed young women. A secretary and a Marine were checking their names off a list as they went in.

Felicity arrived right after Caroline, and noticed the chic pink and black hat. She was wearing a navy silk dress and

jacket, with a matching hat. She felt like her own grandmother. She remembered to put on her white gloves as she
walked in. She was wearing navy shoes, and a navy purse
Araminta had grudgingly agreed to lend her.

The two young Americans filed into a large, elegant room
filled with French antiques of varying periods, most of them
Louis XV and XVI. The upholstery was all in pastel satins,
with heavy antique drapes, held back by thick satin ropes
with long tassels. There were ancestral portraits on the walls
that the ambassador had borrowed from a museum for the
duration of his mission in France, and there were Aubusson
carpets on the floor, also in pastels. A huge crystal chandelier
dominated the room, and there was a long table draped with
a white tablecloth, a heavy silver tea service on the table,
and Limoges china. It all looked very French as the ambassador's wife greeted each of the girls, and her secretary
introduced them. There were thirty-six girls in all, all impeccably dressed, each of them very properly wearing a hat and
gloves. They were from seventeen to nineteen years old, and
looked older in their ladylike outfits. A few of them introduced themselves to each other, others were holding teacups,
or helping themselves to the meticulously cut cucumber and
egg salad sandwiches. Amelia was admiring the scene, as a
delicate young woman with pale red hair in a chic lavender
suit stumbled backward into her, and a small amount of the

tea in her cup spilled on her lavender skirt. Amelia noticed that her hand was shaking, she was so nervous, and she turned to Amelia looking mortified.

"I'm so sorry, I didn't mean to step on you," she said apologetically, and Amelia smiled.

"Don't worry. Is your skirt okay?" Sam Walker nodded nervously and smiled. "I was so busy looking at everything, I didn't realize you were behind me," but she'd had a quick loss of balance which had nothing to do with where Amelia was standing. She was wearing tiny little kitten heels, lavender suede shoes the same color as her suit, and lavender jade earrings, a necklace, and a bangle that her father had brought her from Hong Kong, since it was her favorite color. The lavender jade earrings had tiny diamonds around them.

"It all looks very grand, doesn't it?" Amelia said in wonder. "It looks like Versailles. My mother and I went there the other day so I could see it. The ball is going to be gorgeous. They were building the staircase when we walked through the gardens," Amelia said.

"Is it very steep?" Sam asked her with a look of panic, and Amelia smiled.

"Nothing we can't manage. They don't want us falling on our faces either, and apparently there's a liveried footman at either end of each step. They can always catch us if we trip. And we'll have our escorts. They have to be good for something."

138

# The Ball at Versailles

Amelia looked very confident, and Sam found it reassuring to talk to her. It was nice to know one person in the crowd. They had both noticed that some of the girls were very pretty, others less so. And the ambassadress had made a point of speaking to each of them and welcoming them to France.

"Where are you from?" Sam asked her. "I'm Sam, by the way. Samantha."

"New York," Amelia said with a smile. "I go to Barnard, that's part of Columbia University, it's the women's section. I'm Amelia. Where are you from?"

"I'm from New York too. I go to NYU." Sam wanted to know where Amelia lived but was afraid to ask, in case it sounded too snobbish if she had to admit that she lived on Fifth Avenue.

"Do you like NYU?" Amelia asked her, as a girl in a navy dress and jacket moved past them, heading toward the pastry section on the tea table. She bumped into Sam and turned to apologize.

"I'm sorry," she said, looking flustered, "I was heading for the chocolate éclairs, they were beckoning to me," she said, and Amelia and Sam laughed. They both noticed that she had a heavy Southern accent. She looked friendly.

"Savannah?" Amelia asked her. She had noticed on the list that one of the girls was from Savannah, Georgia, and she thought the girl in navy might be the one.

"Dallas," Felicity said with a broad grin. "My mother wouldn't let me wear my cowboy boots and hat, even if I promised to wear the white gloves. You both look beautiful, by the way," in their mauve and pale blue suits. "Where are you from?"

"New York," they answered in unison, and laughed. They liked the girl in navy, she said her name was Felicity and she looked like fun. And Felicity had forgotten all about the éclair while talking to them. She liked them too. She had been afraid that all the girls would be snobs and would snub her, but Amelia and Sam were both very open and warm.

"You look like New York. So stylish and fashionable. I love your hats. Mine is my mother's. She has terrible taste in hats," Felicity said.

"Where do you go to school?" Sam asked her. "In Texas?"

"No." Felicity shook her head, embarrassed for a minute. "I go to school in Boston." There were many colleges in Boston, but the minute she said which one, it classified her as a freak, and a serious student of subjects most girls hated.

"Radcliffe? Boston University?" Amelia asked her. Sam was too shy to ask.

"MIT," Felicity said, feeling awkward, and both girls looked at her in surprise.

"Wow," Sam said. "That's amazing. I never met a girl who went there. You must be a fantastic student."

"Actually, I go there for the pizza. There's a deli near the school that sells amazing pizza by the slice," she said, and they both laughed.

"What are you majoring in?" Sam asked, fascinated by Felicity. She didn't seem like an intellectual snob, or act like a freak. She seemed very normal and fun.

"I'm heading toward chemical engineering, but I'm thinking of switching to nuclear physics. I haven't decided yet." She looked embarrassed again. "I know girls aren't supposed to want jobs in fields like that, but I've always loved science. My family thinks I'm weird, or my sister does anyway."

"Where does she go to school?" Amelia asked her. She wondered if she came from a family where everyone was involved in science, or maybe were doctors.

"She doesn't. She decided not to go to college, it would have interfered with her social life. We have different interests. She spends a lot of time at the hairdresser. I'm not so good at that," she said, and all three of them laughed. She had wound her braid into a bun under the brim of her hat. The other two girls had worn their hair up too.

"I'm really impressed that you go to MIT," Sam added. "It makes me feel like a slouch. I'm majoring in art history."

"I'm going to major in English literature and pre-law. Both my parents were in publishing. I want to be a lawyer," Amelia said.

"My mom has never worked, and my sister never will.

So that leaves me, the family freak locked in a laboratory somewhere. My father is in land development. He's happy I got into MIT, since it's what I wanted to do. How did you both wind up here?" Felicity asked them.

"By accident, I think. They threw darts at a list of debs, and must have hit my name," Amelia said.

"Me too," Sam said.

"I came out at the Infirmary Ball last Christmas, and I think they may have gotten the list from them. Did you come out there too?" Amelia asked Sam, "or the Junior Assemblies?"

"I didn't. I didn't want to," Sam answered. "I didn't want to this time either. But my father thought I should do it, and Versailles is hard to resist. It felt kind of special," Sam said cautiously, "so I decided to do it."

"I didn't want to at first but then I thought it sounded like fun, and my mom wanted me to do it," Amelia said.

"So did mine. I begged her not to, but she said I had to. I hated the cotillion in Dallas, and big white dresses are not my best look," Felicity said. "I feel better in a lab coat, but here I am. It was easier to just do it, than fight with my parents about it. It makes them happy," Felicity said, looking nervous again, and the others nodded. As a student of MIT, she had a viable excuse not to want to go to a deb ball.

"Well, I'm glad you're here," Sam said to her. "I was worried about not knowing anyone here, or my escort, but now we know each other. It'll be a lot more fun." Felicity had just noticed Caroline Taylor sitting in a chair at the other side of the room. She hadn't moved since they got there and hadn't spoken to anyone.

"Do you think we should go over and say hi to her?" Felicity asked them.

"Why not? Maybe she needs to meet some friends too."

"She hasn't gotten out of that chair since she got here," Felicity commented, and by then she had reached Caroline.

"Hi," she said, and Caroline looked up in surprise, in her pink and black suit with the matching hat. "We came over to say hello. Are you from New York too?" She looked it.

"I'm from Los Angeles," Caroline said.

"They're from New York, I'm from Dallas," Felicity said. She introduced them all by name.

"I'm Caroline," she said, and mustered a weak smile.

"Are you okay?" Amelia asked her solicitously.

"I ate a bad oyster at lunch, and I think I might be dying, but my mother said I had to come."

"So did all of ours," Felicity spoke for them, and Caroline laughed and looked better for a minute.

"Did we all get bullied into this?" Amelia asked them, and Felicity nodded emphatically.

"I did. I figured they'd cut off my allowance if I didn't do it. I tried to get them to let my sister come in my place.

She was dying to, but they wouldn't let us. She's too old, she's twenty-two. So, are we all going to find husbands tomorrow?" Felicity asked them and they laughed again.

"I hope not," Amelia said, adamant. "I want to go to law school. I've got another six years of school ahead of me."

"I have nine or ten for a doctorate," Felicity said, definite.

"I don't know what I want to do later," Sam admitted. "Maybe something to do with art, like work in a museum. But I don't want to get married for a long time."

"I go to USC, and I want to work in film production. My parents are both in the movie business, it's in my blood," Caroline said, looking perkier, as she stood up to talk to them.

"Do you want to be an actress?" Sam looked impressed.

"Hell, no, that's a hard job, and you're never at home. My parents are on location all the time." Caroline didn't admit who they were. She wasn't ready to yet. It changed things when she did.

"So if we don't want husbands, what are we doing here?" Felicity asked them, and they looked blank for a minute. "You realize that every girl here wants to be engaged by the end of the weekend, or by the end of the summer at least. In fact, we're already failures, if we came out at cotillions in our respective cities on Christmas. If we're not engaged by now, seven months later, we have already failed. Do you have boyfriends?" Sam and Amelia shook their heads with a grin. "Me neither.

I've been running track and eating pizza since Christmas, so I've been too busy to meet anyone, and I run faster than they do anyway. And the boys in my class are geeks. I guess I'm a geek too, so that puts me in the 'hard to marry off' category, I'll probably be a burden on my family for many, many years," she said, and they all laughed. "And my sister's not doing so great either. She's been out for four years and hasn't had a single proposal yet. What about you?" she asked Caroline.

"I just broke up with my boyfriend," she said softly, but suddenly, saying it out loud, it didn't seem quite so awful. "But I don't want a husband either, and not a French one. They're probably going to be horribly stuck-up. I hear the prince who would be king, if there was one, is going to be at the ball. But I think he's really old."

"Actually, I wouldn't mind being queen if the opportunity comes up. I might give up MIT if I could be queen, then I could do or wear or eat whatever I want, without my sister ragging on me, and my mother being upset. Sign me up for that guy. I definitely want to interview for that. That would be better than a doctorate."

"I'm not so sure," Amelia said, as the ambassadress's secretary tapped a glass with a knife and the ambassador's wife made a gracious welcome speech to all the girls and wished them an unforgettable night at Versailles. She mentioned that she would see them again tomorrow.

The head of the ball committee was hosting a reception for all two hundred and eighty-six debutantes and an equal number of the escorts who had been assigned to them, to introduce them to each other, with a rehearsal following. And the night after, they would all be at Versailles being presented to international royalty and society, and dining and dancing under the stars afterwards. The ambassadress said that it would be magical.

"And if we don't each find a husband by the end of the weekend, we will each be scarred for life," Felicity whispered to her new friends, and they grinned, and applauded the speech politely. A few minutes later, they all left the embassy to spend the rest of the evening with their families.

The four girls left together and had cars waiting for them that they had to meet up with on the Faubourg Saint-Honoré. They waved to each other as they ran to their cars. The four of them had had fun and were glad they had met each other. And now each of them had three friends, and nothing could be so bad if you had friends to do it with. They were all smiling on their way back to their hotels, except for Caroline, who was feeling sick again. The bad oyster she had eaten for lunch was winning, and when she got to the Ritz, she ran into the hotel, and as fast as she could up the stairs to her suite, before disaster struck.

# Chapter 7

As soon as Caroline got to her room, she was violently sick, but made it to the bathroom, mercifully. She felt better afterwards, having gotten rid of whatever bad thing she had eaten that day. Her mother had made a point of saying earlier that the French were not reliable about refrigeration, and they needed to be careful about what they ate in the heat. Whatever it was, it had made her feel awful, and infinitely better once it was out of her system.

Her parents were out at another fancy restaurant. She knew they were going to La Tour d'Argent, and to the Ritz for drinks afterwards. They enjoyed each other's company and their romantic evenings. They spent enough time away from each other because of their work that their time together was always more precious. After twenty years of marriage, the passion had not gone out of their relationship. It used to embarrass Caroline when she was younger, but she thought it was sweet now. She hoped she had the same kind of marriage they did one day. And that was not going to happen from a one-night meeting, or even two nights, at a ball in Paris. It all sounded very romantic, but she had no illusions about meeting her Prince Charming at the ball. She was doing it to make her mother happy. And she had liked the three girls she'd met that day. They were all different from each other, but they all seemed normal, and open and honest about why they were there, mostly to please their parents. They were all very modest about how bright they seemed, and none of them was looking for a husband, which was a relief. She was sure a lot of girls were, desperate to find a man and get a ring on their finger, so they didn't have to go to school or work. Marriage was the only job they wanted, no matter what they had to compromise to get it. That wasn't how Caroline wanted to spend her life. She wanted to be like her parents and accomplish something on her own, using her mind and her talents, not her wiles to catch a husband as her only achievement in life.

She turned off the light and went to sleep early, still feeling a little queasy, but better than she had before she threw up. She was sure she'd feel better in the morning since whatever she'd eaten was gone now.

\* \* \*

148

Caroline woke up with the sun streaming into the room, rolled over in bed, and sat up. And as soon as she did, she felt sick again. And much to her horror, she threw up again. Her mother walked into the room as she came out of the bathroom, looking pale. And she actually felt worse than she had the day before.

"Are you still sick?" her mother asked, looking worried. "This is not the day for you to get sick. You've got the host committee reception tonight and the ball tomorrow. Caro, you've got to pull yourself together and will yourself to be well. You can do it, I know you can. I'll call the concierge and have him send up a doctor. Maybe he can give you a shot of something. I'll order some ginger ale and crackers and tea. It can't be food poisoning if you're still sick, you must have stomach flu." Caroline was lying on the bed, feeling very nauseous and looking green.

"I don't want to see a doctor, Mom, I'm fine." Her mother was already calling the concierge and hung up a few minutes later.

"He said they use a very nice doctor, and he'll have him here within the hour. What are you wearing to the reception tonight, by the way?" They had brought a few options, and the evening was going to be dressier than the tea at the embassy. It was the first time Caroline was going to meet her escort and Betty wanted her to look fabulous, and there would probably be press there to catch a first glimpse of the debutantes. She had to look her best.

Her mother was not one to be overly sympathetic when anyone was sick. She had shot movies during typhoons, been on ships at sea in storms, and never got seasick. She did her own stunt work when it wasn't too dangerous, and she liked to say that she kept working, dead or alive, so a little stomach flu was not adequate reason for Caroline to collapse like a soufflé. She had a job to do that night: she had to be the most fabulous debutante there, and Betty fully expected her to be.

Caroline felt as though she'd been run over by a truck, and was still in bed when the doctor arrived half an hour later, carrying an Hermès briefcase rather than a doctor's bag. He was wearing a well-cut suit, perfectly shined John Lobb shoes, and an Hermès shirt and tie, and he was very handsome, and charming as he recognized Betty. She introduced him to Caroline and explained what the problem was. She left the room then to check on Josh and make some calls and said she'd be back in a few minutes.

"Some medicine to settle her stomach might be a good idea," she suggested to him, and he smiled. Americans always liked to tell him what to do. He was used to it at the Ritz, and he worked with the other luxury hotels too. He was readily available to them, spoke several languages, and was extremely polite and pleasant to the guests.

He pulled a chair up next to the bed and smiled at Caroline. "So, mademoiselle, what have you eaten in the past twenty-four hours?"

"A bad oyster at lunch yesterday," Caroline said definitively.

"You are certain of that?"

"I think so."

"And you vomited how often?"

"Once last night and once this morning. I felt better after I got sick last night, but worse this morning when I woke up." He nodded, palpated her abdomen carefully, and listened to it with his stethoscope. He was particularly attentive to the lower right, which wasn't painful. Her stomach didn't hurt, she just felt like she was going to throw up. He took her temperature and she had none. He asked her a series of questions, and then asked how old she was.

"Nineteen."

"And you are sexually active?" he asked her, and she hesitated. She didn't want her mother to know, but Betty was still in her own room and hadn't returned.

"I was. My boyfriend and I broke up three weeks ago."

"And your last period was when?" She thought about it. The last three weeks were such a blur, all she had done was cry, and she hadn't thought about her period at all.

"I think it was around the twentieth of May."

151

"And we are now the tenth of July, so you are three weeks late, yes?" She nodded slowly, thinking about it.

"Yes," she said in a small voice, looking at him intensely.

"Which means you could be five weeks pregnant, or seven weeks the way we calculate it, from your last period. I could do a blood test, and we would have the result in two days, or I can send you to a gynecologist and have her examine you, if you wish, to confirm it. I think that could be the problem, Miss Taylor," he said. He could see how shocked and upset she was. She obviously hadn't thought of it. He palpated her lower abdomen again and could feel the slightest swelling. "I think that's a strong possibility."

"Please don't tell my parents," Caroline whispered quickly, in case Betty came back into the room. "I can get a test when I go home," she said, looking frightened and desperate. She had no idea what to do, and Adam wouldn't take her call if she reached out to him, nor care.

"And when are you going home?" he asked her.

"In two or three weeks. We're going to the Hotel du Cap on Sunday."

"In that case, you would be ten weeks pregnant by then, if my guess is correct. Do you wish to wait that long to know?"

"No, but I can't tell my parents, not now. I don't know what to do. Maybe I can get a test in the south of France." He nodded.

"I will give you a prescription to take to a laboratory in Antibes. I could be wrong. I am only guessing. But you seem quite healthy, you appear to have no infection, no fever, and in a healthy young woman your age, a period three weeks late is usually a reliable sign. Did you use protection or not always?"

"Not always," she said glumly. A lot of "not always." They had been careless a number of times, and she had thought they would be lucky because they were in love. She was sure the doctor was right. She was always regular. She hadn't even noticed the missed period, she was so upset about the breakup. She couldn't have his baby now, or anyone else's. She was nineteen years old and not ready to have a child. She would have to have an illegal abortion, and she had no idea how to get one, even when she went home.

"I'm sorry, mademoiselle," he said, closing his bag and putting the chair back where it was. Betty came back to her room then, and Caroline gave him a pleading look not to tell.

"Well, Doctor, what do you think? We have to get her well. She's going to be a debutante at a ball tomorrow night."

"Ah, the ball at Versailles," he said, smiling at Betty. "Well, she must be careful what she eats for a few days. Very light, small meals, and we'll see how she is then. You can see a doctor in Antibes if she's not better. For now, I think she has no danger, but perhaps an unsettled stomach." It was the best he could do. Caroline was an adult, and she had instructed him not to share his suspicions, but she was sure that he was right. She was pregnant, with no idea what to do about it. She was going to tell her parents after the ball, and all hell would break loose. She'd have to tell them about Adam, and she couldn't have a baby. They would have to take her somewhere where abortion was legal. Maybe Japan, or Mexico, or some place they knew about that she didn't. And they would probably never forgive her for it. But she needed their help now. And the situation was absurd. She was going to be presented to international society and royalty, allegedly to meet the man of her dreams and find a husband, when the man of her dreams was already with another woman, had dumped her, and she was now pregnant with his baby. She wanted to cry, but instead she thanked the doctor and Betty escorted him out and came back five minutes later.

"He said you should rest today before you go out tonight, and take it easy tomorrow before the ball. I'm sorry, baby, how do you feel now? At least it's not appendicitis or something serious." It was very serious. She'd rather have had appendicitis than be pregnant. And she felt like an idiot for not noticing the missed period sooner. She lay on her bed, thinking about Adam, and having his baby eight months from now, if she kept it. Everything about that option seemed wrong to her. He wasn't a nice guy, she knew that now. He didn't love her, and she didn't want to have a child with a man who had treated her so shabbily and abandoned her. And a baby wouldn't bring him back, nor should it. She was clear about that.

"I feel better, Mom," she said quietly, and Betty left her to get some rest, as tears slid from her eyes and into her pillow. She dreaded telling her parents, but there was no other choice. She would tell them on Sunday, the day after the ball. She turned over and sobbed in her pillow. This was the worst thing that had ever happened to her, and she was sorry they had come to Paris at all. She wanted to go home.

Caroline was quiet as she dressed for the reception that night. She wore a black cocktail dress, which suited her mood. It was short and sexy, which didn't feel right somehow. But she looked beautiful when she was dressed. Her face was still pale, and her seriousness enhanced her beauty. She looked almost tragic, which was how she felt. Ending a life seemed wrong to her, but having a baby at her age, with a man who didn't love her, was just as bad.

"Oh, my goodness, you're not going to the guillotine, you're going to a reception to meet your escort. Don't look so serious, you're here to have fun," her mother said to her.

155

"I know, Mom, I'm sorry. I'm just in a weird mood." And two days from now her parents would know just how weird, and it would break their hearts that she had been so foolish and cavalier. She thought Adam loved her, she loved him, and she thought nothing bad would happen, and now it had.

"Well, get un-weird," her mother said, smiling at her. "Go and see your new friends, and the other debs, and meet your escort. He might be a very exciting guy," she said. She and Josh had decided to have dinner at the hotel that night, at the Espadon, which was the gastronomic restaurant at the Ritz. And the next night, they would be at the ball. They were enjoying their time in France, were proud of Caroline, and looking forward to a few weeks at the Hotel du Cap, before going back to work in LA. They both had a new film.

The driver from the Ritz took Caroline to the Interalliée club, where the host committee's reception was being held. And she wiped the tears off her cheeks before she got out of the car. She had a real problem to cry about now. The pregnancy she suspected now put everything else into perspective. Nothing was as bad as that.

Jane helped Amelia dress at their hotel on the Left Bank. She was wearing a black cocktail dress too. It was a very pretty dress Jane had found for her, it fit her perfectly and showed off her figure. Amelia was beaming when she left

156

the hotel. She'd been looking forward to the ball for months, but now that she was here it was even more exciting than she thought it would be. Paris added more drama and romance to it. She felt like she was in a movie, as a driver with a Citroën drove her to the Right Bank to the club. She felt incredibly adult and glamorous as she stepped out of the car and walked into the club, with her invitation in her hand. The Interalliée was one of the most beautiful clubs in Paris, with large reception rooms where grand parties and wedding receptions were held. One had a sense of history wherever one went in Paris. And Amelia was happy to see Samantha Walker entering the club at the same time. She was wearing a beautiful draped knee-length white dress. She looked like a goddess, with a cascade of her strawberry blonde curls. She'd gone to the hairdresser that afternoon. She was wearing small diamond studs in her ears, and the back of the dress was bare. And she was wearing silver sandals that laced up her legs.

"Exciting, isn't it?" Amelia asked her, and Sam smiled a wide smile.

"I'm glad I came," she said, feeling more comfortable now that she knew someone there and didn't have to walk in alone. For the first time, Amelia noticed that Samantha had the slightest limp. She was going to ask her if she had hurt herself that afternoon, and then noticed a long scar down the side of her leg and realized that the limp might not be new. You could hardly notice it in her flat shoes, and they walked into the huge room together, where the party was being held. There were already several hundred people there, all young, drinking champagne, and a small group of older people, the host committee, who were surveying the crowd. They knew many of the French debs, but none of the Americans. And they agreed that it was a very handsome group, of healthy, young, well-bred young people, although they knew that many of them would get overexcited after the ball and get up to as much mischief as young people who were less well born. Youth was youth, wherever they had grown up.

Sam and Amelia each accepted a glass of champagne from a waiter carrying a silver tray. There were many of them throughout the room, serving the guests. Sam suddenly pointed across the room to where they saw Felicity standing alone, looking lost, in an emerald green dress, and they headed toward her. They heard snippets of English as they moved through the crowd, but mostly French. The French girls had arrived in groups and were sticking together. Many of them seemed to know each other and their groups kept growing, and throughout the room were little knots of Americans, speaking to each other, and looking intimidated. It took Sam and Amelia a few minutes to weave through the crowd until they reached Felicity, and she was thrilled to see them.

"Oh my God, no one speaks English here. I kept walking up to girls to say hello, and they looked at me as though I was at the wrong party, and I was beginning to think I was. The boys are cute though," she commented, as Sam and Amelia laughed. "I saw a couple of really good-looking guys a few minutes ago. They walked right by me. They all seem to know the girls."

"They all went to what they call 'rallies' together when they were younger. They're organized parties for young people to meet, like school dances but only with fellow aristocrats and fancy people," Amelia explained. The concierge at their hotel had explained it to her and her mother.

"Great, so they all know each other and we're the interlopers here. Where's Caroline, have you seen her?" Felicity asked.

"She wasn't feeling well yesterday, I hope she's not sick today," Amelia said, and ten minutes later, she arrived in a black dress, looking beautiful.

"What a mob scene," Caroline said, breathless when she reached them. "I've been looking for you for twenty minutes. There are a hell of a lot of French people here," she said, sipping a glass of champagne. She was feeling better than she had that morning, after staying in bed all day, and daring to hope that the doctor was wrong. Maybe it was just a flu after all.

They'd been chatting for a few minutes, when a woman in a red suit, with medals pinned to her jacket, got up on a small stage at one end of the room, and told them first in French and then in English, that she was going to call their names, and when they heard their name to come to the front of the room, and they would be introduced to their escorts, whose names would be called too, and they were to remain together until the end of the reception, so they would get to know each other before the ball tomorrow. And there would be a brief run-through of the schedule for the following night, so they would know where to stand and what to expect.

"Here we go," Felicity said, "wish us luck, that we don't wind up with Dracula's nephew, or Jack the Ripper's son." But all the young men looked very handsome in dark suits. They were all slightly older than the girls, and looked to be in their early twenties, which was a good age match with seventeen-to-nineteen-year-old girls. There were a lot of curious glances around the room, and giggling and laughing in anticipation. Some of the French debs had requested specific people to be their escorts, or family members like brothers and cousins, but most of the pairs were decided by the host committee, based on young people they thought would get along. And they tried to make sure that all the

American girls had escorts who spoke English. The escorts had each filled out a short questionnaire that was sent to them in April. It was painstaking work matching them up, and the committee took it very seriously.

Felicity was one of the first girls to be called, and she squeezed through the crowd to the front of the room near the stage. The young man waiting for her there looked older than some of the others, and more like a man than a boy. His name was Pierre Villiers, and he looked as though he had lost at the lottery when he saw Felicity. He was visibly not pleased, as they stepped aside so they could talk.

"Hi, I'm Felicity," she said with a broad smile. "Do you speak English?"

"Of course. I work in an ad agency."

"You're not a student?" He smiled at that.

"Not anymore. My aunt is on the ball committee. They were short of escorts, so she asked me to help. So here I am. I'm twenty-seven. Does that seem too old?" He didn't seem to care one way or another, and he was barely polite to Felicity. He had an arrogant look about him. "Where are you from?" he asked her.

"Dallas, Texas," she said in her Texas drawl.

"I thought you sounded odd. And how old are you?" She could tell that he was annoyed to be assigned to her.

"I'm nineteen, and I'm going to be a sophomore at MIT."

"Isn't that a school for physicists and engineers?"

"Yes, it is," she said proudly.

"Oh my God. My aunt must have been drunk when she did the pairs. I failed physics and chemistry in school, and cheated on all my tests. I still failed."

"I'm sorry to hear it. I enjoy science a lot."

"I find that frightening. Women aren't supposed to have jobs like that," he said bluntly.

"What about Marie Curie? She was a French scientist."

"Clearly, an anomaly. Her husband must have been a weak man." Felicity wasn't sure if he was joking or not. She was somewhat afraid that he wasn't. He stopped talking to her and they listened as the other names were called. He seemed to know a lot of the girls and waved as they went by to meet their escorts. He seemed to know half the room.

Amelia Alexander was called then and Tristan de Bret, and Felicity's escort gave a soft whistle. "I wonder who she knows to get an escort like that. Someone was doing her family a favor."

"Do you know him? Is he nice?" Felicity asked, and Pierre shrugged, with a knowing grin.

"I don't know him personally, but I know the name. His family are the richest people in France. They own all the big important wineries, cosmetic companies, pharmaceutical companies, luxury brands. She should marry him immediately.

Tell her to get pregnant tonight," he said disrespectfully, as though the Americans were there just to marry rich French men, when more likely the reverse was true, and some poor French ones were hoping to land a big American fish in their net. But he had made it quite obvious that rich or poor, Felicity was of no interest to him. He liked pretty women, and it was clear that Felicity's weight disqualified her. He ignored her as he chatted with other people around them, and the debs he knew. In several cases he knew their older brothers. There were definitely in-groups in the room, and outsiders. Felicity saw Amelia making conversation with Tristan de Bret, and neither of them looked too thrilled with each other.

Within a short time, Amelia knew that Tristan was twenty-four years old, studying political science at Sciences Po, one of the best universities in France, and most prestigious. His father was a count, he liked horses and played polo. And he asked Amelia nothing about herself. He seemed to know half the people in the room and talked more to them than the girl he was escorting. There appeared to be no sparks there, and they looked bored with each other.

Caroline was paired with a young Englishman, the second son of an earl. His name was William Brockhall, he was a viscount and declared himself "pauper aristocracy." He explained that they had lots of blue blood and no money. He seemed bright and funny and was twenty-five years old. Caroline had so much on her mind, she didn't listen to anything he said, and barely spoke to him. He could have been the King of England and she wouldn't have cared. She was in the grips of panic that she might be pregnant. Willie Brockhall was a good-looking young man. He was working for a bank in London, in the city, and his charm was wasted on her.

And Sam had been paired with a young man named Quentin Dupont. He spoke excellent English, and had just passed the bar exam at twenty-six, and was going to work for a French law firm. He mentioned that his father was French, and his mother Vietnamese. He was very polite and respectful of Sam, asked her a lot of questions about what she was studying and what pastimes she enjoyed, and made a sincere effort to get to know her. She liked him, and they discovered that they were both only children. His father owned a company that did a lot of business in Asia and had lived in Vietnam for a long time, which was how he met Quentin's mother. He asked about Sam's parents, and she said that her mother had passed away when she was five, and she lived with her father.

The four girls tried to join up, as the escorts were still being announced. Caroline plainly had no interest in Willie Brockhall, who lit up when he saw Amelia, who enjoyed talking to him too. And Tristan de Bret disappeared into the crowd to meet up with friends. He had explained to Amelia that he was supposed to escort his cousin, but she came down with chicken pox, so they had assigned him to Amelia instead, which didn't seem to amuse him, or interest him much before he vanished. And Felicity's escort, Pierre Villiers, disappeared into the crowd too, after making no effort at all to talk to her. He said, "See you tomorrow," and took off, but Willie Brockhall and Quentin Dupont stuck around with the four girls.

There was an explanation after that of how things were going to work at the ball the next day, and in what order, which no one listened to, and most of the debs and escorts left then, and had paid no attention at all to the schedule, and the rehearsal never happened. They were a hard crowd to control, and Willie and Quentin shepherded the four girls out of the huge reception room, and the six of them wound up on the street outside the Interallié club. As soon as they were outside, Caroline took off, with hardly a word to any of them. She said she had to get back to the hotel. In fact, she was feeling nauseous again and she was afraid that if she stayed to chat, she'd throw up on the street, which would be mortifying.

"She hates me," Willie said to Amelia, and she smiled.

"She's kind of aloof with us too," she explained. "I think she had food poisoning yesterday, so maybe she's not feeling well."

"No, she hates me," he said with good humor. "Most people do when they meet me. I talk too much, I ask too many questions, my brother always tells me so, and I always seem to remind them of some wet cousin they hated growing up, or the boy they hated most in school." His description made her laugh. He invited her out for a drink and she accepted, and they took off for Saint-Germain on the Left Bank, to find a friendly bar full of students, which left Felicity with Quentin and Sam, and she could see they liked each other too, so at least two of the American girls had gotten lucky. Willie wasn't Amelia's escort, but Caroline certainly seemed to have no interest in him. She barely said goodbye to him when she left to go back to the Ritz. And Felicity felt as though she should leave Sam to get to know Quentin, so she discreetly extricated herself and left a few minutes later to go back to the Plaza Athénée.

"Well, that was short," Araminta said when she saw Felicity in the living room of the suite. She had just ordered crepes from room service with chocolate sauce, and spaghetti Bolognese, to calm her nerves. "How was your escort?"

"Old and very handsome. He's twenty-seven and works at an ad agency. He looks like a movie star, and disappeared ten minutes after I met him. He knew everyone there."

"You should have spent more time on your diet this spring and kept running track. It might have paid off, and he might have stuck around for more than ten minutes," Araminta said unkindly, typical of her.

"I'm looking for a man who loves me for my mind, not just my body, or my hairdo," Felicity said to Araminta, who was getting a comb-out every day in Paris and looked gorgeous and chic.

"The packaging matters," Araminta said. "Men won't bother to get to know your mind, if they don't like the package it comes with. And most men aren't looking for women who are chemical engineers," she said bluntly. "They don't even know what that is."

"I'll switch majors as soon as I get back to school. How do they feel about nuclear physics? Do you have the lowdown on that?" Felicity asked her ironically.

"I just know that you're not doing anything to help yourself, Felicity. If you want a man, you need to give up ice cream, doughnuts, and pizza, for a while anyway."

"I'm not sure it's worth it," Felicity said pensively.

"You'll have more fun if you lose the weight," Araminta said matter-of-factly. "That's the only reason Mom and I bug you about it. It's for your sake, not ours."

"I'll do it eventually," Felicity said, but she didn't sound convinced. She didn't envy Araminta's life or her circle of friends, and Araminta had never had a serious boyfriend either. Felicity thought she tried too hard and went out with the wrong men. Araminta was all about the packaging, with nothing inside. There was no brain and no heart, once you got past the slick packaging. Araminta rolled her eyes when the room service cart arrived and went back to her own room to apply a face mask, and Felicity ate her dinner in peace, alone in the living room. Their parents had gone out to dinner.

In her room at the Ritz, Caroline had just thrown up for the second time since she got back from the reception. She was panicked thinking about the presentation at Versailles. She couldn't get through an entire evening now without vomiting. And worse than that, she was pregnant with a baby she didn't want, by a man who didn't want her. She cried herself to sleep that night.

And Quentin was a perfect gentleman and took Sam back to her hotel, and they had a sandwich at a table in the lobby while the piano played. He was an interesting person, and she enjoyed getting to know him. Her father came through the lobby, after meeting with an investor over drinks at the bar, and Sam introduced them. Quentin was pleasant and respectful, and Robert asked her about him when she got back to the suite.

"Is that your escort?" he asked her, curious.

"Yes, he's an attorney. He just passed the bar and has a job at a law firm."

"Is he Asian?"

"His mother is Vietnamese."

"He seems very nice."

"He is. His father owns companies in Asia. He's smart, and very polite, and seems nice. I feel better about tomorrow now that I've met him."

"So do I," Robert said to her. He liked Quentin. "Don't forget my dance tomorrow night," he reminded her. She groaned and rolled her eyes.

They chatted for a few minutes and then they went to their bedrooms. She'd had a nice evening with Quentin, and at least Quentin wouldn't be a stranger when she saw him at Versailles. She didn't think the others had been as lucky. She liked Willie Brockhall too. He seemed to be fun, and he was easygoing and unpretentious, calling himself "pauper aristocracy," which was probably true, but he didn't try to hide it. And as a second son in England, he would be poor, even if his father had an enormous fortune. It would all go to his older brother, and he would have nothing, which he said was why he worked in the city, the financial world in London.

Willie and Amelia walked all over Paris that night, after dinner at a bistro. They stopped outside Notre-Dame, and then he took her back to her hotel on the Left Bank at three in the morning. It was a magical night in Paris, even though he wasn't her escort. The hours they spent together had flown. And he was much nicer than her designated escort, Tristan de Bret.

# Chapter 8

Two dozen long-stem white roses in a vase were delivered to Amelia's room at the hotel on Saturday morning. They were from Tristan de Bret, and the card read "Looking forward to tonight. I am honored to be your escort. Tristan." She made a face when she read the card, but the roses were beautiful.

"Wow!" Jane said when she saw them. "He has lovely manners. He must like you."

"He's just being polite, Mom," Amelia said with no emotion. "He hardly spoke to me at the reception, and he went off with his friends."

"You must have made a big impression on him. That's a hell of a lot of roses from a fancy florist, for a guy who's not interested and is just polite. Why don't you give him a chance?"

"To do what? Sweep me off my feet at midnight? We met last night. We didn't talk to each other. He didn't ask me anything about myself. And after he gets me down the stairs at Versailles, and we have one dance, I'll never see him again. What's that supposed to turn into?" Amelia was cynical about it. And realistic.

"So who were you with until three o'clock this morning? I heard you come in."

"One of the other girls' escorts. She wasn't too keen on him, and she went straight back to her hotel. She wasn't feeling well. She has food poisoning."

"So you snatched her guy?" Jane looked disapproving.

"I didn't snatch anyone. We went for a drink, and had dinner, and then we walked around Paris and talked."

"And he didn't send you roses today. Your escort did."

"He's not exciting, Mom. We weren't attracted to each other."

"How do you know that after one evening of walking around Paris, and an hour with the other guy? Paris is a romantic city. It would make King Kong look like a hot date. Don't get carried away by the wrong things, and don't discard someone who might be the right guy if you give him a chance." Amelia had told her mother Tristan's name before the flowers arrived, and it had rung bells for Jane immediately. Even foreigners knew that the de Brets were the richest family in France, and by some amazing turn of fate Tristan had wound up as Amelia's escort, because his cousin had chicken pox and had to back out. It felt like destiny to Jane, but not to Amelia. She thought Tristan was boring, and Willie was fun. And at nineteen, that was all she wanted. She wasn't looking for an engagement to a total stranger, even a rich one, by Sunday.

"You just like him because of who his family is."

"They own all the best vineyards in France, half the industries, and several private banks. And he can afford to send you two dozen roses. That's not a crime, Amelia. You have to grab the opportunities that life gives you with both hands."

"But only if he's rich. Is that the theory? That's disgusting, and I'm not looking for a husband. I have ten years ahead of me before I want to think about getting married. And rich or poor, when that day comes, I want to be madly in love with my husband, and not because he's rich." Jane sighed, listening to her.

"I didn't marry your father for his money. He had some when we married, and he went through nearly all of it by the time he died. I just don't want you to have to struggle. Even if you love someone, that can kill it. It's not romantic to worry about how you're going to pay the next month's rent. My life hasn't been easy since your father died," she said simply.

"You're not doing that either. We live in the apartment Dad bought us. You don't pay rent."

"No, we pay maintenance," and she didn't tell her that if she didn't find a job soon, she might have to sell the apartment, so they could eat and Amelia could stay in college. "I'm not telling you to marry a rich man because he's rich. But I am telling you that security is important. For the last ten years, my life has been a challenge to provide for us. I want a better life than that for you. I don't want you to ever have to worry about money."

"I know, Mom. But I'm nineteen. I don't want to pick the boys I go out with because they have money, so I don't have to struggle one day. And if that's who I fall in love with and I have to struggle, then I will. I'll figure it out, just like you have. We don't lack for anything. I went to the best schools, and I'm in a great college. We have a beautiful apartment. We're here in Paris. We always have everything we need, and you didn't marry some rich drip to get any of it. You did it for us, and if I have to do it one day, I will." Tristan de Bret was an incredible opportunity, and he was exactly what Jane wanted for her daughter. Security, so she didn't have to lie awake at night, panicked about how to put food on the table and pay for school for her only child. The last ten years had taken a heavy toll on Jane, and she realized now that she had done it too well. Amelia thought that everything they had appeared by magic. She had no idea how hard Jane had worked and saved and scrimped and worried to preserve that lifestyle for her and the illusion of security.

"Is that why we're here?" Amelia asked her. "So I can find a rich husband? If that's true, then I guess the purpose of having girls make their debut isn't for a fun Cinderella night, as you put it—in that case, the purpose of a deb ball hasn't changed in the last hundred or two hundred years. It's an auction of young girls, to sell them to the highest bidder. That's not what I want, Mom. I want to be independent, and provide for myself, just like you do. And when I'm an attorney, I will, and maybe I can even help you then, just like you've provided for us since Dad died. But I'm not going to marry, no matter how many roses someone sends me, if he feels like the wrong guy. I'm sure Tristan de Bret is a perfectly nice boy, but I don't have sparks with him, I'm not attracted to him. He's boring. And he wasn't attracted to me last night either." Jane knew that everything Amelia was saying was right, and it was noble, but she also knew how painful it was to barely be able to make ends meet. And now that she was out of a job and had been for five months, desperation was nibbling at her heels, and she never wanted Amelia to experience it, even if it meant being married to a less exciting man.

"And this English boy you walked around with last night is exciting?" Jane looked discouraged when she asked her.

She could feel the de Bret boy slipping through Amelia's fingers. Maybe nothing would come of it, but Amelia wouldn't even give him a chance. She could afford not to, because she had her mother to support her. Jane had given her the illusion of security for ten years, but it was only an illusion, it wasn't real. And they were living much closer to the edge than Amelia knew. For a minute, when Amelia was invited to the ball at Versailles, Jane had thought it was an answer to a prayer, a chance to introduce her to someone suitable, and maybe even much more than suitable, someone who would keep her safe and secure forever, so she'd never have to worry about money. She wanted Amelia to have that opportunity, but the whole idea of it was repulsive to Amelia, and maybe she was right. "I want to meet both of them tonight. And you're right, Amelia. You're only nineteen. You don't need to worry about any of this stuff now. And if Tristan is a bore, so be it. I guess I got caught up in the Cinderella fantasy." She went to hug her daughter, and they clung to each other for a long time.

"You're just freaked out because you haven't found a job yet. You'll probably get a great job as soon as we get home. You're so wonderful and smart, someone's going to hire you. I know it," Amelia said.

She was so young and so innocent and hadn't come up against the unfairness of life yet. She hadn't been turned down for jobs she was qualified for, but a man always got the job, and was paid three times as much money for it. She hadn't been fired after nine years because some man had better credentials, even if he had less experience, but he was a man, and she wasn't, so he got the job. It had been a hard, eye-opening five months for Jane after getting fired, and she was beginning to lose hope of getting a fair deal and a good job. She had been underpaid for years and put up with it because they had almost promised her the job as CEO. And now she couldn't even get a job as a secretary. She didn't see how she was going to continue to pay for Barnard for Amelia, let alone law school three years from now. But something would come along. And Amelia was right, at forty-two, her career wasn't over. It was on pause. But the five-month pause had shaken her faith in herself. The job market favored men. And the ball at Versailles was not going to be Amelia's ticket to an easy life. Jane knew she had been wrong to think that. But she didn't know how else to ensure Amelia's future, or how far they would fall before she found a solution, or a job, or if the job she found would pay enough to support them. For women, there weren't a dozen different ways to secure the future. But marriage was one way. And if Amelia fell in love with a boy from a family with money, it would make her life easier. But the easy way out wasn't always the right one, and clearly marriage wasn't the path to security that

Amelia wanted, and Jane respected her for it. As young as she was, she had morals and principles, and dreams she believed in, and Jane had taught her to have them. She couldn't teach her something different now, or tell her it was all a lie and her dreams would never come true and she couldn't achieve success on her own.

"So, tell me about this English boy," Jane said, sitting down next to her on the couch in Amelia's room.

"He's funny and silly and smart, and he wants to work hard because the English system is terrible, and his older brother will inherit everything, so he wants to make his own fortune. He seems very honest, and he doesn't pretend to be anything he's not. He told me he's poor as soon as I met him, so I didn't have any illusions about him. I told him I'm poor too, even though I have a mother who spoils me rotten, like bringing me to the ball at Versailles. You didn't have to do that, Mom. But I'm glad we came." Jane smiled in answer.

"So am I. I love being here with you." They wouldn't have these times forever, once Amelia was out in the world on her own.

"Thank you for making this happen," Amelia said.

"It sounded too special to pass up," Jane admitted to her.

"It is. And I like the girls I've met so far. Some of them seem stuck up, and I can't talk to the French ones, and they don't talk to us. But the three American girls I've met are really nice. I think one of them has some kind of injury, but I didn't want to ask her about it. She kind of goes off balance every once in a while. She has a slight limp, and I think she has a weak hand."

"That sounds like a stroke, and she's too young for that." Jane frowned.

"I think it was more of an injury, she has a bad scar on one leg. Like she had some kind of accident, or surgery. She's beautiful though, and really smart. She's the only one who really liked her escort. They went out last night too. He's half Vietnamese."

"It's too bad you girls won't see your escorts again after tonight."

"Maybe we'll come back to Paris sometime. And I can see one of the girls in New York, the one who had the accident. She goes to NYU and is from New York. The other two live in Dallas and LA. The one from Dallas is really funny. She goes to MIT. She said she'd come down for a weekend sometime."

"She must be very smart if she goes to MIT." Jane was impressed.

"She is. She has kind of an issue with her weight, and her mother and sister give her a hard time about it. I really like her. The one from LA has been sick the whole time.

She got food poisoning yesterday. I hope she'll be okay tonight." Jane was glad she'd already made some friends among the other debs. In the end those were the connections that would last, not a quick romance with some boy she'd never see again. Amelia had it all right.

They went to lunch at a bistro near the hotel, and walked along the Seine, and then they went back to the hotel. They had already hung up the dress for the ball, and Jane had promised to do Amelia's hair. This was her big night, and as she watched Amelia slip into the bath, and Jane went to press a few creases out of her own dress, she had never been as proud of her daughter as she was now. She was a woman of strong principles and beliefs, and self-respect, even at nineteen.

Caroline had trouble getting ready for the ball that night. She had to stop twice to throw up. The nausea that had overwhelmed her for the past few days had gotten steadily worse. She felt sick all the time now, and it was hard to hide from her mother.

"I want you to see a doctor when we get to the south of France," Betty said firmly, and she shared her concerns with Josh.

"I hope it isn't anything worse than food poisoning. She could have gotten hepatitis from a bad oyster. I don't trust the refrigeration here. They leave everything out in this heat. And she shouldn't be eating oysters in July." He looked concerned, but she didn't have a fever, so it wasn't the flu.

In spite of how ill she felt, Caroline looked exquisite once she was dressed. The white dress with the full ball skirt and the tiny waist made her look like a princess or an angel, her father couldn't decide which. And Caroline was dismayed to realize how tight the waistband had gotten since she'd last tried it on two months before. She almost couldn't get the skirt closed, and once she did, she couldn't breathe. It was going to be a long evening, nauseous and breathless, and she wasn't going to eat, or she was sure she'd throw up. Her mother made her eat some toast and drink some ginger ale before they left the hotel at six o'clock. The debutantes had to be at the palace at seven, and an entire area had been set aside for all two hundred and eighty-six of them to gather, with their escorts.

The presentation of the debutantes was due to begin at seven-thirty, and they'd never had a proper rehearsal. Dinner was to be served at nine, with a light show at dessert once it was dark, around ten-thirty, and there would be fireworks at midnight. The party and dancing were expected to go on until dawn, with breakfast for those who stayed. In all, there were to be twelve hundred guests, two-thirds of whom were young, and the older guests would leave long before the end of the festivities. It was going to be a night no one would forget.

In the car on the way to Versailles, Amelia noticed that her mother wasn't wearing the emerald ring she always wore to formal occasions. It was her best piece of jewelry, and Amelia was startled to see her mother without it.

"Where's your ring, Mom?"

"I didn't bring it," Jane answered smoothly. "I didn't want to travel with it and stay at a hotel. I didn't know if they had a safe for guests or not, and on our driving trip, we're going to stay at some very simple inns. I thought it was better to leave it in the safe at home." She acted as though not wearing it or having it in Paris was unimportant, and Amelia looked at her searchingly and then nodded, but she was quiet and pensive for the rest of the drive to the palace, and then she forgot about it, in her nervousness about the presentation. But something about what her mother said didn't seem right, even if it made sense. She had the uneasy feeling that her mother was lying. And added to her aspirations to marry Amelia off to a rich man, it totaled up to a very disturbing worry about her mother. Amelia wondered suddenly if things were worse than her mother had admitted to her. Maybe being unemployed for five months had taken an even bigger toll than she knew. It was the first time she had ever thought about it and doubted her mother's word. She reached over and held her hand, and they held hands the rest of the way until the magnificent palace came into view, and they both forgot everything else. The magic had begun.

After Felicity got her hair done at Alexandre that afternoon, she bathed carefully, not to get it wet.

After her bath, Araminta and her mother helped her into her dress, smoothed the draped fabric down in the back into the short train, and settled the same panel in front down from her bustline. It effectively concealed most of what Felicity hadn't lost in the last six months. She looked statuesque and elegant, and she hardly recognized herself in the mirror.

"Wow . . . the dress is amazing," Felicity said, looking at herself.

"You look beautiful," Araminta said in a respectful tone. She had never seen her sister look like that, as their mother beamed at her proudly, and their father had tears in his eyes when he saw her.

"You look like a princess," he said to Felicity, and kissed her on the cheek. She felt almost like a bride, and looked like one. All she needed was a veil and a bouquet. She would be carrying the bouquet of white lily of the valley that the ball committee had ordered for each of them. The American debutantes were wearing white, and the French ones would be wearing whatever color they chose. Lower heels had been recommended so they didn't trip on the stairs, but many would wear high heels anyway. It was their escorts' job to keep them on their feet. The young men would be wearing white tie and tails, which would lend dignity and elegance to the occasion. Many of them would be wearing formal attire to that degree for the first time. The debutantes' fathers would be wearing white tie as well, with their medals, if they had any. Royals would be wearing their sashes, and quite a few were expected that night.

The party and presentation were taking place in the orange orchard of the palace, *L'orangerie*. The organizers had put the families and guests of the Americans at tables together, so language wouldn't be a problem and they could enjoy the evening, since so few of the Americans spoke French, and very few of the French guests were fluent in English.

It had taken weeks to work out the seating for so many people, of different rank and importance. And the new Prime Minister and Mrs. de Gaulle would be in attendance.

The parents dropped the girls off in the roped-off receiving area where they'd been told to gather. Once their precious cargo was deposited, the parents went to join the other guests.

\* \* \*

Samantha took her father's breath away when he saw her in the exquisite dress she had had made. She had kept it as a surprise for him until then.

The giant ball skirt swung like a huge bell around her, and the seamstress had been meticulous about the hem. It just barely touched the ground, and no longer, so she wouldn't trip. The debutantes would be walking on uneven ground all evening, in the gardens, in the courtyard, and coming down the stairs. It was treacherous for all of them, and particularly for Sam. She was wearing the shoes with the kitten heel. They looked like Marie Antoinette's delicate shoes, on display at the palace, with the rhinestone buckle peeking out from under the skirt, just enough but not too much sparkle.

An assistant handed out the bouquets to all the girls, and the number was exact.

Pierre Villiers was standing next to Felicity, as they waited for the music to begin to signal that it was time for the procession of debutantes toward the staircase.

"Who was that ravishing girl in the silver dress I saw in the car with you when they dropped you off?" Pierre asked her.

"My sister, Araminta," she said in a flat voice. She could see the lust in his eyes. It was familiar to her, about her sister. Araminta always inspired desire in the men she met, which she was happy to provoke. But it never produced anything more serious once they got to know her.

"You'll have to introduce her to me after the presentation," he said, and Felicity nodded. She didn't care. He hadn't told her she looked beautiful, but she knew she did. The dress made her feel regal. Seeing herself in the exquisite Oscar dress, she got a glimpse of what she would look like if she lost the excess weight and had made a decision that night to do something about it. It was time.

Caroline was clinging to Willie's arm more tightly than he expected, and when he glanced at her, she looked pale but determined. He patted her hand to reassure her, and she smiled wanly. He could see she didn't feel well, and she winced in pain a few times when she thought he wasn't looking.

"Don't forget, you're supposed to be having fun," he reminded her. "Smile as we come down the stairs," he said, and she nodded.

"Thank you for the beautiful flowers," Amelia whispered to Tristan, and he looked pleased. His father had told him it was the correct thing to do. And there was another debutante being presented that night, a French one, in whom he had a particular interest. He had sent her two dozen roses too, and in her case red ones. His father had called the florist for him and paid the bill.

As they waited to start moving, Samantha kept her hand

firmly tucked into Quentin's arm, and after a few minutes, she looked up at him. Her hair was in a sweeping mass of reddish blonde curls, and he had never seen a woman look so beautiful and so innocent.

"I fall sometimes," she whispered to him, getting more nervous by the minute.

"I won't let you," he whispered back. "Can I hold your hand while you curtsy to steady you?" She thought about it for a minute and nodded, and then turned to look at him and smiled. He had understood just enough, and she didn't need to explain it to him.

"That would be very nice. Thank you."

"I'll hold your bouquet when you make your bow," Quentin said to Samantha. She was visibly tense and her hands were shaking, but she looked exquisite in her fairy princess dress. He was proud to be with her, and looked elegant himself in white tie and tails. He had already figured out that her balance wasn't secure at times, and had watched her closely. The problem was subtle, but he had seen it and correctly assumed it was somehow related to the scar on her leg, although she hid it well, and compensated for it artfully. You didn't see the lack of balance unless you looked very hard and watched her for a while. And he didn't care what the committee would think of his holding her hand for the curtsy. They couldn't do anything to stop it. And she mattered more to him than their rules. He wanted her to feel comfortable and safe, and after their brief exchange, she already did.

Then slowly, they finally started moving toward the staircase. Sam had had nightmares about the stairs, but she could feel Quentin's support as they approached them and she was no longer afraid. The liveried footmen with white wigs were in position at the end of each step. And the crier announced their titles and names, first the girls, then their escorts. The escorts wearing military uniforms added color to the crowd.

The French girls went first in their rainbow of colors, and the Americans followed them looking like brides. As it turned out, alphabetically, Samantha Walker was the last one to be presented. She paused just a moment longer than the others, ready to conquer the staircase, with Quentin's help. Her waiting just a few seconds made her entrance more dramatic. A spotlight was on her and cameras flashed, since there were no other girls in front of her to obstruct everyone's view of her.

"Take it slow," Quentin whispered, and she did. She came down one step at a time, and looked as though she was floating, in the gigantic tulle skirt. It was the perfect finale to the presentation. Sam drifted down the stairs, stopped at the bottom, and took a step forward. With a firm grip on Quentin's hand, she made a low curtsy in the direction of the committee, with another smaller bow to the pretender to the no-longer-existent throne, and a nod to the Prime Minister, General de Gaulle, and his wife.

She came up from her bow, beaming, like a figure skater who had mastered the triple axel in midair, and landed solidly and gracefully back on her feet on the ice. She looked at Quentin gratefully, and with smooth steps and her head held high, they went to join the others as the crowd applauded for all the girls, and especially Sam. There was a brief presentation then of a pin for each girl: a gold sun for the French debutantes, and a gold star for the Americans. The sun pin was symbolic of the Sun King who had built the magnificent palace that had survived its challenges in the course of history, and was still standing and more beautiful than ever.

The entire group was allowed to join their friends and families then, at the tables where they were going to dine, and all the guests had watched the girls being presented. Sam handed her father her pin to put in his pocket and introduced him to Quentin again, who shook his hand for the second time and said it was an honor to escort his daughter. They all sat down to dinner then. The debutantes were all at tables in a prominent section where everyone could see them and admire them. They were a gorgeous group of young people. Quentin was at a table near his parents, but he was seated with Sam since he was her escort. Sam met Amelia's mother at her father's table, and thought

Danielle Steel

she seemed nice. Amelia and her escort were at hers. Amelia wanted to introduce her mother to Sam's father, since they all lived in New York. But it wasn't necessary. By chance, Jane and Robert Walker were next to each other, since they had both come alone. And Robert was thrilled to see how happy Sam looked. She was radiant. The presentation had been a victory for her. She had walked those stairs as though she owned them and did it every day.

Just before dinner, the bandleader announced the father-daughter dance, and Robert led Sam away onto the dance floor, and they executed a perfect slow waltz. And then it was the traditional dance with the escorts. Quentin arrived to take Sam from her father, and carefully swept her onto the dance floor, as they circled the room with immeasurable grace.

# Chapter 9

Felicity was at the same table as Caroline, and four other American girls with their escorts. Felicity could see her parents at a nearby table where Araminta was due to sit with them, but her seat was vacant. When the first dance with the escorts was announced, Felicity couldn't find hers anywhere. He had vanished immediately after the presentation without a word to her. She glimpsed him once in the distance during cocktail hour, and he hadn't shown up yet at the dinner table. The meal was about to begin after the first two dances.

"Where's your date?" Caroline asked her in a whisper. Felicity had been left looking abandoned and regal as soon as the father-daughter dance was over.

"I have absolutely no idea," she admitted, feeling lost, as Caroline left the table with Willie Brockhall, who was very

Danielle Steel

gallant when Caroline admitted that she still wasn't feeling well. The evening had been hard for her, she could barely manage to get through the presentation and now the dancing and the meal. The long evening had been planned for young women in search of husbands, not for pregnant women with morning sickness, she thought, and she was trying to be polite to Willie and a good sport, no matter how ill she felt. She'd had cramps in her back and lower abdomen all night, which she thought was probably from throwing up with such force that it wracked her entire body.

Felicity watched Caroline dance away with Willie to a lovely foxtrot. The band was playing the best dance music she had ever heard. They even played some of Frank Sinatra's songs, and some of Dean Martin's. She loved to dance and felt foolish and conspicuous with no partner. She was about to sit down alone at her table, next to Pierre Villier's empty chair, when someone touched her arm and she turned to see who it was, hopefully Pierre returning for the escort's dance. The young man she found herself facing looked as though he'd gotten dressed in the dark. He had a wild mane of curly red hair that formed a bush around his head. He had warm brown eyes, and a cautious smile. He was wearing black tie instead of white tie and tails, since he wasn't an escort, and his tie was crooked.

"I'm sorry. My sister is one of the debutantes tonight, Francoise Trudot, maybe you met her. She has red hair like me.

I'm Raphael, I know Pierre Villiers is your escort. I went to school with him. He spends more time drinking in the bushes with his friends at parties like this than on the dance floor. It's a shame for you to miss this dance, and the music is so good. Would you like to dance with me?" he asked, and she hesitated. She wasn't sure what the rules were about substituting escorts, but the official part of the evening was over, and it was free-form from now on. And she did want to dance. It was nice of Raphael to rescue her.

"Yes, I would." She smiled at him, feeling open to anything in her beautiful dress. She felt like a princess wearing it, and not just some fat, awkward, geeky girl from Dallas, which was how she usually felt.

He led her out to the dance floor, and she discovered instantly what a good dancer he was. She had a great time sweeping around the floor with him, and his English was almost as good as his foxtrot. "You are very beautiful," he said, as the band slipped into the next song and they kept dancing, "and you're a wonderful dancer," he complimented her.

"Thank you, I love to dance, but I don't get a chance to very often."

"Why not?" He seemed intrigued by her, he thought she was extremely glamorous with her fancy hairdo and the elegant dress. She looked like a queen to him. And he was taller than Felicity, with broad shoulders and a sturdy build.

"I study a lot," she said, as she smiled at him.

"Ah, so do I. What do you study?"

She knew that would be the romance killer as soon as she said the word. It was a word no man wanted to hear from a woman. "Engineering," she said, expecting him to stop dancing, drop his arms, and walk off the floor. And instead, all he did was slow down and stare at her. "I have a minor in physics," she said, making it even worse. He was smiling broadly when she looked up at him.

"I go to Polytechnique. I am studying engineering too. But I don't know any women who do. Polytechnique here is a good school for that." This time, it was Felicity who smiled at his modesty.

"Yeah, I know. The best one."

"And you, where do you go to school?" he asked. She was definitely an unusual girl, he could tell that already. He felt sorry for her stuck with Pierre Villiers as an escort. He was a notorious jerk on the social scene, a drinker and a player, a ladies' man and a cheat, and not a respecter of women.

"I go to a school called MIT," she said, "in Boston." And this time he stopped dancing and stared at her.

"Oh my God, no! That is my dream school. You go to MIT? I would hate you, but you are too beautiful to hate, and you dance too well. I applied there for an exchange program, and they turned me down. You are so lucky, and you probably deserve it. I got accepted for a two-year program at Harvard though. I'm a graduate student," which meant that he was somewhere between twenty-two and twenty-four, she guessed.

"When are you going?" She was excited by what he had said. He was going to Harvard.

"I have to be there on September first." He looked very pleased about it, and even more so now that he had met her. He would have a friend in Boston when he arrived.

"I'm going back the week before. It always terrifies people when I say I go to MIT, especially men. Women don't care. They just think I'm a creep and don't want to talk to me. MIT was one of the first schools to take female students, and encourage women in engineering, and as entrepreneurs. They took their first female student in 1870," she said proudly.

"I know. I've read everything about it. I was crushed when they wouldn't take me."

"Harvard is not exactly a slouch school," she teased him.

"It's not MIT," he said. "Can I see you in Boston? I have no friends there."

"Of course. Now you have me. I'll show you around Boston. It's a great city for student life, when you have time for it." It seemed like an incredible stroke of good fortune to both of them to have found a fellow scientist and engineering student. It seemed like the most unlikely place for them to meet, at a deb ball. "My family thinks I'm completely weird," she admitted to him, as a liveried waiter in the costume of the period, a blue satin suit with gold lace trim and knee breeches, set down Pierre's dinner in front of the chair where Pierre was supposed to be sitting. "Do you want to have dinner here?" she asked him, pointing to the empty seat next to her.

"Is this okay?" Raphael asked her. He was a big man and looked like a teddy bear with his red ball of frizzed hair. Felicity felt small next to him.

"Sure, it's fine. I don't think he's coming back. I lost him an hour and a half ago. How does your family feel about you?"

"Happy. I'm their only son, so they have nothing to compare me to. And my sister is quite normal. She's studying to be a biologist. Studies are familiar to them. My father is a cancer researcher at the Marie Curie Institute, and my mother is a playwright and poet laureate at the Académie Francaise. She's quite well known," he said proudly. "They're very intellectual. What about yours?"

"My father is in land development and commercial real estate investments, and my mother is a personal shopper . . . actually, I'm kidding. She just likes to shop, and neither my mother nor my sister went to college, so they think I'm strange. And being an engineer is off the charts as far as they're concerned."

"Why are you here?" he asked her, puzzled. She was a long way from Dallas, with no reason to be that he could figure out.

"In time-honored tradition, I'm here to find a husband. They want to get rid of me. And I don't think Pierre is going to propose marriage by the end of the evening, so I'll have to go back to Dallas in disgrace," she said matter-of-factly, and he laughed at her explanation.

"He's a fool. He should propose. At least he wouldn't be bored. He picks the worst women. All he cares about is how fast he can get them into bed, and then he brags about it. He's disgusting. Why France, for you, I mean?"

"I got invited and my mother thought it sounded glamorous and would build my confidence. And you know, it would be good for trade relations between the U.S. and France, if they got a good price for me. They were planning to sell me to the highest bidder, but I don't think anyone made them any offers. The trip was a total failure."

"No, it wasn't," he said, laughing. "I met you. It was ordained by destiny. I'm sure we're the only two engineers here," he said happily, and invited her to dance again as soon as they finished dinner. The food was delicious, and the band was terrific.

They spent the next hour tirelessly on the dance floor. Pierre Villiers had never shown up to claim his date or his dinner. And Raphael and Felicity were oblivious to the revelers around them. People were getting quite drunk on excellent wine, and everyone seemed happy. So were they. They never stopped talking.

At one of the American parents' tables, Jane Alexander, Amelia's mother, and Robert Walker, Samantha's father, had a long conversation about having only children the age of their daughters, as single parents. They discovered that they were both widowed, and had many things in common. But not all. Robert was a legend with his venture capital firm, and Jane was an unemployed former executive of a publishing house, and acutely aware of the discrepancy of wealth, income, and the importance of their jobs. Robert was an icon in the world of finance. She was just a poor woman looking for work. Or that was how she felt, but he was good company. He sounded sincere about his devotion to his daughter, and they had the same concerns about raising children that age and getting them safely to the starting line of real life, without harm or incident. He asked her to dance, and they both enjoyed it, and continued to chat over dinner.

They commented too on the discovery that the world-famous movie star Betty Wade had a daughter who had been presented with their daughters that night.

"Amelia never mentioned it to me," Jane said, surprised that one of the mothers was a major movie star.

"And Sam didn't tell me. Maybe they didn't know. She's being discreet and they're not on the list of parents." He was looking for them under "W," and Jane found them first.

"She's married to the producer Josh Taylor. There they are, Mr. and Mrs., and the daughter is Caroline Taylor," Jane said.

"She did mention her to me." Robert remembered the name then. "They met at the embassy tea party the other day. Sam said something about a girl named Caroline who was sick. She had food poisoning or something." Jane nodded, impressed yet again by the people they were meeting, including Robert Walker. They danced again after dinner.

Caroline made it through the first dance with Willie. She wasn't having fun but she was managing to hang in. Halfway through the second dance, a lively foxtrot, she got a look of panic on her face, dashed off the dance floor, and was looking frantically for a toilet and couldn't find one fast enough. She literally dove into a small cleared area hidden by bushes, and everything she'd eaten in the past few hours, which wasn't much, splattered at her feet and splashed onto the hem of her dress. She could sense someone standing behind her and didn't care who, and a long arm reached

199

around her and handed her a damp handkerchief dipped in water, and a dry one. She wiped her mouth and her face and turned to see Willie behind her, and felt too sick to even be mortified. Her eyes were watering from the heaving. She took the handkerchiefs gratefully and cleaned herself up, but the bottom of her dress was a mess.

"Thank you," she said in a hoarse voice, as some of the debs hurried past them and made a face. "I'm sorry. I have been an awful date."

"Not to worry, old bean. It happens to me every time I drink rum." Willie felt sorry for Caroline. She looked awful and her makeup had smeared. Her mascara was running down her cheeks, mixed with tears.

"I haven't had anything to drink," she said miserably, trying not to cry.

"That's unfortunate. The wine is really very good. And keep the handkerchiefs. They're my brother's. This is his suit. I found them in the pocket of the tails. He'll never miss them. I actually stole the suit." He smiled and she laughed, and they went to sit on a nearby bench while she recovered her composure.

"I'm really sorry."

"Don't be. I suppose this means that if I propose tonight, you'd turn me down." She nodded with a grin. "What about tomorrow? Any chance?"

She shook her head. "Same response."

"The French really do rush it a bit. We met last night, the presentation tonight, and back to London tomorrow night, which leaves tonight or tomorrow for the proposal. I've never proposed to a vomiting woman before, although I'm sure some must have wanted to, at the prospect of me. It does upset my stomach a bit at times too. Older brother got everything, you know. Beastly British system. Frightfully wrong-footed. I got the Dower House on the estate, but it isn't even big enough for me. My dog hates it. Cats probably died there centuries ago. Dreadful place. So where does this leave us, Miss Taylor? . . . and by the way, is that true that your mother is Betty Wade and your father is Josh Taylor?" She nodded in response. "You might have told me. I've seen all her movies. Do you suppose she'd give me an autograph for my brother's handkerchiefs? No, well, maybe not." He really was a good sport and a nice guy, and in other circumstances she might even have been attracted to him, but not with Adam heavy on her heart, and his baby in her belly, and her need to throw up every five minutes. It had been a hellish few days for her. She didn't even want to go to the Hotel du Cap with her parents. She wanted to go home. To LA.

"I'm going to call it a night," she said to him, and stood up. "I'll go find my parents. You were a wonderful escort, and I was a nightmare date."

"Circumstances beyond your control," he excused her. And more out of control than he knew. "Call me if you ever get to London."

"Or you to LA." She stood up, intending to find her parents and tell them she wanted to go back to the hotel, but when she stood, she felt a knife slice through her, and felt a splash of something fall to the ground at her feet, and when she looked down, there was blood all over her white satin shoes. She tried not to panic but was suddenly in agony. Almost too much to speak. He wasn't sure what was happening, but he could guess.

"Should I call an ambulance?" he asked her, trying not to panic himself.

"No, I don't think so. I just want to go back to the hotel. Can you get my parents? I'll meet them at the car."

"I'll take you to the car, and then I'll get them. You're not walking to the car alone." She didn't think she could. She was dizzy and could feel blood pouring down her legs. Her dress was going to be ruined, but she didn't care. It was the most frightening thing that had ever happened to her. Willie managed to half carry her, with an arm around her, to the parking lot, where her driver was smoking and talking to a group of other drivers, and the Rolls from the Ritz was prominently parked and near at hand. Willie asked him if he had some old towels or a blanket in the boot, and he produced both rapidly, and Caroline spread them on the seat and got in, as Willie looked at her. "Can I leave you now to get them?" he asked seriously. "I think you should go to a hospital, not the hotel. The American Hospital is on the way back," he said. He patted her arm and left her at a dead run to find her parents. He was resourceful and kind and had proven to be a good friend to a girl he hardly knew. He found them quickly at their table, leaned down, introduced himself and explained the situation discreetly to Betty, who looked instantly alarmed, and whispered to Josh, who stood up immediately, with an anxious glance at his wife, and Willie.

"It's nice to meet you both," Willie said politely, "or it would be in other circumstances. Your car is right at the entrance. I was going to introduce myself earlier but you were busy. I'm sorry to meet you like this."

"Thank you very much," Josh said, distracted as Betty scooped her bag off the table. She looked very striking in her red dress, and very much the movie star in a ruby and diamond necklace she had borrowed from Van Cleef with earrings and bracelet to match, and a large ruby ring. They took off half running to the parking lot, and found the Rolls easily, with Caroline inside, leaning back against the seat with her eyes closed. Her parents jumped into the car, with Betty next to Caroline, and Josh in front. Betty told the driver to take them to the American Hospital in Neuilly, as Willie had suggested to her mother as well.

"What's happening?" Betty whispered to her, and tears sprang to Caroline's eyes.

"I don't know. I'm bleeding heavily, I think I'm having a miscarriage." Betty looked like someone had hit her with a sledgehammer.

"You're *pregnant*?"

"I think so," Caroline said in a choked voice, as Betty remembered the supposedly bad oyster and the vomiting.

"Are you sure?"

"More or less."

"How pregnant?"

"About two months."

"And whose is it?" Josh was straining to hear from the front seat but didn't catch it all.

"I'll tell you later. It's over with us anyway. I was going to try and get an abortion when we got home."

"Oh my God," Betty said, and Josh looked grim.

It took them half an hour to get to the hospital, with Caroline squeezing her mother's hand. An attendant and a nurse came out to the car when they got there, and as they moved Caroline into a wheelchair, Betty and Josh could see that the whole back of her dress was soaked in blood. She was hemorrhaging badly, and the attendant and nurse sped her away, while her parents filled out the paperwork for an emergency D and C, and whatever else they needed to do.

Fifteen minutes later, Caroline was on her way to surgery, with a transfusion in process. The attendants raced her down the halls on a gurney as she sobbed. She had already lost the baby, but they needed to stop the hemorrhaging.

Betty sat in the waiting room in her evening gown and jewels and Josh in white tie as people glanced at them as they walked by. And an hour and a half later, as Josh and Betty held hands, the surgeon came to tell them that Caroline was doing well. She had lost a lot of blood, and the fetus hadn't survived of course, but the doctor had only done a D and C and nothing more radical, and her ability to have a baby in future had not been affected.

Betty just cried as she listened. The surgeon said that Caroline was still sedated and asleep after the D and C, and suggested they come back in the morning. After another transfusion and twenty-four hours of observation, she could go home to the hotel either Sunday night or Monday morning. She would need to take it easy for a week or two, he said.

Betty wanted to see her daughter, but Josh said to let her sleep. They left the hospital looking shell-shocked after they thanked the doctor, and the driver took them back to the hotel. He had discreetly put the blood-soaked towels in the trunk with the blanket.

"How could I not know?" Betty said to Josh as she cried, for her daughter and everything that had happened and that she hadn't known. "Why didn't she tell me?"

"Did she tell you who the boy is? Did you know about someone?" Josh asked her, and she shook her head.

"It must have happened while we were on location, someone she met in school," Betty said, heartsick for Caroline to have gone through such a traumatic experience.

"You'd think with her in college, she could manage not to go crazy while we're away," Josh said, ricocheting between anger and sorrow for his daughter, and guilt that they hadn't known. And why didn't she tell her mother? But at least she wasn't pregnant anymore, and had lost it on her own, without doing something crazy and risking her life for an illegal abortion. And she wasn't dead or damaged for life.

They went to their suite at the Ritz and Josh poured them both a stiff drink, scotch neat for him, and vodka for Betty, chilled from the fridge in their minibar. They looked at each other like two shipwrecked people after their drinks, and Betty sat down next to Josh on the couch and he put an arm around her.

"I never thought we'd have to worry about something like that with her. She's always so sensible." They'd never had a problem with Caroline before.

"She's human, she's a woman now, and she must have been in love," she said sadly. "She won't forget this in a hurry. She'll be careful now," Betty said, and rested her head on Josh's shoulder. They sat there for a long time, grateful that Caroline was going to be all right, and then they dragged themselves to bed. The ball at Versailles was a night they would never forget.

When Willie had returned to the table at Versailles, Tristan de Bret was speaking to Amelia's mother and telling her what a pleasure it was to meet them. He was exceedingly polite and well brought up, and Jane was enormously impressed at how mature he seemed. He worked for his father part-time and had a serious job waiting for him when he graduated from Sciences Po. He left after a few minutes to greet some of his friends, and Amelia invited Willie to sit down, and asked him where he'd been and if he'd seen Caroline.

"She wasn't feeling well, so her parents took her back to the hotel. It's that stomach flu she's had all week," he said with a smile.

"I hardly talked to her tonight. I saw you two dancing, and then you disappeared."

"I walked her to the car. The place is vast, it's quite easy to get lost. Her mother is amazing, isn't she?" He changed the subject artfully.

"Totally glam," Amelia agreed with a smile. "She's even more beautiful in real life." And Betty was even younger than her own mother. She had had Caroline very young.

"Would you like to dance?" Willie invited her, and Amelia looked delighted. He stood up and walked her to the dance floor and she looked down and gave a start.

"Willie, oh my God, there's blood on your shoes, did you get hurt or cut yourself?"

"Dreadful! I stepped on a mouse walking Caroline to her car. Disgusting, I assure you, the place is full of them, field mice, I suppose. I stepped down, and splat. Sorry, I forgot to wipe it off my shoes, I was in such a rush to get back to you before someone else rushed off with you. I was quite worried when I saw Tristan back again. He must know everyone here."

"Don't worry about it." Amelia smiled at him, and the look in her eyes said everything he hoped. She had knocked him off his feet ever since they'd met. They began a slow dance to a Nat King Cole song, which the singer with the band imitated perfectly, and in the moonlight, Amelia closed her eyes as they danced, and it felt like the fairy tale her mother had wanted the ball to be for her.

Willie had missed the sound and light show while tending to Caroline, but dancing with Amelia and having her in his arms more than made up for it.

* * *

"It looks like your lovely daughter has two suitors tonight," Robert commented to Jane as she drank champagne and he had brandy with his coffee, and a cigar. All of the men smoked them after dinner and a few of the women, they were the finest cigars from Cuba. It was the perfect end of the meal.

"She's not interested in one of them. He's beautifully brought up, polite, intelligent, an aristocrat, and he sent her two dozen roses yesterday. He's perfect and she thinks he's boring. She's falling for the English boy, who's charming, and admits that his family is dirt poor and lost all their money after the war. He's adorable, but he's just a boy. Tristan is a man." In fact, they were only a year apart, but Tristan had a more adult demeanor, and Willie was more playful.

"I'm not so sure. Tristan has been well schooled in how to impress people, particularly adults. I've been watching him with his friends all night. He's as much a child as the rest of them, and he's a flirt. It's hard not to be impressed by his name, his father's success, and his good manners. But I like Willie. He's real. He's not hiding anything or pretending to be something he's not. A boy like him could go a long way. I'd put my money on him in a race," Robert said, and Jane was surprised. "He'll make something of himself one day. He seems honest. Tristan will ride on his father's coattails and charm a lot of women. The money doesn't matter in the end.

It's all about the man. I think Willie's a good one, if you're looking for a husband for her."

"She doesn't want one," Jane said with a sigh. "She says I've taught her to be independent and her own woman. She doesn't want a man to define who she is or to depend on. She wants to go to law school and make something of herself," she said, and he smiled. He'd had a wonderful evening talking to her.

"Then you've done a good job. We don't want the kind of marriages our parents had, most of them, with domineering men and submissive women, men who didn't know who their wives were and didn't care. I wouldn't even want most of the marriages I see today. I think our girls have the right idea and are going to change the world."

"I hope you're right," she said. She liked him. He seemed like an honest man and a gentle person.

"Would you like to dance?"

"Yes, thank you." He led her out to the dance floor and saw his daughter dancing with Quentin, chatting easily, perfectly at ease, and Amelia dancing with Willie, who was making her laugh. As they circled the dance floor, a girl in a slinky silver dress stumbled out of the bushes and headed to her table, with a good-looking man, who was obviously drunk. They both were. Her dress was visibly askew, and off one shoulder, and the slit on one side of her dress was torn to the thigh.

It was obvious what they'd been doing. And even more so to her parents, as she staggered to the table where her parents were speaking to an American couple from Philadelphia whose daughter had been presented that night too. Araminta sat down, trying to focus, as Pierre Villiers quietly slipped away without a word to Araminta or her parents.

Felicity had seen the whole scene over Raphael's shoulder and gave a disgusted snort. "What happened?" he asked.

"My sister just surfaced, back from the dead. She's drunk out of her mind and was presumably having sex in the bushes with my escort."

"That's his signature move," Raphael said quietly, and glanced over his shoulder to see a pretty but very drunk young woman looking disheveled in a sexy silver dress at the table. "Are you upset?" he asked Felicity, concerned. "He's not a nice guy. He'll never call her again."

"This is her signature move too. In five minutes, my mother will tell me we're leaving." And just as she said it, Charlene gave an anxious wave to Felicity, beckoning her back to the table. She looked livid. It was all too familiar, although Araminta had outdone herself at Versailles, behaving badly, getting blind drunk, and stealing her sister's escort. Felicity no longer cared. She'd had a great time with Raphael.

"May I see you tomorrow, Felicity?" Raphael asked politely.

He looked disheveled, but behaved like a gentleman, and she'd had a wonderful time with him. "We could go for a walk in the Jardins du Luxembourg or the Tuileries Gardens and talk about Boston." He smiled at her. He had had a good time too.

"We're leaving on Monday, but tomorrow would be lovely."

"I'll pick you up at the Plaza at noon." As he said it, the fireworks exploded overhead in a shower of stars and lit up the dancers and the palace. Raphael and Felicity looked at the sky and then at each other.

"Two engineers on a starry night, what could be more perfect," he said, and she laughed.

"I had a terrific time, thank you," she said, and he touched her hand as they both stood up.

"I'm looking forward to Boston," he said, and so was she. It had been a magical night after all, and nothing could spoil it for her, not even her badly-behaved, jealous, drunken sister who had had sex with her escort. Felicity didn't care. She had found the gem in the crowd. Or he had found her. He walked her back to her parents, said good night to her, and to them, and went to find his parents, and his sister and her escort. The Smiths shepherded their daughters back to the car, one barely able to stand up and the other smiling and feeling as though she were floating. They were so angry at Araminta that they didn't speak all the way back to the hotel, while Araminta slept, and Felicity didn't care at all. The ball at Versailles had been everything her mother had promised. Magic.

Jane and Amelia, Willie Brockhall, Robert and Samantha Walker, and Quentin Dupont danced and talked all night, and stayed for the five A.M. breakfast, and left the Palace of Versailles at six in the morning to drive back to the city in their respective cars. Quentin gave Willie a ride back to where he was staying with friends in the 6th, not far from Amelia's hotel. Quentin hadn't had anything to drink in several hours, so he was a safe driver. He was drunk on the evening, not the wine. His parents had left hours earlier, and he had a small Renault that he drove Willie home in. And the Walkers and Alexanders had gone back to their hotels with their respective cars and drivers.

"That was an amazing evening, wasn't it?" Quentin said to Willie. In the past two days they had become friends.

"Best ever," Willie confirmed with a grin, and opened the window for some air. "I think we met the best of the Americans." He was obsessed with Amelia. He had never met anyone like her.

"Felicity is nice too. She looked pretty tonight. What happened to Caroline Taylor?" Quentin asked as he drove. "I saw her parents rush out."

Danielle Steel

"Appendicitis, I think, it had been brewing since she got here. They went straight to the American Hospital," Willie said discreetly.

"Rotten luck for her, to miss all the fun."

The two men drove the rest of the way to the city, lost in thought. They had a lot to look forward to. They already had plans to see Sam and Amelia the next day. The ball was over, and the real excitement had only just begun.

# Chapter 10

illie woke up later than usual, and helped himself to a cup of coffee at the home of his friends. He was staying with an ex-workmate from London, who had moved to Paris, worked at the Credit Lyonnais, and was engaged to a French girl. They had gone to Deauville for the day to see friends.

The first thing Willie did was call the American Hospital and ask for Caroline's room. She answered the phone and sounded tired. She hadn't spoken to her parents yet, and knew it would be hard when she did. She was grateful to hear from Willie, and embarrassed.

"Thank you for last night. I'm sorry you got caught in the middle of all that," she said sadly.

"Are you all right?" he asked. He liked to have fun, but he was a responsible person, and he liked her. She seemed to

215

have gotten into an awful mess, and he felt sorry for her. He could guess what had happened.

"I'm okay."

"Did everything work out all right?"

"It worked out for the best. It's simpler this way," she said cryptically, and he understood and didn't need to know more. He was too well brought up to ask her intrusive questions.

"I hope to see you again if you come to London or if I ever go to LA. It's nice to know I have a friend halfway around the world."

"You do. Take care of yourself, Willie. And thank you again."

"You too, Caroline." They hung up a few minutes later and he was relieved that she had survived the night, whatever had happened after she got to the hospital. It couldn't have been pleasant.

He took a shower and dressed then. He was taking Amelia to lunch in the garden at the Ritz and it was a perfect day for it, with gorgeous weather.

She was wearing a beige linen wide skirt with a crinoline under it, a beige twin set, and sandals when he picked her up at her hotel on the Left Bank. Her mother waved as they drove away. Jane felt better about him after what Robert said. And maybe he was right and Tristan de Bret was a little too smooth. Willie wasn't smooth. He was young and awkward at times, like a big dog wagging his tail. He was sincere and kind and caring. Maybe that was better than just having a rich father.

Amelia and Willie took a walk in the Tuileries Gardens after lunch at the Ritz. They sat on a bench, looking at the Louvre and the children playing in front of them, and he kissed her. They both felt the magic of the night before, and how lucky they had been to meet each other.

"When am I going to see you again?" he asked her.

"I don't know," she said quietly. "I go back to school at the beginning of September, and all I have off after that is Thanksgiving, and then Christmas break. And to be honest, it's a bit of a stretch right now. My mother has been out of work for five months," she said simply, and Willie smiled.

"Mine has been out of work for her entire life, and so has my father, and they're selling the silverware now, and family heirlooms. I'm tired of people moaning about the past. I want to build the future, and have a clean start, without all those encumbrances. I was born before the war, and I remember when it started. I was seven. I was thirteen when it was over. And they've all been crying about the good old days ever since. These are our good days, and I want to make them wonderful. I want every minute to count, and I want to share it with someone I love. I want to share that with you, Amelia, if you want that too. I want to work hard and maybe I'll come to work here in France one day. Or in America. It would be a whole new start. I don't know how I'm going to do it. But I'll come to visit you if I have to swim to get there. I want to make it happen. You're the most exciting woman I've ever met," he said, and kissed her again. It was a lingering kiss filled with longing and meaning. He had the energy and optimism of youth. "I'm so glad we went to the ball," he said afterwards. "It's a ridiculous tradition, bringing people together like that to find someone to love and to marry for the rest of your life, but maybe they're right. We found each other, and now I want to prove to you that I can provide a good life for us. I know your mother liked Tristan de Bret, but he's a jerk, and he'll live off his father forever. I want to give you a good life one day, Amelia, no matter how long it takes me. I know we hardly know each other, but I feel like we were destined to meet. There's a reason why we both went to that stupid ball." Amelia felt it too.

"I'm not in a hurry," she said quietly. "I'm only nineteen, and I have six years of school ahead of me, with law school."

"I don't want to wait that long. I'll figure it out before that," he said smiling, with a look of determination. "And I want to come to see you in August, if I can do it."

"When my mother is working again, I can come and visit you." She didn't want to burden her mother now. Coming to the ball had been expensive, and she had the feeling that her mother was in tighter straits than she admitted. Amelia was worried about the absence of her mother's emerald ring.

"I hardly know you, Amelia, but I'm going to miss you. Write to me, and I'll call you when I can. And one day, you should come to Brockhall Manor, before they totally lose everything and sell it. That will happen eventually. I'm sure of it."

There was nothing more to say then. They knew what they were doing, and what they were going to try to do. And Willie was determined to make it happen. He wanted to come to see her in New York. He didn't want to lose her now that he had found her.

They walked back to her hotel on the Left Bank from the Tuileries Gardens, and bought an ice cream on the way. And he kissed her again before he left her. Amelia and her mother were starting their driving trip the next day, and she was looking forward to it. Willie was going back to London that night. He had to be at work on Monday morning. He had something to work for now, with fresh energy. He had a goal in sight, and a plan for the future. He knew he could do it, and so did she, and when he had his career on track, he would have something to offer her. She had a feeling of peace about him, as she walked into the hotel, and he went back to his friends' apartment to pack. He was still stunned by what had happened, and by meeting her. He had come to Paris for a lark and had met the love of his life. He was sure of it. And so was Amelia. She had never been as sure of anything in her life. She suddenly felt like a woman and not a child. And the Palace of Versailles was the symbol of their future. The ball had been life-changing for both of them.

Raphael picked Felicity up at noon at the Plaza Athénée and they drove to the Bois de Boulogne, so they could walk. He had brought a picnic with him, and a blanket in his car, a tiny battered Peugeot. He had brought a copy of his mother's book of poetry for her, and gave it to her as they lay on the blanket in the grass. And he translated the poems for her. They were beautiful. Then he set the book down and he kissed her.

"I feel like today is the beginning of everything, and I only met you yesterday. You make everything feel like an adventure. My parents didn't want me to go to Harvard. They thought I'd get a better education in France, but now I know why I felt I had to go. It was because of you. I have two years of graduate work there. I want to spend them with you, Felicity." He was only twenty-three. He had a whole lifetime ahead of him, but they were both mature for their age and knew what they were doing and where they wanted to go.

"Maybe you can transfer to MIT after you've been at Harvard for a year, or maybe you won't want to," she said thoughtfully.

"We'll be in the same city. We can study together. I'll be living in the graduate student quarters. And my parents are being very generous," he said, smiling at her, and kissed her again. They had so much to look forward to, and Dallas seemed like such a small part of it to her now. There was a whole wide world waiting for both of them, and all that they could accomplish, on their own and together.

Quentin had invited Sam to come to their home and have lunch with his parents. She had met them the night before, but only briefly, and he wanted them to get to know each other, before she left for America. She was leaving for London on Monday night with her father. He had business there, and had invited her to go with him. She loved visiting London, the museums, the sights, she loved watching the changing of the guard at Buckingham Palace, staying at Claridge's with him, and doing some shopping. Everything would be anti-climactic now after the ball at Versailles, which had been the high point of their trip, of the year, of her life so far. And Quentin said he felt that way too.

She was startled when she saw his house on the rue de Grenelle. It was a beautiful eighteenth-century *hôtel particulier* with a courtyard and a garden. And the furniture was all museum-quality antiques. It reminded her of a tiny corner of Versailles when she walked into the house. His mother was beautifully dressed, and his father was wearing an Austrian loden jacket with wood buttons, and gray slacks. They were stylish, and Quentin's father was very discreet but owned businesses all over Asia. Sam was glad she had worn a skirt and blouse and looked respectable. She loved their contemporary art collection, mostly by Asian artists, blended in among the antiques. And Quentin was excited about his new job as a lawyer.

The Duponts were warm and welcoming to her, and after lunch Sam and Quentin walked through the 7th arrondissement, wondering when they would meet again. She was relieved that she had seen their home and how elegantly they lived. It would make her home less shocking and seem less grand when Quentin came to see her, if he ever did. With his new job in the law firm, he didn't know when he could, and she had her sophomore year at NYU to get through, but they both felt certain that if their paths had been meant to cross now, they would again.

They were sitting on a bench in a small park near his house when he gently broached the subject of her balance and the scar on her leg. He asked her as delicately as he could how it had happened. He had been quick to observe that she had some kind of physical challenge, even though it was subtle and she managed it well.

"If you don't want to talk about it, you don't have to," he said gently and respectfully.

"I'm okay with it. I don't usually talk about it, but you have a right to know." She felt comfortable with him, and safe, which made it easier.

"Was it an accident, or were you born with the balance issues?" he asked gently.

"It was an accident, fourteen years ago. I was five. A truck hit our car. My mother was driving. She was killed instantly, and so was my three-year-old brother. I was badly hurt and in a coma for three months. They didn't think I'd live. My leg was very badly injured, and my arm. I had a head injury, which still affects my balance sometimes, not all the time. I can never predict when it will happen, maybe more so when I'm nervous or tired. Sometimes I just fall down for no reason, which is embarrassing. And at other times I'm fine. My left arm is weaker than the right. And the scar on my leg is from the injury. It gets stiff sometimes. I'm fine now." Quentin looked shocked by her answer, and what she'd been through, and the loss of a parent and sibling. She said it all very simply. It was part of her history now, and she still missed her mother and brother, but missing them wasn't a blinding pain anymore, it was like her limp, gentle and subtle and only acute at times.

"My God, Sam, how did your father get through it? He's a brave man, and you're a brave woman."

"You do what you have to, but it's why he worries about me so much. He's terrified something will happen to me. But you have to trust life. He needs to let me go more. He wouldn't let me stay in the dorm at NYU. He was afraid I'd fall down the stairs. I'm not sure he'll ever get over that, but I'm working on it." She smiled at Quentin, and he pulled her closer to him and held her, wishing he could find the words to tell her that he wanted to protect her too.

"I was so proud of you last night. I knew how scared you were, and I didn't know why. But I wouldn't let anything happen to you," he said. He had a very steady nature and a calm manner.

"I know. I could feel it. I was afraid I'd fall down the stairs and look like an idiot, or a drunk. It's a big deal that my father agreed to come here and let me do the ball. I don't know who was more afraid that something would go wrong, him or me. But I want to get past that. I'm like a bird in a golden cage. I need to make my own mistakes and yes, I fall down sometimes. He can't always be there to protect me, no matter how much he loves me." She was wise beyond her years, and Quentin could sense it. But he was mature for his age too. Being half Vietnamese had been a challenge. His mother's family had been very wealthy in Saigon but had lost everything in the war. And his father's aristocratic French family had vehemently objected to his marrying her, and had cut him off. He had stood by his wife and made a fortune of his own. Quentin was the product of two cultures that were at war within him sometimes.

"It must be very hard for him to let go," Quentin said of Sam's father. Quentin's parents were protective of him too. He had been bullied and tormented at school at times for being of mixed race, but he was comfortable now with who he was, and proud of his heritage. He didn't mind being different. He was at peace with himself.

"It's nearly impossible for my dad to let go," she said. "I've grown up. He has to adjust to that."

"You were perfect last night. You looked like an angel in that dress." He smiled at the memory. He knew he would never forget it.

"I miss my mom a lot at things like that. Everyone else had a mother to help them dress or do their hair or their makeup. I always figure the girl stuff out for myself. My dad has been everything to me for fourteen years. But now he needs to let me grow up and set me free."

"I don't blame him for worrying. The world can be harsh, and dangerous sometimes. I couldn't bear it if something happened to you. Now I want to protect you too." He smiled and took her hand and kissed her fingertips. "You're a very special person," he said.

"So are you," she whispered, leaned toward him and he kissed her. And afterwards he reached into his shirt and pulled a narrow chain out of his collar. It was long and he took it off and held it for a minute. There was a small medal on it.

"My Vietnamese grandmother gave this to me. It has an angel on the medal, she said it protected her during the war. Now my angel will protect you, until we're together again." He put it on her, and it hung low on her chest. The medal was small and the chain very fine. She was deeply touched.

"Are you sure? If it's from your grandmother, you should have it and wear it."

"I'm sharing it with you. I'll give you another angel to protect you one day. This one will take care of you for now." He kissed her then, with gentle lips full of passion and tenderness for her and the story she had told him. Giving her his angel medal was the only way he could show her that he was falling in love with her. He had known from the moment he met her that he was destined to meet her and to know her better. He didn't know when, but he was sure that the time would come and they would see each other again.

They walked some more, then he took her back to her hotel, and kissed her again before he left her. He walked away lost in thought when she disappeared into the hotel.

\* \* \*

Robert had invited Jane to join him for lunch with both their daughters on Sunday, and when she met him at the Crillon for lunch, she apologized that she hadn't known Amelia had other plans. He smiled, and she saw that he was alone too.

"So did Sam. She's having lunch at Quentin's home with his parents. We're leaving tomorrow."

"So are we," Jane said, as they sat at a table in the restaurant. "Amelia is with Willie. He's leaving for London tonight. He has work tomorrow. The ball is over, and all the out-of-towners are dispersing. We're taking a driving trip to visit some châteaux, leaving Paris tomorrow."

"That's a beautiful trip. I've done that, with Sam. My wife also did that trip with me. She loved France. She studied for two years at the Beaux-Arts. She was an artist. Sam has some of her talent, but she doesn't work at it. She's more interested in studying other people's art than her own. We're going to London tomorrow. I have some work to do there, and it's fun having Sam travel with me."

"What would we do without our girls," Jane said with a smile.

"We'd be very lonely people," he said simply. "I know I'll have to let her go eventually, to fly on her own wings, but it's hard. I'm not good at it yet. But I can't keep her tied to me forever. I feel as though a trip like this is tempting fate. Introducing her to people and young men, far from home.

If she falls in love with one of them, seriously, she might want to live here one day. But it wouldn't be fair to deprive her of the possibilities to broaden her horizons."

"I feel the same way about Amelia. Now she's falling for the English boy. And if it weren't him, it could have been Tristan in Paris. And I can't follow her around forever, like her shadow." She had given up a lot of her own life to do so for the past ten years.

He smiled at her after they ordered lunch, and he ordered wine. "I think we're both in the same boat. There is some similarity to our situations with our girls. And now we've opened Pandora's box over here," he said ruefully. "I hope we don't regret it. When are you coming back to New York?"

"In a week. It won't be long. The summer will be half gone by then. Amelia goes back to school at the end of August."

"So does Sam, to NYU. You were braver than I though. I wouldn't let Sam live in the dorms. She's still mad at me about it. I was afraid she might get hurt. She has some issues with her balance. She was in an accident with her mother and younger brother fourteen years ago. My wife and son didn't survive it. Sam nearly didn't, and was in a coma for three months. She has some residual effects, a weaker arm and leg, and some balance issues from a head injury, but she made it, and I'm grateful every day. You have to learn to look forward, not back. It's taken me ten years to realize that.

Coming here was part of that realization. This was so good for Sam, even if she hadn't met Quentin. She handled it beautifully. And so did your daughter. I'm happy they met," he said, smiling at Jane. "I hope you come out to visit us in Connecticut in August, before the girls go back to school. Do you ride?"

"I used to. I haven't in a long time. I used to do jumping competitions when I was younger. I stopped when I had Amelia. And once her father died, I felt like I couldn't take the risk of something happening to me. I'm all she has. It's an awesome responsibility."

"I'm in the same situation with Sam."

They talked of other things then, travel, books, her old job, their college days, which seemed so distant now. He had gone to Yale and Harvard, she to Vassar.

"We have the Ivies pretty well covered. There again, Sam wanted to leave New York for college, and I wouldn't let her. They grow up too damn fast, and now men enter the picture. Foreign ones! We were brave to bring them here," he said, smiling.

"They're all young," Jane said confidently. "Nothing will happen too fast, and if Amelia stays serious about law school, she won't settle down for a long time. This generation doesn't seem as eager to marry as we were. I got married at twenty-two, which seemed normal then. It seems too young now.

I don't think our girls will do that. And the boys they met are too young. They all have time to play for a while."

It was four o'clock when Robert dropped Jane back at her hotel. They had talked for a long time, and he promised to call her when he returned to New York. She wasn't sure if he would call, but it had been nice meeting him in Paris, and he was a very attractive man. It had been lovely having lunch with him. Paris and meeting him was the first fun she'd had in ages, and they had so much to talk about, and in common about their girls.

Josh and Betty were picking Caroline up at the hospital around the time that Robert was dropping Jane off at her hotel. It had been an emotional morning for the Taylors and they didn't discuss it with Caroline until they got back to the Ritz. She looked tired and pale, but serious when she sat down with them in the living room of the suite. There was no avoiding the subject any longer. The drama of the night before had catapulted Caroline and her affair into the spotlight. She wanted to be honest with her parents, but she knew it would nearly kill them to hear it.

"How long had it gone on?" her mother asked her.

"A year, since last summer." Both her parents looked shocked.

"A *year*?" Betty asked.

"It really got heavy when I started at USC. I wasn't home,

230

and I could meet him whenever I wanted." She decided to tell them all of it. She didn't owe it to Adam to protect him. "I'm on academic probation now. I missed a lot of classes. I have fall semester to clean up my act. And I promise I will," she said solemnly. Her father looked even more upset at that news.

"We're avoiding the main issue here," Josh said then. He looked like he had had a very rough night. They all had. "Who is the guy? We have a right to know. Is he someone you met at school?"

"No."

"Does he know about the pregnancy?"

"No. We broke up three weeks ago, and I didn't figure it out until I was here. I thought it was food poisoning, but it wasn't. The doctor Mom called asked me, and then it hit me, and I realized. I didn't know before that. And he still doesn't know. I'm not going to tell him. He's not speaking to me. And he has a new girlfriend."

"That's nice of him," Betty said, furious although she didn't know him. He had a responsibility here too.

"You haven't told us his name," her father reminded her, and instinctively Caroline knew life would never be the same once she did. Her father was liable to blackball him and hurt his career, and they would never trust her again. They already didn't, since last night. But there was no avoiding the truth.

If she wanted to preserve her relationship with her parents, she had to tell them.

"It was Adam Black," she said simply. Her father stared at her as though her head had fallen off.

"The Adam Black we know? The actor? I brought him to our house. Did he make a pass at you and try to seduce you?" he asked, horrified.

"Yes, and I wanted him to. He asked me out, and I went."

"He's ten years older than you are," Josh said, outraged. "You were a kid, you still are." But also a woman, her parents realized now, with a mind of her own, and desires, and a secret life for the past year.

"I know, Dad. But I'm not a child anymore." She had loved a man, conceived a child with him, lost a baby, and could have died or been damaged forever. She had suffered huge consequences for her actions, and she was taking responsibility for it, which made her an adult, overnight.

"No, apparently you're not a child. You're not going to tell him what happened?" Josh confirmed with her, as she had said.

"No, I'm not. I don't want him to know I got pregnant. He won't speak to me anyway. He dumped me for Fay Mallon."

"Sonofabitch," Josh muttered, and Betty dabbed at her eyes with a handkerchief.

"You looked so beautiful last night," she said sadly. "I wanted it to be the happiest night of your life," and instead it had been the worst one. None of them would ever forget it, and the shock of the miscarriage.

"That boy who was your escort was a damn fine guy. He may have saved your life by getting you out of there fast enough and coming to get us," her father said.

"I know. He called me this morning. He won't tell anyone. I trust him."

"I'm going to go to see Adam when we get back, I want him to be aware that I know about the affair, and he'll never get a part from me again. I could have him blackballed at every studio in town." Caroline knew that her father wasn't normally a vengeful person, but he was livid at Adam for the clandestine affair with a girl her age, and his irresponsibility.

Caroline didn't say a word. She had no reason to plead for mercy for him, after the way he'd dumped her. And her father would do what he wanted anyway. He felt personally betrayed by Adam and had helped him in his career. And in return Adam had preyed on Caroline's innocence.

"Is it really over?" her mother asked her.

"Yes, it is. And I want you both to know how sorry I am that I disappointed you and lied to you and took crazy chances. I was really in love with him," she said, as tears filled her eyes and rolled down her cheeks. She had lived through a heartbreak and now a nightmare, and Adam wouldn't even talk to her. He wasn't the man she'd thought he was. She knew that now.

Betty and Josh looked at each other and then at their daughter, and Josh spoke for them both. "Your mother and I are shocked and very upset about this, for you, and for us, as a family. You narrowly escaped a disaster that could have cost your life or impaired your ability to have another baby one day. Fortunately, neither of those is the case. But in future, we want you to be honest with us, even if we don't like what you tell us. You have a right to make choices and decisions. You're an adult. But I don't want secrets and lies anymore among the three of us." Caroline nodded, stunned to be let off so lightly. She got up to hug them and they all cried and hugged and kissed and were relieved that the nightmare was over.

"You'll get over it," Betty said gently. "We all make mistakes and errors of judgment. If it teaches you to be more careful, more discerning, and more honest in future, you'll be way ahead of the game."

"Thank you, Mom."

"Now what are we going to do about Hotel du Cap? Do we want to go there, or go home? We're all worn out, and we've had a hell of a shock. But maybe a vacation would do us all good." Caroline thought about it for a minute and nodded.

"I'd like to go, Dad, if you still want to."

"I'm not sure," he said. "Why don't we think about it for a few hours and decide after dinner." Betty and Caroline agreed, but they were leaning toward yes. The relaxing atmosphere, the extreme comforts, and the healing properties of a real vacation sounded good to all of them, particularly a vacation in the luxury, pampering, and seclusion of the Hotel du Cap/ Eden Roc. By the time they finished a room service dinner, they had come to the conclusion that all three of them wanted to go there. They were going to take another day to relax, and fly down on Tuesday. It felt like the right decision to the three of them, and the start of a new chapter in their lives and more honest relationship with each other. Caroline was officially an adult now. It had come at a high price for her.

Araminta did not get off as lightly with her parents, but she hadn't suffered as much as Caroline, and hadn't nearly died, so she didn't get the sympathy vote for her shocking behavior at the ball.

They waited until Felicity had gone out with Raphael for lunch, so as not to embarrass her or put her on the spot, and then they sat down with Araminta and laid down the law. She hadn't expected it, and she was brutally hungover the day after the ball and claimed she didn't know what she did, which they considered even worse.

Her father spoke for both of them.

"You made off with your sister's escort, so she had no escort for the entire evening, no date at dinner, no one to dance with. You got unbelievably drunk, as you always do at parties, even in Dallas. You ran off with a man you barely know, who may decide to talk about it, thereby humiliating yourself and all of us. You clearly had sex with him somewhere on the grounds of Versailles."

"In the maze," she supplied, as her parents cringed, "and then we couldn't find our way out. He said he knew, but he didn't. Actually, Felicity didn't miss anything. He was kind of a jerk." She sounded callous and not remorseful, although she was somewhat embarrassed.

"And you had sex with him anyway," her father pointed out, "in a public place. You had your dress on cockeyed, and torn, when you got back to the party, so everyone knew exactly what you'd been doing. You humiliated all of us and disgraced yourself. I'm not going to tolerate that kind of behavior anymore. From now on, you will be civil and kind to your sister, who doesn't deserve all the abuse you've heaped on her for nineteen years. If you say one single word about her weight, her looks, what she eats or doesn't, I will tell you to move out of the house," and he looked like he meant it. Araminta was shocked. She hadn't expected her parents to be so harsh. Her mother said nothing in her defense, which was unlike her. She always made excuses for Araminta.

"And in the meantime," her father continued, "for your outrageous behavior here, at an event that was important to all of us, and was to Felicity, I am canceling all your credit cards and your charge accounts at every store in Dallas. You'll either behave like a respectable person, and not some drunken sex-crazed slut, or you can get your own apartment, get a job, and pay your own rent and credit card bills. Is that clear?"

"Yes, Dad, but don't you think canceling all my accounts and credit cards is a little extreme? Felicity says she had a good time, and she didn't like her escort anyway."

"Be that as it may, you made a spectacle of yourself when you rejoined the party, you barely got back into your dress, you looked a mess, your makeup was smeared all over your face, and you were falling-down drunk. All of which crosses the line for me. I won't forget that in a hurry, and you'd better not either." And with that, he walked out of the living room of the suite, into his bedroom and slammed the door, while Araminta begged her mother for mercy.

"And why do I have to be so goddamn nice to Felicity? What does she ever do for me? She got invited to come out at the ball, I didn't."

"So you punished her for it and stole her escort. That's pretty shabby, Araminta," Charlene said in a gentler tone

237

than Bailey had used with their daughter. But for once, Charlene wasn't sorry for her.

"Dad always makes a fuss over her like she's Einstein or a saint or something," Araminta complained. She didn't appear to be remorseful.

Charlene looked at her then, dismayed by who her daughter had become. She was spoiled and heartless, to a frightening degree. "Araminta, if you don't mend your ways and start treating people better and mind your mouth, you're going to be a lonely old woman one day. You have a reputation in Dallas. Everyone knows you're the life of the party, but that mouth of yours is going to get you in trouble. I don't see a trail of men knocking for you at our door. And your sister is a smart, kind, decent person. She's never done anything to hurt you, and you wound her every time she walks into the house and crosses your path. Your daddy is right and that has to stop."

"Would you let Daddy throw me out of the house just for that?" Araminta looked shocked as Charlene leveled an icy gaze at her. Araminta had finally gone too far, even for her mother.

"Honey," she said, in answer to her question, "I would pack your bags and lock the door behind you." Araminta looked crushed.

"I told her she looked beautiful last night," she said weakly.

"And then you made a point of seducing her escort. You're done. Pack your bags. We're leaving for du Cap in the morning."

"And my credit cards? Is Daddy really going to cancel them?"

"He already did this morning. You've got some work to do on yourself," Charlene said. She stood up and walked out of the room, as Araminta sat shaking, hating all of them, and especially that brat of a little sister. Even fat, she got all the treats and all the rewards, and didn't deserve them. Araminta had been jealous of her from the day she was born, and now she had lost her charge accounts and credit cards because of her. It would only make her hate her sister more.

Jane picked up the rented car she'd reserved early Monday morning, and she and Amelia drove an hour to the first château on their list, Fontainebleau, originally built in the twelfth century. It had been added to and embellished by centuries of French kings from Louis VII to Napoleon III. The interior apartments were exquisite and the gardens extensive and magnificent.

After touring the château and its extensive gardens, they drove another half hour to the cathedral in Chartres, stopping for lunch afterwards, and then drove two hours to the Château de Chambord in the Loire Valley. The Renaissance château was enormous, and they only saw a small part of it, with four hundred and forty rooms and eighty-four staircases. By the time they finished the tour, they were ready to check in to a comfortable inn nearby. It had been an exhausting but interesting day, and they were both tired.

Amelia had been thinking of Willie all day, and she called him from a public phone outside the inn where they were spending the night. She had seen him the day before, and she was already missing him. She called him in the office and caught him just before he left. He had stayed later than usual and sounded thrilled to hear her.

"So how are the châteaux in France holding up? That sounds like an ambitious tour your mother has planned."

"It is. It's interesting but exhausting. We visited two enormous châteaux and a cathedral today, and she has two châteaux on her list for tomorrow. She's relentless when she plans a trip. I wish we were still in Paris and you were too."

"So do I," he said gently. What amazed them both was that a week before they hadn't even known each other, and now he was an essential part of her life, and he felt like he couldn't live without her. "Why don't you forget the châteaux and come to London?" he suggested. It sounded like an excellent idea to Amelia. She had no idea when she would see him again. He had said that he would try to get to New York before she went back to school, but he had no vacation due him at the moment, and there was no room in his budget for a ticket to New York. But he was going to manage it somehow, whatever it took. For now, the memories of the ball would have to sustain them. The rest of the summer seemed like an eternity to Amelia now without him, and he wasn't even sure he could come in August. It was just a glimmer of a hope.

They talked for another fifteen minutes until Willie had to leave the office, and then he had to end the call. He was meeting his father at his club for dinner. He had dinner with his father whenever he came to London. His visits weren't frequent anymore. The earl had grown tired of London years before and preferred to stay in the country. Willie didn't like to think about it, but his father was getting older, and so was his mother. They preferred their quiet country life now, which bored Willie to extinction, and he had to force himself to visit them for the occasional weekend.

His parents seemed so cut off from the world now, and their life had gotten so much smaller. His father had made a lifetime of hunting, shooting, riding, running his estate, seeing his friends on neighboring estates, and talking to their tenant farmers. It was the life of a country gentleman. Sometimes he would visit the House of Lords to see his old friends. His archaic lifestyle was part of a lost world and had led them to financial ruin. To Willie, it always seemed like a world that was dying slowly, as the older generation did, and a lifestyle that no longer made sense. His brother was following in their father's footsteps. Fifteen years older than

Willie, he was married, lived on the estate, and had four children. Willie seemed like a child to him. It was becoming obvious to all of them that eventually they would have to sell the estate, probably to a rich American. They still had a little money left, but were barely able to make ends meet, and had just enough to run the estate. It couldn't go on forever, and even Willie admitted he would be sad to sell it. They had so much history there, and happy memories of their childhood. But the place looked run-down and tired now, and was in need of repairs they couldn't afford.

"What have you been up to, my boy?" his father asked him as they ate roast beef in the club's handsome wood-paneled dining room. Willie couldn't tell his father about his job in the city, because the earl didn't approve of it. Work was for commoners, not for noblemen and gentlemen. Willie's brother, Basil, didn't work either, and lived off the estate, as did his wife and children.

"I went to a very amusing event in Paris this weekend, a debutante cotillion given at the Palace of Versailles. Twelve hundred people, nearly three hundred debutantes," Willie told him to distract him, although the earl didn't like the French much, but Willie knew a debutante ball would amuse him, and he'd approve of it. It was familiar to him.

"Any British girls among them?" the Earl of Brockhall asked.

"No, all French and American," Willie said noncommittally.

"It's a shame the queen stopped presenting young girls at court. It's a lovely tradition. That's how I met your mother," the earl said with a nostalgic smile. Willie already knew the story. Willie's mother had been eighteen, and his father had been a member of the Queen's Guards, and they married six months after they met. Their families had known each other for decades and generations. Everybody knew each other then. London Society had been an enclosed entity, with no risk of outsiders intruding on them. Tradition meant everything to them, all bloodlines and titles. Willie's brother was a count and would be the earl one day. And Willie was a viscount, which meant nothing to him. He came from a world that was rapidly disappearing. It had been a wonderful world, but there was nothing now to sustain it. Ever since the war, people had been losing their estates, their homes, their way of life, the treasures they had clung to. Willie felt as though the only way he would have a good life one day was to swim free, and Amelia seemed like the kind of girl he could do that with. He hardly knew her, but she had grown up with strict traditions too, and rules that made no sense to her, and she was as tired of the old ways as he was. All he could think of now was how to scrape up the money for a ticket to New York by the end of August.

\* \* \*

243

The next day, Jane and Amelia continued their carefully planned trip. Jane had researched it thoroughly. They visited the Château de Cheverny, a fourteenth-century castle still owned by the original family. They had begun tours of the château in 1914, in order to support the château, and the tours were immensely popular with visitors from all over the world. The interiors were extraordinary, and Jane and Amelia loved it.

They visited the Château d'Auvers, and the Château des ducs de Bretagne and a number of smaller ones they enjoyed seeing too.

Amelia called Willie every day, which was the high point of her day and his. And while learning about the history of the past, they were dreaming about the future, and couldn't wait to see each other again.

# Chapter 11

Charlene, Bailey, Araminta, and Felicity Smith checked out of the Plaza on Tuesday, flew to Nice in an hour, and were picked up at the airport by two limousines. Charlene and Bailey rode in one, and the two girls rode in the other. Araminta hadn't said a word to Felicity since her father's dressing-down the day after the ball. She blamed Felicity for it and not her own behavior.

Felicity had no idea what had transpired or what their parents had said to Araminta, but she could tell that something major had happened among the three of them, while she was walking around the Bois de Boulogne with Raphael, and kissing him, which had been very enjoyable. She was looking forward to seeing him again in Boston. She wondered if it would turn into a real romance, or if they would just be friends. She hadn't had a date since high school, and the boys she went to school with always turned into pals. They were looking for girls who looked like her sister, but Raphael had definitely shown an interest in her as a girl. Maybe it was just the magic of Paris, or because he was French. But whatever happened, it would be fun to show him around Boston, and hear about the work he was doing at school. She was an undergraduate, and he would be a graduate student at Harvard, but from a scientific standpoint, it would be fun comparing notes.

When she'd gotten back to the Plaza after seeing him, Araminta wouldn't even speak to her. Felicity tried a few times, and then she let it go, and assumed that her parents had said something to Araminta about getting drunk at the ball the night before. She had no idea they had lowered the boom on her to the degree they had and cut off her money. Their father knew it was the only thing she cared about.

But when they reached the Hotel du Cap, the sheer beauty of it, and the endless list of indulgences and comforts, made everything else seem insignificant. They had two beautiful suites in the main building of the hotel, with a sweeping view of the sea and all the yachts anchored right outside the hotel. The yacht owners and their guests came to dinner at the hotel frequently, and had lunch at the Eden Roc, the lower part of the hotel on the water. And the private cabanas for guests staying there allowed one to sunbathe privately, and even have lunch served in the cabana, in total privacy.

Charlene and Bailey went to check out the cabanas soon after they arrived and settled into the larger one for the day. Araminta took over the second cabana, which she was meant to share with her sister. In order to avoid her, Felicity stretched out on a mattress at the pool. She enjoyed watching the other guests stroll by. The women were almost as elegant at the pool as they were for dinner, with their makeup on, their hair done, wearing jewels and brightly colored bathing suits and cover-ups, with high-heeled gold sandals. As always, Felicity felt like a plain brown bird in their midst, among a flock of swans. She was used to it and didn't mind. No one paid attention to her.

The four of them had dinner in the restaurant at the Eden Roc that night. At the end of a sumptuous meal, Felicity eyed the pastry cart longingly, but decided not to brave her sister's comments, and had fruit instead. Araminta raised an eyebrow, but with a sharp glance from her father, she didn't say a word. And Felicity was beginning to think that shedding a few pounds before Raphael arrived in Boston might not be such a bad idea.

It was an unusually quiet meal, with Araminta not speaking to any of them, and Felicity tired from lying in the sun. They all went to bed early, and Felicity stood on the terrace before going to bed, admiring the view, the boats, the lights in the distance, and the moon overhead. It was the most romantic place she'd ever seen, and they loved going there every year. A number of Texans they knew went there in the summer, but none of their friends were there this time.

The next day, Felicity woke early, and went for a walk before going to the pool. She decided to avoid Araminta in the cabana again. She had coffee poolside and skipped the pastry basket. She swam in the pool and met her parents at the restaurant on the terrace for lunch. Her father particularly loved the lavish buffet and helped himself generously. They were all starting to relax after the hectic days before they came. Araminta had stayed in the cabana for lunch alone.

"Is she okay?" Felicity asked her parents, and they exchanged a quick glance.

"She's fine," Charlene said to Felicity, and her father didn't answer. He was still angry at their older daughter, and it was entirely reciprocal. Araminta was livid at having had her wings clipped and her charge accounts closed. Normally, she would have gone shopping in Cannes by then, and indulged herself at Hermès and Chanel, and she couldn't this time, all because of the "little incident" with Felicity's escort at the ball. He had been a bust anyway, and she had never heard from him again and didn't think she would. He wasn't the kind of guy who would stick around. He was strictly a one-night stand, a sexual opportunist. Araminta had had plenty of those before, especially when she got drunk at a party. But she thought it was better than no man at all.

Her parents went back to their cabana after lunch, to lounge and doze for the rest of the afternoon. The comforts of the hotel were so extreme that people came back every year faithfully, from all over the world. It was shockingly expensive, but worth every penny they paid, and anyone who went there could afford it. The people who came there from outside to dine every night were dressed to the teeth, and arrived in Bentleys and convertible Rollses and vintage Mercedes, or Ferraris and Lamborghinis, and the occasional Bugatti.

Felicity was lying half asleep on a mattress at the pool on the second day they were there, in the late afternoon, when she saw a familiar figure walk by, a beautiful blonde girl in a two-piece black bathing suit which showed off her figure. A waiter had told Felicity when she ordered a lemonade that a big movie star had just arrived but he didn't know who.

The girl in the black two-piece suit glanced at Felicity under an umbrella, did a double take, and broke into a smile. It was Caroline Taylor, delighted to see her.

"Felicity! We just got here. I didn't know you were coming."

"We come every year."

"So do we. We just got here twenty minutes ago." Felicity smiled, happy to see Caroline.

"The waiter said some big movie star just arrived. I assume that's your mom."

"Probably. My parents love it here because they don't let the paparazzi in, like they do everywhere else."

She sat down on the edge of Felicity's chaise longue with the mattress on it, under the umbrella. It was a hot day and the sun was bright. Felicity had already gotten some color in two days there, while Caroline looked impressively pale and almost blue-white.

"Are you okay?" Felicity asked her. "I never saw you after you got sick at the ball, and Willie said he thought you were going to the hospital for your food poisoning, and it might be appendicitis. How do you feel now?"

"I'm fine. They took care of it at the hospital. I stayed overnight, and I rested at the hotel yesterday. I feel great." But Felicity could see dark circles under Caroline's eyes. She must have been sicker than anyone thought. She hoped it wasn't serious. She didn't look well. "How long are you staying?" Caroline asked Felicity, happy to see a familiar face. The atmosphere with her parents was still heavy, and it would be nice to have a friend her own age here.

"Two weeks," Felicity answered, equally pleased, as an attendant brought a mattress for Caroline to put on the chaise next to Felicity.

"So are we," Caroline answered. "Where's your sister?"

Caroline hadn't thought much of her when she met her briefly. She thought she acted snobbish and looked cheap, and then she had vanished at the ball and so had Felicity's escort, although she hadn't connected the two. And Caroline had been gone by the time they reappeared.

"She's in the cabana. We don't usually hang out together. She's not crazy about me. I'd rather be here," Felicity said.

Caroline ordered a lemonade, and the two girls chatted. She settled onto the lounge chair next to Felicity and stretched out. Felicity hadn't realized how outgoing Caroline could be when she was feeling well. Felicity had been more drawn to Amelia and Sam, but Caroline was turning out to be good company too.

"Do you want to meet at the bar tonight?" Caroline asked her. People from neighboring homes came there to drink at night, mostly young ones, or they went to the bars and discotheques in Antibes and Juan-les-Pins, or Cannes if they didn't mind going a little farther. The older crowd went even farther to Monte Carlo to drink, eat, and gamble. The Riviera was lively in summer and a magnet to people with money.

"Sure, that would be fun," Felicity readily agreed.

"Should you ask your sister?" Caroline asked.

"She won't want to be with me," Felicity said simply, which Caroline thought was strange, but didn't pry.

Caroline asked if she had seen the other two girls before she left, and Felicity said she hadn't. "Amelia was going on a driving trip with her mom, to visit châteaux, and they left Monday morning. And Sam was going to London with her father." She hesitated and then looked mischievous. "I did have lunch though with a guy I met when my creep of an escort went MIA. The new guy saved me from total humiliation for the escort dance. His sister came out with us, I never met her, but he was very nice. He's going to be a grad student at Harvard this year. I'll see him in Boston, so that might be fun."

"Whoaaa . . . the plot thickens. Is he cute?" Caroline hadn't noticed Felicity dancing with him. She felt too ill and was in too much pain to notice anyone. It was shortly before she started to hemorrhage and collapsed.

"No, not really. He's got weird hair, but he's really smart, and he seems nice. And he didn't faint when I said I'm studying chemical engineering, because he's an engineer too."

"Sounds like a match made in Heaven," Caroline said, leaning her head back against the chair. She was still tired, and probably still anemic. The idea of starting a romance with anyone filled her with dread, but she was glad that Felicity had met someone. She wasn't an easy match, and they sounded meant for each other.

"It never clicked with you and Willie Brockhall, did it?"

252

"I wasn't in the mood," Caroline said. "I just broke up with my boyfriend. I think I'll stay out of the dating scene for a while." A very long while. She had been badly burned.

"I think he and Amelia really hit it off," Felicity commented.

"I'm glad," Caroline said. "He's a really nice guy. He called the next day to see how I was. He got my parents for me the other night and told us what hospital to go to. It's all kind of a blur now." She smiled at Felicity then. "But I'm glad I met you, and Amelia, and Sam. I hope that somehow we can see each other again when we go back to the States. Maybe I can come to New York during a break and we can all get together."

"That would be more fun than Dallas," Felicity said, and easier for the others, since she was in Boston, and the other two in New York.

"Wouldn't it be amazing if something came of it for any of us? You and the French grad student at Harvard, Sam seemed to like her escort, and it sounds like Amelia and Willie hit it off. I know she didn't like her escort. But wouldn't it be exciting if any serious romances came of it? It's a long shot, but I love that idea," Caroline said.

"It's not likely, but you never know," Felicity said, thinking of Raphael. They sat talking until it was time for them to dress for dinner. Caroline said she was going to have room service that night. She was still tired. Felicity had to dine with her family in the main restaurant at the Eden Roc.

"Do you still want to go to the bar after dinner?" Felicity asked Caroline before she left the pool area.

"Sure. Why not? I'll just put on some white slacks and a silk blouse after I eat, and I'm good to go." Felicity thought that Caroline was so beautiful, she could have worn a paper bag over her head and a bedsheet and she'd look gorgeous.

Felicity left with a wave, as Caroline lay on the deck chair, thinking about her. She was so bright and such a nice girl. She wondered what was up between her and her sister. Felicity needed to lose some weight, but what difference did it make? She was good company, funny, and a nice person. Caroline was grateful to have a friend there, someone her own age to hang out with. Things were still delicate between her and her parents, and Felicity didn't want to be around her sister, so it was good luck for both of them to have found a friend, and a nice opportunity for them to get to know each other, since Caroline had been under the weather during the days leading up to the ball. She seemed much more outgoing now.

Felicity and Caroline met at the bar that night, and both sets of parents were happy that their daughters had visited with a friend. Felicity cautiously invited Araminta to join them, just to be polite, and she refused. She wanted nothing to do with Felicity, whom she saw as the author of her current troubles with her parents, and Felicity was delighted to go without her. After dinner, she walked up to the bar at the main part of the hotel to meet Caroline. The hotel looked like a small château, and the bar area on the terrace was crowded with people. The older ones stayed inside, to enjoy the air-conditioning. The younger guests and people who came from neighboring villas congregated on the terrace and chatted from table to table, drinking champagne on a beautiful, star-filled summer night. Several young men attempted to join them, but both girls just wanted to talk quietly between themselves. But on another night, Caroline thought it would be fun to go into Juan-les-Pins for a drink, and walk around. The next two weeks were going to be fun, which neither of them had expected. It was a wonderful aftermath from the ball, and whatever else happened with the men Felicity and the others had met, they were both happy to have a new friend. The ball had turned out so much better than any of them had expected, even for Caroline now.

Felicity swam every morning in the sea, and in the afternoon in the pool. The two girls played tennis, and they went dancing in Juan-les-Pins with a group of young people staying at the hotel with their families. One group was from Oklahoma, another from Houston, and Felicity explained to Caroline that it was oil money. Caroline's mother was the only American movie star there, and Brigitte Bardot, the sexy young French movie star, spent the weekend during their stay. She was with her husband, French movie producer Roger Vadim, and there had been rumors in the French press recently that they were splitting up, so everyone was fascinated to see them there, and watched them constantly. They kept out of sight in their cabana, but the girls glimpsed them occasionally.

Felicity and Caroline saw her at the pool, and every man in the place was staring at Bardot's body and even Caroline said she was jealous of her. Felicity was too, and she doubled her swimming regime every morning after seeing her. Bardot was the ultimate sex kitten and only twenty-four years old.

Both girls agreed that their two weeks at the hotel were going by all too quickly, and they were happy to be there. Araminta had managed to find her own circle of friends who were in their late twenties and early thirties, and she enjoyed hanging out with a more sophisticated crowd and spent as little time as possible with her parents and sister. There were things for all of them to do there. They were only together for meals.

Within a week of their arrival, Caroline looked healthy again, and was in good spirits. She realized that however painful the night of the ball had been for her in every possible way, the end of the pregnancy was a blessing.

*　*　*

Sam always loved trips to London with her father. She loved traveling with him. And she loved the dignified atmosphere at Claridge's, and the elegant, often old-fashioned stores, full of beautiful items. The silver animals at Asprey, the antiques, the jewelers, the dress stores. Harrods was a feast and she always found pretty clothes there. Her father gave her carte blanche and she didn't abuse it, but she had lots of fun while he conducted his business. At the end of the day, she had high tea at Claridge's, when she got back from her shopping adventures, and felt very ladylike and grown-up, eating delicate little perfectly made sandwiches, with scones, strawberry jam, and clotted cream. And when he wasn't busy with clients and associates, she met up with her father for dinner.

Quentin called her every night at the hotel, and she loved talking to him. He told her about his new job, and she told him what she was doing.

"I know this sounds silly, because I didn't know you a week ago, but I miss you," he said cautiously, afraid to sound foolish.

"I miss you too," she admitted, shy for a minute, but comfortable with him most of the time.

"I wish I were there so we could have dinner together. I like London. It's always exciting, like New York."

"I love it too, and it's fun to shop here. My father has had a lot of meetings, so I've had time to myself."

Danielle Steel

"My parents really enjoyed meeting you. Thank you for having lunch with them."

"I was flattered to be asked."

"I'm trying to find out when I can come to visit you. They won't give me time off for a while at the law firm." It was a new job for him.

"I'll be busy at school anyway. My father says he'll have to come back here again before the end of the year. Maybe I can come with him. He has business in London, but I could make a quick trip to Paris while he's here."

"We'll figure something out," he said, and they talked on the phone for an hour every night, as she learned more about him, and they shared their private dreams and hopes for the future. "There are some beautiful photographs of the ball in *Paris Match*. And accounts of it have been in the papers. I think every newspaper wrote about it. You should get *Paris Match* though. I'm not sure, but I think there's a picture of us during the Escort Dance. There are a lot of people in the picture, but I'm pretty sure it's us." She was excited to hear it, and loved the idea of having a picture of them. She was wearing his angel medal and hadn't taken it off since he gave it to her.

After their call, she went down to the magazine shop in the lobby and bought a *Paris Match*. The ball at Versailles was on the cover. She hurried upstairs with it, lay on the bed, and examined every photograph avidly. She studied the one he

258

had mentioned, of the Escort Dance, and she was sure he was right. They were in the distance, dancing, but she recognized his height, and her hair color, and her dress. She was looking up at him, smiling, and they looked graceful and young and happy in the photograph. She wished the photographer had been closer. But there were five hundred and seventy-two people dancing, all of the debutantes and their escorts, so it was remarkable that Quentin and Sam could recognize themselves at all, but she was sure they were right. The rest of the photographs were beautiful, and showed off the palace, the light show, the fireworks, the first debutantes coming down the staircase to be presented with the liveried footmen bordering the stairway, and the first girl in line doing a deep curtsy to the ball committee. They had captured all the most important moments. It was a tribute to French history and a remarkable event. She left the magazine open on the dresser with the page open to the Escort Dance.

Robert finished his meetings on Friday, and on Saturday morning, after dinner at Rule's the night before, which was a tradition for them, he and Samantha flew back to New York. They went straight to Connecticut instead of the city. It was blazing hot, and the next morning, in shorts, sitting at the pool, it felt strange to be home. So much had happened since they left. She had made new friends, been presented to French society, had fun in Paris and London, and Quentin had entered her life. It was a lot to digest. Quentin was startled by it too, although less had happened to him, and he was in his home city. But being at Versailles, with flaming torches lining the path for the cars that arrived, the guests wearing remarkable dresses, the debutantes, some in jewel-colored dresses and the Americans in white ball gowns, was like a trip back in the past for all of them. It all felt like a dream now. And what Sam remembered most was the feeling of being in Quentin's arms and dancing. She hadn't felt unsteady at all, and the other thing she remembered and knew she would never forget was when he kissed her the next day, sitting on the bench in the little park. It was a memory she would cherish forever. She touched the little gold medal on the chain when she thought of it, just to remind herself that he was real, and she hadn't dreamed it.

Jane and Amelia landed at Idlewild International Airport in New York on Sunday morning, and took a cab to their apartment on Fifth Avenue. They had five suitcases, including the one that Amelia's dress was in, carefully wrapped in tissue paper. Gloria, their cleaning woman, had left them enough food to eat at home on Sunday, and Amelia walked around the apartment, as though trying to get her bearings. Everything suddenly felt new and unfamiliar, so much had happened. She found her mother making a pot of coffee in the kitchen.

"I feel like Cinderella after the ball," she said to her mother, as she sat down at the kitchen table and glanced around their cozy kitchen. "It's all white mice and pumpkins now," Amelia said, and Jane laughed.

"I feel the same way. I just realized I have to cook dinner tonight, or we'll starve. There are no bistros or quaint little inns between châteaux. No evening gowns, no balls." And she would have to call the employment agencies the next day, still looking for a job. "It was a wonderful trip," Jane said, happy they'd done it, and dreading resuming her job search the next day.

"Thank you for making me do it, Mom. I never thought it would be that much fun, or that special." The Infirmary Ball in New York in December paled in comparison. And Jane thought it was worth every penny it had cost her, even the emerald ring. She had no regrets, and Amelia looked happy too.

She went to unpack her suitcases, and the doorbell rang that afternoon. It was Western Union, with a telegram from Willie. Amelia smiled when she read the message. "Welcome home. See you in August. Love, Willie." He had wanted to send her flowers but had decided to put the money toward his savings for a ticket to New York and sent the telegram instead. She loved it.

"Who was at the door?" Jane popped her head into Amelia's room and inquired. Amelia's ball gown was spread out on her bed, a magnificent memory she would probably never wear again. But the dress had been worth it too.

"A telegram from Willie Brockhall," she said with a shy smile, and her mother walked over and hugged her.

"Well, Cinderella, it looks like you may have gotten your handsome prince." Jane had gotten used to the idea, and he really was a nice young man.

"He's only a viscount," Amelia corrected her mother, and Jane laughed. She went back to her own suitcases then, wondering if the romance would cool and they'd forget each other in the coming months. Anything was possible with young love. They might each meet someone else who struck their fancy, or perhaps only one of them would. They might not see each other for a year or two or longer, and a natural process would simply dissolve their feelings for each other, or maybe it really would last, and they'd see each other again.

Amelia knew that it was much more than her mother believed, and that they'd meet again. She didn't try to convince her. All she needed was to know it herself, and for Willie to make it happen, if he could scrape up the money for a ticket to New York.

# Chapter 12

Sam called Amelia first thing on Monday morning, and invited her to lunch in the city. She was going in with her father, who said he had a mountain of things to do in his office.

"Where do you want to have lunch?" Amelia asked her.

"Should we be grown-ups or kids? We could have lunch at The Plaza if you want, or there's a deli on Madison Avenue that makes good sandwiches and salads."

They opted for The Plaza. There would be plenty of time for delis when they were back at school. And it was fun to get dressed up for lunch.

"How was London, by the way?" Amelia asked her.

"I had a really good time. My dad was busy, so I had a lot of time to shop and play. What about you? How was your trip with your mom?" Sam asked her. "How were the châteaux?"

"Big, and old. Versailles was better. The rest were beautiful, but we saw a lot of them. Two or three days of it would have been enough, not six. My mom gets kind of obsessive about culture," Amelia said, and Sam laughed. "This was château summer. Last year it was horticultural shows. She kept buying plants and at the end of the summer, the apartment looked like a greenhouse, and we had to give some of them away. The year before, we went to bird sanctuaries all over the state, and a famous one in Florida. I'm a little scared what next year might be." Jane sounded like fun to Sam, who had met her but didn't know her well. There were times when she ached for a mother, but only her mother, not someone else's. But she had a great father, and Amelia barely remembered hers, so they all had their blessings and their losses, and each of them had one good parent.

They both looked lovely and appropriate when they met at The Plaza. Sam was wearing a pink linen summer dress with a matching jacket, and pink sandals, and Amelia was wearing a sleeveless white pique dress that looked great on her with the tan she had acquired on the car trip through France. They'd had enough outdoor lunches and walked around enough château gardens to pick up some color. They were two beautiful young women having lunch in the Palm Court. They each had an enormous salad and iced tea. It was Sam's favorite place for lunch and one of Amelia's, and while they were still in Paris, they had discovered that they lived only a few blocks away on Fifth Avenue, which seemed like a remarkable coincidence. They lived three blocks apart.

And inevitably, they talked about Willie and Quentin, and wondered when they'd ever see them again. The thought that they might never see them, and that it would prove to be complicated and too expensive, hadn't occurred to them yet. The odds of survival of a long-distance relationship between Paris, London, and New York at their ages were slim to none.

Jane had waited until Amelia left for lunch to call the round of agencies she had been calling before. It was too humiliating to have Amelia hear her make the calls. She expected the same answers she'd been getting for five months, that there was nothing suitable for her skill level, and she was overqualified, but she kept checking, and they said they'd call her if anything suitable came up.

She got exactly that answer from the first two agencies, but the third one asked her to hold for a minute. The agent came back on the line quickly, with a file in her hand.

"I was going to call you today. I called last week, and your cleaning lady answered. She said you were out of town until Sunday. I've got something on the books that isn't what you wanted, but it's an interesting job. The CEO you'd report to is a woman. She's kind of a character, and I've worked with her before and I like her. I think you might too."

"What kind of job is it?" Jane asked, not sure if she liked the introduction as a job that the agent already knew wasn't what she wanted.

"It's varied. You've got all the skills they require, and the salary is good, in the high range of what you want."

"Don't keep me in suspense. It's part of a high-wire act in the circus, or a dog walker, or a switchboard operator." There were so many jobs that she'd been offered that she didn't want, and mostly they didn't want her.

"It's Number Two at a magazine," the agent said simply. "Assistant Publisher, Executive Director. Good title. It's chaotic," she said honestly, "but magazines are. The editor in chief is sixty-eight years old. She says she doesn't want to retire, but that can change. It's an old magazine with a new look. It was sold five years ago to a French group, and they've given it a whole new twist. They publish some pretty interesting articles and have a very decent circulation. It's not *Vogue* or *Bazaar*, but it's respected. It's called *Chic* now, formerly *Women's World*. It was more like *Ladies' Home Journal* before, kind of a housewife magazine, now they're shooting for a higher-end group of working women.

Fewer recipes, more beauty, intelligent contributors, and good advertisers." Jane thought about it and tried to keep an open mind. It was very different from a staid publishing house, but it was a job, and she needed one desperately. It didn't sound like something she'd hate doing.

"What's the salary range?" Jane braced for bad news, and the agent gave her the figure in a flat voice, as Jane's eyes opened wide.

"Did I hear you right?"

"Their owners are the biggest publishers in France." The salary was a little more than double what Jane had been making at Axelrod and Baker when she left.

"Oh my God. When can I see them?"

"I'll call them. You got back in the nick of time. The CEO is going back to France on vacation for a month on the first of August. You got in just under the wire."

"Have they seen anyone else?"

"No one's been in town. But you were top of my list anyway. I was saving it for you." Jane had tears in her eyes as she listened. Even if she hated her boss for some reason, how bad could it be with a salary like that?

"I haven't worked at a magazine in twenty years, and I only stayed for a year," she reminded her. "All my experience is in book publishing."

"Something tells me you'll like this better. It sounds like

a lot more fun. The CEO is French but entirely bilingual. But you don't need French to work for them. Their whole staff are Americans, except for the CEO. She's been here for fifty years. She went to college here. And her husband is American. I'll call them now, and I'll get back to you," she said, as Jane sat rooted to the spot in her kitchen, staring into space, praying she'd get the job. Financially, it would solve all her problems, after five of the worst months of her life.

Her phone rang ten minutes later.

"Tomorrow, ten A.M. I don't need to tell you to be on time. She's punctual."

"I'll sleep on their doorstep if that will help."

The agent could hear the nervousness in Jane's voice. Getting fired had shaken her faith in herself. It had been so unexpected and undeserved. Phillip Parker had stopped calling her months before. He had felt so guilty when she couldn't find another job. They'd had a number of problems with Ted Hughes, the new CEO, who was heavy-handed with the owners, who didn't like him. Jane would have been a much better choice for CEO, and worlds cheaper, since Hughes was a man. And he was upsetting the staff, but it wasn't her problem anymore.

*Chic Magazine* occupied three floors in a new building on Seventh Avenue. The offices were clean, sleek, understated, modern, and elegant, and had been designed by a prize-winning French architect and interior designer. They were expecting Jane when she arrived, and kept her waiting less than five minutes, before she was led down a long, wide hall to a corner office. The CEO's secretary had come to get her, and a small thin woman stood up when Jane arrived, and invited her in with a smile. She was wearing a black linen skirt and a crisp white shirt. She had snow-white hair and a great haircut. Her eyes were a piercing blue, and she had a big onyx bangle on her wrist. She looked like what she was selling: chic. Jane was wearing black too, which seemed like a safe bet for the interview.

Pascale Winters invited her to sit down, and she barely had an accent when she spoke. She had gone to Columbia School of Journalism, and had been the fashion editor of *The New York Times,* then the Sunday magazine, before switching to other magazines. She looked straight at Jane when she spoke. Her eyes were lively, and she had a gentle voice. She was very dynamic and seemed years younger than her age.

"I got fired by *Vogue,*" Pascale said immediately. "It was my first big magazine job after the *Times*. I thought it would kill me. I was crushed. The editor in chief didn't like me, and I got fired after a year. I just want you to know that it happens to good people sometimes, and it's not the end of the road, and certainly not at your age."

She liked Jane's resume and said so. She respected her steadiness and loyalty more than the company she had worked for had, which sounded dull to her. "You know publishing. How do you feel about fashion?"

"I have no professional experience in the field," Jane said.

"We want strong editorial content, good articles by good writers. We want to respect the intelligence of our readers, no papier-mâché snowflakes or recipes unless they involve brandy, truffles, or caviar. We're a magazine for women with style and brains and imagination. No subject is too controversial if it's interesting. We have no prejudices or preconceived notions. I don't care what color our readers are or even if they went to college. Lots of smart women don't. In other words, anything goes," Pascale said with a smile, and Jane felt as though she had been pushed out of an airplane and wasn't sure if she was wearing a parachute. But it was exciting and innovative, it had a European flavor to it, and yet it was very American. It sounded like the magazine respected women, and liked them, and it was run by a woman reflecting what women wanted, not a man telling them who they should be, and what they should want.

"We want to appeal to married women, divorced women, widows, single women and single mothers, *all* women, of all ages. And style refers to many things, not just what they wear. It's how they think, how they live, what they read, what they say." Pascale was a strong, ener-getic woman, and her strength was contagious. Jane was excited just listening to what she had to say.

They toured the art department, and the layouts were gorgeous. The art director was a man. The features editor was a woman, the beauty editor was a man who was Ethiopian and beautiful. Everything Pascale said inspired Jane to want to be more and do more. It made her old job seem antiquated and limited, and clearly they didn't respect women even though it was owned by women. In the end, they hadn't respected her, or valued her, and had dumped her for a man. Jane didn't consider herself a feminist, but she believed in equality, justice, and fair treatment for all. She was a humanist, and believed in treating people well, men or women.

"How does it sound to you?" Pascale asked when they got back to her office. "I will tell you that I will always listen to your ideas. I may not agree with you, and I have strong opinions, but I'm always interested in hearing new ideas from my team. And you'll bring a fresh new perspective since this is all new to you."

"It's incredibly exciting," Jane said, and Pascale smiled.

"I think you'd do well here," Pascale said. "You can grow here, and discover your own opinions, and voice. The kind of publishing you were doing is repressive, and entirely run by men. One day that will change, but it hasn't yet. I like to push in that direction, but it takes time. Fifty years from now, it will be a different world, maybe even in twenty, or ten. But right now, the old ways still dominate. I want to change that." Jane nodded. She had been a victim of the old ways when she got fired. "It won't happen overnight. I want to be the pioneer of the new."

"You already are," Jane said, in admiration of what Pascale represented and was trying to do. And she hoped that she was up to the job. That much freedom was scary. There were no limits. She would need courage and imagination to do a good job, and to stretch her mind, not just rely on what she already knew. Her experience would serve her, but she had much to learn, which was exciting.

Pascale quoted the salary to her again, which still stunned Jane. "I want to be here when you start, and I go on holiday in a week. I'll be away for three weeks. Shall we say you could start on August twenty-first, *if* you want the job?"

"I do. I would love it." It was more than anything she had dared to hope she'd find.

"I want you too." Pascale stood up then, the interview was over. And Jane didn't know it, but Pascale had called Phillip Parker and asked him for the truth about Jane. He had raved about her, and said she had gotten a bad deal when she left. Pascale had no qualms about hiring her after that.

Pascale shook Jane's hand, and the deal was done. She said that the personnel department would contact her with the details. Jane was in a daze when she left, and stood on Seventh Avenue grinning, looking at the building where she was going to work. She had a *job*! Everything was going to be okay. They had made it. They had survived five months of terror, and her feet were on firm ground again. Their life was secure. She could pay for college and everything else, even some luxuries they hadn't had before. She wanted to jump for joy. She took a cab home, and the phone was ringing when she walked in the door. It was the agency calling to congratulate her, and she thanked them profusely for having the vision to put her forward for the job. She hung up a few minutes later and the phone rang again. It was Robert Walker, and she was startled to hear from him.

"You sound very happy to be back." He could hear the elation in her voice.

"I am. I just got a new job, and it sounds fantastic."

"May I ask where?"

"Something called *Chic Magazine*."

"I've heard of it. It sounds like fun."

"It will be. And how are you? How was London? How's Sam?"

"We're fine. We just got back two days ago. I was busy in London, but Sam's good about entertaining herself. May I

273

make a bold suggestion? Can I take you to dinner to celebrate your new job, or would that be inappropriate and an intrusion?"

"No, it would be lovely." She was touched. She was going to celebrate with Amelia, but she liked the idea of celebrating with him too.

"Is tomorrow too soon?"

"No, it's perfect."

"Terrific. I'll pick you up at seven-thirty if that works for you."

"That would be wonderful."

"Sam tells me you're right up the street from us. I'll walk up to get you and we can take a cab to dinner. I look forward to it, Jane."

"Thank you," she said softly, thanking her lucky stars for all the good things that had just happened to her. Sometimes a bad thing had to happen to make room for a good one. And suddenly it felt as though getting fired had been a gift, to make way for something new. She hung up after Robert's call, finished unpacking, and was waiting impatiently for Amelia when she came home from seeing one of her friends from school.

"You look happy, Mom."

"I am. I have a job, at twice my old salary. I start in four weeks." Amelia let out a whoop and hugged her mother and they danced around the kitchen, as Jane laughed. The five months melted behind her like a bad dream. Life was going to be good again. Even better than before.

Jane's evening with Robert Walker was like a date in a movie, and unlike any other first date she'd ever had. He was interesting and smart and fun, and a perfect gentleman.

They had a drink at Jane's apartment, and he admired the view and the small but elegantly furnished rooms. They were already comfortable with each other by the time they left for dinner. He took her to a very elegant French restaurant, which was a short cab ride down Fifth Avenue, for a delicious meal in gorgeous and very grand French surroundings, with fabulous flowers. All the waiters and headwaiters knew him well. They gave him a discreet corner table, and they touched on many subjects, and spoke about their children and their marriages. Jane was honest about the failings in hers, and how the war had destroyed Alfred, which led to his suicide, leaving her alone with Amelia, and the past ten years of struggling, her old job, getting fired and what the new job meant to her.

And Robert talked about how much Samantha meant to him and how he had almost lost her, and the struggle it was for him to let her fly now, which he had mentioned before.

They talked about the things they liked to do, he made her laugh, and they teased each other about what mother hens they were, and how they dreaded their daughters becoming independent and having their own lives one day. They had both put all their eggs in one basket, while fully recognizing how dangerous that was, but it was inevitable in their circumstances, with the traumatic deaths of their partners. They had more in common than they'd realized when they met at the ball.

They walked back to her building after dinner, in the warm night air, and when they got to her address, he invited her to come to Greenwich on Saturday and bring Amelia. They could have a nice relaxing day at his farm, and Jane accepted with pleasure.

"Good night, Robert. Thank you," Jane said when she left him. He touched her arm, but didn't kiss her or ask to come up, and she didn't invite him. Neither of them could see the road ahead of them, only a short distance, but the road they were on seemed surprisingly comfortable, and easy to walk together, easier than alone. After the doorman closed the door behind her, Robert left and walked home.

Sam was in her room reading when he walked by her bedroom.

"Business dinner tonight?" she asked him. "You look nice." He had worn a new pink Hermès tie for the first date he'd had in a long time, and a dark blue suit and white shirt.

"I had dinner with a friend. I invited your friend Amelia

and her mother to Greenwich for the day on Saturday, if that's all right with you." He hoped it would be, and Sam's face broke into a smile.

"That's a great idea. I was going to ask you if we could invite them out." Robert and Sam were going to spend the month of August there, as they did every year, and he would come to the city now and then to work. It was a perfect way to end the summer. "Thanks for inviting them, Dad."

After he headed to his own room, she suddenly wondered if the "friend" he had dinner with was Jane, but it seemed too soon for that, and unlikely, although she would have liked that too. But they'd just gotten back, and she couldn't imagine him taking her out so quickly, if he ever would. He was smiling when he got to his room, thinking of the evening he had just spent with Jane. He thought it was as perfect as she did. And a day at the farm with her and her daughter sounded good to him too. He was enjoying getting to know her, little by little, and he liked what he knew so far. He wanted to take his time to discover the rest. There were so many facets to her, and as she undressed a few blocks up the street, she was thinking the same about him. Father, businessman, financial wizard, widower, friend. They were both having fun, which was all that mattered for now.

# Chapter 13

The day that Jane and Amelia spent with the Walkers was better than any of them had expected. Robert spent the morning driving Jane around the farm to show her everything, and the horses in their extremely well-kept stables. There were cows and sheep, and a small dairy, some vegetables they grew, the pastureland for the animals. It was a real farm and he loved it. He had his own tractor, which made Jane smile. He said it relaxed him from the tensions of his work, and he loved spending time there. Everything was impeccably kept, and it was a beautiful working farm.

After their tour, he left his car at the stables, and they walked back through the orchards until they reached the house. It was a lovely, very large farmhouse that he had built when he bought the farm. He had his own wing, and Sam had hers at the opposite end of the house, and there were several guesthouses close by on the grounds.

"Maybe you and Amelia would like to spend the weekend sometime. It's a wonderful contrast to life in the city." He looked relaxed and happy as he walked with her. He seemed very different from the sophisticated world-class businessman she had met in Paris and dined with in New York. He was wearing well-worn cowboy boots, jeans, a blue checked shirt, and a cowboy hat. The look suited him as well as his impeccably tailored British suits, and Hermès shirts and ties. It was just a different side of him. She had worn white jeans, a white T-shirt, and sandals, and hadn't expected his farm to be quite as rural, but Amelia loved it. And the two girls were already sitting at the pool when Robert and Jane came back from their tour. It was a gorgeous place.

"Not quite Versailles," he said with a smile, but he was proud of his farm too. Since Jane had never seen his mansion in the city, she didn't realize how extreme the contrast was.

His chef made them burgers and French fries for lunch, with sliced cold chicken if Jane didn't want a burger, a big green salad, a selection of pies made from their fruit grown on the farm, ice cream sundaes for the girls if they preferred them, and a plate of homemade brownies and cookies.

After lunch, they all lay by the pool. Jane and Robert

talked quietly under an umbrella, and the two girls were giggling and laughing at the other end, keeping their secrets to themselves. They acted like two children together, and Jane and Robert smiled as they watched them.

"It will break my heart if she ever falls for one of these European guys and moves over there. It was one of the things I was worried about letting her do the ball at Versailles," he admitted to Jane.

"Nothing is forever at their age," Jane reassured him.

"Or at ours," he reminded her. They had both discovered that in their marriages with unexpected endings.

"They had fun at the ball, and a little romance added spice to it. Who knows if they'll ever see those boys again," Jane said. It was the second time he had mentioned it, so she knew he was worried about it.

"I'm not so sure it's as lightweight as you think. Quentin has been calling Sam every day, from Europe."

"They'll get tired of it. Long distance is hard enough at our age, and impossible at theirs. Willie is a nice boy, but he can't afford to come over and visit Amelia."

"There are no lengths to which a man won't go when he wants a woman," Robert said, still worried.

"They're not fully men and women yet, they just look like it. They're still kids most of the time."

"The Brockhall boy is younger, I think he's twenty-five.

Quentin Dupont is twenty-six. I was younger than that when I married my wife."

"I was twenty-two, and my husband was twenty-four. But that was twenty years ago. I think we still have some time to enjoy them before they run off and leave us," Jane said, and smiled warmly at him. "You have a wonderful place here."

"I enjoy it a lot. I love spending time here, the animals, and growing things. It's the perfect counterpoint to the rest of my life, stuck at a desk. I enjoy sailing too."

"I used to love to sail when I was a kid. We went to Maine in the summers for a week or two. Those are nice memories to have when you grow up. All of the things you do with Sam, the trips, being here, will keep her close to you."

"I hope so," he said, and she could see how close to his daughter he was and how much she meant to him. They were both possessive about their children, more so than most parents, and she understood what motivated him. The fear of losing her kept him close.

At the end of the day, Robert asked Jane if they'd like to stay for dinner. He hadn't realized how much he'd enjoy her company and how easy she was to be with. She had enjoyed it too, but it was a long drive back to the city, and she didn't want to overstay their welcome.

And then the girls surprised them, and Sam begged both Jane and her father to let Amelia stay the night, and it was obvious she wanted to. The girls were relishing their new friendship. Their school friends were still away for the summer, and the ball at Versailles had created a bond between them. Robert added his invitation to Sam's, and Jane hesitated, but the invitation appeared to be sincere and she finally relented. He said that Jane could stay too, in one of the guesthouses, but she didn't want to overdo it and impose. She finally agreed to let Amelia stay, and he promised to take good care of her, and bring her home on Sunday night. Amelia looked delighted, and they hurried into the house to go up to Sam's room, as Robert walked Jane to the car.

"Will you be all right, driving home alone in the dark?"

"I think I can manage it." She smiled at him. "You made my daughter too comfortable. She'll never want to leave now."

"She'll be tired of us by tomorrow and happy to come home." They were both happy to see their girls get along. They were like puppies or young colts playing together.

Jane thought about the day as she drove home, and what life might have been like if she'd been married and not the only parent Amelia had. Both girls seemed hungry for what they didn't have. Sam liked talking to Amelia's mother, and Amelia looked admiringly at Robert, and could see what Sam had and she'd been missing.

\* \* \*

283

It was an hour-and-a-half drive back to the city, and Jane was pleasantly tired when she got home. The day in the sunshine and the outdoors on a farm had been relaxing, she was sure Amelia was having a great time, and she was grateful to Robert for letting her stay. The girls seemed to be forming a fast friendship, and it seemed nice to Jane that they lived in the city and could pursue it, although they'd both be busy when school got started.

She had just undressed and was about to get into the bath when Robert called, and he was quick to reassure her.

"The girls are fine. They're watching a movie on a projector we have. I just wanted to make sure you got home all right. I'm sorry you had to drive home alone." She'd been doing everything alone for the past ten years. This was no different. She was used to it.

"It's a nice drive. It was relaxing. You really have a wonderful setup there. Thank you for making it such a nice day for us. Too nice. Now you're stuck with my daughter."

"We love having her. And they're having a great time. We made popcorn for the movie." He was a good father, she liked that about him.

Jane puttered around the apartment on Sunday, and Robert and Sam dropped Amelia off at six o'clock. She thanked them warmly. Jane invited them to come up for a drink, and Robert said he had to get home and get organized.

He had a tough week ahead. They left to go home, and Amelia told her what a great time she'd had, how much she liked Sam, and she said Robert had been very nice to her too. She reported then that Sam was crazy about Quentin, and he was calling her every day from Paris. He was planning to come and visit her, but he didn't know when.

Jane didn't hear from Robert again for another week, and he invited them back to the farm again, and Amelia to spend the weekend. It was just as pleasant as it had been before. And he invited Jane to dinner in the city again, the night before they left for the farm for three weeks. It was even nicer than it had been before. They went to a little Italian restaurant, and were the last ones to leave. She was starting her new job in less than three weeks and they talked about it.

"I hope I do a decent job. I have no real experience with magazines, just books."

"You'll adjust," he assured her. He had bought a copy of the magazine and was impressed by the quality of their features.

"I have a lot to learn," she said modestly. He liked her humility and the fact that she didn't seem to be in competition with him. She wasn't trying to prove anything, she just wanted to do a good job in her new position. It was a very different job from the one she'd had at Axelrod and Baker.

Once they'd settled in at the farm, Sam invited Amelia to spend a week there, and Amelia begged her mother to let her go. Jane didn't want them to feel that they were imposing, but she finally agreed, and spent the day there when she went to pick Amelia up at the end of the week. It was another enjoyable day with them, and both Sam and her father seemed sad to see Amelia leave.

After that, Jane's life moved into high gear again. She hadn't worked in six months and had been around all the time, and she was starting her new job the week after Amelia came home, and she was going back to Barnard and the dorm in a week. The timing was good. Pascale had warned her that she might have to work late at times, especially when they were putting the magazine to bed for the following month.

When Jane started, the job was as exciting as she had hoped, and she worked late every night the first week, trying to catch up. On Saturday, she settled Amelia into her dorm room. She had the same roommate as the previous year, so she was happy. Jane got everything hung up and put away, and arrived home at eight o'clock that night. She lay down on her bed, exhausted after hauling boxes, bags, and suitcases all day, and a trunk, and setting up a small refrigerator. Amelia's roommate's father had put in a small sound system, and Jane loaned her an electric typewriter that she didn't use anymore. When the phone rang, she was almost too tired to answer it, but she did.

"You sound as tired as I am," Robert laughed at the other end. "Moving-in day at the dorm?"

"Yes. But you said Sam isn't in the dorms."

"She isn't. She had orientation, there was a seminar for parents, a second orientation with parents, a meet-and-greet. A lunch, a tea for her department. I've been all over that campus. Nothing was in the same building. We walked miles today."

"I set up a refrigerator and carried a trunk up three flights of stairs." She laughed, with no sympathy for him. "All you did was eat cookies and listen to department heads make speeches."

"That's exhausting too. How in hell did you manage to carry a trunk up three flights of stairs?"

"I paid her roommate's twelve-year-old brother five dollars to help me do it."

"Sounds like a good investment. I was going to ask you if you want to go out for dinner. Sam is still at school with her friends. She won't be back till late. But it doesn't sound like you're up to it."

"You'd have to carry me to the elevator. I don't think I could get off my bed without major assistance."

"Tomorrow maybe? I'm hardly going to see Sam for the rest of the semester."

"Or Amelia. She only comes home for clean laundry or if she's sick, during school. Tomorrow sounds good. It's Sunday. I seem to be working late every night."

"Are you enjoying the new job?" he asked her.

"I love it. But it's a whole new world from my old one."

"It's a long way from Versailles, isn't it?" he said, and she laughed.

"It certainly is. None of the mothers of those debutantes work. But I'm happy to be back in a job. I was going crazy without one." And going broke.

"I would too. I'm looking forward to seeing you tomorrow. I have to go out to the West Coast this week to meet with a venture capital firm there. We're doing a joint deal." He was even busier than she was, but she had enjoyed the evenings she spent with him.

He picked her up the next night at seven, and they had an easy Sunday night dinner at P.J. Clarke's, and talked about their daughters and their work. It was nice having a friend. He held her hand when he walked her back to her apartment. They always had a nice time. She hadn't had a bad time with him yet, and he gave her good advice about her job, which she appreciated.

As they approached her building, she asked him if he wanted to come up for a drink. She had some trepidation about it. She wasn't sure where they were going, if it was a friendship or something more, or how deep in she wanted to get. It would be awkward if it didn't work out, and spoiled the friendship between the two girls. He seemed to be as careful as she was. They stopped walking when she asked him about the drink, and he looked at her gently and touched her cheek.

"I'd love to, but I have to get up at five in the morning to catch my flight to San Francisco. I'd love a rain check for when I get back. I enjoy spending time with you, Jane. I don't want to spoil anything between us, or screw anything up."

"Neither do I," she said, relieved by his honesty, and he put his arms around her and held her. They had been walking along the outer wall of Central Park.

"I really like being with you," he said. "I haven't felt like this in a long time. I feel so comfortable with you." She nodded as he held her. It was how she felt too, and then he kissed her, and there was a gentleness to his lips on hers that she hadn't expected. The kiss grew more passionate, and they were both breathless when they stopped. They had been seeing each other regularly for a month and a half. The time had drifted past them, and they weren't keeping track, but they'd been meeting consistently ever since Paris. "Maybe I think too much," he said softly, "and we need to just let things happen." He kissed her again after he said it, and then they walked slowly to her building, with the doorman standing guard outside. The doorman turned away not to embarrass them. He had seen them kissing across the street like two teenagers.

Robert looked down at her and smiled. "Maybe that just clarified things for both of us. I wasn't sure what path we were on. I think we just made that clear," he said, and she laughed. "To be continued," he said. "I'll be back on Friday. I think we need to try that again." It sounded promising, and Jane's heart was beating faster, as she kissed him on the cheek and he waved and walked away. He was still smiling. He felt like a schoolboy suddenly when he was with her. He had been afraid to get too deeply involved ever since he'd met her. And he suddenly realized it was already too late for that.

When Amelia headed for class, and hurried down the stairs of her dorm in Hewitt Hall on the first day, there was a telegram on the bulletin board for her. She saw it as she rushed past, took it off and read it, and her face broke into a smile. "Won the lottery. Bank holiday in England. See you Friday night. Love, Willie." She had no idea how he'd pulled it off, but the following Monday was Labor Day and she had a three-day weekend. She didn't care how short his visit was going to be, she was excited about seeing him, and he had kept his word to come to New York to see her. She put the telegram in her purse and hurried off to class. She had a required math class she was taking, and an English Lit class after that.

The first week seemed grueling, after three months off. She hadn't done well on the math quiz, and she already had two books to read for her English Lit class, but she had no intention of studying the following weekend.

Amelia was mildly panicked about where Willie was going to stay, and hoped he didn't think he could stay in the dorm with her. The rules were stringent about that. And she didn't want to ask her mother if he could stay at the apartment. He sent her another telegram on Tuesday, which put her mind to rest. "In case you're wondering, staying with a friend in Greenwich Village. Arriving in time for dinner Friday. Meet me at his apartment?" He had written the friend's address and phone number. It was at the opposite end of the city from her dorm. "Dinner to follow." The message continued. "Entirely aboveboard. Scout's honor. Love, Willie." She nearly danced in the street, she was so excited. Her mother called her on Wednesday night, to ask her what she was doing for the long weekend, and if she was coming home, and wanted to do anything with her, or had plans of her own.

"Willie's coming for the weekend," she said, and Jane was startled.

"From London?"

"He's staying with a friend. I don't know how long he's staying. But I want to see him."

"Of course," Jane said, sounding subdued. She hadn't expected him to actually show up. It sounded more serious than she'd thought. "Don't do anything crazy," Jane said.

"Of course not, Mom." Amelia sounded offended by the suggestion, and she'd always been sensible before. But no man had ever flown all the way from London to see her. That was heavy stuff. "What are you doing?"

"I don't know. I wanted to check with you first." Robert had invited her to dinner on Saturday, after he got back on Friday night. And he had said that Sam was going to stay with friends on Long Island, so their daughters had their own plans, which left them free to do what they wanted. And he said he was staying in the city that weekend.

Jane accepted dinner with him the next time he called her. And she was faintly worried that Willie would sweep Amelia off her feet, but she knew she had to trust her. She couldn't follow her around.

When Friday came, Amelia could hardly sit through her classes. Subsequent telegrams had set their meeting time at seven o'clock at the apartment where he was staying in the Village, and then they would go to dinner in the neighborhood, he would be exhausted by then anyway, with the time difference. And they had Saturday and Sunday to spend together. He was leaving on Sunday to be at work on Monday morning. It was the most romantic thing anyone had ever done for her. She called Sam and told her, and she was excited for her friend.

"What are you going to do with him?" Sam asked her.

"I don't know, whatever he wants. We'll have two days together." It occurred to her that she hardly knew him, but it felt as though she had known him all her life, and he was coming all the way from London to see her. And he had told her it was "entirely aboveboard."

"Will you stay with him at the apartment?" Sam asked her in a whisper, so no one would hear her on the phone.

"Of course not," Amelia answered nervously, but she was wondering about it herself. She didn't want him to think that she was fast or a slut, but every time she thought of him, her whole body seemed to melt, and she didn't know if she could resist him. She didn't want to get pregnant either. She knew girls at school who had, and any solution available to them had been a nightmare to contemplate. She couldn't let anything like that happen, and she knew he wouldn't want that to happen, or to take the chance. They'd seen each other three times in their life, but their correspondence had been passionate and loving in the month and a half since. They had moved forward very quickly from where they started, and there was no doubt in her mind that she loved him and that he loved her. "I'll stay at the dorm," she said, as much to convince herself as Sam.

"You have to tell me everything on Monday. I'll be back on Monday night from Long Island." Sam was staying with a friend from NYU. And two other girls were coming too.

She wished Amelia good luck. At six o'clock on Friday night, Amelia was dressed and ready. She was wearing a black pencil skirt and a white V-neck sweater with high heels and a purse her mother had given her, and white gloves. She walked to the subway near her dorm and rode it all the way downtown to the Village. She had looked up the address on a map, since she didn't know the Village well and addresses were hard to find. She walked to where it was. Her hair was long down her back. The weather was still warm.

It was a quarter to seven, she was early, but she didn't want to stand alone in the street. The crowd eddying around her looked like students, and ordinary people who lived in the neighborhood. It wasn't far from the NYU campus, and there were coffeehouses and restaurants everywhere. The building looked a little dilapidated, but not shockingly so. She rang the bell. She had never gone to a man's apartment before, but she didn't want to meet him at her dorm. She could have met him at home, but she didn't want to do that either, with her mother hovering in the next room and coming in to check on them every five minutes. And at the last minute, she had signed herself out as going home for the holiday weekend. She was planning to go back to the dorm, but just in case something got complicated or she decided to go home after all, she wanted the freedom to do it, so she signed herself out until Monday, for the whole holiday weekend.

She stood there waiting for a minute, and he buzzed her in without asking who it was. He knew, and she hurried to the second floor, and her breath caught when she saw him in the doorway waiting for her. He was wearing a blazer and a shirt and tie, his hair was as blond as hers, and he looked so incredibly handsome it took her breath away, as he took two long strides to meet her, and without a word he took her in his arms and kissed her, and there was no doubt in either of their minds what their feelings were. They were a man and a woman in love, with everything that entailed. She followed him into the apartment, and he kissed her again, and led her into the tiny, shabby living room, and she sat down on the couch next to him.

"Oh my God," he said, staring at her, "I was starting to think you were some kind of dream, or an illusion, or I had imagined you, but you're real. And you're so beautiful, Amelia, it hurts to look at you. I've thought about you every minute since Paris."

"So have I," she said, smiling at him. "I didn't think you'd come."

"It took a little wangling. Today is a bank holiday so I got the day off. I got a great deal on a ticket, so here I am."

"How did you get the apartment?" He was resourceful if nothing else. It wasn't pretty, but it was a place to stay for free.

"I have a friend whose brother is studying here. He's away for the weekend in the Hamptons. It's some kind of holiday here too. He left the keys with the building manager, she gave them to me, and here I am. Do you want a drink before we go to dinner?"

"All right." Willie was staring at her again. This was so different from the deb ball. They were alone and it was real, in a tiny apartment. He was taller than she remembered and even better looking, and his arms around her felt wonderful, and when he kissed her, she felt as though she was floating away.

He walked into the tiny kitchen and found a small bottle of champagne in the fridge. He opened it and poured them each a glass. The living room was just big enough for a couch, a desk, a coffee table, and two chairs, and the bedroom was the size of the bed. She sipped the champagne, and he set his glass down and kissed her again.

"I feel as though the minutes are already ticking away, and I don't want to waste a minute with you. Do you want to go to dinner now?" She nodded. There was nothing else to do in the tiny apartment and she felt shy for a minute being with him, and very grown-up, meeting a man this way. A man who had flown all the way from England to see her. She still couldn't get over it. He had kept his promise. He had come when he said he would.

They finished the champagne in the two glasses, and he picked up his keys, and she followed him out of the apartment, and tucked her hand in his arm when they got to the street. There was a small Italian restaurant across the street. He pointed and she laughed. It was all so romantic and fun. They walked into the restaurant and sat at a small table. In the end, they ordered pizza. She wasn't hungry and it was after midnight for him, but he looked wide awake.

"What are our plans for tomorrow?" he asked her when they finished the pizza.

"Whatever you want to do. Museums, the Statue of Liberty, Central Park, we can go to my apartment and see my mom. Have you been here before?" She didn't know that about him.

"Twice, a long time ago. I went to the top of the Empire State Building, and the Statue of Liberty. The park sounds nice. Where do you live?"

"Way uptown from here. I live in the dorm during school, I don't know what my mother is doing this weekend. I wanted to be with you, Willie."

"And I came to see you." He held her hand under the table. "Do you want to come back to the apartment and talk for a while?" He was in an unfamiliar city and wasn't sure what to do. "Do you want to go to a bar and have a drink?" A bar would be noisy. It was Friday night and there would be a lot of people getting drunk, and it would be hard to talk.

"Maybe just talk for a while." She wanted to settle down quietly, her heart was still fluttering. He liked that idea too. They went back to the building across the street after he paid for the pizza, and she followed him up the stairs. The shabby little apartment looked familiar when they saw it again. They sat down next to each other, and he kissed her again. And the moment he kissed her she felt as though she was home in his arms. He couldn't keep his hands off her and she didn't want him to. She was lying on the couch next to him, knowing she should stop, but unable to, as he unbuttoned her skirt and it fell away from her, and he slid a gentle hand under her sweater. He let out a low growl of desire and pulled away from her.

"Amelia," he said in a hoarse voice, "I don't want to do anything you don't want or will hate me for later. I didn't come here for this. I came here because I love you, but I have to admit, it's damn hard to keep my hands off you," he said, and kissed her again. With her skirt unbuttoned, her white lace underwear was exposed and her garter belt, which aroused him so unbearably that his trousers could barely contain him, and she felt him against her.

"I want you too," she whispered, and it was all he needed to hear. He unclipped her garters, rolled her nylons down and took them off. He took off his own clothes and then he kissed her, and they lay there naked, and he stopped and looked at her.

"I want to remember this moment forever, in this ridiculous ugly apartment. Everything looks beautiful to me when I'm with you." He scooped her up in his arms then and walked to the tiny bedroom and laid her gently on the bed, and stopped again. "You don't have to do this. I'll love you even if we don't." Resisting her was becoming an impossibility for him, but he left her and walked across the tiny hall to the bathroom, pawed through the shaving kit he had left there when he showered and dressed, and came back with what he needed. "I don't want you to get pregnant," he whispered to her. He still remembered the horrible scene with Caroline at the ball, with blood splashing on the ground. Then he tenderly and gently made love to her, making it as painless as he could for her. He was sure she was a virgin without asking her. He held back as long as he could, and had protected her. And then he adeptly saw to it that she came too, and she was startled by the force of it, and of him as he let out a roar of unbridled pleasure. He had tried to make it as memorable as he could for her, and afterwards he held her close to him and worried about her. He didn't want it to be a bad memory for her.

"Did I hurt you?" Willie whispered to her, leaning on one elbow to look at her beautiful face. She was smiling at him with such a look of love and tenderness that it brought tears to his eyes.

"Amelia, I will love you forever. And one day, we will do it all right. I promise to love and care for you till the day I die." He had never loved another human being as he did her at that moment.

"I love you too," she said peacefully, and they lay there for a long time, whispering in the dark. "Do you want a drink?" he asked her. "The bloke only has scotch and ice cubes. We drank his champagne. If I'd known this would happen, I would have saved it." She laughed and he loved the sound of it.

"I don't want a drink. I don't need one. I just need you," she said, and a little while later, they made love again. She became a woman that night in his arms, and in the morning, they showered together, and then they went out to breakfast, and he ate an enormous meal, and couldn't stop smiling at her. She was hungry too, and after they ate, she said she had to go back to school and get some clothes. They rode the subway together.

"I should have gotten a hotel room," he whispered to her on the subway. "I didn't think you'd be staying with me. I didn't think I could be that lucky," he said. They got out at her stop, and she went to her dorm, while he waited downstairs in the lobby. She was back five minutes later with everything she needed to spend the night with him. She came downstairs wearing blue jeans and a sweater, and had a skirt in the bag in case they went out to dinner.

They went back to his borrowed apartment then, and dropped off her clothes, and then they walked around the Village together. They bought ice cream from a Good Humor truck, and sat in Washington Square Park, watching the people, and then they went back to the apartment and made love again.

"I want to take you to a decent restaurant for dinner," Willie said when they got out of bed again. "I have to at least feed you," he said, and Amelia laughed.

"Do you like Chinese food?"

"Love it."

"I know a place where all the students from NYU go." It wasn't far from the apartment, and they went there and had a feast, talking about everything and making plans far into the future. They devoured each other with their eyes all through the meal. When they'd eaten everything, they went out and walked again. There were people playing music in

301

Danielle Steel

Washington Square, and they discovered an Italian street festival, and people were talking and laughing and dancing in the street, and he danced with her. Amelia knew that whatever happened between them later, this would always feel like their wedding day to her. Willie bought her a bouquet of roses and won a teddy bear for her at the street fair. They bought more ice cream, and wended their way slowly back to the apartment, and made love. She fell asleep in his arms as he watched her in the moonlight and gently touched her face and stroked her hair. And then he nestled beside her, feeling her warmth next to him, and he knew it was the best day of his life, it didn't get better than this.

# Chapter 14

When Robert picked Jane up at her apartment on Saturday, he was dressed casually and he had told her to do the same. They went to the "21" Club for dinner, and he told her about his trip to San Francisco. He had gone to meet with another venture capital firm, to discuss a very large joint investment they were making, combining two funds for a deal of epic proportions. It was fascinating listening to him explain it, and he made the complexities of the deal very simple to understand. Listening to him, Jane understood the magnitude of his legendary reputation and the kind of investments he made, and she could see how much he enjoyed it. The trip had been successful and the two firms had come to an agreement. It had been a good week's work and he was pleased.

Then they went to the Hotel Carlyle for a drink, a favorite of both of theirs. It was close to their homes, and a pianist was playing popular songs in the background. The maitre d' knew Robert and tucked them into a corner table in the bar. It was fun being with Robert. Jane loved his versatility from rancher/farmer, to devoted father, to financial legend in his professional life. There were dozens of sides and facets to him, and he was never boring.

They stayed late talking and listening to the music, and then walked toward Fifth Avenue from the hotel, in the direction of Jane's apartment, a block west on Fifth Avenue.

"Where's Amelia this weekend?" he asked her, as they walked past the shop windows on Madison Avenue.

"She stayed in the dorm. It's a big weekend for her. Willie Brockhall flew in from London to see her."

"Wow," Robert said, impressed. "He's a man of his word. As I recall, he told her he'd visit her in August, he just made it. That's a big deal for a guy his age. He doesn't make a big salary where he is. He must be crazy about her."

"It seems like it," she said, and Robert looked at her.

"You're skeptical?"

"No, but I'm worried. They're both so young, madly in love, and I hope she doesn't do anything crazy. It'll be a long time before he can support a wife and kids. And long distance is hard to maintain. I just see a lot of struggles in her future if she casts her lot with him. His family is on the decline. They have a crumbling estate. He has a small job, and a big heart, and big ambitions, but nothing happens overnight. Add a wife and kids to all that and she'll be helping him for a long time, to climb out of the pit his family put him in as a second son. The crumbling estate will belong to his brother, who leads the life of a country nobleman and doesn't work. Amelia is going to be working for many years to support all that. It's a lot to expect love to overcome. I'd hoped for an easier life for her, not even a grand life, but just an easier one."

"And if he's the guy she wants?" he asked gently.

"Then he's the one she'll follow into the sunset, and I guess they'll figure it out." She tried to be philosophical about it.

"What if he comes to work here?"

"He'd have a better shot at making a decent living and getting his family off his back, and I wouldn't be three thousand miles away if she needs a hand. But she'll do whatever she decides to do. She's head over heels in love with him. That's dangerous territory for a young girl with stars in her eyes. I was there once too. And I suppose we would have made a decent life of it if the war hadn't changed all that. My husband came back from the war destroyed, and he never recovered. It killed him in the end, as surely as if they'd shot him on the beach in Normandy on D-Day. He was already dead when he came back."

"The war destroyed a lot of good men," Robert said quietly.

"At least Amelia won't have to deal with that. I just hope she doesn't want to marry him before he figures out his own life. She's too young to get married anyway."

"They might make it, you know. Sometimes those young marriages work, if they're determined enough and on the right track."

"I hope they are, if it comes to that. She fell in love with him at the ball. It's early days yet."

"I'm concerned about Sam and Quentin too. He seems to be hanging in. He still calls her almost every day from Paris."

"At least they both fell for decent boys who are crazy about them, not like the creep who ditched that poor girl from Texas and wound up in the bushes with her sister." Robert shook his head, remembering the night of the ball.

"There were all kinds of possibilities that night. I think our daughters may have gotten lucky and wound up with good ones."

"Young love," Jane said with a rueful smile, and tucked her hand into his arm. Somehow Robert always made the world seem like a less dangerous place, even for her daughter, and for her. He was a born protector. "Young love is scary, it's so blind sometimes."

"Maybe that's not such a bad thing. Maybe you have to be a little blind to take a chance on love. The young haven't cornered that market. A little of it isn't bad at our age either. If you only look at everything that could go wrong, you'd never get up in the morning. A little blind faith never hurts. You have to believe in each other. And at our age, you have a better idea of what you're getting. You just don't know what curveballs life will throw at you. But with a little luck you can dodge the curveballs, or survive them." She smiled and nodded as they walked toward her building. Robert pulled her closer to him then. "I seem to recall that you owe me a rain check for a drink from last week, before I left for San Francisco. Any chance I can cash that in now?" He looked up to the heavens and held up a hand. "I think I just felt a few raindrops." She was smiling at what he said.

"Yes, we have a special on rain checks tonight. And you have a good memory. You did ask for a rain check the last time I saw you, and as I recall, I agreed."

They walked past her doorman with a determined step and rode up in the elevator, and she let him into her apartment and turned on the lights.

"I love your apartment, Jane, everything is beautiful, and the whole place makes one want to sit down and stay, or curl up with a good book by the fire."

"I'm glad you like it," she said warmly, and he kissed her before they sat down in the living room. "Champagne or brandy?"

"Maybe just a glass of white wine, if you have it."

She got a bottle out of the fridge in the kitchen, and he opened it for her and poured some into two glasses, and they went back and sat down, and as soon as they did, he kissed her.

"I love being with you," he said quietly, "you always make me feel happy, and you make me want to see more of you." They kissed again after he said it.

"You make me happy too. Happier than I've been in a long time." And now, with her new job, she felt secure again. It was a good feeling, after five months of anxiety and panic. But she and Amelia had gotten through it.

"You deserve to be happy," he said, setting down his glass on the coffee table and putting his arms around her. He took her breath away when he kissed her. They had had too little time to indulge themselves, with their daughters around so much of the time. "We need time for us," he said to her. "I've been thinking about that a lot lately. I want to go away with you somewhere." He kissed her harder then, and felt her body under the sweater she had worn, and touched her breasts with gentle fingers. His mouth was devouring her then, and he took her sweater off and she helped him out of his clothes, as he unzipped the pants she had worn for dinner that night. A minute later she was naked as he admired her in the soft lamplight, and she took off the rest of his clothes and devoured him gently as he lay there, swept away by her passion and his own. She led him to her bedroom, and they lay on her bed fitting together, blending together, needing each other, starving for each other, having poured their love into others for so long, needing it for themselves and each other now. He felt as though he had become part of her as they made love, and they clung to each other, breathless, when it was over.

"Oh God, I wanted you so much," he whispered to her. He had never wanted any woman as much. "You're so independent and you work so hard at standing on your own, I was afraid you'd never want me. I've wanted you since the first time I saw you at the ball, and I was afraid to show it and tell you. Thank you for wanting me now."

"Thank you for wanting me." She smiled at him. "I was so afraid to want you. I was afraid I wasn't good enough. You're such a big person, you deserve someone better than someone like me."

"There is no person better than you, for me," he said, as he held her and started to make love to her again. There were no words to tell her how much he loved her. All he could do was show her. He wanted to be there to protect her, so she didn't have to be so brave all the time. She was the bravest woman he'd ever met, and he needed her to make him brave too.

He held her in his arms after they made love, and wanted to hold her forever, and then she giggled and looked up at him.

"What are we going to tell our daughters? I don't think it occurs to them that we could fall in love too."

"I don't think we'll have a problem with either of them." He smiled and pulled her closer. "They may think they've cornered the market on love, but we got there first and we need it more than they do. We don't even need to tell them for a while. They're busy with their own affairs. They'll figure it out about us sooner or later. I think they want us to be happy too. They're going to fly off to their own lives any minute, and after they do, we'll still have each other." She loved everything he said to her, and everything he did to her, and everything they were together.

They slept in each other's arms that night, made love in the morning, made breakfast together, and suddenly Jane was glad that Amelia was living in the dorms now. It was time for her and Robert to have a life. They had paid their dues and had earned everything they had together.

Amelia and Willie spent their last two hours together in the apartment, making love and making promises, and plans for the future. It had been a perfect weekend.

"I'll come to you during Christmas break," she promised him. "Probably right after Christmas. I need to spend it with my mom, and I'll come to you after that. I'll figure out how to pay for a ticket somehow," just as he had to visit her.

They washed the sheets in the washing machine in the basement and made the bed, and Willie had bought their unseen host a full bottle of decent champagne, and they left him a note of thanks. And as they left the apartment together, they looked at the small rooms and the well-worn furniture, and the finest suite at The Plaza wouldn't have looked more beautiful to them.

Willie held her for a last time on the street and kissed her.

"Remember everything we said," he told her seriously. "I meant every word of it," and she did too. He hailed a cab then and got in, to head for the airport. Amelia stood there until the cab turned a corner and disappeared, and then she walked to the subway and went down the stairs to go back to her dorm uptown, and as she sat down on the subway a few minutes later, thinking of him, she knew that in those two days with him, she had been changed forever.

Robert stayed with Jane on Sunday night. Sam wasn't due back from Long Island until Monday. He didn't need to account for his whereabouts. He owed no one any explanations, and he needed to be with Jane for another night.

He didn't want to be away from her now, and wherever he was with her would be home from now on. It was painful leaving her to go back to his own house on Monday.

When Felicity arrived in Boston at the end of August, Raphael was due to get there five days later on Labor Day. He had signed up for the furnished housing available to graduate students, and Felicity had promised to help him move in. She picked him up at the airport with a van she'd borrowed, and saw him waiting for her on the sidewalk outside the terminal, with two duffel bags, a suitcase, and wearing a heavy back-pack. He was wearing cut-off jeans, high-top sneakers, and a brand-new Harvard T-shirt. She couldn't miss his mane of red curls as he stood waiting for her. She was happy to see him and they were both smiling as she stopped the van and helped him load everything in. They blocked traffic and people were already honking at them when he dropped everything and kissed her. Cars were backing up behind them, people were shouting, and Raphael didn't care. He smiled at her, and looked ecstatic to see her. He had been waiting for this day ever since he met her. They had been writing to each other all summer.

He looked at her oddly as they left the airport and she headed for the Harvard campus in Cambridge.

"You look different," he said, and she pretended to concentrate on the flow of traffic.

She had lost eighteen pounds in the last six weeks in Nice and Dallas. She had given up ice cream, doughnuts, and pizza, which had been the mainstay of her diet for the last five years. She still had more to lose but it made a big difference in her appearance. She had started running track again the day after she arrived and had lost three more pounds. Having lost twenty-one pounds, she was halfway to where she wanted to be.

"Did you do that for me?" He looked shocked.

"Maybe. I did it for me too. It was time."

"I love you the way you are. You don't need to do that for me." It was visible evidence that she cared about him, and so was showing up at the airport with a van to help him. She thought he could bring more with him than he had.

"I didn't love me the way I was. That's how I got that way," she said, as he looked out the window of the van, excited to be there with her. Being in Boston to study was the dream of his lifetime. He wanted to see everything now that he was here.

"How are your classes?" he asked her.

"Pretty good. I think I'm switching majors next semester."

"Nuclear physics?" he asked, and she nodded, smiling. They spoke the same language and he understood her. It was a relief to be back in Boston, as far away as she could get from Dallas and her toxic sister. Their father had finally given

313

Araminta back her credit cards after a month, and she was only slightly less rude to Felicity than she had been previously. It no longer mattered. Felicity didn't care. She knew that Raphael loved her, and her parents did the best they could. They couldn't control Araminta and her jealousy. As Felicity began to lose weight, Araminta got meaner. It was part of the fiber of her being. She was a miserable person, and Felicity had finally understood that it had nothing to do with her. It was just who Araminta was. She was a nasty human being, unhappy with her life, always ready to envy and blame someone else.

As they approached the Harvard campus, Raphael could hardly contain himself. Felicity had gotten a map of the campus and surrounding area, so she could find the housing he'd been assigned to. He'd gotten what he requested, a studio apartment without roommates. She had a sophomore single at MIT. As an undergraduate and a female, she had far more restrictions than he did. The single was exactly what she'd wanted, so she could study in peace, and she had sent her fridge back to the rental company as part of her resolution to finally lose the weight. She kept no food in her room now.

"How far is Harvard from MIT?" he asked her.

"One point one miles," she said with a smile.

"I have to buy a bicycle tomorrow." He wanted to see

everything, go everywhere, be with her, share it with her. The familiar sights of the Harvard campus came into view, as he saw the Johnston Gate and looked at it with wonder. It was real now.

When they got to the graduate student housing, she helped him unload his bags and carry them upstairs. They each took a duffel bag, and he took the suitcase and backpack. When they unpacked, she saw that he had brought a number of his French textbooks with him, to refresh his memory on the subjects he'd be studying.

They unpacked everything, and she drove him around the campus so he could see where everything was, and then she drove him to MIT. He looked like he was in Mecca. MIT was a holy place to him, and Harvard a close second. All his dreams were coming true. She couldn't show him her dorm room, but she showed him everything else. They had dinner at the cafeteria and visited the library and the student union, and then she took him back to Harvard. He kissed her before she left him alone to settle in, and finally get some sleep. It was two in the morning for him by then, but he was too excited to sleep. He didn't want to miss anything.

He called her in her dorm half an hour later. When she got to the phone, he told her how happy he was to be there, and what it meant to him that she'd been there to help. His English was good, with a heavy accent.

"You should be asleep," she told him. She was as excited as he was.

"I'm too happy to sleep. This is the best day of my life." It was one of the best of hers too. Overnight she had become a girl who had a boyfriend. She loved him, and she loved her school. It was a gift from the Universe. After years of feeling out of place and misunderstood, she finally had a man who cared about her and understood her, loved the same things, and didn't make her feel like a freak.

She returned the van with a delicious-looking chocolate cake to thank its owner, and rode her bike over to Harvard in the morning to have breakfast with him. She had given him the map so he could find where his classes were, and he was reading it diligently.

"It's too bad you can't take classes with me," he said wistfully when she got up to leave.

"You're four years ahead of me." She laughed at him. He always looked disheveled and surprised and excited about life. She could tell he hadn't bothered to brush his hair when he got up, and she loved the way he looked. There was a touching innocence about him, and such a bright mind.

"I'm sure you could follow along if you tried," he said confidently. He had great faith in her and a profound respect for how smart she was.

He bought a bike during his lunchtime, and came to see her at MIT that afternoon, after her last class. They had dinner together at a little deli on campus and he thought the food was delicious. Everything pleased and delighted him, especially her. And he thought her sexy and even more beautiful with her new look. She was beginning to understand him and know him through their letters and now in person. He was one of those people who saw the bright side of everything, and the good in all, which made it a pleasure to be with him, instead of the people who complained all the time, like her sister, or even her parents, who were good to her and well-meaning, but judged everyone by how rich they were, or what they had and how they looked. Raphael looked a mess, his sweatshirt was faded and torn, his jeans had holes in them, his sneakers ancient, but he was the best person she had ever met.

When Sam came home from Long Island on Labor Day night, she'd had a nice weekend but was happy to be back. Her father was in his study, going over some papers on his desk. She stopped in to give him a hug. He was happy to see her, and smiled as soon as she walked into the room. She thought he looked tired, but he was in a good mood. She hadn't seen him in a week, since before his trip to San Francisco. She had left for Long Island on Friday, and he had returned that night.

"Did you have a nice weekend, Dad?" She hoped he wasn't too lonely. She had hesitated about going to Long Island. She felt guilty leaving him alone.

"Very," he answered, and didn't elaborate. There were some things he didn't share with her, but not many. In his mind she was still a child, and he was protective of his relationship with Jane, and would be even more so now.

"Does that mean you worked all weekend, or had some fun?" she teased him. He had told her he was staying in the city, and not going to the farm, which had surprised her. He liked going there whenever he could.

"A little of both," he said noncommittally. "What about you? Good weekend?"

"Nice." But it was always comfortable to get home, and she already had a paper due that week. "I missed you." It touched him when she said it, and he wondered when he and Jane should tell their girls what was happening. Not yet. It was too soon, and he wanted to savor the ecstasy with Jane first. But eventually, they would tell them. He had a dreamy look in his eyes when he thought about her, and Sam smiled as she left his study to unpack. "Get some rest, Dad, you look a little tired." She assumed he had worked hard in San Francisco. It didn't cross her mind for a second that there could be another reason. Robert and Jane had slept little during the weekend and had put the time to good use. He smiled as Sam went to her room.

As soon as she got there, she called Amelia in her dorm. She was out of breath when she got to the phone. She had run from her room to take the call at the phone in the dorm hallway. She had talked to Willie earlier before his flight took off, and she thought he was calling back to say it was delayed. She was startled that it was Sam and not Willie.

"Tell me everything," Sam said, and Amelia laughed. It was a happy sound, full of guilt and delight. She was still on a cloud after their weekend. She knew it was wrong to have slept with him, they weren't married, but it felt so right too. He had protected her all weekend, so she wouldn't get pregnant.

"I'm standing in my dorm hallway," Amelia reminded her.

"Damn," Sam said, frustrated. "Was it great?"

"Better than that. It was as close to Heaven as I'll ever get."

"Oh my God! You did it! Amelia, you're insane."

"I didn't say that!" Amelia corrected her. "It was wonderful, that's all."

"You didn't have to say it. You sound drunk."

"I'm not. I'm just happy." She lowered her voice so the entire hallway and girls walking by didn't hear her. "He's just a wonderful person. He's as terrific as I thought." She had had the faint worry that it would be different or disappointing when she saw him again. Communicating by letters and telegrams wasn't the same. Quentin called Sam almost every day, but he could afford to, Willie couldn't.

But he had turned out to be even better and more loving than she had remembered and dared to hope. Sam was happy for her. Amelia loved talking to her about him, because she had met him, and he was real to her.

"When is he coming back?" Sam asked her.

"He isn't. It was a big deal for him to come this time. I'm going to try to save as much of my allowance as I can and go over during Christmas break. I might ask my mom to help me, as part of my Christmas gift. I'd go right after Christmas." It was more than three months away, and her heart ached thinking about it, but it was the best they could do. She had another idea that she wanted to explore and suggest to him. But she needed her mother's permission to do it, and she didn't want to ask her yet. Listening to her, Sam realized how lucky she herself was, she could do almost anything she wanted and money wasn't an issue. Her father was incredibly generous, and it wasn't a problem for them. She knew from Amelia that she and her mother had to be careful, and money had been very tight for them for the past six months. Quentin was discreet about it, and financing things wasn't an issue for him either, but he had a job and couldn't just take off whenever he wanted. He said he didn't have vacation days available until November, which seemed like a lifetime away to them. So, she and Amelia were in the same boat, with men they loved, far away in another country.

Sometimes Sam wondered if it would kill their relationships in the end. But Quentin said they just had to be patient and adult about it.

"When can I see you so we can talk?" Sam asked her.

"Next weekend for dinner?" Amelia suggested.

"Why don't you come to Greenwich for the weekend? We're going next week."

"I'd love to. I have to check with my mom. I ditched her all weekend, and she's lonely on the weekends. I felt kind of bad, but I told her I was busy. She's nice about it, but she probably had a pretty awful few days. I may have to spend it with her, or part of it anyway. I'll let you know."

"Ask her to come with us. That'll keep my dad busy so we can talk. They get along, and she might enjoy it. My dad likes her, and you and I will have plenty of time to talk." It sounded like a very effective way to kill several birds with one stone, for the two girls to be together, and meet family obligations too. "I'll ask my dad," Sam said, "and then you can ask her. I'm sure he'll say yes. I hope she doesn't just want you to herself, and want you to stay in the city," Sam said.

"She likes spending time with you guys, and she loves the farm." They hung up a minute later. Two other dorm residents were waiting for the phone, and Amelia apologized and went back to her room, happy with the plan.

Sam went back to her father's study a few minutes later.

Robert was still there, putting his papers back in his briefcase to take to the office the next day. He looked up when Sam walked back into the room. She stumbled for a second in the doorway, and then steadied herself. She had been a lot better recently. The stumbling was happening less often.

She got right to the point. "Can we have Amelia and her mom come to Greenwich next weekend?" she asked bluntly, and he looked up with a schoolboy grin Sam paid no attention to and didn't even notice.

"Sure. Of course. Whose idea was it?" He was curious what Jane might have said to her daughter.

"Mine. I invited Amelia for the weekend, and she feels bad about leaving her mother. She said she gets lonely on the weekends, and she didn't see her this week. Amelia was busy, so she thought she should see her next week." It amused him how little she knew about them, or imagined.

"Sounds like a great idea," he said blithely. "Put her mom in the big guesthouse. It's a little farther away from the main house, but it'll be more comfortable for her. Amelia can stay with you in your room, as she did before." He had it all worked out. It was perfect. The girls were playing right into their hands. He couldn't wait to tell Jane.

"Okay," Sam agreed. "You guys can play cards or talk or something, and Amelia and I can hang out. Maybe you can take her mom riding."

"We'll figure something out, to stay out of your hair," he teased her.

"Thanks, Dad," she said, and went back to her room, as he sat at his desk smiling after she left. He called Jane and told her, and she laughed too.

"Those two could run the world. It sounds perfect."

He lowered his voice. "I'm going to put you in the guest-house, not in the main house, so I can be there with you, and sneak back to the house before the girls get up. They sleep late anyway," and he was an early riser. It was a perfect idea.

And Sam didn't tell him that Willie Brockhall had just visited Amelia for the weekend. She didn't want her father getting nervous about Quentin. He was uneasy about her phone romance with a man three thousand miles away. She knew that her father was hoping she'd lose interest in him, but she was more in love with Quentin every day. And her father didn't need the reminder of Amelia's romance, and that long-distance relationships did work out sometimes. She was going to tell Amelia to be discreet about Willie's visit too.

The weekend in Greenwich at the Walkers' farm turned out even better than Robert had hoped, once Sam told him about the plan. Jane stayed in the guesthouse farthest from the main house. As soon as the girls went to Sam's bedroom at night, where Amelia was sleeping with her in her giant king-sized bed, Robert slipped quietly out the back door, and walked across a field down a narrow path, and joined Jane for the night. They slept and made love and watched the sun come up together. She made breakfast for him, and they went on a sunrise ride. He gave her a very docile horse, and he took her to the far reaches of the property. They were closer day by day, and the girls spent very little time with them, except at meals. They wanted to be alone to speak freely about the men in their lives without their mother and father within hearing distance.

The weekend became a model for them to follow in future, and met all their needs, Jane and Robert's to spend time with their respective daughters and still be together, and even sleep in the same guesthouse on weekends. The far guesthouse became their weekend love nest, and the girls never suspected anything.

Jane and Robert talked about it one day.

"We have to say something to them at some point. I don't want them to feel that we lied to them for months when we finally do tell them," Jane said. But they also liked keeping their romance to themselves. It made it more private and more special, but they also knew that they were walking a fine line with their daughters' trust in future. The right time to tell them hadn't become clear to them yet. Sometimes Jane wondered if it ever would.

# Chapter 15

Halloween was fun on all their campuses. Amelia at Columbia, Sam at NYU even as a nonresident student, Raphael at Harvard as a graduate student, and Felicity at MIT all wore costumes and went to parties, and ate trick-or-treat candy, except for Felicity, who had lost another ten pounds, and was within nine pounds of her goal and refused to do anything to jeopardize it. They all had fun. And Caroline sent them all a picture of herself in the original costume of the witch in *The Wizard of Oz,* complete with green face and pointy hat. Her mother had borrowed it from the studio, and Caroline had won a prize at USC for Best Costume and Best Makeup.

She said she was doing well, and told the girls that she wasn't dating anyone and didn't want to. She was working hard at getting off academic probation and putting all her effort into that, and thought she'd be off probably by Christmas. She said she was hoping to come to New York either during Christmas break or in February, and wanted to see them all then. Sam said she thought she sounded very serious, but she'd had a hard experience with Adam. They didn't know about the rest, but she had been very subdued in her correspondence to them after the ball. Felicity was the closest to her after spending time with her at the Hotel du Cap. But they were all looking forward to seeing her whenever she came to New York.

Raphael had particularly enjoyed Halloween, because it was all new to him since it wasn't celebrated in France. He had come up with a very creative costume, as a foreign student at Princeton. He had worn a Princeton T-shirt he found at a garage sale, wore a blazer and a tie with it, and gray flannel slacks he bought secondhand, slicked down his hair to look remarkably preppy, and carried a life-sized plush tiger around with him, with his face painted like the French flag in blue, white, and red stripes. It made everyone who saw him laugh, and those who didn't know him thought he was putting on the French accent, which made it even funnier because it was real. Felicity went as Superwoman with curves in all the right places for the first time in her life. She was thrilled with her new figure and showed it off in a leotard from her ballet class, which she was doing for exercise now instead of track and enjoying a lot more. And Raphael was enjoying her new look too, and was happy to eat all the candy people gave her that she refused to touch.

He had a little trouble getting the blue, white, and red face paint off the next day, particularly the blue he'd used, which turned out to be waterproof and hard to remove, and half his face looked bruised when he went to class, and his physics professor asked him if he'd gotten in a fight and been punched in the face for wearing the Princeton costume, which delighted Raphael. He was thoroughly enjoying his American experience, and he and Felicity were together as much as possible, biking between their two campuses, even when it snowed.

The day after Halloween, Quentin called Samantha, and she told him all about the party she went to, dressed as Minnie Mouse, and he explained to her that the first of November was All Saints' Day, a holiday in France, so he had the day off from the law firm where he worked. He said he had good news, and told her he had a week's vacation coming up in three weeks, and he wanted to come and visit her. She was thrilled when she heard the news, and then did a quick calculation. Thanksgiving fell in the week he wanted to come, and she wasn't sure how her father would feel about it.

It was an important day to them, and having no other family except each other, they usually spent the holiday at the farm alone. Holidays were still hard for her father, even fourteen years after her mother and brother's deaths.

"Could you come a week earlier or later?" she asked, and sounding disappointed, he said he couldn't. He had to take the week he'd been assigned.

"I'll ask my dad tonight," she promised. She would have preferred a time when they could buffer his presence a little, and include others. Having Quentin visit her for a week would make it very clear to her father how serious they were about each other, and she had a feeling he wouldn't be pleased.

She broached the subject with Robert that night at dinner, with delicacy and caution.

"I spoke to Quentin today," she started gingerly, and her father smiled.

"That's not an unusual occurrence," he said, tolerant as long as Quentin was three thousand miles away. He was still expecting them to lose interest in each other, but that hadn't happened yet.

"He's planning to come to the States," she said, pushing peas and mashed potatoes around her plate with her fork.

"For work? He must be doing well at the law firm, if they're sending him out on international work," he said.

"Actually, he's coming on vacation," she said in a small voice, and her father looked directly at her.

"Is he coming to see you?" Robert asked her, as his eyes bore into hers like fact-finding lasers.

"He might be . . . yes, actually, he is." She waited for the storm to break, and it didn't. There was a long silence at the table.

"What are you asking me, Sam?" He could tell there was more to it, and she was always open and honest with him.

"The only time he can come is Thanksgiving week, and I'd like to see him." Robert didn't answer her for what seemed like an eternity, while he weighed the pros and cons of his decision as quickly as he could. If he refused to let Sam see Quentin, he knew it would heighten their romance, and he had no real objection to him, except that at twenty-seven, he was a man, not a boy, and he lived in Paris, three thousand miles away, and Robert didn't want to lose his daughter to him. But stopping her, or trying to, would only make it worse. In an instant, he decided to put the outcome in the hands of the Fates.

"Would you like him to join us for Thanksgiving?" he asked her, and she nodded.

"Yes, Dad, I would." The look of love in her eyes, for another man, and the trust he also saw of her father melted his heart and touched him profoundly.

"Then ask him to join us. Explain to him that it's an important American holiday about family, and welcoming others at our Thanksgiving table. He's welcome to spend it with us." Quentin had already told her that he would stay at a hotel, so it was not a question of asking to have him stay at the house, which would have made Quentin uncomfortable too. She felt a rush of gratitude toward her father for his answer, jumped up from her seat, and went to hug him.

"Thank you, Dad, it really means a lot to me, and will to him too." That was precisely what Robert was afraid of, as he expressed to Jane when he saw her later that night, when he went to her apartment for a glass of wine and to make love to her.

"She's serious about him," he said to Jane, as they lay in bed afterwards, talking about it.

"I think she is," Jane agreed with him. It had been going on for almost four months now, since the ball. "Amelia is serious about Willie too, but fortunately neither can afford to think about marriage. It's very different in Quentin and Sam's case." She agreed with Robert now, there was serious risk there. Robert had discovered that Quentin's family was very wealthy, and Quentin had a good job at the law firm that employed him.

"I hope he's not coming with anything serious in mind and it's just a visit. Maybe it'll cool off when they see each other," but he didn't believe that and neither did Jane now. It sounded serious to her too. "They'll want to do things in the city while he visits, so I guess we won't do Thanksgiving at the farm this year. Would you and Amelia want to join us for Thanksgiving? I've been meaning to ask you anyway." He rolled over on his side in her always-welcoming bed and kissed her. There was nowhere on earth he'd rather be now. Their affair had gone on for two months.

"We'd love it," Jane responded. "It wouldn't be an intrusion?"

"On the contrary. It'll take some of the steam out of just Quentin being there, and Amelia knows him too. It might make things easier and more relaxed. You have a way of making things seem normal and less dramatic."

"We would love to be there." She answered for Amelia too, and knew she would be thrilled with the invitation, rather than just dinner with her mother, which wasn't much fun by comparison.

He told Sam the next day that he had invited the Alexanders, and she was as delighted as he knew she would be.

Thanksgiving was over three weeks away, and Quentin and Sam were counting the days until they would see each other again. It gave the holiday this year much greater meaning to Sam, and Robert was facing it with trepidation and a chill running down his spine each time he thought of it.

* * *

Felicity made the decision the week before Thanksgiving. She'd been mulling it over for a month. It was a bold move she would have never dared to do before, but it was something she knew she had to do for her own mental health and personal growth. Raphael had something to do with it, but it wasn't because of him. But his being with her would make it easier. The worst part would be telling them, but she knew she had to do it. She and Raphael were lovers now. They had both been virgins, and she knew she had grown up in the past few months, ever since she decided that she didn't care what her sister did or said anymore. She had started to lose the weight after that. She had decided not to let any more poison into her body, through her mouth or her ears. Araminta was just too toxic to be around.

She called her mother a week before Thanksgiving and told her she wasn't coming home this year. She didn't say the decision was forever, but in her mind it was. But one year at a time would be easier for her parents to accept. Her mother was shocked when she told her, and then she cried, which made Felicity feel terrible. But it was either them or her this time, and she had decided to do what was best for herself, for the first time in her life. She had always done what they wanted her to do, and they had never protected her from her sister in nineteen years.

"I can't come home, Mom," she said. "I can't sit there and

listen to her and let her insult me and be rude to me and degrade me. You can't stop her. I see that now. She's too old to punish. It's better for me to stay here. I'll be fine, Mom. And you will be too. You won't have to worry all day about what she's going to do or say, or if she's going to ruin Thanksgiving for all of us by beating me up."

"That's terrible," Charlene said, still crying. "What will you do for Thanksgiving? You should be home with your family." Felicity didn't want to say that she had no family, and the way hers behaved was not how she wanted to spend the holiday.

"They do a big Thanksgiving dinner for all the students who stay here, all the international students, and a lot of the ones from around the country who can't afford to go home."

"I can send the plane for you," Charlene said, missing the point entirely, as usual.

"I don't want the plane, Mom, and I don't want to come home. It's not your fault, or Dad's, or about you." But it was about them, and how little they had understood her and not defended or protected her enough. And now, she wanted to be in Boston with Raphael, and not with them. It felt good to be free from the pain she knew she would have to endure if she went home. And she wasn't even overweight anymore. She only had five pounds left to lose. It had never been about her weight, it turned out, it had always been about how much her sister hated her, which her parents chose to ignore and which they thought would fix itself. It hadn't. And now Felicity needed to do what was good for her. Being with them wasn't it.

"I'll talk to you soon, Mom," she said, and got off the phone as quickly as she could, before it degenerated into a long discussion about what was wrong with their family, and how it would change. It wouldn't, she knew that now.

"Did you tell them?" Raphael asked her when she saw him that night.

"Yes, I did," she said, smiling at him. She felt lighter than air. And she was happy with him. The heavy burden she had carried for so many years, her sister's jealousy and viciousness, had been lifted from her, and she had shed it like her excess weight. "I love you," she said, and put her arms around his neck. They made love in his room, because the rules were different at Harvard for graduate students, and his room there was their love nest. It was home to her now, and he was her family now, the only one she wanted at the moment. And best of all, she knew that she could take care of herself.

Quentin arrived in New York on the Saturday before Thanksgiving, and checked in to the Mark Hotel. It was a small, trendy, chic hotel where a lot of Europeans stayed, close to the Walkers' home, and he had stayed there before and liked it. He was nervous and excited to see Samantha, and had been wide awake for the whole flight, thinking about what he was going to say to her, what it would be like seeing her again. He had never been seriously in love before, and it made everything that happened between them seem more important. He wanted to do it right, and he knew that her father was worried about her. He was eager to have Robert meet his parents so he could see that Quentin had a solid family. He was sure their fathers would get along, they were both powerful businessmen, used to getting their own way. He was glad that his parents had met Sam, and approved of her. They thought he was young to be so serious, and she was even more so, but they had faith in his judgment, and respected how much he loved her. They had dealt with their own parents' disapproval, and wouldn't do that to him. It would cause damage that could never be repaired later. They genuinely liked Sam, and found her mature for her age.

Quentin called her from his room at the hotel, and it was thrilling to know that she was only a few blocks and not an ocean away.

"When can I see you?" he asked, breathless with anticipation and excitement.

She was just as excited as he was. "Now, if you want. Do you want to come over, or should I meet you at the hotel? Are you hungry? They have a good restaurant at the Mark." She had lunch there sometimes, or she and her father went to dinner there when their cook was off. "Or we can go for a walk, and then come back here and have something to eat. My dad is in Connecticut for the weekend. He'll be back tomorrow night."

"I want to say hello to him of course."

"He figured we'd be busy. Why don't I come meet you, and we can go for a walk, unless you want to eat first."

"That sounds great, I'll meet you downstairs in twenty minutes. I'll just take a quick shower and change. And Sam, can't wait to see you."

"Me too." His English was flawless, and he was relieved to hear that her father was out of town and he had a reprieve for a day before he had to see him. He was happy to be alone with her for the next two days and to get used to each other again. Talking on the phone was different than being able to put his arms around her.

Robert was in Greenwich with Jane, and Amelia was studying in the library at Barnard. The girls still knew nothing about them. Robert was as nervous about seeing Quentin as Quentin was about seeing him. Jane was trying to calm him down and thought the weekend at the farm would do him good. The cook was off, and Jane was staying in the main house with him. It was nice being there alone without the girls, which was rare.

\* \* \*

When Quentin got to the lobby, Sam wasn't there yet. He was wearing a blazer and slacks and a warm topcoat, he wanted to look respectable for her. He walked outside into the chill November air, glanced toward the park, and saw her walking toward him in a sure steady gait, with just the slightest hitch to it. She was wearing a fluffy pale blue mohair coat, and a white cashmere knitted hat, and she smiled when she spotted him, and he walked rapidly toward her. He reached her first, and pulled her into his arms and held her tight and then he kissed her. His kiss told her everything that he was too moved to say. He couldn't stop smiling and kissing her, and then they walked slowly toward the park. It was a cold, sunny day, and the park looked beautiful. The last of the red leaves were falling off the trees, and the city was alive with energy. The atmosphere was contagious, as she tucked her hand into his arm, and they walked through the park, and then looped around and came back to her house. She had seen how beautiful his home was, so she wasn't embarrassed to have him see hers, no matter how imposing it was. She took him upstairs to the library, and there was a fire lit. They took off their coats and he took her in his arms again.

"Do you have any idea how much I love you?" he whispered to her. "You are the love of my life." They were soulmates. They both felt it, and she felt peaceful and full of joy with him. It was a light feeling, like floating. She felt like a Chagall painting come to life, with a happy couple flying through the sky with the moon and stars, and often the woman was a bride. And then she realized that she felt like a bride with him. She already felt married to him even though she had hardly seen him. But she knew that she was already his.

They sat by the fire for a long time, talking and drinking tea, and then they made dinner from what was in the refrigerator, since the cook and much of the staff were off, with her father away for the weekend. Quentin lived in a big house too, although hers was bigger and more daunting, but he seemed totally at ease, and it was nice to be alone at last, and see him in person after four months apart.

They cuddled on the couch in the library again after dinner, and then he admitted he was tired, and he left her to walk the few blocks back to the hotel. He was lost in thought, thinking about her.

He didn't try to take advantage of the fact that her father was away, or ask to sleep with her and see her bedroom. He was saving her for something much more important and didn't want to spoil it. He wanted it to be right in every way.

He could barely tear himself away from her when he left, and she closed the door softly behind him, and walked up the stairs with a smile on her face, his kisses still fresh on her lips.

* * *

Quentin and Sam ran all over New York, doing all the things he wanted to do. They went shopping, went to museums, visited galleries, walked all through the city. She spent every moment with him she could. She had no school that week so she was free, and on Monday night, Quentin had dinner with her and her father at the house. It went better than Sam had dared to hope, Quentin was serious and respectful. He paid homage to the deep love he knew Robert had for his daughter, and he invited Robert to lunch the next day. Her father had been impressed by that too. He had suggested the "21" Club, which Robert liked. She was startled when Quentin invited him, and Quentin told her afterwards it was the correct thing to do, since Robert had invited him to join them on a major holiday. It was the only way he could reciprocate, and show his gratitude.

When she met Quentin later that afternoon after his lunch with her father, she asked him what they had talked about, and he said business mostly, politics, venture capital. "Men things," he told her, and she made a face.

"Don't be such a grown-up," but seeing more of him, she could tell that he was. He was a man, not a boy, and he behaved like one. Later, Robert told her that Quentin was a very fine young man. She felt as though they were in collusion against her and was annoyed.

"Don't treat me like a child," she complained to Quentin,

but he didn't, he treated her like a woman he loved. She could sense that he was someone she could count on, like her father. She hadn't known what to expect from Quentin when he first arrived. She had guessed that Amelia had slept with Willie when he was there. But he was a different kind of man, and in some ways still a boy. Amelia was still hoping to see Willie after Christmas but hadn't saved all the money for the ticket yet, so it was still up in the air. But Sam and Quentin had talked about sleeping together, and he didn't want them to do something they would regret later. He wanted to do things right, and they spent hours kissing, but he wouldn't go to bed with her. She wasn't sure what she would have done if he had pressed her to, but she felt even more comfortable knowing that he wouldn't, even though at times it was hard for them to resist.

The Thanksgiving meal they shared with Jane and Amelia was beautiful and perfect in every way. Quentin was a perfect gentleman, and told some funny stories once he felt comfortable in the group. Robert said grace at the beginning of the meal and they talked about all the things they were grateful for. The food was superb, in an all-American style. The turkey was perfect, the stuffing was exceptional, and there were three different kinds. There were also cranberry jelly, creamed spinach and string beans, mashed potatoes and gravy, and popovers, which Sam always loved. And after the meal, Robert and Jane sat by the fire and talked, and the young people played cards and shrieked with laughter and accused each other of cheating. It was a wonderful, warm family day, and everything Thanksgiving was meant to be.

Sam had shown Quentin when he arrived that she wore his angel necklace every day. Finally, Jane and Amelia went home, and Quentin left with them. He was coming back in the morning, to take Sam to see the tree at Rockefeller Center. It had been decorated, but wasn't due to be lit for another week, so Quentin would miss it, but Sam wanted him to see the tree anyway.

"Thank you for a beautiful Thanksgiving, Dad," Sam said to her father as they walked up the stairs to their rooms. Her father was quiet, and he put an arm around her and kissed her, and there was something very bittersweet about it. She had the feeling that he was missing her mother, but she didn't ask. And at least Jane was good company for him as a friend. "And thank you for letting me have Quentin, and Amelia and her mom." He nodded and walked to his room with a slow smile.

She was ready when Quentin picked her up at eleven o'clock the next morning. He was flying back to Paris on Sunday, so they had two more days together, and no plans to see each other again. But she was grateful for the time they had now.

The tree at Rockefeller Center was majestic and beautifully decorated, and the skating rink below it was crowded. Watching them always made Sam wish she could still skate, she had loved it as a little girl and used to go skating with her mother. But those were memories best left undisturbed. She didn't want to be sad. Being with Quentin made her happy, and she wanted to keep it that way.

"Do you want to light a candle in church?" he asked in front of St. Patrick's, and she hadn't thought of it, but she liked the idea. She always went to midnight mass with her father on Christmas Eve and lit candles then.

They walked into the vast cathedral together and stopped at a bank of candles. Quentin put money in for both of them. Sam lit candles for her mother and brother, her father and Quentin, and turned to see Quentin looking at her tenderly.

"Will you marry me, Samantha?" he said softly, and she stared at him. At first, she thought she must have heard him wrong.

"Are you serious?" she whispered back, as the candles lit their faces and she looked beautiful with her titian hair, it looked like burnished gold.

"Yes, I am," Quentin smiled at her.

"Don't you have to ask my father first?"

"I asked him at lunch, and he said yes. I love you, Sam. Will you be my wife?" She opened and closed her mouth, too overwhelmed to speak for a minute, and then she nodded and threw her arms around him, and he kissed her and held her tight. "I promise to love and protect you and keep you safe for the rest of my life," he added, and there were tears rolling down her cheeks when she answered him.

"Yes, yes, I love you and I'll protect you too." She hadn't expected it, and he took a small dark red velvet box out of his pocket. The box looked very old, and he opened it, and she saw an antique diamond ring, with a large round stone in the center, and her eyes met his in amazement.

"It was my grandmother's, the one who gave me the angel necklace you're wearing. She would have wanted you to have this too." Quentin's mother had given it to him before he left Paris, when he told her what he intended to do in New York. He had his parents' blessing and her father's. He slipped the ring on Sam's finger, and it fit perfectly. His grandmother had had small delicate hands like Sam. She stood staring at it in astonishment and kissed him again.

"Oh my God," she said, looking at him. "I'm engaged! When are we getting married?" She hadn't even thought about what it meant yet. And she realized then why he didn't want to sleep with her. He wanted to do everything right and wait until they were married.

"I was thinking next summer, a year after the ball where we met." It was eight months away, but it would take that long to plan the wedding. "Your father said it's up to you, whether you want to get married in Connecticut, or in the city. There will be a lot of details to think about," and as he said it, her eyes filled with tears and he pulled her close to him.

"I miss my mom," she whispered. "I just realized I don't have a mom to help me plan a wedding, or shop for a dress, or help me get dressed." He held her for a long time, in the peace of the church, thinking of the future and the past, and then they walked out of St. Patrick's into the sunlight, with his arm around her, holding her steady as they walked down the cathedral steps, engaged.

# Chapter 16

Christmas was incredibly hectic, more so than usual. Once Sam and Quentin were engaged, Robert sent the notice to *The New York Times*. The focus leapt immediately to the following summer, there was much to talk about and decide. They picked the date. They were getting married on the eleventh of July. The ball at Versailles had been on July twelfth. It was Quentin's suggestion and seemed like a good one. Sam wanted to get married at her home in the city. Her parents had given parties in their home for two hundred, with seated dinners and dancing, but she and Quentin didn't want that many guests. Without her mother present, Sam wanted a smaller wedding and they were trying to keep it to a hundred. They both had small families, and wanted to keep it intimate. And Jane had delicately offered to help Sam with the wedding details that her mother might have done otherwise. Sam was grateful to accept her offer. She had no female relatives to advise her.

Amelia was stunned by the news of the engagement when Sam told her. Sam called Felicity and Caroline, and they were thrilled for her. She was the first of the debs in their little group to get engaged. Felicity and Raphael had years of studies ahead of them, before they could think about marriage, maybe in their late twenties or early thirties. They didn't mind waiting. Caroline was still feeling gun-shy after Adam and hadn't started dating yet. Adam had broken up very publicly with Fay Mallon, and had called Caroline, but she didn't want to see him again, and hadn't returned his calls. She knew she would date again and meet the right man one day, but not yet. She wasn't ready, and was concentrating on school. She had just come off academic probation at USC.

"I'll be a hundred years old before Willie and I can ever get engaged," Amelia said wistfully to Sam. "We'll be too poor to get married, unless he gets a better job and I'm a success as a lawyer. And that's years away. It'll be ten years from now if we're lucky." She was beginning to understand now what her mother had meant by wanting her to fall in love with a man of means. But she hadn't fallen in love with a rich man. She was in love with Willie, and they had to make the best of it and be creative. Even seeing each other was a challenge. She had managed to scrape together almost enough money to pay for a ticket to London, and her mother had given her the rest. She was flying the day after Christmas. She could hardly wait to see him. She hadn't seen him since Labor Day. She was spending a week with him, and he was planning to come to New York in the summer. It had taken time to convince her mother, but Jane had agreed to let Amelia apply for her junior year abroad, and do it in London, which meant that she and Willie would be together for an entire school year, if she was accepted in the available programs in London that Columbia approved of for credit. It was their only hope of being together, and it was still nine months away. It made their week together after Christmas even more precious. She wouldn't know about whether she'd been accepted for her junior year in London until February. Their life together was a waiting game between visits, with five more years of school ahead of her.

Robert and Sam were flying to Paris the day after Christmas too. Robert wanted to meet Quentin's parents. He was only planning to stay for a few days, and planned to be back in New York in time to spend New Year's Eve with Jane. They were going to the farm to celebrate quietly. Sam was staying in Paris for ten days with Quentin and his parents, to continue to solidify their plans. Sam had promised her father that she

# Danielle Steel

would graduate from college, and she would be living with Quentin in Paris for her last two years of school. She was going to transfer to the Sorbonne, and do her junior and senior years there, and she had to apply when she went over now. And Quentin wanted to look for an apartment with her. There was so much to do.

"Your mother did two years of college in Paris," Robert reminded Sam, which made it sound more familiar, and she had a feeling her mother would have liked that idea for her. It was all falling into place, and she and Jane were going to shop for wedding dresses when she got back from Paris. Sam had asked Amelia to be her maid of honor, and Felicity and Caroline to be her bridesmaids. She felt closer to them now than her old friends from school. And she hadn't gotten very close to her classmates at NYU as she didn't live in the dorms and wasn't part of the campus social life, since she went home every night. And now she was going to live with her husband in Paris. Quentin was going to continue looking for an apartment for them in the spring if they didn't find one when she was in Paris. And she'd probably have to go back again, for the apartment and transferring schools. Quentin's bachelor pad was just too small. It was a lot to think about, with calls back and forth to Paris every day to discuss it.

Sam spent Christmas Eve with her father as she always did, and Jane and Amelia visited them on Christmas Day.

348

Jane was looking very chic these days, now that she worked for a magazine, and the job was as exciting as she had hoped it would be, and Pascale had promised it would. It was an exciting, invigorating, creative atmosphere. She loved working with Pascale. She was a wonderful teacher, mentor, work partner, and friend.

When they came to visit on Christmas Day, Amelia was excited about her trip to London to see Willie. She was leaving the next day. She had lost weight from all the meals she didn't eat and saved the money to pay for her ticket to England.

Willie was going to take her to Brockhall Manor while she was there, so she would finally see it, and meet his parents and brother. Willie had warned her to bring "woolies" and warm clothes since there was no heating in the Dower House, only what was provided by the fireplaces. He had booked a small room for her in a hotel he knew in London, where she could get messages from her mother if necessary, but she was staying at his flat with him. Sam envied her that, but she knew that her visit to Quentin's parents would be respectful and supervised, and she wouldn't have the freedom or the experiences that Amelia did. But she was getting married, and Amelia wasn't. They each had their lives to pursue in the best way they could.

\* \* \*

When Amelia landed at Heathrow airport, Willie was waiting for her, and hugged her so tight she couldn't breathe. "Good God, woman, I thought you'd never get here. It's been nearly four months," but she was there now, and they were going to live every moment to the fullest. They raced home from the airport. His flat in Notting Hill was small and charming, with books stacked everywhere and a friendly mess, and five minutes after she got there, they were in bed, making up for lost time. All she could do was pray now that she'd be accepted to do her junior year abroad in London. They would have a whole nine months together then. All she wanted was to be in London with him now. They could hardly wait.

When Sam and her father got to Paris on the same day Amelia arrived in London, they stayed at the George V again. They were invited to the Duponts' for dinner that night, and Quentin took Sam to his apartment for a glass of champagne first, and they almost wound up in bed making love, but he came to his senses before anything dramatic happened and forced himself to stop. The next seven months until their wedding were going to be the longest in his life, but he knew that respecting her was the right thing to do, whether she wanted him to or not, and some of the time, she didn't. He was already discovering that she was much more hot-blooded than her cool, shy, reserved demeanor suggested. It promised delights and surprises for their honeymoon, and a lot of cold showers until then.

The dinner with Sam's father and Quentin's parents went well, even better than the engaged couple had hoped. The two fathers had many interests in common, centered around business, and Quentin's mother was lovely to Sam. She treated Sam like a daughter of her own. They assured Robert that they would all take good care of her. He admitted that he was planning to visit her often, and they said that he would always be welcome. It went better than anyone could have hoped. And he left two days later, to meet Jane in New York. They went straight to the farm in Connecticut the day after his return, and he admitted to her how sad he was that Sam would be living in Paris, no matter how nice Quentin and his family were. He was happy for Sam, but nostalgic about losing her. The house and his life would be empty without her.

"I'm going to be in the same boat with Amelia," Jane said. "Unless something changes. As soon as they can afford to, she'll be married to Willie and living in England. If they're still together, she'll want to move to London when she graduates. And she'll be there for junior year next year. She's almost gone now. She literally starved for the last four months so she could pay for a ticket to see him. I finally gave her some money for the trip before she disappeared entirely."

Going to the farm in Greenwich with Jane was like going home. She was familiar to Robert now, and provided peace and joy in his life. After four months together, it felt more natural to be together than apart, and his house seemed empty and lonely without her now whenever she left to go to her own apartment, when Sam was around. He still thought of his late wife at times, but he finally had a sense of peace about her, as though she was in a tranquil place and wished him well. It had been a long time coming and freed him to build a life with Jane. A life which their daughters remained completely unaware of. Robert was still zealously guarding their secret. He didn't want anything to disrupt his life with Jane, and he was afraid that one of their daughters might object. But Sam was focused on her wedding, and Amelia on getting to England whenever she could to see Willie, and Jane didn't think that either of the girls would cause a problem for them. Robert wanted to wait and tell them after Sam's wedding. And after that, Sam would be in Paris, and presumably Amelia in England for a year, and they couldn't interfere with them. It was going to be a long wait until they told them. Jane left the decision up to Robert.

They saw the New Year in with champagne at the farm, and then went to bed right after midnight. The pleasure they shared grew daily, as their love for each other deepened, and he never said it, but in some ways Jane suited him better than Diana had. They had more common interests, and she was wonderful to Samantha. And Jane was fulfilled and enjoying her job.

The months between January and July flew by. In January, as soon as Sam got back from Paris, Jane and Sam found the perfect wedding dress for her. It remained a dark secret and was kept locked in one of the guestrooms in Robert's house. It was the most beautiful dress Sam had ever seen.

In February, Amelia was accepted to do her junior year abroad in London, for credit at Barnard, which was a huge relief to her and Willie. They would be together for nine months until she returned to New York for her senior year. And then they would be apart again.

In March, Quentin found an apartment in the 7th arrondissement overlooking the Seine, and in April, Sam went to visit it, and she loved it. She had much to decide with him about how to decorate it, which took several weeks to organize and make the first decisions about their home.

By April, all the wedding plans were set, everything was decided, ordered, and in place. In May, the invitations went out. It was official, for real. Sam had picked out the bridesmaids' dresses at Saks, in the palest blush pink that looked beautiful on all three girls, and they would be carrying bouquets of roses the same color. Caroline asked if she

Danielle Steel

could bring a date to the wedding. She was dating a doctor in LA, a young plastic surgeon, and she sounded very happy. He was fifteen years older, but her parents liked him and didn't object.

Jane was going over the lists of menus from the caterer with intense precision one weekend in Connecticut when she got a call from Pascale, her boss at *Chic*. It was ten o'clock at night.

"I've made a decision," Pascale said with determination. Jane waited for what would come next. She had learned by then that Pascale was somewhat impulsive, but once she made a decision, she never changed her mind. And she had her most creative inspirations late at night or on the weekends. She frequently called Jane at midnight, and once at two A.M. to tell her that she wanted to change the look of the beauty pages.

"What's the decision?" Jane asked with a smile. She loved working with Pascale and had learned a lot from her in a short time.

"I'm retiring. I want to retire while I can still travel and have fun with my husband. I never thought I'd retire at all, and I realize now that I'm missing out on time with him. Working this hard is necessary and a good thing at your age, not at mine." She sounded very definite. Jane wasn't sure whether to take her seriously or not.

354

"Pascale, you can't retire," Jane said firmly. "The magazine won't be the same without you. There's no one like you. Take a vacation, take a sabbatical, but do *not* retire."

"I've made up my mind, and picked my successor," Pascale said in her subtle but still present French accent. Jane couldn't imagine who it was. She had been this route before with a new CEO who cost her her job. "I want to leave by the end of the year. You will have my job as editor in chief. I want us to make the decisions together starting in September. Get ready. Your daughter won't be here in the fall, so you have no excuse not to take the job. It's not open to discussion," she said and hung up, and Jane looked at Robert in dismay. He had heard her side of the conversation and all he could guess was that Pascale was quitting.

"She's retiring? Maybe she's right. Did she say who's taking her place?" Jane looked unhappy. She didn't want to be CEO anymore. She liked her job as it was. Being second-in-command had its advantages. All the responsibility and headaches weren't on her shoulders.

"Me," she said, shocked about it. "I don't want all the problems that go with being CEO. I love my job the way it is now." And she loved spending time with Robert. She had time for him now.

"I have another idea," he said, smiling at her. "I have a job for you too. Full-time, overworked, underpaid, but greatly appreciated. You've done a great job with the wedding, and you've been so good to Sam. I want to offer you a job now," he said, looking smug.

"You want to hire me? As what? Event planner? Robert, I'm helping because I love you and Sam. I don't want to be a wedding planner or a party planner. You need someone young to do that. I'm not even sure I'm good at it."

"You're great at it, and you are young." She looked hesitant. She loved him immeasurably, but she didn't want to work for him. It would be too awkward. It was hard enough keeping their relationship in the closet as it was. He bent down and kissed her, as she set the menus down for the wedding. "I want you to be my wife. This craziness has gone on long enough. We've been together for nine months and known each other for ten. Sam loves you, I love you. I think Amelia likes me. I don't know why we're hiding anymore. No one is going to be upset. I want to marry you, you can plan the wedding, any place, any time, any way you want. Will you marry me, Jane?" he asked, and went down on one knee in his bedroom as she stared at him in amazement. She hadn't thought marriage was an option. They had never discussed it, only romance.

"Do you mean it?"

"Yes, I do. I should have asked you months ago." He stood up and kissed her again.

"When?" she asked him cautiously. "I can't plan two weddings at once." She was too stunned to think clearly.

"You probably could. Let's just get married quietly with the kids. I want to live with you openly, I'm tired of hiding. Will you marry me?" She was smiling, looking at him.

"Wow, yes, a marriage proposal and a job offer all in five minutes."

"You can take whatever job you want, just be my wife, Jane." He looked pleading and she put her arms around him and kissed him. "Let's do it soon. We can tell the girls tomorrow when we go back to the city."

"Are you sure?" He was moving quickly.

"Completely sure," he said, smiling. He looked ecstatic.

Jane called Sam and Amelia before it got any later and invited them to dinner the following night.

"To talk about the wedding?" Sam asked, she was swamped with the wedding and school. "I have finals next week. But I can do an early dinner tomorrow," she said. She was grateful to Jane for all she'd done for her, as much as any mother.

"And I need to talk menus with you," Jane said. "I don't think fish is a good idea, too many people are allergic." Quentin wanted sole and lobster as a main course.

Amelia was packing up her dorm room, but she promised to come for an early dinner too.

Robert was in a jovial mood all the way to the city. The girls arrived on time. Before dinner, Jane looked sheepish as she started explaining it to them, and Robert took over.

"You're in love with Quentin, Sam, and we're happy for you. We think he's a wonderful guy," and then he turned to Amelia. "And you're in love with Willie, and we like him a lot too, and we hope you two can work it out." Both girls smiled when he said it. "And we're in love too. I'm in love with your mother," he said to Amelia, "and she's in love with me," he said to Sam. "We've been sneaking around, and now we want to get married. Soon. Now. We thought you should know." He leaned over and kissed Jane. Both girls were laughing at his blunt delivery, and so was Jane. He made it simple, easy, and uncomplicated.

"Why didn't you tell us?" Sam said. She had suspected it once or twice, and then decided she was wrong. Robert and Jane had been very discreet.

"I don't even know now, maybe we were embarrassed to be in love at our age, or we thought you'd be upset, or something like that. I hope you're not upset, because we're happy," Robert said, "and we love you both immensely. We're a family already."

"When are you going to do it?" Amelia asked them. She was smiling, and happy for her mother.

"Sometime before Sam's wedding," Robert said. "Just the four of us, maybe at the farm."

"Do you want to do it at our wedding?" Sam offered generously, and she meant it.

"We don't want to steal your thunder. That's your day," Jane said definitely.

"And I don't want to wait that long," Robert added.

They managed to put it together in two weeks, and on Memorial Day weekend, on the thirtieth of May, Jane and Robert were married by a local minister at the farm. Jane wore a simple white cotton dress from Chanel and carried a bouquet of white flowers from the garden. They exchanged simple gold wedding bands. And the cook made a delicious lunch afterwards. There was no fuss and no fanfare. They said their traditional vows in front of their daughters, who were their witnesses.

Jane moved into the house the following week. Within days, it felt like she had always been there. Sam was warm and welcoming, and helped her get settled. The ripples from the ball at Versailles had spread far and even included Jane and Robert . . . Quentin and Samantha . . . Amelia and Willie . . . Raphael and Felicity . . . and who knew how many others. It was amazing to contemplate. The seeds had been planted at Versailles a year before, and one by one they were flowering. Spring was in the air.

# Chapter 17

Samantha's wedding was perfect in every way. Every detail turned out right. Her dress was a work of art with layers of organdy, a high neck, long full organdy sleeves, and a train that floated behind her, and her veil was a whisper of almost invisible tulle all around her and over her face. Robert had tears in his eyes when he saw her, and Quentin was speechless for a moment. She gracefully came down the grand staircase in their house, and she went from her father's arm to Quentin's. Robert took his place next to Jane in the front row of seats. She was wearing a long beige lace gown with a matching coat over it. The color was perfect with her blonde hair. The pale pink dresses looked lovely on the bridesmaids. Quentin wore the same white tie and tails he had worn at Versailles. Robert and Quentin's father and all the male guests wore black tie. Quentin's mother wore a very chic navy gown with long sleeves.

Jane had the florist fill the house with lily of the valley, and their delicate fragrance filled the air. The house was cool from the air-conditioning, even though it was July, and the doors to the garden were open, for those who wanted to revel in the warm July night.

The service itself was simple and serious, their vows traditional and heartfelt, although Sam had chosen "love, honor, and cherish" rather than "obey." All their hopes for each other and their marriage were seen on their faces as they gazed at each other tenderly, and they exchanged narrow gold wedding bands, which were a rite of passage for both of them. Jane noticed that Samantha no longer looked like a child. She was a woman accepting fully all that that entailed, now and in the years to come. It was the beginning of a journey, and a life, just as it was meant to be, and none of the hundred guests watching them took it lightly. They spoke up clearly when asked if they would support this marriage.

For Sam, it had begun in a white ballgown, and had led to a white wedding gown and a veil exactly a year later. She had all the demure grace of a loving young bride.

Robert and Jane had begun the same journey in a simpler way six weeks before, but with just as much love and deep dedication to each other.

There was no detail missing, there were no mistakes. And the memory of her mother and her brother were with Sam on that day, and with Robert, blessing them for the years ahead. Jane had promised to walk with him through life's trials, just as Samantha was doing now.

When the minister declared Sam and Quentin husband and wife, and Quentin kissed her, Robert had tears in his eyes. And a moment later, there was a jubilant cry from all the guests, and the champagne flowed freely until dinner would be served.

As they stood drinking and talking to friends, Felicity was telling the other bridesmaids that her sister had just gotten engaged. Araminta was marrying a fellow Texan, an oil man with a huge ranch just outside Houston. He had children older than Araminta, and she was going to be his fourth wife. Felicity didn't envy her. She never had. He would probably suit Araminta and give her the status and self-confidence she had craved for years. She was getting married at Christmas, and Felicity thought she might go, out of curiosity and as a gesture of good will. There were going to be eight hundred guests, and their mother was busy planning the wedding. Felicity had already decided to move to France with Raphael when he went back in a year, and she might transfer to the Sorbonne like Sam, for her senior year of school, or Polytechnique. Felicity had taken French classes for Raphael, and was almost fluent.

They all liked Caroline's new man. He was the current favorite plastic surgeon to the stars. He treated Caroline well and seemed like a genuinely nice guy. There was no talk of marriage, yet. Caroline wanted to graduate from USC before thinking about marriage. She was in no rush.

Amelia was about to begin her big adventure in England for her junior year in six weeks, and she planned to come back to Barnard for senior year, to graduate with her class, before starting law school. She was planning to apply to Columbia Law School, and hoped she'd get in. But she had two more years of college to complete first.

The girls were all talking about their plans. They seemed more grown-up, more worldly, and wiser than they had a year before at the ball at Versailles. They were grown women now, not just young girls.

Robert gently touched Willie's sleeve as he listened to the girls and beckoned him to come with him. He led him to his study and closed the door.

"Beautiful wedding," Willie commented. "I'll be on a cane by the time we get to ours," he said ruefully.

"I have a proposition to make you," Robert said. He had liked him from the moment they met, and he trusted his instincts. "I've done a little research and you're doing a good job where you are. They'll never pay you decently. They're too steeped in tradition and the old ways. I know you want to be in England this year with Amelia there. She's doing that year abroad to be with you. I think you need a bit of a helping hand here. She'll be coming back to New York a year from now for her last year at Barnard. I'm prepared to offer you a job, starting next June, or sooner if she comes back earlier. And I don't see why she can't be married while she completes her senior year. If you want to get married next summer, you'll have a job you can support a wife on, if you want the job, to learn about venture capital with me. You'll make about five times what you're making now, to be crass about it. I've talked to Jane, and she approves. You don't have to be tied down in England if you don't want to be. And with a decent job, you can get married and Amelia can finish school as your wife, just like Sam's going to do in Paris. If you can hold out for this year, while she's in London for junior year, I think things will be much easier for you a year from now. Sometimes, Willie, we all need a bit of luck and a helping hand." Willie was a bright young guy, and Robert felt comfortable with his offer of a job in a year, as Willie stared at him and his face turned bright red. He looked as though he was going to cry or kiss Robert, as Robert patted his shoulder and poured him a real drink from his bar. Willie took a long sip and stared at his benefactor.

"Do I have your blessing to ask Amelia's hand in marriage?" he asked.

"Yes, but you'll have to ask her mother too. She's my step-daughter now, but that's still out of my jurisdiction," Robert said with a smile. "With a decent job, you won't have a problem with her mother. We know you love each other, and it doesn't feel right to make you wait another two or three years to get married when she finishes school. And she can go to law school while you work for me. I think a wedding next summer should do it, don't you?" Willie nodded frantically, and couldn't wait to tell Amelia, and then he looked sheepishly at Robert.

"I was going to ask her now anyway. We were going to keep it a secret if we got engaged, but we would have had to be engaged for years, without your job offer. I would never have dared to ask you for a job, although I'd thought of it."

"So had I, and now it's done. You have a job waiting for you here as soon as you both come back from England." Willie followed Robert out of his study, with a look of awe on his face, and went to look for Amelia to tell her. She was talking to her mother with a serious expression, and looked very pretty in her bridesmaid dress.

"What are you going to do with the apartment, Mom?" Amelia had just asked her. It made her sad to think of her mother selling it. She had grown up there. "Are you going to sell it?"

Her mother spoke to her in a low voice so no one else could hear. "I'm saving it for you," she said quietly.

"For me?" Amelia looked surprised and confused.

"Robert is talking to Willie now," she went on, "about a job. I'm sure Willie will tell you about it. If you still love him in a year, you could get married, Willie could work for Robert while you finish school, and I think our old apartment would be a perfect place for a young couple. You'd even have room for a child or two." Robert had talked to Jane about the job before he made the offer. He had suggested it to Jane, and it changed Willie's prospects considerably. Willie could afford to get married with a good job, and Jane preferred to have Amelia married in New York, rather than starving in England with a penniless aristocrat. Married to Willie, she would be a viscountess, but it was more important that he could support himself, and a wife and family. And in the old apartment, they would be living nearby, only a few blocks away. "I'm going to miss you this year," Jane said, as Willie approached them. "We'll come to visit you, and I want you home for Christmas," she said firmly.

"You won't have time to miss me," Amelia said with a grateful smile. She was thrilled about the apartment. "With your new job at the magazine, you'll have your hands full. I'm proud of you, Mom, and happy for you with Robert." Jane still had misgivings about the job as CEO and didn't want Pascale to leave. It was going to be an enormous responsibility heading up the magazine, and she hoped she could do a decent job. She wasn't sure she knew enough yet.

"Congratulations on your new job," Jane said to Willie as he came to stand next to Amelia. He had so much to tell her.

"Thank you," he said, still deeply moved by the conversation he'd just had with Robert. "It changes everything."

"That was our intention," Jane said, and smiled at them both, as she drifted away to talk to the other guests, while Willie and Amelia shared their news, with a bright future ahead of them. The ball at Versailles had been magic after all.

Willie looked at Amelia, still in shock at his good fortune. He had met the woman of his dreams at Versailles, and now suddenly doors that had been closed opened magically. "I have something to ask you." He couldn't wait a minute longer. He had planned to talk to her that night after the wedding about getting engaged in secret. Now they could get engaged openly, thanks to Jane and Robert.

"What was all that about a job offer?" Amelia asked him. So much was happening at once, in the midst of Sam's wedding.

"I'll tell you later. Will you marry me, Amelia Alexander?"

She smiled at him. "My mother just told me she's giving me her apartment so we can get married and have children there."

"And Robert is giving me a job. We can be engaged for the next year and get married next summer," he said in a voice still filled with disbelief. "Will you marry me?" he asked, desperate for her answer.

"Yes," she said, and he kissed her, and then pulled a small round black velvet box out of his pocket and opened it. There was a small but brilliant ruby ring nestled on the velvet. He put it on her finger, and it fit. She was staring at it in amazement, as he looked at her proudly, and Sam walked up to them. She saw the ruby ring immediately.

"What's that?" she asked them both.

"We just got engaged," Amelia said, beaming. "Versailles brought me luck too," she said, and the three of them laughed. "And I even got a sister out of it," she said, and hugged Sam. Sam was happy for them. They deserved it. She went to find Quentin then, to tell him about Willie and Amelia, and across the room she saw her father kissing Jane. They looked happy too. There had been two weddings so far from that fairy-tale night a year ago, with another wedding to come next year. And maybe Raphael and Felicity one day. The ball at Versailles had done its job after all. As it turned out, an ancient, seemingly outdated tradition was part of the modern world and had brought the right people together. Destiny and history had worked their magic on a night that had brought them joy and blessed them all. It had changed each of their lives forever, just as their mothers had promised it would.

# UPSIDE DOWN

Oscar-winning actress Ardith Law is a Hollywood icon. While her long-time partner is away filming, Josh Gray, an actor waiting for his big break, is employed as Ardith's assistant at her Bel Air home. When tragedy strikes he becomes an invaluable support, stirring up conflicting feelings in her for this younger man.

In New York, Ardith's daughter Morgan is swept off her feet by Ben Ryan, one of the country's most famous TV news reporters. Though two decades her senior, she falls headlong for his charms. But, when a blackmail scheme puts his career – and their relationship – on the line, she doesn't know where to turn.

It's time for both women to find a way to follow their hearts – because finding true happiness with the right partner has nothing to do with age.

**Read on for an extract . . .**

# Chapter 1

The line of limousines snaked down the driveway of the Beverly Hilton hotel at a snail's pace to drop off stars and starlets, producers, directors, ingénues, the famous and the infamous and the unknowns and wannabes, desperate to be seen at one of Hollywood's most glittering annual events, the Golden Globe Awards. The greatly respected award was second only to the Academy Awards. At sixty-two, Ardith Law, one of Hollywood's biggest stars for the past forty years, had won three Golden Globes so far. And she had two of the Academy's coveted Oscars to her credit as well. This was an evening she never missed, as much to pay her respects to her fellow actors as to be seen herself. It was one of those things one had to do. It was expected, and you had to keep your face out there if you wanted to continue to get work, and your face had to look damn good or you'd better not show up!

Ardith was known for the variety and depth of the roles she accepted, and the quality of the movies she starred in. Occasionally, she took a small, unusual part if it intrigued her, which happened from time to time, but as a rule, she only took major starring roles. She was an extraordinary actress with a huge talent and a well-deserved reputation. She was picky about the parts she took. She wanted to be in movies with depth and merit, which weren't always easy to find after a certain age. She looked exceptionally good at sixty-two, was still beautiful, and unlike nearly every actress in Hollywood, she had had no "work" done. She preferred to keep her own natural face and left it to the makeup artists on set to correct whatever needed attention. And she was never afraid to take an important part if it aged her beyond her actual years.

Ardith wanted roles with substance that stretched her to the limits of her abilities. She turned down most of the easy parts. Although, for the past two years, there had been no offers. No one dared to cast her in minor roles, and producers knew that her agent, Joe Ricci, would turn them down before the offers even got to her. But once she turned sixty, there had been no appropriate parts for her. She read scripts constantly, looking for the right roles, but hadn't seen any she wanted to play. Her high standards and perfectionism on set had won her the reputation of being difficult or a diva, which wasn't entirely true. She was an extremely dedicated actress and demanded a lot of herself and everyone she worked with. So now and then, when others fell short, forty years of the best parts available and producers who would do almost anything to keep her happy had led to rare but memorable outbursts that supported the notion that she was a diva. She was above all a consummate professional, and a star to her very core. It wasn't about ego, but more about wanting to be the absolute best she could be in every role, at all times. She hated working with lazy actors, and she hated stupidity and phonies. She was true to herself and her high standards in every way. She was an honest woman, and a great actress more than a diva, no matter what people said who didn't really know her. Her career was vital to her sense of well-being and purpose. She had missed working for the past two years but preferred it to accepting roles in second-rate movies. She was waiting for the right film to come along, and she knew that eventually it would. In the meantime, she read every book and script she could lay her hands on.

Her personal life had always taken a back seat to her career, and it still did. She had one daughter from an eight-year marriage that began in her twenties. She had been married to one of Hollywood's biggest producers, John

Walker. They had been a powerful pair and had made several movies together, which had been legendary box-office successes and enhanced both their careers. It had been a tumultuous but creative match, which also produced their only daughter, Morgan, who was now thirty-eight years old and a plastic surgeon in New York.

Morgan had avoided the Hollywood scene all her life, and chose medicine as an exciting, satisfying alternative. It suited her. She was a partner in a successful practice of plastic surgeons, with two senior partners who had worked together for years. One was close to retirement, the other was in full swing, and Morgan was the only woman they had ever invited to join the partnership. One of the senior partners also taught at Columbia medical school. They set the bar high.

Ardith wished now that she had spent more time with Morgan when she was younger, but her own career had been white-hot then, and she was too often away on location and away from Morgan, and didn't deny it. Ardith had missed all the important moments and landmarks in Morgan's life, the school plays, her first prom, her first heartbreak, many birthdays, and it was impossible to catch up. She felt guilty about it now but there was no way to make up for it, or relive the past. Once Morgan was an adult, the two women were very different. Morgan respected her mother's career but had never enjoyed it, and the differences in their personalities and respective careers were hard to bridge now. They spoke often, out of duty and respect, but agreed on very little. Morgan had few memories of her father, who had died when she was seven. There had been scandal around her father's death, which had troubled her for years.

John Walker had died in a tragic helicopter accident, which was even more traumatic for Ardith because he was killed with the young woman he was rumored to be having an affair with at the time, a budding actress who was appearing in one of his movies and whose career he was shepherding. She was twenty-two, and Ardith was thirty-one then. The letters she found after John's death with his protégée confirmed her fears and suspicions about their involvement. Ardith had never forgiven him for it. The press had turned his death into a lurid event. Morgan knew the story once she was older, and had harbored illusions about him anyway. His films remained as tributes to him, but his reputation as a womanizer lasted after his death. Ardith knew it wasn't his first affair by any means and had said as much to Morgan. He could never resist the actresses in his films. Ardith had never married again and had no regrets that she hadn't. It was an experience she never wanted to repeat, as she had no desire to be married to another cheater and she didn't want more children. Morgan was enough to deal with on her own, and their relationship had never been easy, and less and less so when Morgan grew up. She'd been rebellious in her teens, and angry about the parents she didn't have. Ardith readily admitted that although she loved her daughter, motherhood wasn't her strong suit. Morgan agreed. Ardith hadn't been prepared for how much she had needed to give a child, especially after her father died. They occasionally had a good time together, but they didn't see each other often anymore. Ardith had the time to give her now, but Morgan didn't have the interest or the availability. She was busy with her career as a physician in New York, and her mother was proud of her, but Ardith still had her own life as a star in L.A. Morgan was single at thirty-eight and said she didn't have time for a husband and children, or even dating. Her work and her patients were her priorities. In some ways she was like her mother—her career came first. And the tables had turned. Ardith hadn't made enough time for her when she was a child, and now Morgan made no effort for her. It was a cycle they couldn't seem to break, and Ardith had accepted the fact that it was too late and they would never be close. They existed on the periphery of each other's lives. And living on opposite coasts, they saw too little of each other to heal the damage of the past. They had the occasional nice dinner together, and then Morgan flew back to New York, and they didn't see each other for months.

For the past twelve years, Ardith had found comfortable

companionship with William West, who was almost as big a star as she was. He had been a readily identifiable hero over a fifty-year career, even longer than Ardith's. He had never won an Oscar, and hadn't taken the challenging roles she had, but audiences loved him. He took parts that endeared him to his fans. Since he wasn't as demanding about the parts he played, he worked more often than Ardith, and still did one or two pictures a year. He was leaving in two days for England on location, playing a worthwhile role, although he was no longer the romantic lead. At seventy-eight, he was healthy and energetic and wanted to continue working, even in slightly less important parts. He had no desire to retire.

Ardith always said that the sixteen-year age difference between them didn't bother her. When they'd gotten together, she was fifty and he was sixty-six, still a handsome man, and a star. They had their careers in common, and he was kind, attentive, and good company. He had slowed down a little in the past few years, but other than the handful of pills and vitamins she handed him every day to keep him healthy, he was in surprisingly good condition for his age. No one knew what would come later, but for now he was doing fine and still working. He hadn't been as wise with money as she was. He had never commanded the salaries she did and was grateful to be living in her home in Bel Air for the past ten years. He contributed a small amount to expenses, but Ardith didn't expect anything from him. He had been married and divorced twice, to actresses both times, had only stayed married briefly, and had no children, which kept things simple. He had always been friendly to Morgan, but she was already doing her residency at Columbia by the time he and Ardith got together, so Morgan's relationship with him was cordial but superficial. She had no complaints against him, he was friendly and polite and good to her mother, and he had appeared much too late to be a father figure to her. She said she had no need for one, and she found him somewhat narcissistic, like most actors, more concerned with his own looks, projects, and problems than anyone else's. Ardith was used to it and didn't mind, and they were each the longest relationship either of them had ever had. After twelve years, they had become a legendary Hollywood couple, and were always seen together. It wasn't a great love affair and never had been, but it was companionship for both of them. They had each other and weren't alone or lonely.

When the car finally stopped in front of the Hilton, Ardith stepped out of the car in a long sleek black satin gown, which molded her impeccably maintained figure. She had a white fox wrap on her shoulders, was wearing a diamond necklace and earrings she had borrowed from Van Cleef & Arpels, and her blonde hair was combed in a smooth, elegant bun. She looked dazzling, and the press went wild when they saw her, flashing her picture, shouting her name, waving to catch her attention as Bill West stepped out behind her in an impeccable tuxedo. She smiled and waved like royalty at the mass of photographers and the fans hovering near them at the edge of the crowd, and she and Bill glided smoothly inside to make their way down the red carpet before the dinner and award ceremony began. Once Ardith and Bill were in a room or a crowd, all eyes were on them. Most people assumed that they were married by now, but they weren't, and she still had no desire to be. She said there was no reason for it, although Bill reminded her from time to time that he would prefer it, but he was of a previous generation. And she always pointed out that at this point marriage wouldn't change anything. They had lived together for ten out of twelve years, and there was no additional benefit to marriage, except emotional reassurance she didn't need. Ardith was a strong, self-sufficient woman and preferred her life that way.

Bill had beaten prostate cancer five years before, which had left him healthy and cancer-free but unable to perform sexually, which she accepted. She was young to give up sex, but it was a sacrifice she made for him. The relationship they had suited her, and him as well. She couldn't imagine meeting someone else now and having to adjust to a new man. She had had enough men in her life and was satisfied to have

Bill West be the last one. They were both Hollywood icons and thought to be the perfect couple. In some ways, being with a man his age aged her, and in others it made her feel young. They seemed right together in everyone's eyes, including their own. He was the perfect supporting actor to her, the star.

They spent half an hour going down the red carpet, then made their way to their table, where they would have dinner and watch the awards. The Golden Globes were important and often predicted how the Oscars would go two months later. Ardith and Bill were seated at a table of comparably major stars, and the TV cameras sought them out constantly. They would be under close scrutiny all night, and Bill had already told Ardith he wanted to go home right after the awards and skip the after-parties. He still had a lot to do before he left for England two days later, and he didn't want to stay out late, although she would have enjoyed it. She didn't want to go to the parties without him, so she planned to leave with him.

Ardith and Bill both accurately predicted who would win that night, and approved of the foreign press's choices, and after making their way back through the photographers, they escaped without attending any of the parties and were back at Ardith's house in Bel Air before midnight. Ardith had already packed most of what Bill would need in England, but he kept adding to it, afraid she had forgotten something. She was going to pack his various medications in his brief-case, with notes about what to take when. He fell asleep with his arm around her that night, with Oscar, Ardith's tiny white toy poodle, on the bed next to her. She took him everywhere, which Bill had objected to at first, but he finally got used to him. Ardith claimed the dog was her soulmate, and his constant presence was non-negotiable.

Ardith was an early riser and was already at the breakfast table the next day when Bill appeared in a navy cashmere dressing gown with navy satin lapels. She looked up and smiled when she saw him. She read the *Los Angeles Times, The New York Times,* and *The Wall Street Journal* every day. She had an insatiable hunger for knowing about the world around her, more so than Bill, who read *Variety* for news of the film industry, which was all that really interested him. He said that he left Ardith in charge of world news, and was sure she'd let him know if the stock market crashed or a war broke out, and she promised she would.

"Did you sleep well?" she asked him, as she did every morning, with a tender look.

"I did." He smiled at her. "I hate to leave you for two months," he said wistfully, as she poured him a cup of coffee. But he had no desire to retire either. He enjoyed his work and loved going on location. It made him feel busy and alive, and important. "I had an email from the producer this morning. Your assistant starts tomorrow, when I leave." As part of his contract, and to induce him to go on location for two months, the producers would provide an assistant to help Ardith with all the small tasks Bill did for her. He worried about her being alone for so long with no one to help her and felt mildly guilty leaving. He was still a bankable name and to keep him happy, the producers agreed to provide Ardith the assistant, she had guessed probably a young actress they knew well who wasn't currently working and needed the money. And she was grateful for whatever help an assistant would give her. She was expecting a female assistant. She had a housekeeper who came daily during the week, and left dinner for them if they weren't going out. Ardith often drove herself around town, but used drivers too. She drove Bill when he had appointments, or he took an Uber. She thought an assistant might be superfluous, but Bill wanted her to accept it. It was free and an add-on to his contract, which his agent had negotiated. It was a perk for her to share, so she agreed somewhat hesitantly. Since it wasn't Ardith's contract, they didn't offer her the opportunity to interview whoever they hired. She was mildly worried that an unknown assistant might be more of an annoyance than a help, but she could always fire her if she didn't like her, and it made Bill feel as though he had done something special for her, so she hadn't argued about it.

"Did they tell you anything about her?" Ardith asked, as she poured skim milk into a bowl of cereal for him. She watched his diet more carefully than he did. He would have preferred bacon and fried eggs, which she didn't allow him. There was a responsibility that went with being with a man his age. She was as much a nurse as a girlfriend.

"No, they didn't," he said about the assistant. "I'm sure she'll be very nice. You can send Oscar to the groomer with her," he said, a task which he personally didn't like. Oscar had never been overly fond of Bill. Oscar knew who his friends were. Bill wasn't a "dog person" and Oscar knew it.

"I don't mind taking him," Ardith said breezily.

"What are you hearing from Morgan these days?" he asked her. He was impressed by Morgan's medical career. Even though they weren't close, Ardith frequently asked her for medical advice, which Morgan was loath to give her. Ardith checked on all of Bill's medications with her daughter, to be sure there weren't dangerous side effects the doctors hadn't informed him of.

"Nothing much. All Morgan does is work," she answered his question.

"No man in her life?" He was sorry she hadn't met someone by now, at thirty-eight. He thought she should make some effort in that direction, as she wasn't getting any younger if she wanted a husband and a child. Bill had old-school views on every subject, particularly women and relationships.

"She says she doesn't have time," Ardith said. She had stopped reminding her daughter of it herself. It was up to Morgan if she wanted marriage and kids. It didn't look like it so far, and she loved her work. Morgan had never been very interested in marriage. "She's thinking about going to Vietnam this fall, to work on a special project, pro bono, helping kids with burns. It sounds awful, but noble."

"She's a good girl," Bill said admiringly, and left the table a short time later to finish packing. Ardith drove him all over town to do last-minute errands, and they were both exhausted that night when they went to bed. He had to leave the house at six A.M., as the producers were having him picked up for a nine A.M. flight to London. He was getting VIP treatment all the way, due to his age and status.

The alarm went off at five, and he was ready to leave when the car arrived. He looked lovingly at Ardith as they stood in the doorway, she in her nightgown, and Bill elegantly dressed for the trip.

He looked every inch a movie star, in a dark gray suit, blue shirt, and navy tie, with a well-cut navy overcoat, and a hat that made him look very dashing. He was excited to be going to work on a film for two months, and to have a good role, but he was sorry to leave her. She had promised to visit him in three weeks, and she was looking forward to some time alone while he was gone. She was planning to spend a night in New York on the way, to visit Morgan if her daughter had time. The plan wasn't definite yet. Morgan didn't make plans far in advance and said she was swamped at work.

"Try to behave while you're gone," Ardith teased Bill. "Don't fall in love with the star."

"You too," he said, and kissed her. He had more to worry about than she did, but they were faithful to each other. She stood waving from the doorway as the car pulled away, and she envied him for a minute. She would have liked to be leaving to work on a film on location, and hoped she would be one of these days, for the right movie. It made Bill feel useful and engaged to be working. He had three suitcases for his elegant suits, and a fourth one just for shoes. He had friends in London he planned to see when they had breaks, and he wouldn't be on set every day. The role wasn't too physically demanding, unlike the projects Ardith usually signed on for, which required months of preparation. His career had never been as demanding as hers. He was the only actor she'd ever been involved with who wasn't jealous of her and didn't punish her for her success, which was one of the reasons their relationship worked so well. He had never been resentful of her fame. Bill was easygoing, comfortable with who he was, satisfied with the degree of success he'd achieved, and didn't want more than that. Unlike Ardith, who had always pushed herself hard, physically and mentally, with the roles she took, always wanting to achieve more. It was why she had won two Oscars and he hadn't, and he didn't mind that either. At seventy-eight, he was just happy to still be in the game and to have work at all. He had never been as ambitious or driven as she was. They were a good fit that way.

She went back to bed, thinking about him after he left, happy for him that he would be working. It was an impressive cast, which would be fun, and a famous director whom Bill had worked with before.

She fell asleep, woke up two hours later, showered, and put on a green face mask she didn't like applying when Bill was at home. It made her look like the witch in *The Wizard of Oz*. Then she sat down to breakfast with the papers she read every day. She was halfway through the *Los Angeles Times* when there was the sound of an explosion outside, or some kind of major disturbance. She looked up in surprise, peeked through the blinds of the kitchen window, and saw an enormous motorcycle head straight for the house and spin around with a spray of gravel. The biker riding it looked like Darth Vader or a Hell's Angel, in a helmet with a black shield that concealed his face, a black motorcycle jacket, torn jeans, and biker boots, and he sat staring at the house for a minute, looking as though he was going to kill someone if he got inside. Benicia, the housekeeper, came running up to Ardith, looking terrified.

"He looks like a Hell's Angel, should I call the police?" she whispered, while Ardith tried to evaluate the situation and just how dangerous the biker was. He looked like a rough customer. Oscar was barking frantically from the noise the biker had already made with the Harley.

"Where are the panic buttons?" Ardith asked, whispering too. The rider looked menacing as he slowly got off the enormous motorcycle. You heard about guys like him, who broke into homes or held people at gunpoint while they robbed them in broad daylight.

Benicia took a panic button out of a drawer and handed it to Ardith, as she continued to watch him, wondering if he was armed or going to break a window to enter the house. It had never happened before. She didn't like guns and didn't keep one in the house, although Bill thought she should, for an event such as this. Burglars and criminals in the Los Angeles area were known to be pretty bold. Ardith was holding the panic button in her hand, about to press it, while watching what the fearsome-looking biker was going to do. He took the helmet off, and she saw that he was unshaven, with a face covered in beard stubble, and had longish hair that looked as though it hadn't seen a comb in months. He had a powerful build, and she had visions of him tying them up while he robbed the house. He didn't look like a drug addict, more like a thug. He was in good shape, with broad shoulders. He walked away from the kitchen windows, strode up the front steps, and rang the doorbell, which wasn't what she expected at all. Or maybe robbers were just that brazen now, they rang the front doorbell, grabbed you, and tied you up. She hit the panic button as soon as he rang the bell and tiptoed to the front door to get a better look at him through the peephole. He was just standing there, and she knew the police would arrive in less than ten minutes. Ardith told Benicia to stay in the kitchen—she didn't want her house-keeper getting hurt—and stood on the opposite side of the front door, wondering what to do before the police arrived. Bill had been gone for exactly three hours and they were under attack. She remembered then that he had told *Variety* that he was leaving town for two months on location, which she didn't like. Not that he would be any match for the hoodlum on their front steps, who was built like a body-builder and looked about thirty years old, if that, probably younger.

"Who is it?" Ardith shouted through the door, curious what he'd say, and trying to sound fierce herself. Her throat was dry, and she was shaking, but the adrenaline rush of fear made her brave.

"It's Josh Gray. Ms. Law's assistant," he said, sounding much meeker than Ardith as she let out a gasp and felt her knees go weak.

"You're *what*?" She unlocked and pulled open the door and stared at him, in her bathrobe and bare feet, with her hair piled on top of her head, and her face green with the forgotten face mask. She and the fierce-looking alleged assistant stared at each other in disbelief.

"I'm her new assistant . . . your new assistant," he said, hesitantly, assuming she was Ardith Law. "I'm supposed to start this morning. Mr. West's producer sent me."

"And you came to work looking like *that*?" she said with blatant disapproval. "I thought you were going to break into the house and kill us. And you're supposed to be a woman."

"Sorry, they sent me. For two months." Oscar the toy poodle ran into the hall from the kitchen and barked frantically at the man. Ardith could hear sirens in the distance, and in less than a minute, two squad cars arrived and four officers ran toward them with guns drawn, as Josh Gray looked panicked.

"Hands in the air," the police shouted at him, as one of them pushed him to the ground and he lay facedown on the lawn. Ardith looked embarrassed.

"I'm sorry," she said to the officers, as two of them stared at her. "It was a misunderstanding. I thought it was a break-in, but it was just my assistant coming to work." She tried to look starlike and sound charming and casual, as Josh looked up at them from the ground in shock, and she caught a glimpse of herself in the hall mirror and saw the green face mask she had forgotten. "Oh my God. I'm really sorry." The police withdrew quickly, and Josh got to his feet and stared at her. She was unrecognizable with the green goo on her face, but she was obviously Ardith Law. It was a hell of an introduction to his new boss, and he hadn't wanted the job anyway. Josh was an actor, out of work, his next movie had just been canceled so Bill's producer on the film assigned him to Ardith as an assistant for two months, which Josh had been dreading.

He had read about her reputation as a diva and had no desire to be her cabana boy for two months, but he was being paid to do it and he needed the money, since the sci-fi movie he'd been hired to do hadn't happened. But this was a lot worse than a bad movie. He was forty-one years old and had been acting in second-rate movies for the last ten years, and waiting on tables. He was still hoping for his big break, and it hadn't happened yet. Ardith Law was clearly not it.

"Come in," she said to him sternly, "before the whole neighborhood sees us." She picked up Oscar, Josh walked into the front hall, and she shut the door hard behind him. "What are you doing coming to work on that *thing*? You'll terrify the whole neighborhood. I thought you were a Hell's Angel."

"So you called the police?" He was still stunned at what had happened.

"You look dangerous. And why didn't they send a woman?"

"I think they were going to, but she got a part on some teen vampire movie, so you got me instead. The sci-fi movie I was supposed to do got canceled so I was free. I have a friend in the producer's office. He set me up for the job."

"Great. You look like Darth Vader. You can't come to work on that thing," she told him as he followed her into the kitchen, and Benicia stared at them both, unable to understand why Ardith had invited their attacker into the house.

"I don't have a car," he said politely, wondering if she was crazy, or just weird with the green face.

"Take an Uber. My neighbors will kill me for that racket. I can give you a car to drive while you're at work."

"What exactly am I going to be doing?" he asked, looking worried. "They said you needed an assistant while Mr. West is away."

"Exactly. You can take the dog to the groomer, pick up packages, do errands for me. Whatever I need," but having a male assistant was going to be a problem. He couldn't come into the room when she was undressed or take orders while she was in the bathtub. He wasn't what she wanted at all, and they had never told Bill they might send a man. He was almost useless to her.

"I'm not a trained bodyguard," he warned her.

"I don't need one. Or I didn't until you showed up. You scared poor Benicia to death," she scolded him. "And you have to come to work decently dressed, you can't run around town looking like a Hell's Angel. Do you have a jacket, like a blazer or something?"

He nodded. "Do you want me to wear a suit and tie?" he asked dismally.

"No, a proper shirt, clean untorn jeans, and a jacket will be fine, and real shoes or running shoes, no axe murderer boots." She looked at him with disapproval. "Do you like dogs?"

"I've never had one." Oscar was still barking, and Josh didn't look enthused at the prospect. "Does he bite?"

"Only people he doesn't like," Ardith said curtly. "He weighs three pounds. You don't need to worry about him." As she said it, Oscar bared his fangs and looked more like a rabid guinea pig than a dog. Josh looked miserable.

"Do you want me to go home and change?" She considered it, still in her green face, which she had forgotten again while berating him. He had upset them all, even the dog.

"You're fine for today. Try not to scare us to death

tomorrow." He nodded, still remembering when he had been lying facedown on the lawn minutes before, with two armed LAPD officers pointing their guns at him. "I'll get dressed. You can run me into Beverly Hills to do some errands, that way I won't have to park."

"Fine." He nodded, still stunned by the first moments of his new job. The next eight weeks seemed frightening, given what he'd seen so far. A crazed mouse of a dog, a boss with a green face, armed police forcing him down on her front lawn. If he could have hit his own panic button, he would have. This was a lot worse than he had feared. She wasn't a diva, she was insane, and he was stuck with her for the next eight weeks. A drink to calm his nerves would have been appealing, and then maybe she'd fire him and he wouldn't have to deal with her for the next two months. But for now, he was on the hook, because his damn movie had been canceled and he had to be an errand boy to a lunatic. He wanted to run screaming out the door, but he knew he couldn't. He needed the money to pay his rent. Benicia looked at him suspiciously as he sat down at the kitchen table and waited for Ardith to reappear so he could drive her somewhere. As far as Josh was concerned, she needed an exorcist, not an assistant, and as he waited, he reached down to pet the frenzied toy poodle, who bared his fangs at him again, aspiring to be Cujo.

"Be nice," Josh whispered to him. "I'm not liking this any more than you are. I promise not to bother you if you don't bite me. Deal?" Oscar hesitated for a minute, stared Josh in the eye, uncurled his lips, and marched off to find his mistress, while Josh wondered what the production company would do to him if he quit on the first day. It was very tempting, and he reflected on whether he'd need a tetanus shot if Oscar bit him. This was definitely a high-stress job, and not at all what he'd expected. But how much worse could it get? At least the cops didn't shoot him, but he couldn't bring his Harley to work, and he had to dress to cater to her. It was possibly the worst job he'd ever had, and diva didn't begin to describe it. A diva with a green face and a savage toy poodle. He couldn't wait to get home, smoke a joint, and have a martini. It was going to be a very, very long eight weeks working for Ms. Ardith Law!

If you enjoyed

# THE BALL AT VERSAILLES

you'll love these other titles by
Danielle Steel

# SECOND ACT

The courage to begin again . . .

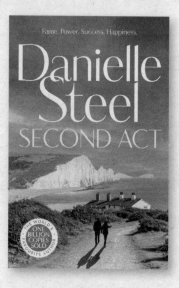

When Andy Westfield, the head of a prestigious movie studio, unexpectedly loses his job, he takes a break from Los Angeles and rents a luxurious home on the south coast of England. There he meets local woman Violet Smith. Violet leaves the manuscript of her unfinished novel lying around one day, and Andy is captivated by a story that begs to be adapted for the big screen. Could this be the miracle they've both been looking for?

# HAPPINESS

**Happiness is a choice.**

When Sabrina Brooks learns that she is
the sole heir to a historic manor house in
Hampshire, she is forced to cross the Atlantic
and see the property for herself. Sabrina
learns about her family history – and the
secrets her father kept from her. She starts to
fall in love with the manor and its beautiful
gardens. And she cannot help but enjoy the
company of the devastatingly handsome but
complicated lawyer who acts as her tour
guide . . .

# PALAZZO

## Dreams do come true . . .

After a tragic accident, Cosima Saverio
assumes leadership of her family's haute
couture Italian leather brand at just twenty-
three. Success comes at a cost, and her needs
are always secondary . . . until she meets
Olivier Bayard, the founder of France's most
successful ready-to-wear handbag company.

But, as her brother's gambling addiction
spirals out of control, Cosima is forced to
make an impossible choice. Is there a way to
rescue everything she has fought for – before
it goes up in flames?

# THE WEDDING PLANNER

## A day to remember . . .

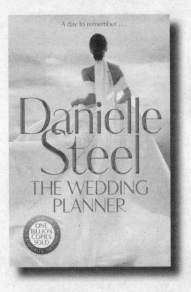

Faith Ferguson is one of New York's most
sought-after wedding planners. Realizing
dreams is part of why she loves her job.
But weddings aren't always champagne
and roses, and Faith herself has come
close to marriage twice – with disastrous
consequences. She loves making magic
happen for others, yet believes it isn't
meant for her. But maybe the saying 'never
say never' is true . . .

# Danielle Steel

Have you liked Danielle Steel on Facebook?

Be the first to know about Danielle's latest books,
access exclusive competitions and stay in touch
with news about Danielle.

www.facebook.com/DanielleSteelOfficial